Prai

"With keenly human observations and pitch-perfect banter, *Pick-Up* is a rom-com that completely delivers. I'll be daydreaming about Sasha and Ethan for a long time to come."

—Annabel Monaghan, national bestselling author of *Same Time Next Summer*

"Sexy, smart, and sweetly satisfying, *Pick-Up* is the perfect escape. I read it in one night and never wanted it to end!"

—Meg Cabot, #1 *New York Times* bestselling author of *Enchanted to Meet You* and *The Princess Diaries*

"Nora's New York–set romance is like the city itself—bright, vibrant, and full of character. You won't be able to put *Pick-Up* down."

—Sarah MacLean, *New York Times* bestselling author and host of *Fated Mates* podcast

"Filled with smart banter and swoon-worthy moments."

—*Woman's World*

"Debut romance author Dahlia makes good use of the enemies-to-lovers trope, and Sasha and Ethan are realistic parents and thoroughly enjoyable characters. Readers will be rooting for them and hoping for more from this new author."

—*Booklist*

"Snappy dialogue and a unique narrator structure bring Dahlia's introspective novel to life . . . Readers will love this unique blend of romance and relationship fiction, perfect for fans of Kate Clayborn and Emily Giffin."

—*Library Journal*

"A pitch-perfect rom-com . . . Dahlia leads readers on a delightful journey, replete with snappy prose, appealing characters, and wit. Fans of enemies-to-lovers rom-coms won't be able to resist."
—*Publishers Weekly*

Backslide

Also by Nora Dahlia

Pick-Up

Backslide

A Novel

Nora Dahlia

Gallery Books

New York · Antwerp/Amsterdam · London
Toronto · Sydney/Melbourne · New Delhi

G

Gallery Books
An Imprint of Simon & Schuster, LLC
1230 Avenue of the Americas
New York, NY 10020

For more than 100 years, Simon & Schuster has championed authors and the stories they create. By respecting the copyright of an author's intellectual property, you enable Simon & Schuster and the author to continue publishing exceptional books for years to come. We thank you for supporting the author's copyright by purchasing an authorized edition of this book.

No amount of this book may be reproduced or stored in any format, nor may it be uploaded to any website, database, language-learning model, or other repository, retrieval, or artificial intelligence system without express permission. All rights reserved. Inquiries may be directed to Simon & Schuster, 1230 Avenue of the Americas, New York, NY 10020 or permissions@simonandschuster.com.

This book is a work of fiction. Any references to historical events, real people, or real places are used fictitiously. Other names, characters, places, and events are products of the author's imagination, and any resemblance to actual events or places or persons, living or dead, is entirely coincidental.

Copyright © 2025 by Nora Zelevansky

All rights reserved, including the right to reproduce this book or portions thereof in any form whatsoever. For information, address Gallery Books Subsidiary Rights Department, 1230 Avenue of the Americas, New York, NY 10020.

First Gallery Books trade paperback edition October 2025

GALLERY BOOKS and colophon are registered trademarks of Simon & Schuster, LLC

Simon & Schuster strongly believes in freedom of expression and stands against censorship in all its forms. For more information, visit BooksBelong.com.

For information about special discounts for bulk purchases, please contact Simon & Schuster Special Sales at 1-866-506-1949 or business@simonandschuster.com.

The Simon & Schuster Speakers Bureau can bring authors to your live event. For more information or to book an event, contact the Simon & Schuster Speakers Bureau at 1-866-248-3049 or visit our website at www.simonspeakers.com.

Interior design by Julia Jacintho

Manufactured in the United States of America

10 9 8 7 6 5 4 3 2 1

Library of Congress Cataloging-in-Publication Data has been applied for.

ISBN 978-1-6680-8413-7
ISBN 978-1-6680-8414-4 (ebook)

For Megan, who takes the cot,
and Rachel, who shares the bed.

Prologue

BOTH

BACK IN THE DAY

Tonight, they are charmed.

Nellie feels it like a charge.

Tonight, instead of barking "Too many people!" and peeling out, the first cabdriver that pulls over on Seventy-Ninth and Broadway takes all *five* girls without hesitation, like it isn't illegal. Like he can't deny the magic.

And he doesn't get annoyed. Not even when Nellie settles onto Cara's lap to fit, her hand flat against the taxi's ceiling to protect her head each time they hit a pothole or stop short at a red light. Even though Sabrina, Cara, Nellie, and Sabrina's two other random friends have clearly already drank too much fizzy Zima and fruity Alizé. Even though, as the city blows past in trails and Cara starts to hiccup, they laugh and laugh and laugh.

Still kind of like children, though they imagine otherwise.

Tonight, the list girl hops off her stool, opens the velvet rope, and lets them through without an arched eyebrow or a wait. Compliments

Nellie on her skintight crop top, baggy jeans, and platform Docs. (Nellie's decision to freeze her ass off without a coat was *obviously* solid.)

The nine-foot-tall bouncer in a leather jacket that smells like cigarettes and cowboy almost smiles as his eyes barely graze their fake IDs and he pulls the absurdly huge door open.

They step through into inkier black.

Torch sconces line the walls, and Nellie is reminded of Gothic estates. She is reading *Jane Eyre* in AP English. But school—her cheerful classroom with Shakespeare quotes tacked to the walls—is a world away, though it's technically only thirty blocks uptown.

Here, she is a different person. Here, there are different rules.

The music grows louder and louder as they strut down the hall. It sizzles in their chests. Layers of Biggie. Mary J. "Murder She Wrote," like a reggae anthem.

Like they're strutting into a coliseum. Like it plays for *them*.

And then Sabrina, shiny black hair dramatic against her pale skin, pushes the heavy crimson curtain aside—and they have arrived.

The two girls they barely know instantly disperse. And Cara glues herself to Nellie's side as they stop to take it all in—while Sabrina, always fearless, runs up to the boys she knows. The ones from her school who invited them to the party. They're standing with other boys who are decidedly not from any high school—older, grittier, with oversized hoodies and appraising eyes. Sabrina stands on tiptoe—in her new nose piercing, bandeau top, and Carhartt overalls—and kisses the boys each on the cheek beneath their Yankees and Stüssy caps. One by one by one.

Nellie waves casually to the two she has met with Sabrina before. One short and stocky with brown hair; one tall and stocky with blond. They nod, too cool to smile.

This is not the girls' first time at one of these parties, thrown by promoters their own age and filled to capacity with posturing teenagers, drunk on freedom and, somehow despite being underage, flowing liquor.

Like the overstuffed cab, *technically* illegal.

But the grown-ups in their world are too busy with wars and political affairs and murderous former football stars to care.

The helicopter parents have not yet landed. It's still latchkey all the way.

The dance floor is packed. Bodies in motion. Pressed together and teased apart. Bodies, bodies everywhere.

In baggy jeans. In bamboo earrings. In fades and slicked-back ponytails.

In platforms. In Princess Leia buns. With flannels around their waists and Ring Pops in their mouths.

The bass invades them all like a subway car thundering into a station. A pleasant rumble to the core that doesn't apologize.

Possibility hums.

The ground is sticky. A smell of malt liquor and CK One permeates—just this side of rancid. The scent of bad behavior.

Nellie takes one more scan of the space. And just like that— the lights strobe, but time stands still. The music, the bodies, the sweat. It all disappears.

When she sees him, he is in a spotlight. At least, he is to her.

He is sitting a distance away on a raised platform that she will remember as a stage. He wears cargo pants and a thin white T-shirt, and he leans over his legs, his elbows resting on his thighs, as he nods to the music.

His baseball cap is slightly askew. Maybe on purpose. And maybe that's a little douchey, she allows herself to admit. But it doesn't matter. Because nothing can counteract his effect from moment one—his tan skin, his twinkling eyes, his toned arms straining against the cotton, the killer smile he flashes when a friend nearby cracks a joke. He is beautiful, admittedly. But mostly it is just *him*. Though she can't explain it. The way, through her lens, he glows brighter than everyone else.

It takes her a moment to realize she's being talked to. Yanked on. By someone else.

"What?" she asks, distracted, loath to tear her eyes away.

"Let's go get a drink!" Sabrina is demanding. And Nellie shifts her gaze back to her friends, suddenly conscious that she has been staring. At a full stranger.

Still, she misses the lovely view.

But Sabrina is bopping in front of her, ready for takeoff. Tugging on Nellie's arm.

Cara—dark skin aglow in the strobes above her more demure striped tank top and baggy jeans—nods like *let's go*. She is the shy one. She is also the wild one. But she needs a minute—and probably a drink—to get her sea legs.

That tall blond boy from Sabrina's school comes up behind her now, apparently all smiles once his friends aren't looking. Mocks her dance moves with a hand at her waist, and she leans back into him, swats him and laughs.

He has light eyes and light lashes. He is a clown. And he is trouble. Anyone who bothers to look can see that.

Nellie touches Sabrina's arm to get her attention.

"Who's that?" she asks, gesturing with her chin toward the other boy, the suddenly deeply important one, still sitting on the platform. She's surprised at herself for asking out loud. But she *must* know.

Sabrina shrugs, looks up at her blond friend, points at the mystery man and then at Nellie. "What's his name again? My friend wants to know."

Sabrina mostly ignores the social scene at her school, opting to hang with Cara and Nellie instead. It tracks that she doesn't recall.

The tall boy can't hear her question above the music. Or at least he acts that way, gesturing toward his ear in confusion as he takes the opportunity to step closer to Nellie. He lays a large hand on her shoulder and leans in. "What did you want to know?"

She stands on her tiptoes to reach his ear. "Who is *that*?" she asks. "In the white T-shirt. Sitting on the stage."

"Oh, that?" He shrugs, his breath—almost his lips—brushing her ear. On another night his proximity might have affected Nellie, raised her curiosity and even interest, but she is single-minded in her focus now. "That's just Noah," he says. "I told him not to wear that wack hat."

"Totally," Nellie says. She must save face.

Noah.

Mercifully, the tall boy doesn't ask why she wants to know. Maybe girls are always asking about Noah. She wouldn't be surprised. Instead, he grabs her hand and pulls her in the other direction toward the bar. And, since she can't just stand there staring all night, she surrenders to the velocity. But, as they begin to weave through the room of partygoers, she allows herself a single glance back.

He is still there. That boy. *Noah.*

And that's when he looks up and, from a distance, their eyes lock. His mouth drops open. He tilts his head, like she's a question. Like maybe he knows her. But does he?

Their chests rise and fall together, pulses quickening, pupils swelling. And then, just as quickly as they each came into view, they are blocked by a mass of other teens. She thinks maybe she sees him crane his head, trying to look beyond the crowd. But no luck.

For the rest of the night, as they each navigate the room, dancing and shout-talking and blurring edges, they glance around periodically for a glimpse of each other. But Noah and Nellie don't see each other at the party again.

Tonight, they never speak. But still the world teeters—and then tilts on its axis.

1

NELLIE

TODAY

I text Cara, checking my corners.

> Nellie
> Even the airport is nice. Too nice.

And it's true. Except for the part where I pretend to resent the loveliness.

Though I have always blamed Northern California for stealing my best friend away from me, in this moment, my grudge is wavering.

I have to admit, this is a delightful change. I have traded unspeakably repulsive subway cars—full of New Yorkers beaten into near submission by winter and left with resting frowns—for manicured cheer. Clean lines, clean floors!

An embarrassment of sunlight is falling through the skylights at SFO like spilled lemonade. Careless in its abundance. Like there's always more where that came from.

Isn't San Francisco supposed to be gray?

I pit stop in the bathroom en route to baggage claim. Inside, there are bag hooks that aren't broken and fully stocked toilet seat covers and paper towel dispensers that actually dispense paper towels.

There are trash receptacles marked COMPOST and LANDFILL. What are these marvels?

There are fellow bathroom users who smile at me by the sink for no apparent reason—just friendliness?

I guess this is living the good life.

And if I wasn't about to knowingly walk into the darkest depths of hell, just weeks after my well-ordered life took a nosedive, I would be elated.

I eye my reflection with hope, then resignation. I took an early morning flight and I look like it. My gray sweatsuit is cute but rumpled. My liner has smudged under my eyes in the way it does. My hair, always wavy and untamed, is an indented tangle from the sleep mask I used on the plane.

Sorry. *Tried* to use on the plane. It's hard to sleep when you're being rammed repeatedly by a beverage cart. The flight attendant either had a vendetta or a suspended license.

Cara texts me back:

Cara

You're here!

I am. I am here. And, if I could hop on a plane back to the East Coast grit and grunge, I would. Even though it feels like a relief to be somewhere else. Even though I am in desperate need of a break—some lightness. Some abundant lemonade of my own.

I need a minute to recalibrate. But there is no avoiding the inevitable.

Although I am all storm clouds, I text Cara:

> **Nellie**
> ...

This week is about her, and I will not be the one to bring her down. I am an adult. *Mostly.* I can handle this. *Maybe.*

But she is not fooled. She texts:

> **Cara**
> Are you nervous?

My body has been vibrating with anxiety for weeks. But I lie:

> **Nellie**
> Me? No! It's not MY do-over un-wedding celebration.

Cara and her husband, Ben, never had a "real" wedding—or so she keeps insisting. Faced with the prospect of a shotgun ceremony, they eloped to city hall. Now, several years and kids later, they've invited their closest friends to a vineyard compound in Sonoma County for the intimate shindig they never had.

Their closest friends. Including *him.*

Why Ben, always so delightful, stays tight with the devil I will never know. *Blackmail? Brainwashing?*

Swinging my tote back onto my shoulder, I follow the signs to baggage claim to retrieve my admittedly monstrous suitcase. It's large and in charge. But how else was I supposed to cope with this disaster?

In the months leading up to this trip, I may have ceded control of my credit card to my anxiety. Let's just say, when it comes to what to wear . . . I have *options.* And debt.

In equal measure.

And that recklessness began to feel exponentially ill-advised about three weeks ago, when—during our standing Monday morning meeting—my boss gave us senior staff members a heads-up that the magazine would be folding after only two more issues. And that news of that development would be public soon.

Now, scrolling through work emails I will willfully ignore all week on my phone, I let myself admit that, before reality fully set in, I had experienced a fleeting wave of relief about my job ending. Maybe the magazine *was* feeling a little tired; maybe *I* was feeling a little tired. Maybe I'd been squinting at that reality—my need for more stimulation, for change—for more than a while now.

Then I remembered that I like to be able to pay my rent. And that I have to show my face at this un-wedding thing and act like I'm not a basket case.

I pick up the pace.

Weaving through the terminal, I pass gourmet markets and chocolate shops. A yoga room! There are travelers in line for elevated takeout—spicy Korean rice bowls, massive burritos piled with fresh green avocado, radishes, and tangy limes, smoothies with ingredients like cacao and transformative adaptogen dust.

I don't know what that is. But who cares? I'm in California! And I clearly need to transform.

I exhale. For a moment, I can almost, *almost* forget what's coming my way.

Maybe he won't make it, I reason, letting hope rise in my chest against my better judgment. Maybe his flight will get canceled, permanently—or, better yet, he'll get hit by one of those motorized luggage carts and fall into a coma. You know . . . temporarily, of course. So I don't have to feel bad for him.

I smile at the thought. Then I park myself by baggage carousel five and wait. I scan my surroundings for tech bros, this being close to Silicon Valley, but, while there are a few nerdy white boys of indeterminate age in big ugly sneakers, there are mostly preppy older ladies in pressed button-downs with tight lips and Goyard bags.

My phone dings again. Cara is not going to let me off the hook.

Cara

Nellie! You CAN talk to us about this. About him.

I quickly respond:

Nellie

Just because I can, doesn't mean I want to.

Cara

He was your first love!

Nellie

I don't have a first love. If anything, I have a first hate. And I feel good about that.

Cara

That's not a thing.

Nellie

It is now.

I can just see her rolling her big brown eyes in frustration at me, then pursing her lips to the side as she contemplates how to move the needle on getting me to talk.

The needle is going nowhere.

After a beat, she types:

Cara

> So, what's the plan? If not introspection, sharing, and catharsis?

That's an easy one.

Nellie

> Total avoidance.

Cara

> Not going to be possible.

Nellie

> Anything is possible. If you believe.

The dots appear, then disappear. Then appear again.

She is losing patience with me. Or she would be, if she wasn't Cara and the most tolerant human on earth.

I exhale. I'm sure she's worried that I'm about to ruin her whole celebration with my bullshit. I'm not quite sure why since it's semi out of character, but Cara is clearly putting *a lot* of stock in this trip she's planned for us all—checking, rechecking, and triple-checking every detail. And to be honest, she has no clue the amount of emotional baggage I am currently carrying. It makes my giant suitcase look like a fanny pack. There is so much I am saving for a more appropriate time. And most of it has nothing to do with Noah. But, right now, I need to offer her reassurance. Because her stress about this potential complication is no good. I can't have that.

I text:

> Nellie
> Don't worry, CB!

CB is short for Care Bear. Sabrina and I gave Cara this nickname in drunken celebration after she *finally* dumped a particularly simpering boyfriend who called her "Funshine" earnestly after one of the *Care Bears* TV characters—a major red flag. (Cara had more than one simpering boyfriend before Ben.) But the name also seemed to match her maternal instincts. She is our mama bear.

So, I continue:

> Nellie
> Please don't stress! I'm just fine and I will behave. 😇 This week is about you having fun and celebrating the love of your life and drinking a lot of alcohol. But, like, the classy kind.

> Cara
> And leaving my kids at home! Don't forget that!

I grin.

> Nellie
> And leaving your kids at home.

A piercing shriek announces that the baggage carousel is about to begin moving. It rotates five feet, then stops dead in its tracks. False start.

Same, dude. Same.

I roll my shoulders, tight from contorting myself into something approximating a comfortable position during the flight. Extra legroom my ass.

The truth is my right shoulder has bothered me on and off since high school when I damaged my rotator cuff during our senior trip to France. I would like to say I was skiing down a black diamond in the Alps when I took a dramatic tumble, but I was actually tearing a chunk off a deeply stubborn Parisian baguette.

It was so good. I still kind of think it was worth it.

My phone serves up another alert. I'm hoping it's Sabrina this time, the third on our "Funshiners" text chain, to chime in on my behalf. She and her wife, Rita, are driving up from LA, and should have already arrived. And she is suspiciously silent on this topic.

Historically, she loves to rail against Noah. And basically everything else.

But it's Cara again.

Cara

BTW as a reminder: there will be a driver holding a sign with your name on it at the curb.

She has alerted me to this fact many times. She and Ben are providing airport transfers for all their out-of-town guests. She is the organized one of our trio, the diligent one, the math-brained one, and the one who, despite all of that, is the first to volunteer to down a shot, pop a mushroom cap, see what comes her way.

At least she was, pre-kids.

Cara

Are you sure you're okay?

Nellie

Cara. I'm fine! I promise.

Cara

Just, I get it if you're not. And I'm here if you need me. Confronting the past isn't easy. Old habits die hard.

Nellie

Not my old habit. He'll never die. Like the other cockroaches, he will outlive us all.

Cara

Nellie!

Sabrina

Oh, yeah. Nellie, you sound TOTALLY fine.

Oh, *now* Sabrina appears?

Nellie

Hey! You're supposed to be on my side!

Sabrina

> What side is that? The delusional side?

Nellie

> No! The I-hate-him-too-but-know-Nellie-is-mature-enough-to-ignore-him-with-grace-and-ease side!

Sabrina

> Hmm. Right. Grace and ease ARE your specialty. Tell me again about that time you got so drunk you tried to throw up in a tiny water bottle?

Nellie

> That never happened.

Sabrina

> I saw it with my own two 👀

Nellie

> As far as the rest of the world is concerned, THAT NEVER HAPPENED.

Damn. This is the problem with having lifelong friends. They've seen it all—and they don't let you forget it.

Sabrina

Fine. And yes. Of course I'm on the Noah Sucks Ass team.

Cara

Oooh. I like that. The NSA!

Nellie

That acronym might be taken.

But Sabrina is not done:

Sabrina

But you know, Nellie, it might help if you finally told us WHY we hate him. Aside from the fact that he's an entitled jock who once took your maidenhood.

I gag while speed-typing:

Nellie

Maidenhood? I think I just threw up in my mouth.

Sabrina

Better than in a water bottle.

I can practically see Sabrina shrug, all attitude. Her black lob grazing her shoulders.

Surely to defuse any tension, Cara types:

Cara

> I bet you're really wishing Alfie was here, Nellie. I'm so sorry he couldn't come.

I give her message a thumbs-up. It's all I can muster in answer.

Nellie

> Uh, oh. Gotta go! Bags are coming. Bags, bags, bags!

The bags are not coming. In fact, some of my fellow travelers have given up, sinking down to the floor against enormous blue cement pillars as they wait. Like they might live here now.

I sigh with resignation. In truth, I am not sad Alfie is absent, even if he would have served as a convenient buffer. But I don't want to get into that with my friends. Right now, he would be complaining about something—the pathetic snack selection on the plane, the luggage delay, the fact that people on the West Coast are not from the East Coast.

Not that some of those things aren't annoying, but sometimes it's better to accept your circumstances and make the best of things rather than torture the people around you. Suffer in silence. Or go silent so others don't have to suffer through your bullshit.

Griping doesn't make adversity *more* tolerable.

It isn't until the luggage starts dropping down from that trapdoor in the sky and rotating around the carousel that I do sort of wish he was here, for manual labor's sake. The airline—in its infinite wisdom—has decided to combine bags from two flights willy-nilly, one from New York City and one from Portland, Oregon. The carousel is a full-on culture war in the making. New Yorkers elbow their way up to grab their belongings, while Oregonians shoot them horrified looks. As a stout woman in a Brooklyn's Finest T-shirt pushes aggressively to the front, a young skater dude nearby mumbles "Chill" under his breath.

She whips around. "*You* fucking CHILL!" she snaps, her finger in his face. His eyes bulge.

That's when I spot my suitcase. *Hallelujah!*

It is giant. It is green. In fact, a while back, Alfie nicknamed it the Jolly Green Giant during a semi-joking rant about my overpacking habit. And it stuck.

An expert in crowd weaving, I work my way to the front of the group, a bit ahead of the bag, my shins braced against the metal frame for leverage. My suitcase is behind some other luggage in a kind of de facto second row, though. So, as it nears, I have to lunge toward it. Only Brooklyn's Finest thinks I'm trying to cut in front of her and she boxes me out, so by the time I grab on to my bag's handle, it's for dear life. It's too heavy and too far away to yank from its position, but I will not let go.

My bad shoulder is not amused.

Just when I lose my grip and almost topple onto the carousel, along for the ride with the Saran-wrapped duffels, I watch a disembodied strong hand grab the Jolly Green Giant by the side handle and lift it easily off the revolving death trap. I can't see this heroic human through the mess of people, but I exhale and push myself to standing, grateful.

See? There's still kindness in the world! Or thieves. Who steal bags. One of those.

Ducking through the crowd, I spot my luggage waiting peacefully to the side, away from the fray. See? No one stole it! I'm so relieved that I race up with a singular focus. "Hello, Beautiful!" I say, and caress it as I repeat "Thank you, thank you, thank you" about a million times.

It's not until he says "You're welcome" in a deep throaty voice that I realize. And slowly look up, dread settling over me.

It's *him*.

For just an instant, I white-out. There is a rush of air that moves through me like a sonic boom. It steals my oxygen, then returns it too quickly. I wheeze. Then work to regain my composure.

Noah stands before me—of course, the picture of good health and relaxed ease. Not only has he made it here to Northern California coma-free, but he looks like he just spent a day at a spa instead of on a packed flight. His hands in his pockets, he is refreshed. Groomed. Handsome as hell. *Bastard*.

It's only then that I realize my mouth is hanging open. I shut it like a trap.

"Hey, Nell," he says.

"Eleanor," I correct him. Because he doesn't get to use a nickname.

"Okay, *Eleanor*." He rolls his eyes. His beautiful hazel eyes—that I want to rip out of their sockets and use as ping-pong balls, I remind myself.

A small part of me, an almost physical pull at my core, has an impulse to hug him, feel the comfort and warmth his body once gave me, pressed up against mine. This man—a grown-up version of the boy I knew so well. I am stunned by the sense that I know him still, every mannerism, every impulse, every freckle. He feels like . . . family. And so much more.

Luckily, the other part of me, that hates him with the fire of a thousand suns, is way stronger.

"I see you still have a lot of baggage," he says.

"I see you're still a cocky tool," I reply.

And we're back!

He flinches, visibly. Lifts his chin in the direction of my bag. "Um. You're welcome?"

"Um. You're not?"

"Well, this is delightful," he says, frowning. "Can we at least be civil?"

"Sure," I growl, crossing my arms over my chest. "If you stay away from me—and my stuff."

Now his mouth drops open. Now *he* is incredulous.

It gives me a real jolt of satisfaction.

"Dude," he says, his hands raised palms up. "What's your problem? I was just trying to help. I figured maybe you'd have trouble . . . 'cause of your rotator injury. I imagine it's still an issue." He gestures toward my bad shoulder. And he's right about which one it is.

"Nope," I lie, though deep down I experience a twinge of recognition and, fine, maybe the tiniest bit of hurt. *He knows me.* Just like I know him. Or he *knew* me. Before he trashed everything.

He doesn't know me now, I remind myself. Because I cut him out of my life. With good reason. "The rotator cuff is not a thing."

You don't know me.

"Okay. That's great. I was just trying to help."

"Well, don't. I'm not your concern."

"Fine." He shrugs. "I guess old habits die hard."

Why do people keep saying that to me?

I glare at him. "If only that were true."

He stares down at my face for a beat, long enough for me to shift uncomfortably as warmth shimmies up my spine, then he shakes his head in disbelief. "Well, I can see you haven't changed."

"You say that like it's a bad thing." He fixes me with a look. But I will not be deterred. "Why are you even here?" I ask, motioning toward the baggage carousel. "Aren't you flying in from somewhere else? Like Newark? Or Hades?"

He glares back at me. And it's a look filled with ire, but just this side of smoldering. I can too easily recall a different version of that fierce focus on me, in a very different scenario. I am blindsided by a flash in my mind to skin against skin.

I try to blink it away, but it persists.

There's a burst of heat at the back of my neck.

Damn. It would be helpful if he didn't look so good. But Noah's skin is tan and smooth except for some perfect stubble, his hair is short like I always liked it, and, in the intervening years, some of his boyishness has transformed into something more rugged and chiseled.

"I was just cutting through to exit," he says. "I flew here private—with the team." *Private. With the team.* Like it's no big deal.

Is there no justice in the world? No wonder even his white T-shirt looks crisp. And hugs his biceps when he . . . *ugh.*

I change course: Why is he flying with a team? This is confusing to me since I know he isn't playing sports, though he had all that promise. Because wasn't that where all the problems began?

"What team?" I sneer. *Why does he just assume I know about his life?*

"Oh. The Dodgers. For the last few years, I've been working for them and living in . . ." He hesitates, then mumbles, "LA."

"In LA?!" I say with alarm. More than I'd like. The last thing I want him to think is that I care.

But LA? Of all the fucking places? My insides twist, ringing out a slow drip of bile.

What is he—some stupid sports marketing bro?

I have done my best to avoid keeping tabs on Noah. And, let me just say, that is a feat in this day and age. Last I heard, when I ran into a girl I knew from high school who didn't know enough not to tell me, he was living in Cleveland. And I liked thinking of him there, getting fat, bald, and pasty under gray skies. Meanwhile, he was busy jogging up canyons and getting Hollywood tune-ups—in *my* onetime city!

He bites his lip as we eye each other, like he at least has the sense to feel a little ashamed.

My gaze catches on his mouth. And, when I finally meet his eyes, I watch them drop down to my mouth too.

Ugh! I've got to get away from this man!

This is not how I wanted things to go. It's all wrong. I had plans, dammit! I was going to float out onto the estate's veranda under the gauzy light of dusk in one of my new dresses, the embodiment of effervescent hate-glam. I wanted to look past him, *through* him—like the ghost he is—as he stared at me longingly from the other side of the reclaimed wood deck, all night long. Under a canopy of majestic redwoods, I wanted to toast with Prosecco and laugh with my girls and ignore him into desperate submission until he skulked home early and got a jump on that coma.

Instead, I am staring at his handsome hateful face, feeling the vestiges of our past burn through me, fresh and raw. Like a brand-new smack to the face. And I am doing it in a sweatsuit with a red kiss appliqué on the upper left-hand side.

"We've got to go," I mumble as much to myself as to him.

"We?" he repeats, like maybe I mean him. I can't read his expression. Surprise? Disdain? Hope?

Maybe it's just confusion.

"*I've* got to go," I say. "Me. And the Jolly Green Giant."

2

NOAH
TODAY

"Sorry—the Jolly Green what?"

"*Sorry*. From you? Hilarious!"

Neither of us laugh.

The forest-green suitcase is almost as tall as Nell. Which isn't saying all that much. And as she begins to drag that heavy-ass thing alongside her, the world's slowest and saddest attempt at storming away, I catch her flinching in pain.

Ah-ha! I knew that rotator cuff injury would still be a problem.

I let myself feel smug for a second. Then, I sigh inwardly. I obviously need to carry the stupid thing for her. But what's the likelihood that she bares her fangs and bites me before I can get close enough to grab it?

This is the problem with this infuriating woman. She's stubborn as hell. Would barely accept help even when she liked me . . . let alone now.

On the flight up, I was genuinely hoping we could see each other and keep it chill this week. Maybe laugh about the past—how it's ancient history, anyway. Meet as benign acquaintances.

When I spotted her at baggage claim, I legit thought it was a good sign—a chance to ease the tension before we arrived at the property and were surrounded by our shared past.

But seeing her is more confusing than I imagined. She's just as maddening as always. Her words sting just as much. And, worst of all, she's just as hot. I can't tell if I'm more attracted to or irked by her, but whatever I'm feeling, it's not anything like benign.

The past doesn't feel so past.

Her thick hair is longer than I've ever seen it and streaked with a million shades of light brown and blond. Back in the day, she used to wear it pin straight, and even then it drove me crazy. But now she's letting the waves fly—and it's next level. I'd been kind of hoping she'd let herself go over the years or even over-injected her face until she looked like someone else, *everyone* else, at least in LA—but, of course she didn't. She's Nell. She's beautiful. Natural. Sprightly. And she's annoyingly fit.

Even in sweatpants and high-tops, her style is on point. And though she looks a little tired, her sleepy eyes—that crazy gray color I've never seen on anyone else—call to me in a way I don't want to feel. I'm not here to wipe that smudge of makeup from under her cat-like eyes with my thumb, though every inch of my body thinks I am. I'm not here to untangle her necklaces. That hasn't been my job for years.

C'mon, man. You know better than that.

Grabbing my own reasonably sized suitcase, I follow behind her as she tries to sprint toward the automatic glass doors. I coach myself not to check out her ass. I should not. I will not. And yet, I do. And judging by what rockets through me, it's a huge mistake.

But I only have a beat to tamp that shit down because she's racing ahead of me. Injury or no, she will not be stopped. She is intent on escaping me and I'm surprised to feel a pang of hurt.

And that pisses me off.

"Hey, Nell. *Eleanor*. At least let me help with your stupid . . ."

"Jolly Green Giant," she says without glancing back.

"The Jolly Green Giant is jolly. That thing has more Hulk vibes." Or maybe that's her.

We make it through the automatic doors and outside onto the curb, and she blinks against the light. A cloud cover has started to move in, that kind of overcast filter that feels brighter than straight sun. Clusters of other travelers are huddled near their baggage, awaiting pickups. Normal travelers. Who don't loathe each other.

I slide my sunglasses on—I'll take any barrier between us.

Why am I still standing here?

I tell myself I am acting on a sense of basic decency instilled by my mom and older sister. Nell is a woman alone, she's lugging a giant fucking monster of a suitcase, and she is clearly hurt. It doesn't matter if she's a demon in disguise. Or that she thinks I'm a horrible person—and, around her, I start to wonder if she's right.

Maybe it was a mistake to come to this thing alone.

An older man in a uniform with an official-looking airport employee badge passes by. "Excuse me," Nell calls out sweetly—like she's an entirely other human being. "Sorry to bother you, but do you know if car service pickup is here or . . . ?"

He pauses and grins at her, mistaking her for a normal person—a pretty, polite woman who doesn't stomp on people's hearts and eat them raw. "Right across the street here, miss. You need help with that bag?"

"Thank you so much, sir. No, I've got it," she smiles.

"Are you sure?"

"I can help her," I say, stepping forward.

"No," she snaps. "You can't."

"I could if you weren't impossible!" I say, losing my temper. "That thing is clearly too big for you and your shoulder is obviously messed up."

"You're obviously messed up!" she snipes back, full of venom.

"You're right. I am. 'Cause for some reason I'm still standing here!"

The airport employee is looking between us like he's watching the most un-fun tennis volley. Like he's unsure whether it's safe to leave or if, since we're acting like children, he should send us to our rooms.

"Miss," he says, tilting his head and eyeing Nell meaningfully. "Are you alright?"

Oh, that's just fucking great. Now I'm a predator.

Thirty minutes ago, I was sitting in a quilted cream leather seat on a private jet eating a legitimately decent steak, feeling pretty damn good about my life. That's what Nell does to me—in five minutes flat.

"I'm fine," she says with resignation, her shoulders dropping. "It's okay."

The man nods and heads off, glancing over his epauletted shoulder twice to shoot me a warning look. Like he knows where I live.

I groan, everything in me deflating at the prospect of the coming days. I'm doing this for Ben, I remind myself. For Cara. They deserve a week without the stress of . . . us.

"Listen," I start.

"No, thanks," Nell says, avoiding eye contact. "Pass!" Like I've just offered her a piece of gum instead of begun a sentence.

I look to the bleached-out sky for strength. Why does she insist on picking up where we left off, so many years ago? Has nothing changed?

That's when, across the street, I spot a silver-haired driver in his mid-sixties wearing a tailored suit and holding a rectangular sign that reads NELLIE HURWITZ.

I catch the guy's eye and wave. He throws his hands up like *there you are* and hurries over.

"Your driver is right here," I grumble.

She chances a look up at me from beneath her dark lashes but doesn't speak.

"Listen, we need to find a way to be okay this week," I force myself to say, my throat tight. "For *them*."

She sighs, big. Tips her head back, then rights it, her hair falling over her face. Everything in me wants to brush the rogue strands aside, but I don't.

"Fine," she nods. "But this would have been a lot easier with you in a coma."

"Excuse me?"

But the driver has hustled up and is taking that insane bag from her. And she is at least letting him.

"Hi!" he says. "Apologies. I thought pickup was at baggage claim, but the bags took so long I got worried you'd carried on and I'd missed you! And then I checked over there, but then you were here and now . . . well, now let's get you to Sonoma for a glass of vino before the traffic gets the better of us."

"Sounds great," Nell says.

The driver examines her behemoth luggage. "Wow. This is a big one. But it'll fit."

"That's what she said," Nell and I mumble in unison under our breath. We look up at each other in surprise. I see her almost start to laugh, but then she presses her lips together to suppress the smile.

There were reasons why we liked each other. Reasons we made sense. Even though we seemed different on paper.

And they weren't all raunchy jokes.

"Are you coming too?" asks the driver.

"No!" Nell yelps before I can answer. "No," she repeats, turning to me. "We are *not* sharing a car."

I shake my head. *What the hell.*

"I'm not trying to take the ride with you, Eleanor. I rented a car."

"Good," she says, visibly relaxing. "Then why are you still here?"

"I just stayed to help you."

She looks me up and down with a scowl, like I am decades late. Which I guess I am. "I'm not the one who needs help."

And, like so many years before, she turns and leaves. And I am left, confused and angry, staring helplessly at her back as she recedes.

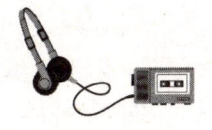

3

BOTH
BACK IN THE DAY

Cara and Lydia have no plans. And Nellie is jealous. Jealous like a sixteen-year-old afraid to miss out on even the *least* promising social interaction. In truth, Nellie exists in a constant state of FOMO, though the acronym for it does not yet exist.

It's spring in New York City. Warmer but not warm. The breeze smells fresh and damp, stirring with new beginnings. Pink magnolia and white cherry blossoms explode from fragile branches, embarrassing the surrounding dogwood trees—still naked and thorny.

Thorny like Lydia, who Nellie doesn't even like.

Lydia is Cara's leftover from nursery school—a kind of obligatory-family-friend-appendage who Nellie would prefer to exorcise. She doesn't go to school with any of them and yet, somehow, she constantly pops up, her curly red hair and freckled skin accented by bright-red lipstick. And, whether it's because she sees Nellie as a threat to her childhood friendship with Cara or just can't suppress her snark, she throws relentless barbs.

"I've been looking for a sweater exactly like this!" Cara exclaims, fingering the soft sleeve of Nellie's oversized black cashmere V-neck as they walk downtown on Broadway. They lug matching JanSport backpacks, heavy with textbooks and in various states of disrepair, cluttered with quippy pins or tagged with Sharpies.

"Yeah, it's kinda fly," Lydia allows. "Is it, like, vintage?"

"No, I don't think so," Nellie says, looking down to examine it. "It was my brother's, actually."

"Oh, yeah," Lydia nods. "That makes sense. 'Cause it looks kind of old and worn out."

Fucking Lydia. Nellie just rolls her eyes.

Nellie may act cavalier about her outfit, but there is nothing left to chance about the distressed sweater over the white V-neck Hanes T-shirt, tight black stretchy miniskirt, and requisite late nineties blue six-hole Doc Martens. She cares what she wears maybe even more than the average teen. Actually, she cares about aesthetics and design in general—all things visual. Which is why instead of having no plans like Lydia and Cara, she is headed to her weekly drawing class right now.

"Do we have to walk her *all* the way?" Lydia asks Cara like Nellie isn't standing right there. Like she can't hear every word. "I'm tired."

"Lydia!" Cara giggles, lagging a couple steps behind, so she can playfully place her hands on her friend's back and push her forward. Lydia leans back into Cara's palms until she almost trust-falls backward. They both dissolve into laughter.

Very funny. They're going to make Nellie late.

"You guys . . ."

"Coming, coming!" Lydia says, rolling her eyes, like Nellie is such a buzzkill. "Let me just get a cigarette." And, while Nellie taps her foot, impatience strumming through her, Lydia takes her sweet-ass time flipping her bag off one shoulder, unzipping a front pocket, then a side one, sliding a Newport Light 100 out, and then rummaging for a lighter.

She finally lights the thing and takes a heavy drag, her red lipstick leaving a ring around the filter like the mark of the devil.

If any of the adults walking past disapprove, they don't show it. Pedestrians rush down the sidewalk on either side of the girls, headed toward meetings and appointments scrawled in Filofax organizers. The tech-savvy among them return pages via pay phones. People actually look where they're going.

This pre-Y2K world is a simpler place than it will be soon.

"I can just walk myself," Nellie blurts out finally, working to keep the irritation out of her voice. "Really. I'm a big girl. I'm all good. *Bye!*"

She's not bluffing. She really wants to leave. She edges away down the street.

"No way, Nells!" Cara says. "We *want* to walk you! Otherwise, we have to go back and start our homework."

"We don't *have* to start our homework," Lydia quips, dragging on her cigarette and blowing an ineffectual ring—more like a blob of smoke. "We could go to the Meadow. I heard the cast of *The Real World* has been chilling there. They, like, rollerblade on the bike path nearby."

But if she thinks she can distract Cara from her schoolwork, she doesn't know her old friend as well as she imagines. Cara is up for a party—but only after her calculus is done.

Nellie relates to this. The need for vigilance.

The threesome turns the corner onto Seventy-Fourth Street, east in the direction of Central Park on a mostly residential block, and stumbles into an optimistic stretch of sunlight. Cara tilts her head toward the sun and sighs. *Heaven.*

New York winter was long. Had lost its charm ages ago.

The snow had yellowed—with the help of enthusiastic neighborhood dogs—and the last vestiges, small patches of ice, still cling to the dark soil of sporadic tree wells.

It isn't that Nellie doesn't appreciate the warmth. She does. It is a balm as it warms the top of her head. But nothing is icier than arriving late to drawing. That means being on the receiving end of a disappointed look—through horn-rimmed glasses—from the teacher, Sharon, a bony frustrated artist with limited patience.

"Guys . . ." Nellie says, preparing to say goodbye and run ahead no matter how Cara resists, "thanks for walking me, but I'm just going to . . ."

But then she stops midsentence, her mouth dropping open slightly. Because, through the glare of afternoon sunlight, she sees a trio of boys walking toward them like a hormonal mirage. And she recognizes them instantly, as if from her imagination.

The boys from the party.

The tall one. The short one. The one she saw only from afar, but who—since she spotted him—she's been thinking about nightly in bed as she waits under her too-heavy comforter for sleep to turn her thoughts to dreams. Who she has endowed with an imaginary personality that probably bears no resemblance to the *actual* flesh-and-blood boy. Who she feels like she *knows* because of how much he has occupied her thoughts.

She has looked for him at other parties since that first one—desperately, pathetically. No dice.

She's looked around the neighborhood too. Because even though she doesn't know these boys *really*, she knows them vaguely as one of the other groups of kids from this corner of the city. She never paid them much mind before. But she knows they think they own the Upper West Side just like she, Cara, and Sabrina do.

No doubt, they also eat Gray's Papaya hot dogs with tangy mustard and sauerkraut over a greasy orange counter, also suck tart striped candy sticks down to fine points from the Broadway Nut Shop, where nothing ever tastes quite as good as the store smells. They too order whatever is still hot—crusty on the outside and pliable on the inside—from H&H Bagels. They sit on the same stoops, avoid the same bird shit splatters on the same green park benches, eat funnel cake dusted with powdered sugar from the same street fairs. They probably smoke blunts and drink tall boys on the border of Riverside Park, by the same stone wall where Nellie perches daily.

They have been living parallel lives.

So, why shouldn't she spot her mystery guy here? On her turf? She's never seen him specifically here before—she would remember—but then she didn't know to look.

It's been long enough now, since the party though, that she has (until this very moment!) convinced herself that maybe he doesn't exist at all. That she has exaggerated him so greatly in her mind that he no longer resembles any actual boy. Perhaps she passes the *real* him daily without recognition because she has built him up so much in her mind. Because there is no way he's as hot as she remembers, no way his smile is as easy, no way he glows as bright.

But here he is now. Like she finally manifested him. Sauntering toward her flanked by his friends, hands in his pockets, in a kind of lazy meander that can only come from having nowhere to be.

And he is just as magnetic as she recalls. No. He is *more*. Because there is no baseball cap this time. His hair is buzzed short. And he's taller than she realized. Over six feet. Golden tan in the light of day. Lean and muscular in an athletic way.

He is chewing gum, his jaw popping. And even that looks good on him.

As they come to a stop in front of each other, she is overwhelmed by a full-body flush, irrationally sure he can read her thoughts. Surely, he—and all his friends—will know that she spends every night in the dark wondering about him, reinventing him.

She averts her eyes, looking anywhere else.

"Hey!" says the tall blond one. Damien. That's his name. "I know you! You're Sabrina's friends, right?"

It's funny for him to pretend he's not sure. It's a manipulation; a power play. Like he's too cool to have fully engaged. They'd hung out that whole night at the party—drinking, dancing, shouting above the din, repeat. Now, he looks from Nellie to Cara for recognition.

Cara nods, overcome by quiet. She shifts on her feet, bites her nails. That's how she rolls with new people. How she clams up.

Nellie has no choice but to speak for them both. "Yeah," she humors him. "We met at that club."

"No doubt," he says, bobbing his head. Which sort of makes no sense. But then he laughs. At himself maybe? At them? It's hard to tell.

Which Nellie also thinks is by design.

It's all a little obnoxious.

"I remember!" the short boy chimes in, shooting them an untempered smile—open for business.

He seems unapologetically sweet in his striped orange, white, and yellow Hang Ten T-shirt. Like human candy corn.

Lydia clears her throat. Like, *hello?*

"That's Lydia," Nellie says, fighting the urge to roll her eyes. "You guys didn't meet her at the party. Because she wasn't there."

Oh, blessed night.

"I wasn't there." Lydia drags on her cigarette and lowers her lashes, like she's some screen siren and not a seventeen-year-old in a Champion sweatshirt with a small pimple on her forehead.

"Nice to meet you, Lydia." Damien eyes her and laughs in an unreadable way again—is he mocking or flirting with her? "I'm D. We missed you . . . even though we don't know you."

"You have no idea what you missed," she says.

His eyebrows quirk upward. "I bet that's true."

It takes everything in Nellie's power not to visibly gag.

In the wake of that bizarre exchange, there's a lull as the members of the group eye each other. A car rumbles by, blasting Snoop. "Ain't No Fun." It's a strange kind of situation—no Sabrina to connect them, no alcoholic lubrication, no real knowledge of each other.

"So," says Damien, the mouthpiece, doing his job of filling the dead air. "Where's Sabrina at now? How come you're not with her? Did you ditch her? You can tell us."

Is he making fun of Sabrina or them or no one at all? Nellie can't tell and it makes her uneasy.

"You guys saw her at your school more recently than we've seen her," Nellie says, shrugging. "How come *you're* not with her?"

Damien smirks. "She's too cool for us."

Nellie looks him up and down, purses her lips. "I can see that."

And he scratches his head, like he can't decide how this exchange is going.

"Sabrina has piano on Tuesdays!" Cara forces out at a near shout. It is abrupt. And she looks like she regrets her awkward attempt. Like she'd like to crawl back into her shell.

"Sabrina plays piano?" the short one says. "That's cool." He shrugs at his friends. "Who knew?"

"I think there's probably a lot we don't know about Sabrina," Noah says, joining the conversation at long last.

Finally. His actual voice.

To Nellie's relief, it is throaty and low. Matches his whole demeanor. And it feels like somehow she already knows the timbre. Plus, there's something about his tone, the glint in his eye, the genuine warmth of his smile, that feels in deep contrast to Damien's slip-and-slide vibe. Noah is, as she has suspected, the kind of person whose attention feels like a heat lamp shining only on you.

"That's probably true." Nellie smiles small at him. "Sab is kind of a mystery—even to us sometimes."

His gaze lingers on her for a second, flits down to her mouth and back up. To avoid scaring him off, she pulls her own eyes away. She stares at a Dixie cup in the gutter, a discarded cigarette butt snagged in a sidewalk crack, focuses on anything else for fear of obviously gaping.

"So, where are you guys going?" the short one asks. *What was his name again?*

"Nowhere," says Lydia. "Fast."

Ugh. This girl.

All three boys widen their eyes and exchange glances.

"I have drawing class," Nellie says, squinting at the black Swatch on her wrist. "And actually, I'm late."

As much as she doesn't want to leave Noah's presence now that she has finally found him again, she *really* must go.

The drawing classes are not cheap. And her parents remind her of that every time she misses one.

"You draw?" Noah asks Nellie.

"I like to, yeah."

"She's being modest!" Cara manages to pipe up. "She's *amazing*."

Nellie smiles at her friend, genuinely touched. Cara is her biggest cheerleader.

"Wow," Noah says. "That's dope. It's like figure drawing or . . . ?"

"Alright, then," Damien interrupts. "Noah, dude. She said she's late. Maybe let her go instead of asking for an art history lecture. Sorry. Not 'her.' *Nellie*, right?" Despite his feigned ignorance, Damien clearly knows her name.

"D, don't be a dick." Noah shakes his head, lacing his hands behind his neck and stretching his arms out like he is sunning himself. His shirt rides up above his baggy jeans, revealing a strip of hard skin above an elastic Calvin Klein band. A bolt of heat scorches through Nellie's body at the sight.

She tears her eyes away again. But the image is already stored in her memory bank. For all eternity.

She has broken up the party. The boys nod goodbye and weave past the girls on the sidewalk, heading the opposite way. But, at the last minute, Noah turns back around.

"By the way, I don't think I actually got to meet you guys at the party either," he says, leaning in slightly. "I'm Noah."

Oh, I know.

"Hi," Nellie says. "Nice to meet you." All formal. Like this is a cotillion and not a littered street corner.

The sun kisses his forehead, his cheeks, his neck, so that he glistens. He winks like he knows. "Hope to see you soon . . . Nell."

Nellie can only nod dumbly as he shoots her his winning smile, turns, and saunters away.

She exhales. Now she is irrevocably late. But just catching a glimpse of that boy—that *Noah*—feels worth a billion dirty looks from her teacher. He is just as Nellie remembers from that night. He isn't like the boys she's friends with and has dated before. He looms larger, incandescent, *more*.

Now in something of a daze, she sighs as she and the girls resume walking. She's actually only a few town houses away from drawing class now.

"Okay!" she says, exhaling. "I'm out for real."

She kisses Cara on the cheek and stupid Lydia too, and she starts toward the steps.

"How come that boy was staring at you?" Lydia barks, before Nellie can get to the top.

Nellie whips back around. "Which boy?" she asks, her heart suddenly pounding. "The blond guy? Damien?"

"No. Not him. The cute one. With the shaved head. And the six-pack." Cara shoots Lydia a look, mock scandalized. "What? Are you saying you didn't notice?"

"No, I noticed." Cara grins.

A rush of joy washes over Nellie, leaving her feeling refreshed, like she's just emerged from a cold lake into the summer heat. "He was looking at me? Are you sure?"

"Definitely." Lydia frowns.

Nellie looks to Cara for confirmation. "Yup," she nods. "I saw it too."

Nellie's heart is bursting at the seams. Almost too full. So full that she's tempted to run back and hug Lydia for saying this, stink face and all.

Maybe not.

As Nellie runs up the final steps to class, behind her, she hears Lydia gripe, "Maybe she had something in her teeth."

Gleeful, Nellie laughs and jogs to the door. Nothing can tamp down her joy, her insides twinkling.

As the boys turn the corner, Noah glances back as nonchalantly as he can, just in time to watch Nellie disappear inside the doors, swallowed up by a building whose interior he has never seen. He is oddly desperate to know what world exists within, what halls and passageways with tiled floors, what pulpy drawing pads perched on easels and still-life vases stuffed with chaotic carnations. What smudges of charcoal and smells of turpentine. And he has the distinct sense that—in the admittedly very short period he has known that Nellie exists on this planet—he has already lost sight of her too many times.

4

NELLIE

TODAY

The drive to wine country is drop dead.

Enough so that it distracts me for a while from my angst. *Mostly*.

When my driver, John, and I leave the airport in our gargantuan black SUV with its perforated leather seats—presidential motorcade style—the skies quickly morph to full white. In the distance, clouds obscure the crests of green hills.

San Francisco is not totally unknown to me, though I have never quite had my bearings here. So, I am hit by a wave of nostalgia and even longing as I gaze at these vaguely familiar streets. When I lived in LA in college, more years ago than I care to count, I used to come visit Cara here regularly to spend Saturday nights crashing house parties and kissing random boys, and Sundays wandering indie boutiques in Hayes Valley. We gorged ourselves on hangover dim sum. And, *okay*, maybe once when Sabrina was also in town, I threw up in a tiny water bottle not far from here.

It's hard not to mourn those carefree days. That sense of possibility sure beats the stress of my current employment situation, the worries of adulting. My friends and I met up for holidays and long weekends and for no reason at all, driving back and forth on the 5 freeway between here and Southern Cali like it was nothing, as long as we had ample chips and mixtapes in tow. Let the truckers honk their hearts out.

It feels like eons ago—and like yesterday. Just like it felt to see Noah's face.

It has been actual decades (over two and a half, I flinch) since he and I last crossed paths. I don't know what I imagined I'd feel when I saw him. Anger, sure. Distance, definitely. Satisfaction, ideally—if he was balding and paunchy enough.

No such luck.

Instead, I am shocked by the freshness of the wound. Humiliated by it, even. By the sense of knowing him and of being known, which feels delusional after so many years of not speaking. By the lapsing into old rhythms, even antagonistic ones, so automatically.

It should be old news.

And I was angry, *sure*. But, I realize now with horror that it was less because of the original injury and more a sense that, with his actions, Noah had robbed us of so many years we could have had together. And, even worse, that as he stood in front of me, hands in his pockets, completely *fine*, he didn't appear to be experiencing the same sense of loss. While I was tossed into some zero-gravity atmosphere, floating untethered through space and time, he had his feet planted firmly on the ground. Didn't even seem thrown.

Which is so annoyingly *him*. To let everything roll off his back, to take the situation in stride. Like it's all no big deal.

Like none of it meant anything to him. And, of course, why should it? We were literally teenagers. Just kids.

I'm the one who needs to get a life, after all these years.

But he could at least have had the decency to look like shit.

I'd had relationships since ours, of course, after I had taken some time early on in college to lick my wounds. Alfie and others—and for longer stretches. Shared apartments, shared jokes, shared pets. But somehow all that life experience seemed to vanish into the ether as soon as I saw Noah's face.

Now, John and I come to a stop at a red light alongside a driverless car, as if to underline the passage of time. The past is past. This is the future.

Wake up.

We wind up, down, and through the hills of the city, past precious pastel town houses pitched at unnatural angles, artisanal juice shops, and seedy corners tagged with graffiti and littered with debris. We pass through Golden Gate Park, green and lush with white dogwoods and cherry blossoms in bloom, and pass over Golden Gate Bridge with views of Alcatraz juxtaposed with crisp white sailboats in the glimmering distance. We coast through the arched rainbows of the Robin Williams Tunnel and are transported to quieter Sausalito with its houseboats and untamed fields of yellow grass. We head toward dreamy bohemian Marin.

And all the time, I am vibrating.

And then, suddenly, things are pastoral. There are farms—with hay bales and grazing velvet horses—that give way to redwood forests at their back edges, surely harboring mystical secrets. And then the clouds lift. Like they never existed at all. And we are in the full bouquet of wine country. Cheerful grapevines rise toward the sky on all sides, sunning themselves in neat rows as far as the eye can see.

And I exhale. Because it is basically a prerequisite to arriving in this part of the country.

"We're here," says John as we pull into the gravel driveway at what Cara and Ben and the driver himself keep referring to as "the estate."

"Great!" I say, but it comes out flat.

Because, as excited as I am to see Cara and Sabrina and Ben too, and as gorgeous as it is here, dread has settled leaden in my stomach.

I don't move. The driver glances back at me. Pulls off his aviator shades.

He is probably accustomed to customers who exit his car once they arrive at their destination.

"Are you okay?" he asks, his blue eyes crinkling. Because even he—this stranger—can tell I'm off. And that is not good.

"Is it that obvious?"

He smiles warmly. "I have daughters."

"Ah."

I can do this, I tell myself. I can be just fine. I can face the past and then leave it there. I can make it through this trip. I can avoid Noah-who-must-not-be-named and I can celebrate my best friends and then I can fly home and figure out how to rebuild my life into something I want it to be.

John steps out of the car, pops the trunk, and, with a bit of effort, pulls out the Jolly Green Giant. As I climb out too and circle to meet him, I notice my suitcase looks pretty banged up in the light of day. A little less jolly.

"Can I take this in for you?" he asks.

I shake my head, forced bravery rising in my chest. "I'm good."

He nods and rotates the bag toward me, so that I can easily access the handle. "Listen," he says. "I don't know what's going on. We don't know each other. But I can tell you the thing I always tell my girls: You are stronger than you think. And then some. You've got this."

I've got this.

His words reverberate through me. And I realize he reminds me of my own dad, who I could really use right now. I almost start to cry right then and there. My God, I'm a mess.

"Thank you, John." I smile, my vision blurred.

"Also," he says, leaning in. "The wine helps."

And that I know is true.

Before I can fully thank him, I hear my name ring out from behind me and I swivel toward the voice. There is Cara, on the threshold of the property, arms raised above her head in celebration. And, despite my misgivings, a wave of relief washes over me.

"You're here!" she practically sings.

Yup. I am. I am here. Whether I like it or not.

She drops her arms. "Be honest: Do I look okay in this? Because I feel like a character out of *Laurel Canyon*."

And I can't help but smile, the knot in my chest loosening ever so slightly. Because she is glowing, a vision of California bohemia in an Indian block-printed maxi dress and Birkenstocks—a stark contrast to her usual more tailored and preppy striped tops. She is trying something out.

"You look great. *And* like a character in *Laurel Canyon*."

She purses her lips, rests a hand on her hip, and I rush toward her for a giant hug. And it's just what the doctor ordered. My best friend.

She smells like vanilla and her—and it's as comforting as anything could be.

When we finally release each other, she turns and leads the way deeper into the property. "I can't wait to show you around!"

"Great!" I say. "But where's your VW bus parked?"

She shoots me a death glare and we both dissolve into laughter.

I should have let John carry my bag. That's my first thought as I drag the Jolly Green Giant along the cobbled path. Though it's sprawling and stunning, I think "estate" is not quite the right word for this place, which feels rustic in the most upscale and contained way. Because there is nothing stuffy or grandiose here. It's beautiful but barefoot—every breezy detail considered.

No needs left behind.

The path is lined with an organized pandemonium of wildflowers against low stone walls—white clovers, violets, the friendliest daisy fleabane. Bees and butterflies flit harmoniously from bloom to bloom, sharing an abundance of nectar. It's a free-for-all!

We walk by an understated indoor/outdoor dining area with twinkle lights strung from the trees above, and a spacious pool surrounded by plush loungers and sharp white umbrellas. Behind that is a row of small slatted buttercup-colored bungalows, clearly individual guest rooms.

On our way past the chicken coop and vegetable garden, I catch a glimpse of a tall blond man in overdetermined sunglasses and a too-hipster short-sleeved button-down coming around a corner. I haven't seen him in years, but I'd know him anywhere. *Damien.* I duck my head and discreetly hustle behind Cara before he spots us, my heart pounding. It's one thing to confront these blasts from the past; it's another to do it while airplane grime is still clinging to your clothes.

I am not ready to contend with him.

Gesturing toward the adjoining biodynamic vineyard and orange grove like a spokesmodel for artisanal living, Cara leads me beyond a spa wafting the scent of neroli to a larger barn-style building—also in slatted yellow—that she explains is the main manor house.

Renting this property must have cost a pretty penny. Ben and Cara both work in tech and all that implies, but still . . . they have gone all out.

Again, it occurs to me that this is all a little unlike Cara, who tends to be sensible, responsible, austere. This event, while being mostly symbolic, is clearly important.

It's a reminder not to ruin it for her. I will not be a flaming ball of rage. I will be measured, calm. I will fake it like nobody's business.

For once, *I'll* be the chill one—not him.

"This is where Ben and I are staying," Cara says of the big house. "And our closest people."

"That's me, I think," I say, raising my hand. "Is that me?"

She grins. "That's you, you maniac."

I lug my bag up several steps to the front porch, where cherry-red Adirondack chairs await beneath rotating ceiling fans.

"Do you want some help with that?" she asks, eyeing me warily as I pant and heave and try to ignore the increasingly intense throbbing in my injured shoulder. "I can help you—or there should be some staff members around here somewhere."

"I'm good," I assure her, raising a hand to stop her. "Really."

"If you say so."

Once I make it to the porch, she opens the front doors and we step into an airy parlor. Only there is nothing stodgy about it as the word suggests. The ceilings are lofted and a mile high. There are windows everywhere, inviting the outside in, especially at the back where the house bellies up to actual woods. The furniture leans Danish modern and is appointed with warm neutrals and pops of neon. French blue and lilac bud vases—that I suspect are made by local Heath Ceramics—abound, filled with the same wildflowers I spotted on our walk through the property.

Everything smells like spring.

Except maybe post-plane me.

There is a staircase to my right, leading to what I imagine are more glorious rooms. "Cara, this is gorgeous," I gush. "But please tell me I don't have to carry the Jolly Green Giant up those stairs."

"No, no, you're good," she titters, tucking her hair behind her ear.

But she doesn't move to show me the way. And, looking at her more closely, I realize she seems nervous.

"Hey CB, I'd love to wash my face," I say. "Maybe shower. Which way is my room?"

She is avoiding my eyes.

"Dude. What's up? Seriously. Out with it."

She exhales sharply. "Okay, so, because Alfie didn't come with you and you're . . . single for the trip, I had to put you in one of the smaller bedrooms. Well, meaning, a room with one of the full-size beds. We have the main suite, and I gave Sabrina and Rita the other king room in the house."

"Okay," I shrug. "That's totally fine. Don't even worry! I'm happy to take the kids' room or whatever."

"Great," she says, though she's still biting her lip like she is not relieved.

"Okay?" I say.

"Okay," she agrees.

She turns, tentatively, and begins guiding me off to the left, stopping in front of a door marked THE POPPY SUITE.

"Oh! It's a suite," I say, delighted. I am doubly fine with a small room if it has an adjoining living space. "Sweet!"

"It's a suite alright," she nods, turning the knob.

Inside, the room is as breezy and bright as the rest of the house. The ceilings are tall, the floors are a beautiful light wood in wide slats. We are greeted by plush rugs in muted pinks and corals in a full living room with a cushy couch and a Pendleton throw blanket folded over a modernist leather ottoman. There's even an old-school record player and an assortment of vinyl on a bookshelf along with the usual array of worn vacation house books, but also beautiful bound copies of classics. I peep *The Great Gatsby* and *Franny and Zooey*. A kitchen area to the left boasts an espresso machine and a countertop bearing a pretty box of tea. The wine fridge looks fully stocked as well.

"This is lovely!" I say, meaning it. But then I glitch on Cara's anxious expression again and wave my hand in her general direction. "Why does your face still look like that?"

I know my best friend. And something is up.

She takes a deep breath as if to steel herself. "There's one teeny-tiny catch . . ."

"This is your room," I hear a male voice say as I whip around to find Ben walking in . . . with Noah close behind him.

Of course.

Noah looks from Ben to me and then back to Ben, his mouth falling open.

My stomach drops and begins to churn like an ancient washing machine.

With alarm, I turn to Cara as she points her fingers in opposite directions. "There are two rooms," she says. "Separate rooms. Like totally separate."

Ben scurries over to stand by her side, either in her defense or out of fear. The two of them eye us like we're rabid raccoons. They are more powerful together.

The silence in the room is deep as Noah and I absorb this information—and it extends until Cara can't take it anymore.

"The thing is, I'm so sorry and I know neither of you want to share a suite, but you're our best friends and we really want you close by us and this is really the only option unless we give Sabrina and Rita one of these rooms—but then it's a smaller bed and that doesn't seem like a good solution for a couple. So, I totally understand if you don't want to do this and, if either of you want to switch with someone who's in a separate bungalow on the grounds, you totally can. We really understand. And I am so, so sorry!"

She pauses to catch her breath like she has just run a sprint.

I truly cannot believe my best friend would put me in this situation. Knowing how I feel about *him*. It's a total nightmare. As much as it can be a nightmare to be in a beautiful suite in wine country—which, to be fair, isn't that much of a nightmare. And I am about to say all this out loud when Ben puts his arm around his wife, looks from me to Noah, and says pointedly: "Cara did her best. And she's been *really* worried about this."

And that instantly takes me down a notch. Because, of course, I catch his drift. This is Cara's week. Ben's week. And here I am already causing them unnecessary stress.

Against my better judgment, I steal a look at Noah. And though he is tense enough to be running his fingers continuously over his hair, I can see him processing this the same way I am. Begrudgingly, I catch his eye. We always had solid silent communication and that has not changed, even after all these years. I know we're in agreement before he speaks.

"Please don't worry, Cara," he says. "We're grown-ups. We have one hundred percent got this." He looks at me. "Right, Nell . . . *Eleanor?*"

Everything in me wants to turn around and do the whole journey in reverse. Call John back to the estate and have him whisk me in the opposite direction through the rainbow tunnel—perhaps to a pot of gold—and across the bridge to the airport, where I will take off like a rocket, never to return. But this is Cara's trip. Ben's trip. And I will not be the one to ruin it. So, instead, I clear my throat, gather my strength, and will the corners of my mouth to curve into a smile.

It may look terrifying, but it's the best I've got.

"Yes. Don't worry. We are all good. It's *all* good. We got this."

Even using the word *we* gives me agita. But I grin my way through it so hard that my face starts to hurt. When the happy couple finally leaves the suite, Cara glancing back three hundred times to check to see if I am truly okay, I am relieved to see them go.

The door clicks shut. I let my face fall. And then it's just *him* and me. Noah. Me. Alone. Together.

There's a moment of silence as we consider each other, resigned.

Then, he opens his mouth to speak and I put up a hand. Like I am a crossing guard and he does not have the right of way. It's my right hand and, as my shoulder rotates, I involuntarily wince from pain.

I don't need to know what he's going to say to know that I don't want to hear it. No thanks.

"Don't," I bark before he makes a sound and, without a glance back, I cross to my room, the Jolly Green Giant rolling close behind.

5

NOAH
TODAY

These days, I never drink heavily. It's not worth the three-day hangover.

But tonight I'm tempted to skip the glass and stick my head under a wine barrel's faucet instead, so I can mainline the stuff more quickly. Not because the wine is good—though it is. And not because I'm psyched for my friends and a much-needed vacation—which I was. But because I am desperate to get out of my fucking head.

Oaky. Full-bodied. Notes of cherry and tobacco. I don't give a shit. I just want to numb out.

It's never fun to hang out around someone you have beef with, but this is more than that. It's . . . shit I don't even want to consider. What's going on inside my brain right now is some kind of twisted mental time travel. It's like I'm falling down a black hole into that tempestuous period when I was eighteen, with as little perspective as I had in that actual moment.

It's like my hindsight has evaporated.

To make matters worse, Ben and Cara are loyal, dedicated. So many of the guests at this gathering will be people they befriended back in the day, people I've also known for years. It's all making the past feel more present.

If it was possible to shake myself and remind myself that I'm an adult, even a functional semi-happy one, I'd slap some sense into my stupid ass. But that's not a thing.

So . . . alcohol.

When Nell emerges, I'm into my second glass of some local pinot noir, but it does nothing to quell the strumming that riots through me at the sight of her. After the harrowing discovery that we're going to be roomies, we managed to avoid each other. In the afternoon, I spent more time than made sense scanning "Cara & Ben's Un-Wedding Itinerary"—printed and placed at my bedside—as I grasped for a foothold in reality. Mostly, it included detailed attire suggestions and QR codes that linked to songs representing each of the six days' themes. (Day 1: *Arrival!* Song: "Welcome to the Jungle" by Guns N' Roses.)

Welcome to the jungle, we take it day by day
If you want it, you're gonna bleed, but it's the price you pay

Seemed about right.

This evening, I slipped out first—and I swear I heard Nell cry out in pain through the wall when I crept toward our suite's main door.

What the hell is wrong with me? Why am I eavesdropping on this woman? I am a goddamn adult. I need to act like one.

Now, Damien tracks Nell's movement across the patio with his eyes, raises his brows at me. This is his first time catching a glimpse of her since we arrived.

I turn my back to her. Act like I don't see. Like I don't know what he's suggesting with his look. Like I can't feel her there, behind me, like a live wire.

He smirks. Like *please*.

He's not going to let me pretend I don't give a shit. Of course not. He's Damien. He loves me, but he also loves to torture me. My asshole brother from another mother.

I am a collector of people. That's what my older sister, Henrietta, always says. Only she uses less flattering words like *hoarder*. She groans every time I mention Damien's name or tell some admittedly shameful story about another one of my aging high school boys—other than Ben, who she loves.

"You need to spring-clean," Henny groaned during a recent call. "Make space. Set them free in their natural habitat to roam . . . to custodial court or a seedy bar at eleven a.m."

But dissing those guys outright, even the shadiest of them, feels disloyal. Like denying a part of myself. So, I try not to judge. I keep in touch.

They—Damien especially—have been good friends to me in their way. They stuck by me in tough times. Not everyone did.

Nell didn't, though I can see it was more complicated than that now.

So, I take their calls. I hang out when I'm back in New York. I do them favors, here and there.

"She still looks tight," Damien says now, assessing Nellie from afar.

And I don't like the way he's looking at her.

I've never liked the way he looks at her, I let myself admit.

I know what he's seeing without turning my head. Because, whether I wanted to or not, I memorized everything about her the instant she walked into the party—her jeans that fit her ass like a glove, a satiny tank top that dips low, and a white cable-knit cardigan in case she wants to wrap herself in a protective hug. Classic Nell.

"I guess she looks okay," I allow. I swig from my glass. 'Cause that's how you're supposed to drink wine, right? Chug it in giant gulps? All classy?

"You guess?" He is disbelieving.

I shrug. Roll my eyes. "Of course she looks good, D. Doesn't make her any more pleasant to be around."

Damien looks past me again. I watch him catch her eye over my shoulder. Nod and wink in greeting. "I beg to differ," he says, his gaze still on her. "I think it makes her plenty pleasant."

I shrug again. Suit yourself.

I am a shrugging machine.

"You think you guys will hook up?" he asks, still distracted by Nell. His eyes remain not on me.

"Hard pass," I say. And mean it.

Now, he's the one who shrugs. Like *more for me*. Like he might have a chance with her. Like he might try. I know he wouldn't dare, which is why I don't dignify the gesture with a response. And even though I feel like throttling him, I have zero legs to stand on.

I sigh and try to surrender to the surroundings. Ben and Cara have asked us all to gather on the slatted deck outside the estate's restaurant for this first official event. D and I are hanging toward the edges as daylight begins its retreat. The air smells like fresh ferns, like a forest after a rain. Like something fertile and real.

Like there might be hobbits nearby.

Damien leans back against the wooden railing. Not a care in the world. The dress code was described as casual. And I followed instructions in my favorite denim button-down and army-green slacks. But he's wearing one of his signature looks—like some kind of Boyz II Men throwback in baggy chinos and a vest. Like maybe he and Travis Kelce share a stylist. I have never understood his taste, but he does him. And women don't seem to mind. I'll give him that.

"Dude. This is a trip," he says, eyeing the crowd. Ben and Cara have not invited family since this is not *actually* their wedding. I sort of hoped they might as a buffer. I've always liked Ben's parents and sister.

"No way, man," Ben told me over the phone last week when I asked. "We're hoping to actually *enjoy* this trip."

Instead, they have convened a group of close friends. Some I recognize from other events throughout the years, ones that Nell missed since there was an unspoken rule that only one of us attended (usually based on whether it was more of a Ben or a Cara thing). Ben's college buddies, his work friends. Some people who I assume belong to Cara in the same capacity. I imagine there's a parent friend or two—couples they met on the playground or at preschool pickup. But I figure I'll spend most of this trip chilling with D. We talk occasionally, text off and on, but I don't get to see him that often since he still lives in New York. So hanging with him sounds just fine.

Or it did. Before he started ogling Nell like a hot fudge sundae with all the toppings—except nuts. Nobody wants nuts.

His eyes bulge suddenly, and I finally can't help but turn around to follow his gaze. But it's not Nell he's looking at now. It's Lydia. *Fucking Lydia.* Walking up the steps and onto the deck, her red hair as ablaze as ever, and instantly I know this situation has gone from bad to worse.

"Fuck," I mumble under my breath, whipping back around to face the trees. Maybe if I stand really still, she won't notice me. I glance around for somewhere to hide—behind a giant redwood or, better yet, back in my room.

Nope. My room is not a safe space either.

Damn. I'm not used to stressing like this. It's not how I roll.

Damien grins. He lives for this shit. The ultimate drama queen.

If I make it through this trip alive, I will count myself lucky. I rub a hand over my hair, gulp down more wine.

And then Damien is waving and gesturing someone over and I can't even bring myself to turn and see who it is because it can only be bad news.

"Hey! Whattup guys?" Cara says, landing beside me. And I heave a sigh of relief as I open our circle to include her . . . and, *dammit*, Nell too. Relief null and void.

Nell glances up at me, nods curtly. I guess this is her trying for Cara.

I am instantly buzzing from head to toe, as I try to ignore the effect her closeness has on me.

"Not much," Damien says, waving his hand to reference the surroundings. "Except this place is fucking next level. So dope."

"It is, right?" Cara agrees. She's beaming and it's a little contagious, even to me, mid–stress spiral. She seems so happy, her eyes shining. "I'm so glad this is finally really happening! It feels like we've been planning forever—and now we're really all together!"

Cara throws an arm over Nell's shoulder and squeezes, and I watch Nell wince, even as she shoots her best friend a pained smile. Her shoulder hurts. And it's obvious.

Is that why I heard cries from her room earlier?

"We are!" says Nell, toasting the air with her full glass in the other hand. "We are definitely together!"

I can't tell if she's doing a poor performance of happy or if I just still know her well enough to see she's actually peak miserable.

Maybe like recognizes like.

Damien focuses his gaze on her—again. Tips his chin up. I know this look. It's his Ryan Gosling special. "Hey, Nellie," he says, his tone smooth and velvety. "It's been too long."

"It has!" she says, as they exchange kisses hello on the cheek. "It's good to see you."

A wave of irrational jealousy crashes over me. On what planet is she sweet to Damien and a fucking demon to me?

He gets a peck and I get a middle finger.

"You look exactly the same," he's saying.

"Well," she smiles, despite herself. "Not exactly."

"You're right," he says, his eyes raking down her body. "You look even better."

And then she blushes. She actually fucking *blushes*. All pretty and demure. And I can't fucking believe what I'm seeing because Nell never fell for Damien's game back in the day. She was the first one to call bullshit—even to his face. She complained about him to me all the time. And now she's aglow under his gaze while she avoids mine?

If anyone is going to look down her low-cut top, it should be me!

Since when did the earth become the sky?

And I am nodding along to what Cara is telling all of us about the history of the estate and the incredible biodynamic wineries in the area, listening vaguely to Nell and Damien respond, comparing notes about the places they've heard we should visit. But I am absorbing none of it thanks to the rushing in my ears.

On the outside, I might seem calm. But, in my head, there is an ocean in tumult.

"Is that the spa building?" Nell asks. She tries to raise her arm to point and visibly grimaces, grabbing her shoulder in a way that you'd have to be blind to miss.

"Oh no!" Cara says. "Is it your rotator cuff again?"

Nell chances a real glance up at me for the first time since we've been standing here and I raise my eyebrows. *Shoulder's not a thing anymore, huh?*

"Yeah. I don't know. It's no big deal."

"You need to let Noah look at it," Damien says.

And Nell half laughs like he's kidding. Like he's made a bad joke and she's playing along.

"No, really," he says. "You know he works for like the Dodgers and Clippers and shit, right?"

"Right." She smirks up at me. "What are you? Like the ball boy?"

Damien opens his mouth to answer her, but I put a hand on his forearm to stop him. "If she wants to believe I'm a nothing, let her," I murmur. What the hell do I care?

There was a time when I believed that, too.

"Yeah," I nod to Nell. "I'm a ball boy. With the rest of the children and the dogs."

"Well," she says. "The dog part tracks."

I glare at her hatefully and she glares back at me. So much for civility.

"You guys, I'm so sorry I put you in the same suite!" Cara blurts out, her brow furrowed. "If you want to switch, *please* tell me. It's not too late!"

Damien's eyes go wide. He lets out a sharp guffaw. "Wait. No way! The same suite? You two?"

"Yup," I say. "Us two."

"Damn," he says, pointing. "It's on."

"Nothing is on," Nell says. "Ever."

"We have very separate rooms," I mumble at the same time. "Thank God."

Damien takes another look at Nell, scanning her from head to toe like he's a fucking MRI machine I'm about to smash. He shrugs. "I'll switch with Noah."

"Really?" Cara says, hopeful.

"Sure," he says. "I'll take his room, no problem. I'd happily share a suite with Nellie. We can catch up on old times. Watch movies on the couch. Eat popcorn. Bond."

Nell's eyes widen. Despite the tension between us, she casts a panicked look my way. Thank the Lord. She is still in there somewhere. And she has no interest in alone time with Damien.

"No, thanks," I say. "I already unpacked."

And I see Nell exhale just as I hear a female voice behind me purr, "Then let me help. I'll switch with Nellie. Noah and I have *always* gotten along. Swimmingly."

Go fish.

And there is Lydia in all her ginger glory, sucking her teeth from behind bright-red lips. And if I thought Nell's top was a little low cut, Lydia's makes it seem church-worthy, dipping down to reveal an expanse of freckled cleavage that commands center stage.

Nell's expression goes from relieved to pinched in an instant. A shot of something like anger, but maybe even pain akin to when her shoulder spasmed, crosses her face and disappears before it goes stony.

I hate this closed look even more than the angry one. She is shut down. I want to reach over and brush a thumb across her cheek to flip the switch back on. But the instinct is just muscle memory, so I stay put.

She doesn't acknowledge Lydia's offer. Or Lydia at all. And I'm grateful. I don't want to share a suite with her either. Lydia is not a fan of boundaries, and I need space more than anything right now.

"I see Sabrina," Nell says. To Cara. To Damien. To the people to whom she actually speaks. And then she races away to anywhere else, taking a deep sip of wine as she goes.

We all watch her leave. Damien lets out a low whistle. "Wow," he says. "It's like not a day has passed."

I think he may mean this in a good way. But it is in no way good.

"Except Ben and I are married with kids," says Cara, desperate to keep things light. "And Sab is with Rita. And Nellie has Alfie, of course."

I snap to attention at that.

"Alfie? Who the hell is that?" asks Damien. And I'm grateful he asks because it means I don't have to.

"Her fiancé!" Cara says, like it's the most obvious thing in the world. Like Alfie is the easiest answer on *Jeopardy!*

"Fiancé?" we all say at once—even Lydia.

And now my heart is pounding again. Even though this is a good thing, right? This takes the pressure off. This means Nell will be hanging with some guy the whole time and we can fully ignore each other.

Damien scans the deck. "But where is he? I want to check this dude out."

"Oh, he couldn't come," Cara shrugs, frowning. "He had a work thing. He's a big-deal political journalist. Nellie's usual type."

Her usual type. Brainy. High-achieving. Not like she sees me—the ball boy.

If Cara knows she's said something triggering, she doesn't show it. And we all nod like this is no big thing. *Fiancé.* The word stutters in my brain like a scratched record.

"So, you guys are the single crew!" Cara adds, as if this is a good thing. Damien nods, thoughtfully. Lydia looks up at me, lasciviously. And I just try to breathe.

My normal life, the one in which I feel like a full human and people take me seriously and I have friends and coworkers and successful interactions, is receding further and further from my consciousness, so that I am already having trouble connecting with it.

It's like I'm aging backward in the worst possible way.

From a distance, I see Nell huddling with Sabrina and Rita, her tried-and-true friends, and I kind of wish I could be there too. There was a time when I would have been. When that would have been my inner circle too. It's magic hour, and the light is settling over the women in swaths of tangerine. Fairy lights twinkle over their heads, wound around the branches of overarching trees. Maybe it's just me, but Nell seems to actually glow.

And I am reminded of the first time I saw her, across a crowded club. Like she was my north star, lit from within.

Something wrenches in my chest.

I don't know why it should matter if she's engaged. We're practically mortal enemies. But, for some reason, it does. My insides are glitching. I try to push the feeling aside, remember what a pain in the ass she is, remind myself that I've had long-term girlfriends too—but it won't budge. Sensing my gaze on her, she glances up. Meets my eyes. Gives me a questioning look, like, *what?* Then shakes her head clear and goes back to her girls.

I feel an icy palm rest on my forearm like a wake-up call. Lydia. Her nails long and sharp. "Single is more fun anyway," she says. "I can't wait to get the lowdown on you."

And in that moment, I know for sure it's going to be a really long week.

6

BOTH

BACK IN THE DAY

The smell of weed permeates. The air—if there is any remaining—is cloudy with smoke. The room, a hotbox.

Though it's the middle of the day on a Saturday, the space is dark, shades pulled down to block out the sun.

Nellie has only tried pot once before, with a camp friend on the girl's family farm in Wisconsin. There, they'd been perched on grassy knolls surrounding a placid lake in summer. Dandelions abounded at crooked angles in place of people. It was peaceful, serene, silly.

Even the pot, which came from her friend's father's stash, seemed somehow wholesome.

Though urban legend says you never feel high the first time you smoke, they'd shared a whole joint and Nellie definitely got stoned. What else would explain why—when after a while they had to push to standing, brush the grass off their shorts, and make their way back to the family home for early dinner—she literally couldn't stop laughing?

But even that felt fine, if mildly out of control. Mostly Nellie recalled the warmth of the waning sun on her shoulders as they dug into the world's most delicious pasta salad and hot dogs around a picnic table by a vegetable garden.

This. Today. At some kid's apartment who she doesn't know—the short, stocky sweet one whose name she can never recall (*Ben? Benji? Bill?*)—feels totally different. For one thing, there are no dandelions. Only disheveled teenage boys in every direction, in clothes so oversized on their wiry frames that they evoke laundry piles. In the dim bedroom with too many lava lamps (is there such thing as too few?), they slouch in corners. On an old couch below Wu-Tang Clan and Knicks posters. On the floor by a collection of still-boxed action figures and *Star Wars* figurines. In a desk chair that swivels as one boy keeps spinning in it.

Brain trust.

There are girls here too, but only a few. Nellie, Sabrina, and Lydia (who Cara left them to babysit when she ran to her model U.N. meeting). And a couple others from Sabrina's school, whose names entered and exited Nellie's consciousness within seconds of hearing them. Jen and Jenny, maybe? Jess and Jessica?

Nellie is sitting on the floor against one wall next to Sebastian, a boy Sabrina has wanted her to meet. The reason Sabrina dragged her here.

Even now, Sabrina, who sits on her other side, keeps nudging Nellie and raising her eyebrows like, *what do you think?*

Why doesn't Sabrina date him herself?

He is more grunge than hip-hop. More flannel than Fubu. Supposedly a sensitive boy, full of poetry and pain. His tattered skateboard—laden with stickers and tags—leans up against a nearby wall.

He's not Nellie's type, but he's definitely good-looking, with scruffy auburn hair and chiseled, almost pretty features that remind her of Brad Pitt in *True Romance*.

And that almost, *almost*, makes up for the fact that he's boring as hell and has a resting expression like someone just murdered his puppy.

"So, like, do you like music?" he asks.

"Yeah," Nellie says. "I like music." Because she is human. And humans like music. And food. And air (preferably not polluted like a head shop).

"My favorite band is The Smiths." He frowns with what she imagines is enthusiasm. " 'Cause they're, like, mad *real*, you know?"

Nellie nods. She does know. The Smiths are in fact a real band.

"Um, you're in your own band too, right?" Nellie tries, searching for common ground.

"Word. Yeah. I'm in a band."

"That's cool. What kind?"

"What kind?" His brow creases. This question has stumped him. "What do you mean?"

"Like, what kind of music do you guys play?"

"Just . . . kind of like the Smiths. It's hard to explain."

Is it though?

Sabrina nudges Nellie again. Scoots closer to her, so that Nellie is forced to press her other side right up against Sebastian's arm and hip. She glances surreptitiously over and assesses him—his trucker hat and Carhartt jeans. The wallet chain that hangs between his back pocket and his belt.

Ugh. The dreaded wallet chain. Has the world ever seen a more hard-trying accessory?

She tries to ignore it.

She wants to like this dude. *Really* wants to like him. 'Cause he is very hot. And also, she is mired in a dry spell of roughly . . . her whole life. But he is making it very difficult to like him. Because he has the personality of wet cardboard.

It will take her years to understand that this brand of skater boy is her diametric opposite on the spectrum of human personality, a type to whom she can never connect. Literally *ever*.

Now, the bong makes its way back around to them and, like last time, she readies to pass it along without partaking. She liked her one pot experience, but she doesn't feel like she needs to relive it socially, alcohol being so much more predictable and loose. But then she looks at Sebastian and he looks blankly back at her and she realizes his eyes are intensely bloodshot and she thinks, *Huh. Maybe if I smoke pot too, we'll be on the same wavelength?*

Maybe she can smoke her way into his heart—or at least his pants.

So, she brings her lips to the bong's damp hole, trying not to think about the number of teenage mouths that have been there before. Ignoring the dank stench of the water inside, she lets this boy bring his lighter to the bowl. It blazes orange, sizzling with heat, as she inhales an enormous hit.

Too enormous. Like by a lot. So that she fears for a brief moment that her lungs might collapse. Instead she launches into a deeply unsexy coughing fit, as Sebastian looks on encouragingly.

"When you cough," he says, "it makes the effects stronger."

This is what it takes to make him smile?

She nods vigorously, like she is totally fine with coughing up a lung and trying to ignore the searing pressure in her chest. Also: *Stronger?* Is that what she wants?

And nope. Nope, it isn't. Because within minutes what was previously dull but benign feels horribly conspicuous and awkward as she slouches against the wall and wills the high to end.

No wonder Sebastian can't form a coherent sentence. Now that she's high, she can't form any sentence at all.

This isn't at all like lounging on the banks of the Door County river. This isn't at all like running her bare feet through the grass, a sense of freedom and abandon as she stretched out and shut her eyes against the breeze.

Nope.

This feeling is more akin to being trapped in a middle seat in a miniature airplane during apocalyptic turbulence.

She is dying to turn to Sabrina and tell her what's up—to beg for help—but her bestie is embroiled in some deep conversation with this other artsy girl, Chloe something, with lots of tongue pierces and black lipstick. And as a now socially inept human, Nellie can't figure out how a normal person would interject.

The back of her neck flashes hot. Her heart is pounding. Full panic descending.

Are the boys in the room multiplying like bacteria? The space feels like it's shrinking.

And, oh, no! On top of the high from the bong hit, is she getting an exponential contact high from the smoke in the room?

"Hey, I remember you!" booms a voice from above her, interrupting her spiral. She looks up to find that blond kid, Damien, standing over her, his palm outstretched.

Oh, God. Not this guy. Not now.

"What's up, *Nellie?*"

He says her name like she should be impressed that he knows it.

Given no other option, she manages to unfreeze and make a feeble attempt at a pound. But she doesn't answer audibly. Words are not an option.

His hand is sweaty.

"What's up, dude?" he says, examining her face from above, his sharp features venturing closer to her own. "Cat got your tongue? Or whatever the fuck that expression is. Is that right? Cat got your tongue? It sounds weird now. Cat. Got. Your. Tongue."

It does sound weird. But not as weird as Nellie is feeling. She has to get out of here. Immediately.

With Damien distracted by this linguistic brain teaser, she pushes to standing and, wobbly, chances a glance down at Sebastian. "I've got to . . ." She never bothers to finish the sentence. Instead, she tiptoes her way out of the room, careful not to trip over outstretched legs or strewn backpacks. Having thus escaped into the foyer, she scans the area for the kitchen, crosses to it, and finds it blessedly empty.

Phew. She is not saved, but this is something, at least.

She finds and fills a glass to the brim with cold water, chugs it, and then tries to catch her breath.

Okay. She is okay. She will be okay.

This will end.

Right? Oh, God. What if it never ends? What if she feels this way forever? What if the pot is laced with acid and she is eternally altered like that boy she'd heard about who thought he was a glass of orange juice and spent the rest of his life afraid he might spill?

Her gaze drifts to the window with a view of Riverside Drive—the familiar stone wall, the collage of tall trees in the park, goofy with overlapping leaves like giant green sheepdogs. All she needs to do is get herself out there in the sunlight and away from all these people. All this smoke.

But how? First thing, grab her stuff. Second, make an excuse.

I feel sick? No. Too much fuss.

I forgot I need to get home. Maybe. It's believable. Her mom is on the stricter side.

Third, find the elevator, press the button, pray not to get stuck, act like a normal human around any other tenants, exit the building with an awkward nod to the doorman.

Then burst into fresh air, blissfully alone.

She can do that. If she can move from this safe spot back into the other room. *The other room.* She rotates toward the sink and fills the tumbler with more water. Then she leans over, propping her forearms on the edge and her head in her hands, and groans.

"Um, hey, are you okay?" A voice from the entrance. Gravelly, low.

She looks up. Blinks. And it's *him*. Noah of club and sidewalk fame.

Oh Lord. Not him. Not now.

Why didn't she realize he might be here? With Damien and the short stocky kid?

"I'm fine," she squeaks, pivoting and leaning back against the counter like this is no big deal. But she misjudges the distance to the sink and almost topples over. He bounds through the narrow kitchen and catches her as she teeters. And the conductive heat of his hands on her lower back and arm is, for just an instant, a distraction from the chaos unraveling in her mind.

He peers into her face, close enough so she can stare in wonder at the yellow flecks in his hazel eyes. "You don't seem . . . fine?"

She considers trying to play it off. Pretend all is okay. But, as she steadies herself against the counter and he (regrettably) removes his hands and takes a step back, she realizes she has already humiliated herself enough to render her forever unattractive in his eyes anyway. So, she's honest.

"I'm too high."

"Oh," he says, a look of pity coming over his adorable face. "That sucks. Does this happen to you a lot?"

"What? No! If this happened to me a lot, I would never have taken the bong hit in the first place!"

"Right, right. That makes sense. I didn't know if you were, like, a stoner."

Fantastic.

"I actually don't normally smoke pot," she says.

"Because?"

"Because I'm scared of something like this!" To clarify, she adds: "I am not, like, *chill*."

He suppresses a laugh, like this last fact is obvious, then brings a finger to his mouth like he's having a thought. "You're really freaking out, huh?"

"I'm really freaking out."

"Don't freak out."

"I mean . . . okay?"

He studies her intently, his eyes narrowing. "I think I can help."

"Really? Can you turn back time? Can you find a way? Can you—"

"Who are you? Cher?"

Without waiting for an answer, he turns and opens a cabinet above them, rifling through its contents with his arm outstretched, so that his shirt rises to expose that smooth strip of skin above his Marky Mark boxer briefs. *This again?* She wills her eyes up, up, and away, but it isn't her fault—the drugs made her do it!

If he catches her gawking, he doesn't let on as he pulls a box of Cheerios down from the shelf.

"Cereal?" she asks, ignoring all the tingles.

"Yup." He nods, all seriousness. "It's a little-known fact that Cheerios can cure literally any ailment."

Nellie eyes him doubtfully. "A cold?"

"Obviously."

"The flu?"

"Sure."

"Leprosy?"

"I mean, I haven't tested that one. But seriously, I don't understand the exact science of it, but apparently oats can temporarily raise your glucose levels, which—when blended with the protein in milk—can make the high shorter."

He looks so damn earnest, holding out that cereal box, that she figures it's worth a shot. And anyway, what choice does she have, because he is already pulling down a bowl and grabbing a quart of milk from the fridge and so, *yes*, she is going to eat a bowl of cereal in a stranger's apartment with the boy she's been fantasizing about for months.

Maybe she's hallucinating?

"Is this weird?" she asks, glancing around this unfamiliar kitchen with its French blue tiles and sugar jar in the shape of Garfield. There's a vintage tin sign propped against the backsplash that reads: Fresh Strawberries.

He rifles through more drawers looking for a spoon. "Is what weird?"

"Me eating in Ben's kitchen when I don't even really know him."

"Who's Ben?"

"Your friend. The guy. The person who lives here."

"His name is Clark."

"Wait, really?" Her eyes widen. She jogs her memory. Had she used his name when she said hi?

Noah grins and hands her the spoon, gesturing toward the now-full bowl of cereal on the counter. "Nah. I'm just fucking with you. His name is Ben."

"Really?"

"Maybe."

"Hey," she says, bending to take her first bite, which turns out to be kind of heavenly. "Don't mess with me. I'm in a vulnerable state."

"Fair enough," he says, holding his hands up in surrender. "But it's hard to resist."

Hard to resist like the adorable, crooked smile on his face. His eyes, twinkling in amusement at her expense. The way his arms flex when he crosses them over his chest and watches her eat.

She takes a shuddered inhale.

"Ben is cool," he says. "He won't care. Also, you're pretty cute. I don't think he'll mind you being in his kitchen."

She's pretty *cute*? Cute like a drooling bulldog? Or cute like she's hot?

At this point, probably the bulldog. Let's be honest.

So maybe she screwed up her chances with this guy forever, she thinks, but, as she closes her eyes and takes bite after bite, at least she is having the best bowl of cereal of her life. Why doesn't she eat Cheerios more often? *They are delicious.*

And is it her imagination or does she feel the bedlam in her head starting to quiet as she eats and, if she's honest, as she talks to this boy? This Noah. Who, even from a distance, she had known was special. Who is now standing next to her, his lean but muscular biceps popping as he absently checks his beeper.

"I'm Nellie, by the way," she mumbles between bites.

"Hi Nellie."

"We've actually met before." Is this weed laced with truth serum? If so, she's in trouble.

"We have?"

"Yup. On the street. Outside my drawing class."

"When you were not high."

"When I was not high. Or eating cereal. When I was a happy, well-adjusted person who wasn't going to have to be institutionalized and could hold a conversation."

"Wow," he says. "I'm so glad I got to meet you at least once before the downfall."

Nellie nods. "Me too. I was an excellent human."

In no time, the bowl is empty of all but the dregs (which she has just enough self-control not to pick up and drink). And she feels notably better.

"Thanks for this," she says.

"It's not my cereal," he says. "It's Clark's."

She shoots him a mock dirty look.

Noah points his thumb toward the kitchen doorway. "Want to come back with me to the other room? I can escort you safely."

"No way," she shakes her head. "I'm better, but not *that* much better. I can't interact with others. I can only talk to you. For the rest of eternity."

He shrugs, takes a step closer to her, so they are only about a foot apart. "That works for me."

And they are standing there, eyeing each other not quite shyly, the air between them percolating like steam from a kettle, when Sabrina calls Nellie's name from the foyer just outside the room.

"In here!" Nellie calls.

Though she is grateful for her best friend, who she wanted so badly only minutes before, now she mentally wills her away.

To no avail.

Sabrina pops into the room, her eyes widening ever so slightly when she spots Nellie with this random boy she knows from school.

"Hey Noah," Sabrina says. "I didn't realize you were here."

"Yup. Just . . . talking to your friend Nell."

"She's a good one," Sabrina says. "Too good."

"Seems that way," he agrees.

Behind her, Lydia snorts.

"I think we're gonna take off," Sabrina says to Nellie. "If that's okay? You can stay if you want."

"Me? Stay? Here? Without you? Nope. Not a thing."

There is no way in hell. No matter how cute this boy is.

Sabrina laughs. "Okay. I guess not, then." She frowns, lowering her voice. "And I guess Sebastian wasn't the future Mr. Hurwitz?"

Noah's lips part, as his eyes narrow. "Sebastian? For her? Them together?" He shakes his head, gesturing toward Nellie. Draws a hand across his neck—like it's a death sentence.

"Why not?" Sabrina demands. "He's hot."

"Yeah!" Nellie adds, a little more indignantly than she intends. "Why couldn't he like me?"

"Oh, he could like you. I'm sure he *does* like you. But not as much as he likes weed. You'd have to carry Cheerios with you everywhere you go."

"Cheerios?" Sabrina's brow furrows, reasonably. Then she shrugs and takes Nellie by the hand, leading her out of the kitchen. "Whatever. We gotta go."

"Later, stoner," Noah says.

If he waves goodbye, Nellie is gone before she can see.

The girls wait for the elevator in a hallway that smells of simmering garlic from some other, more civilized apartment.

Sabrina scrunches her nose. "What was all that about Cheerios?"

"Long story," Nellie says.

"That's the guy we ran into on the street a while back, right?" Lydia asks.

Nellie nods, turns to Sabrina. "Honestly, I think I might be more into someone like him than that Sebastian guy."

"Who? Noah?" Sabrina asks, eyebrows raised. After all, Nellie hasn't confided anything about her obsession, even to her closest friends. And Sabrina wasn't even around when they met on the street.

"Yeah," Nellie sighs, propping herself against the pockmarked wall. "Unfortunately. Since I just totally humiliated myself in front of him." She looks up at her friend, hesitantly. "Do a lot of girls like him?"

Sabrina bites her lip. "Honestly? Yes. A lot of girls like him. *All* the girls like him. And I think he likes them all back. He's like . . . a jock. Like a white-hat frat boy type, sort of. You guys have nothing in common."

"Duh," Lydia snorts again. "He's hot." She twists a strand of her hair around her finger like she's trying to cut off blood flow. "No offense, Nellie, but, like, he's kind of out of your league." She turns and presses the already illuminated button again, leaving Nellie's heart to drop behind her.

Noah grabs a handful of Cheerios before he leaves the kitchen. He's eating them out of his hand as he walks back into Ben's crowded bedroom and leans against the doorjamb. This is one of those classic New York apartments, old and stately, but in need of some love. Paint is chipped along its deco edges.

Mostly, this gathering is a sausage fest. Dudes everywhere. Most of them high as kites. Hip-hop blares, loud and careless. As Noah scopes out the room now, his eyes can't help but wander toward Sebastian and he feels an unwelcome—not to mention irrational—pang of jealousy rise in his chest.

He coughs to clear it.

What is wrong with him? He's known Seb since they were eight years old and in Little League together. He's a good dude. A nice guy.

But not good enough for her.

The words reverberate through him, unbidden, and he shakes his head like that might reset his thoughts, like his brain is an Etch A Sketch.

He knows girls think Sebastian is hot. I mean, he's a good-looking guy. Even Noah can see that. But don't girls say that about him too?

Nellie had seemed defensive about Sebastian liking her. Did that mean she liked him back? That she was hoping something *would* happen between them?

The thought takes the wind out of his sails. Noah slouches, defeated.

But then he catches his faint reflection in the glass of a framed *Goodfellas* poster, mounted on a nearby wall. Ben is so obsessed with mafia movies; he basically thinks he's a mobster instead of a nice Jewish boy from the Upper West Side.

Noah runs a hand over his short dark hair, then down along his cheek and chiseled jaw. He looks alright. Maybe not like Sebastian. But decent.

"Hey, pretty boy! If you can stop gazing at yourself long enough, we got next ups for *Street Fighter* as soon as Ben loses, which is any minute . . . 'cause he kind of sucks balls."

"Hey! Fuck you," Ben scowls at Damien, though even his scowl is good-natured. "I don't suck. Your mother sucks."

"Your mother sucks too," Damien grins. "My dick."

Noah shakes his head at the chorus of *oh shit*s and *damn*s that emanate from the homeboy peanut gallery. It doesn't take much when they're this fucked up.

"I'm in," he says to Damien, though, truth be told, he isn't in the mood for video games. He's sober, for one thing, which he always is during baseball season—and that makes these guys seem like fools. But he also feels antsy, on edge. Like he can't sit still.

This is not his usual mode. Nellie has thrown him for a loop.

"I'm in," he repeats anyway.

"Into what?" comes a husky voice from beside him. Noah turns to find that redhead—Lydia, maybe?—standing too close to him with a hand on her hip. "Into me?"

She laughs, like she might be kidding or she might not, depending on his response.

"Oh, um." He is at a loss. Because no. Not into her. So, he pops a Cheerio into his mouth instead of answering. It tastes like a better time. In the kitchen. With that girl Nell. Just minutes before.

Why had he pretended he didn't know who she was when she said that they'd met before?

He knows who she is. He does. He *knows*. He's known since that night at the club, when he first spotted her looking at him from across the room through the flashing lights and ambient shadows. He's known for sure since he watched her disappear into her art class weeks back, better places to be.

So why had he lied?

He shouldn't have. He should have said he knew. He should have kept her talking, taken advantage of the moment. Because what were the chances of him going into Ben's kitchen to grab a glass of juice and finding her—this girl who keeps popping up in his mind—there alone, in Technicolor? Just waiting for him. Smelling like orange trees. Her straight thick copper hair falling in her face as she covered her eyes and tried to right herself. Her wolf-gray eyes, like none he'd ever seen before, flooded with panic. In need of help he was actually able to offer?

Regret settles in, dark and heavy.

"Hey, didn't you just leave with Sabrina?" he asks Lydia now.

"Yeah, but I came back. They were being so wack! They were just going to chill on a stoop on West End." She looks him up and down in a way that feels both clumsy and deeply suggestive. It makes him want to put on and zip up his hoodie. "Things are more interesting here."

But they aren't. Not for Noah. And suddenly he realizes he has no interest in staying. He'd rather be sitting on a stoop. He'd rather be wack. With Nell.

"I'm out!" he calls into the room, throwing a peace sign to Damien and anyone else who cares.

"Out? What?! But we're next! Dude, what the fuck?"

But he is already slamming the apartment door behind him as he pushes the elevator button—one, two, three times—like that might actually speed things up.

When the elevator finally comes, it's packed with people— an elderly woman, a middle-aged bald man, a girl around his age in pajamas with a basket full of dirty clothes. And it stops at what feels like *every* floor, including the mezzanine laundry room, as he taps his foot impatiently and does his best to smile and look friendly and not too tall and intimidating.

Finally, he bolts out of the building like it's on fire, realizing only then that he doesn't know which way to go. Uptown? Downtown? He has no clue where Nell lives or in what direction the girls may have headed.

He arrives on the corner, breathless, looks up and down the manicured avenue toward rows of prewar buildings for any sign of them. No luck.

Shit, he curses. Wipes his forehead with the back of his hand.

And that's when he spots a small figure, alone, about a block away, receding into the distance. *Nell*. Apparently, she and Sabrina had abandoned their stoop hang. He can't say why he feels like this is his one and only chance, like if he doesn't speak now, he will forever have to hold his peace. But he does.

Call it lack of impulse control. Call it instinct. Call it teenage hormones run amok. But he jogs across the street, slowing to a speed walk as he nears her.

Sensing his presence, Nellie stops, swivels, and looks up in surprise, her eyes still a bit glassy.

A nearby doorman standing under a pristine awning eyes the scene, assessing if Noah is friend or foe.

"Hey," Nellie says, squinting like she is trying to see Noah through a haze. "What are *you* doing here?"

"Well," Noah says, a little winded. "I realized you forgot something."

His first instinct had been relief at spotting her, at not having lost her, but now, as he stares into her beautiful, confused face, he realizes he's a man without a plan.

No plan *at all*.

"I forgot something?" She slips a hand into her jean shorts pocket, pulling out her gum and keys and exhaling to find them there. "What did I forget?"

"Cheerios," he offers, holding out his palm, where only seven or so *o*s still sit. "They lower cholesterol—and make you less high, so. I wouldn't want you to be without them."

She looks down at his hand and then up at his face and grins. "Straight from your hand, huh?"

He flushes. "I like to think of them as *handpicked*."

She laughs and the sound—and the fact that he elicited it—floods him with warmth, eclipsing his embarrassment.

"Very thoughtful of you to be so concerned for my health," she says. "And my sanity."

"Well, I take health class *really* seriously."

"As you should. Five servings of fruits and vegetables a day!"

"Especially during baseball season."

She blinks up at him. "You need to be healthy while you watch baseball?"

"I need to be healthy while I *play* baseball."

"Ah," she sighs, dropping her lids closed for a moment. "That makes more sense."

She didn't know? It's not that Noah consciously uses his athleticism as social currency, but of course he's aware that being the star of the team, the way he performs, makes him shiny in some kids' eyes—in some *girls'* eyes.

But Nellie doesn't even know that he's a star player. He can't rely on his prowess as a crutch. Maybe he couldn't have anyway. She's the kind of girl who likes art classes and books and freaks out from one hit of pot. When he says he plays ball, people's interest is usually piqued. They ask him what position he plays or his favorite pro team (an unholy tie between both the Yankees and the Dodgers, oddly), but she looks completely unmoved.

He shuffles his feet, suddenly nervous again. Forces his hands into the pockets of his low-slung jeans. She doesn't know shit about him. What if now she thinks he really is some kind of oats-obsessed idiot?

"I'm kidding," he blurts out, as she looks up at him expectantly. "I'm not, like, uptight about health. I mean, I'm healthy. In a regular way."

"As long as you're not healthy in an irregular way."

She shoots him a flirty smile, which he wants to return, but he feels like he's losing the thread of this conversation, slipping deeper and deeper into some kind of social quicksand.

And it doesn't help that he is so distracted by her pink lips, by the way she bites the lower one periodically as she listens. By the way her crop top stretches across her chest, layered gold necklaces a bit tangled above. By the curve of her waist, smooth and toned above frayed jean shorts.

This isn't like him at all. Normally, Noah can win anyone over—talk to *anyone*. Charm anyone. But now he has gone blank. He can't think of a single thing to say.

The silence is torture.

"Anyway," Nellie says, eventually, glancing down the street in the direction she'd been walking. "I guess I should head home."

"Totally," he says. "It's getting late." Which it is not. At all. It's still the full light of day.

She cocks her head slightly, glances up at the brilliant blue sky. "Right. Well, thanks again," she says, holding her hand out expectantly.

It takes Noah a beat to realize she's asking for the Cheerios. As he drops the cereal bits into her palm, his fingertips graze her skin, putting every nerve in his body on alert. And that minuscule contact makes him instantly desperate for more. To run his hands through her hair, over her shoulders, her back, scraping down her hips, up her thighs and under her . . .

What is happening to him?

He is losing his goddamn mind.

She takes an *o* between her fingers and pops it in her mouth, letting it rest for a moment on her tongue. She closes her eyes, obviously still a bit stoned.

He watches, rapt. Trying to tamp down what's coursing through his body.

"My God, Cheerios are good," she sighs—and it is almost like a soft moan. "I'm definitely adding them to the grocery list." When she reopens her eyes, they're shining. "Hey, thank you, by the way. For real. You really helped me back there."

"At Clark's house?"

"At Clark's house."

"No problem," he says, almost bashful. "Anytime."

"Be careful what you offer."

"I stand by it. *Anytime.*"

He holds her gaze for a beat, tension humming between them like a live wire. And, in that instant, he lets himself believe that maybe he's not the only one who feels it.

"Alright," Nellie says, finally. "But next time I smoke too much pot, don't be surprised if I send up a flare."

"I'll be on the lookout."

She smiles, hesitates, gazing down at the sidewalk and then back up at him. "Okay. Well . . . bye."

"Bye," Noah says. Stupidly. Moronically. Idiotically.

Like a fucking fool.

And, as she starts to walk away, he turns to leave too, making incidental eye contact with the nearby doorman. The man shrugs from under his cap, looking a little disappointed. Like, *you win some, you lose some—and today you lost.*

Why is this happening? Noah is never this way. Sure, he's liked girls before. Made out with many. Dated a few. But this girl . . . this is different.

And he doesn't even know her.

It's not even because she's hot. Even though she is. There's just something about her.

He takes one step. Then two. Then he thinks, *fuck it*. And he pivots back around.

"Hey, Nell!" he calls out.

And she turns around, looking—could it be?—hopeful.

"Yeah?"

He jogs back toward her, so they're only a couple feet from each other. He is reminded of the moment in the kitchen, right before Sabrina walked in. The electric pull between them as they drew closer.

The air between them thick.

"I was just thinking, flares don't work that well. So, we should probably exchange numbers. You know, in case there's an emergency."

Her cheeks flush, pink. And though she tries to restrain it, her million-dollar smile wins out.

"That would be smart," she agrees. "In case of emergency."

And only after a full minute of staring at each other dopily do they realize they don't have a pen.

"Here," says a deep voice from a few feet away. The doorman digs into his blazer's inside pocket and pulls out a shiny ballpoint. He hands it to Noah with a wink.

Nellie pulls a piece of gum from her pocket, unwraps it, pops it in her mouth, and hands Noah the foil, matte white side up.

Leaning the paper against a scratched-up blue mailbox, they both scribble their phone numbers. He rips the wrapper in half, and they each pocket their jagged scraps.

"So, next time I get super paranoid, you're the first person I'll call." Nellie smiles, fiddling with the fringe of her shorts against her upper thigh.

"Okay. But that's gonna be soon, right?" Noah says. "Like, should we run back upstairs and roll a blunt? Start another freak-out?"

"Now?"

"Well, the thing is, I'd kind of like to talk *tonight*."

And he's back. Back in his swagger. Thank God.

Still, he holds his breath while he awaits her response.

"Oh," she says, surprise and then amusement in her eyes. "Sure. Try me. After all, I might still be feeling the effects of today."

"So true."

And then he leans down and kisses her on her soft cheek, not in a perfunctory sort of way, but with intention, so that he can take a beat to notice her orangey perfume again. He watches her shiver slightly at his touch as he slowly returns to his full height.

"Talk to you later," he says.

"Talk to you later . . . Noah."

His name on her tongue threatens to take him down.

And when they part ways, both turning back at least once to steal a glance, he feels like he just hit a game-winning grand slam. Maybe even a season-winning one. He feels that light.

A warm breeze blows past, rustling the leaves of the English elm above.

Eyes twinkling, the doorman nods as Noah returns his pen, and he nods in response.

And making sure that precious gum wrapper is safe in his pocket, Noah heads back the way he came. *Now* he could go for some video games.

Then he needs to get home. He's got a phone call to make.

7

NELLIE
TODAY

When I feel his eyes on me from across the deck—sense him like I always could—I can't help but turn to catch him. And when our eyes lock, I feel like I'm falling down a wormhole into a different me. A me from decades past—who still thinks brown lip liner and matte lipstick is a good idea. Who communicates with this man across rooms. And, for just an instant, I kind of want to keep falling.

Maybe Noah just happens to be surveying the scene when I look up. Maybe I'm reading into his expression—which seems to hold all the things at once. But the familiarity of those changeable hazel eyes, the way I *know* them like I know my own even after all this time, how they become conductive with that soft blue denim shirt—I feel something slip inside me and I have to look away.

I still light up under his gaze. And it's no good.

We are stuck in that suite together. Because I cannot with Damien. That's too close for comfort in a different way. I don't want to live on guard. But I also cannot complicate things even more.

The anger feels safe. Like an unshakable boundary. *Keep the anger*, I tell myself.

Though I'm pretty sure that's not what the life coaches say.

I shake my head clear. Shake Noah out of it like a pebble from a shoe. It's just the passage of time, running rampant through me, pushing my buttons. Creating that ache in my chest.

With that small act, I feel a sting radiate from my upper arm. It wasn't until I tried to get dressed for evening cocktails earlier that my shoulder lodged an official complaint. Or maybe I just didn't notice the severity of the flare-up until then because, before that, I was busy reeling.

Now, Sabrina catches whatever flickers across my face before I can quite return to normal. She catches everything. Even a thing like this—that isn't a thing.

She tilts her head. "So, I know you've got Alfie at home but how is seeing *him* again?" she asks, lowering her voice, as her wife, Rita, sets off for another drink. Rita drinks like a fish and holds her liquor like a beast.

I steel myself for the interrogation. "Seeing who again?"

Sabrina gives me an impatient look.

"Fine," I say. "It's fine."

She arches an eyebrow. And it's a good one. Extra dramatic above her cat-eye liner. The best in the biz. "Fine?"

"Fine."

"Fine like fine, but really not fine?"

"Fine like . . . just fine." I take a swig of my rosé. Not because I'm stressed. Because I'm *thirsty*.

"Seeing your first love again for the first time after decades? After you had an epic fight that exploded everything to the point where you won't even tell your best friends the details to this day? That's 'fine like . . . just fine'?"

"Yup," I nod, resolved to mean it. "Fine like more than just fine, in fact. Fine like seeing old photos of yourself with a heinous haircut and wondering how you ever thought bangs were a good idea."

I don't mention how, despite my best intentions, I spent the late afternoon lying in bed, listening for signs of Noah from his nearby room, or the jolt of illicit pleasure I got when I heard the muffled chords of "Welcome to the Jungle" playing from a distance and knew he was lying in his bed listening too.

I don't mention how I could feel him near me like radiant heat as we stood in the same circle a few minutes before, which was anything but *fine*. How it sent pins and needles skidding across my skin. I don't mention how *fine* he looks. And I definitely don't mention the push and pull thrumming through me now—sadness, anger, humiliation, excitement. Honestly, I couldn't describe it even if I wanted to. And I don't.

Sabrina eyes me, pursing her lips. "So Noah is just a bad haircut?"

"Pretty much," I say, then swivel to grab a spicy tuna canapé off a passing tray to prove how fine I am. "One that grew out eons ago."

"Um. Okay. Well, for the record, I thought you looked cute in bangs."

"No one looks cute in bangs."

I don't even believe that. And Sabrina isn't buying what I'm selling. But Rita has returned double-fisted and that's a lucky distraction for me.

I run a hand through my hair. My current hair. Which I took literal great pains to refresh post-plane. Lifting my arm to use a curling iron was a true feat with my messed-up shoulder. I'm hoping copious alcohol is a cure for muscle strain.

"Who's the redhead?" Rita asks, gesturing across the deck to where Lydia is hanging off Noah's arm like a giant bangle. He has the good sense to look uncomfortable. I look away.

"Oh, that's just Cara's old friend Lydia," Sabrina says.

"She looks . . . shy," Rita deadpans.

"Demure is the word," says Sabrina.

"Venomous is the word," I snipe.

Rita shifts her gaze to me, and I shift under it. Where Sabrina is all sharp eyes and wit, Rita is a horizon line—the most even-keeled person I know. She just sees the thing and says it. Sabrina is dark shadows, copper liners, and bold lips. Rita thinks lip balm passes for makeup. Sabrina is all cat, Rita is all dog. And that combination—of uncanny scrutiny and unflinching honesty—is terrifying, especially if you're holding back as many secrets as I am. These two can sniff anything out.

"Somebody doesn't like Lydia," Rita says, finally.

"Many people don't like Lydia," I grumble. "Entire countries probably. Continents. Planets."

Sabrina turns to Rita with a smirk. "But especially Planet Nellie. Though she'll never say exactly why. I mean, Lydia has always been kind of a hater. But at some point, Nellie's irritation ratcheted up to total disdain."

Rita leans in toward me. "Well, give me the gossip. Why don't we like her?"

I appreciate the *we* so much. Rita, as always, is deeply loyal and ready to climb on board. But I can't begin to get into that history. Not now, when I'm teetering on the brink. "We don't like her because she's the worst."

Dropping all pretense of subtlety, Rita shifts her gaze behind me and openly stares, cocking her curly head to one side.

"So, it's not because she's trying to hump your ex?"

I can't help but turn at that, too. Indeed, Lydia has Noah pinned against the balustrade, her palm creeping up his denim-clad chest. He looks like he'd like to climb over the railing and jump, broken bones be damned. But who can tell for sure?

And fine, *yes*, I am a little irate at the sight. But it's not because he's my ex. Not at all! Why would I care about what he does?

It's because I am a big fan of that shirt. And it's too nice for her creepy claws.

I clear my throat. "Nope. Not because she's trying to hump my ex. That's ancient history."

"What's that thing," asks Sabrina, bringing a fingertip to her lip in mock contemplation, "about history repeating itself?"

"I don't know," I say. "But it involves doom."

At that, we all resume staring at Noah and Lydia. The last gasps of daylight are beginning to fade and flatten, pink to mauve to purplish gray.

Rita toggles her head. "She's not unsexy though."

Sabrina elbows her. "Excuse me!"

Rita puts her hands up in surrender. "Sorry, sorry."

"But yeah," Sabrina admits, eyeing Lydia too. "I can see how if you didn't know her before, you might think that. She has maybe improved with age."

"Not her personality."

Noah's gaze darts over the crowd like he's a cornered animal looking for safe passage. He catches Rita's eye. She waves enthusiastically. He shoots her a genuine smile of momentary relief, then a hapless shrug. She laughs, gives him a thumbs-up.

Then he catches my eye, and I look away.

"Should we rescue him?" Rita asks.

"No," I say. "We hate him too."

"We do?"

She looks to Sabrina for confirmation, genuine confusion on her face.

"Yup, yup." Sabrina nods vigorously like *of course we do*. "That's right. We are card-carrying members of the NSA."

"The National Security Agency?"

"Team Noah Sucks Ass."

I watch Rita take this in. Frown. "But isn't there that whole 'do no harm' thing with doctors? Isn't it our duty to save him, so he can go on to save others in the future?"

"No," Sabrina shakes her head. "That's not to save doctors. That's for doctors to save us."

"I don't think that's right."

"I'm confused," I sigh. "Who is a doctor in this scenario?"

"Noah!" the two women answer in unison. Like it's the most obvious thing in the world. Like he has a stethoscope tattooed on his forehead.

"Jinx!" yells Sabrina, then she turns to me. "Wait. Are you telling me you didn't know that? Like you legitimately have *never* googled him?"

I shake my head. Nope. Have I been tempted? Of course. But I have never given in. I knew it would only make me feel bad.

"Wow," Rita says. "How is that possible? You're a hero among women."

"No more stubborn—or disciplined—a grudge holder has ever lived." Sabrina grins, raising her glass for a toast like it's a tribute. "To us. To CB and Ben. Let the insanity begin!"

I think that ship sailed hours ago—at least for me. Noah is a *doctor*? I am so confused. Like a podiatrist? Or a dentist?

I think about my work debacle. The fact that I'll be out of a job in a matter of months. I'll freelance, I know. I'll figure it out. But he's a doctor . . . and I am *unemployed*.

And it's as we clink glasses, with this new information processing through my cerebral cortex, that I think to ask, "Wait, Rita. How do you even know Noah? When did you meet him?"

But then there's a tinkling like fairy wings reverberating through the air and Ben is climbing up to stand on a wobbly chair to make a toast—suggesting that perhaps he has already had his fill of wine. So, we turn toward him, as Rita slides an arm around Sabrina's waist and Sabrina tips her head onto her wife's shoulder.

I am so grateful for them and so happy for them and so alone in that same moment.

Until I feel someone settle in beside me too, place a strong hand on my shoulder. I don't know who I'm hoping to find. But when I look up, it's Damien grinning down at me like the Cheshire cat. And that was definitely not it.

Ah, well, beggars can't be choosers.

"I hear you're getting hitched," he whispers.

At first I don't know what he means—there's so much roiling through my brain and home feels so far away. But then I play catch-up. Understand. Cara must have mentioned Alfie. So, I smile. And nod.

What's one more lie?

"Too bad," he says.

"Is it?" I whisper.

"Maybe not," he reasons, a glimmer in his eye. "There's always time for a last hurrah."

I look up at him with profound confusion or maybe it's disgust—because on what planet? Certainly not Planet Nellie.

But then doubt creeps in. Is he talking about Noah? Or himself?

There's no time to find out. Which is probably for the best.

"Friends, Romans, countrymen—and women and those that identify as . . . well, Roman people," says Ben.

He has definitely had too much pinot. His purple-tinged teeth are a tell.

I throw back the rest of my wine. If you can't beat 'em, join 'em.

I will my focus to Cara's shining face as she stands to the side, looking adoringly up at her husband. Even in his silly state.

This will all be worth it for her, I tell myself as I exchange my empty glass for a full one from a server's passing tray. She's got so much on her plate. She's seemed so stressed lately on the rare occasions that she can make time to talk. She deserves to let loose.

I can bask in her joy. And, if I'm lucky, the rest will be a blur.

When I wake up the next morning, there's tempered light relaxing through my gauzy curtains. Like it's just so damn mellow.

Good. For. You. *Sunshine*.

I am also seeing things through a hazy filter. So there.

But I am not weightless or airy. Nope. To the contrary. Everything in me weighs ten tons.

My head, sure. That's heavy as hell from too much wine.

Reality coming to call. That's plenty leaden.

But, above all else, it's my shoulder that I quite literally cannot move.

Damn.

I can't help but see it as the physical manifestation of my current mental state. Frozen in place. Unable to move forward. Mired in a portion of the past that I would much rather forget.

For a minute, I just lie there and let my eyes close again. The rest feels like an uphill battle.

Eventually, I blink my eyes open again and use my good arm to reach over and grab the itinerary from my bedside table. Today reads: "Day 2: *Out on the town!*" Apparently, we're taking a day trip to "wander quaint shops" and, if we choose, stay for a "craft brew tasting and organic pizza feast." I scan the code for today's song. Not surprisingly, it's another throwback—though a bit mysterious considering the plans. "Pack the Pipe" by the Pharcyde.

> *Now I have to play the part of the adviser*
> *Because the bud is just a tasty tantalizer*
> *The bud, not the beer, 'cause the bud makes me wiser*

Steeling myself, I let my eyes drop closed again. If I made it through last night, I can make it through this whole trip, I tell myself. I can hide behind Sabrina and Rita. I can chat with Cara's boring college friends. I can drink more wine—if I can stomach it again. Most importantly, I can avoid *him*.

And I can keep my spinout to myself.

Only, can I really? Because I could swear I dreamed about Noah's stupid denim shirt. And him tugging it off his broad shoulders. Or—ugh, worse—was that a drunken daydream while I was still in that liminal state between sleep and wakefulness, hearing him return to his room with a click of his door shortly after I climbed into bed? I cringe. Why was I envisioning what he was doing on the other side of our living room? Like I don't violently hate him.

Lord help me.

It's safer to open my eyes. So I do.

With my good arm, I reach over to a switch by the bed and turn on the light.

And, in the full illumination, I have to admit the room really is sweet. Even from my compromised position. Against the backdrop of white vertical shiplap walls, the furniture is unfussy and neutral, the couch a cushy textured oatmeal linen. A cheerful green-tea throw collapses neatly over one arm. You can almost hear it yawn and stretch.

Sprigs of lavender, buckeye pods, and their wildflower friends jut from a speckled bud vase, quirky and upbeat. Like they've been gathered by nymphs from a nearby meadow. On the coffee table, which looks like reclaimed wood without being blocky, is a ceramic dish bearing house-made salted caramel truffles—each also adorned with sprigs of lavender and rosemary.

And if I wasn't hungover enough to dry heave, I would start my day with one. It is vacation, after all.

Everything feels rustic but pristine and it's an occupational hazard—my art director brain that never fully turns off—that makes me instantly think about how I might switch out the thistle rug and add an additional bedside lamp. Then this would be a lovely place to shoot.

Great natural light.

For people with actual *jobs*.

But no time for that. Because I have to attempt to drag myself out of bed and get myself dressed—with one functional arm. It's been years and years since my shoulder hurt like this, and I can only vaguely remember what to do about it—especially while far from home.

Now, I pad through white barn doors into the bathroom, equally bright and cheerful, with a contemporary egg-shaped tub that is most definitely calling my name later in the trip. According to a letter-pressed card by the sink, even the marbled hand soap is made on-site.

I manage to brush my teeth and smooth my hair a bit, at least. I bury my nose in that soap—notes of berries and simpler times. Then I return to my bedroom in search of coffee. Sadly, when I check out my little snack nook, there is only tea. But lord knows I'm not going into the common area and risking running into *him*. So, as much as my hungover body is dying for a heavier dose of caffeine, I make myself a sad cup of Earl Grey, dunking the tea bag with my one good hand.

Clasping my mug, I slide open the glass doors and step out onto my private patio.

It's lovely. Which is a theme here. The air is warm and fragrant. Under a tree canopy, Adirondack rocking chairs overlook vineyard fields, neat green rows that seem to smile up at me as they reach toward the sun. I place my cup on a simple side table as I walk toward the railing to get a better look. The sky is an unmarked blue that's reserved for only the most special San Francisco days but is de rigueur here. And I am so consumed with the view that, when a low voice murmurs "Morning" from behind me, I startle and almost fall to my death off the deck.

I whip around to find Noah sitting in a chair to my left, and I do it too fast to remember to be mindful of my arm. Before I can decide whether to respond politely or growl at him, I am clutching my shoulder and yelping in unbridled pain.

Apparently, this terrace is less private than I thought.

He jumps up and crosses to me, setting his coffee cup down.

Of course *he* has coffee. See? I am overachieving. Even through the pain, I can resent him.

"Where does it hurt?" he asks, standing in front of me. All tall and . . . ugh.

"It doesn't," I squeak.

He doesn't even bother to shoot me an impatient look. "Nell—Eleanor. Whatever your name is. *Where does it hurt?*"

At a loss, I gesture with my other hand toward my shoulder.

"Sit for a second, okay?"

I am resigned.

I let Noah lead me to one of the rocking chairs. I collapse into it in defeat as it reverberates.

He kneels in front of me. And, as he settles in, I take the opportunity to observe him from above. He's in a gray T-shirt and athletic shorts, both a perfect fit. And he has clearly recently returned from a run because they're both clinging to his body ever so slightly.

Maybe he doesn't play sports anymore, at least not in hopes of a career, but he has definitely kept himself in fighting shape. The California sun has done him well too. His chest is lean. His arms are toned. His legs are tan, except where I note—with a pang—a large scar at his knee.

He leans toward me and it takes everything in my power not to back away. He smells like men's deodorant and freshly brewed coffee and . . . him. And his proximity is doing something unholy to me even through the pain. It has been a beat since I've had decent sex. Things with Alfie had been strained for a while—and, if I'm honest, he was never the most thrilling in that department anyway. It was all kind of rote, and he was never very interested in taking direction. But this is something else—something age-old and unfinished coming to call. I cross my legs and will my eyes away from Noah's defined arms, chest, and legs and back to his face.

Below a creased brow, his eyes scan me like I might be feral. Like he isn't sure how to approach. Can he help me? Will I bite?

Against my will, I feel a pang of affection. And coupled with the other pangs shooting through me, it's a problem.

We both exhale. The air around us seems to still.

"Can I touch you?" he asks, quietly, gently.

Fuck.

"Why?" I demand, scared for a moment that he has read my mind.

Noah cocks his head to one side, his expression amused. "So that I can check out your rotator cuff?"

"Right. Fine. I guess so." I roll my eyes.

"Okay," he says. "First, you're going to have to let go."

It is only in this instant that I realize I've been clutching my shoulder with my opposite hand. I slowly release my death grip and exhale sharply, the searing pain dissipating the tiniest bit.

And that's when I remember that I'm wearing a threadbare, oversized Whitney Biennial T-shirt, which I cut at the neck and sleeves years ago, and a pair of black underwear. And that's *it*. No bra. No pants.

For Christ's sake. How will I survive any of this?

It's too late to turn back now.

All business, Noah lays a tentative hand on my shoulder, carefully feeling around the joint and muscles. It's the first time he has touched me in decades, and I have to hold my breath not to react to the sweep of his fingertips against my skin.

What is wrong with me? Have I suddenly developed a hormonal imbalance? That must be it. The plane travel has somehow thrown my body into a pubescent state of horniness.

But I will not respond. So, my ex-boyfriend who I despise—but who has remained insanely hot—is touching my body. *No. Big. Deal.*

I will an image of my pediatrician, Dr. Shapiro, into my mind to remind me that this is just a run-of-the-mill medical exam. Noah is just like Dr. Shapiro. Except three decades younger and with less ear and eyebrow hair.

I do not want to bone Dr. Shapiro. So, I will not want to bone Noah either. I am oh so well-adjusted.

He asks me to try to raise my arm. Lifts it carefully himself, and I flinch.

"So," I say, eager to distract myself, "not a ball boy, huh?"

"Nope. Not a ball boy."

"You're a doctor?"

"Yes."

"Like a real one?"

Noah smirks, still focused on examining my shoulder and upper arm. "Yes."

"You went to medical school and everything?"

"Yup."

"Not a correspondence one? Not for-profit? Somewhere good?"

"Johns Hopkins."

I try not to act impressed. Even though I kind of am. "I think I've heard of that."

He glances up at me with a small smile, then goes back to work. "Nothing gets past you."

Noah was never academically inclined. I was the studious one. In school, he got away with the bare minimum. But I guess in the intervening years he turned that around. Applied all that dedication to baseball to something else.

Whatever. He still sucks.

"So, what, you're like . . . a chiropractor?" I ask.

At that, he stops and looks up at me, indignant. "You think I'm a *chiropractor*?"

"What's wrong with that? It's a real job!"

"It's a real job. It's just not a real doctor."

"Wow," I say, raising my eyebrows. "Someone's a snob."

Also, someone is defensive about their medical pedigree. Now I've got him where I want him:

"So, like, are you a physical therapist then?"

"No. I am not a physical therapist."

"A veterinarian?"

"No. But in this moment, it feels like experience wrangling wild animals might be helpful—or at least sedating them."

So funny. I smile sweetly through gritted teeth. "So, what then? You're a personal trainer?"

He stops and looks up at me. "Do you actually think a personal trainer is a type of doctor?"

"No," I say, adopting my most innocent expression. "But Damien said you work with sports teams. I know how *flexible* you are with the truth. So, I figured maybe you were using the word 'doctor' loosely."

At this, he finally loses patience. "I'm a doctor. An *actual* doctor. Even if that's hard for you to believe." I'm getting under his skin, and I am loving it. Score one for Planet Nellie!

"Okay, got it," I shrug. "So, like, an RN? I hear registered nurses can do almost everything a doctor can."

"Nell!"

I am enjoying his indignation and the way my needling is making him flushed. But also, my injury is currently in his hands, so it occurs to me that maybe I want him less frustrated and more focused. Plus, something is gnawing at me about what he just said—how it would be hard for me to believe he made something of himself. And it occurs to me that he mumbled something similar under his breath yesterday—about how I thought he was nothing.

I have believed a lot of things about Noah in my life, but that is definitely not one of them. On the contrary, for a long while, I thought he was everything.

Why would he think that?

"Okay," I say. "I give. What kind of doctor are you really?"

"I'm an orthopedic surgeon," he mutters.

A *surgeon*? A motherfucking surgeon? For professional sports teams? That's what he's been doing all this time in La La Land, while I thought he was working a thankless office job in the big-box-store-filled suburbs of some cloudy city?

But I guess it makes sense. At least a little bit. Because while the Noah I knew was mostly beloved for his athleticism and charm, he was secretly a gifted artist, too. That was the part of him I liked best, a part reserved mostly for me.

Different small motor skills.

In fact, though I didn't get this T-shirt on an outing with him and instead as part of a thank-you gift after I worked on an editorial spread about the artists of the Whitney Biennial, I could have. Because even as teenagers, we wandered museums and galleries together, sharing a love of aesthetics like so many 1950s milkshakes.

"How did that happen?" I finally blurt out with more force than I intend.

He looks at me like I am a full moron. "Magic," he deadpans.

"Magic," I repeat, because I don't know what else to say. The truth is, though I won't admit it now, I am truly curious about his trajectory. After all, last time I saw him, he had a dramatically different vision for his future.

In another universe, at another time, I would have told him how proud I am of him. How amazed I am, but also not at all surprised.

How I knew his future would be boundless, no matter what happened to his original dream.

But I can't say any of that now.

How can you miss someone and hate them at the same time? Is the person I miss even in front of me—in the body of this man, this *surgeon*—or does he no longer exist?

Emotional tornadoes may be swirling through my head, flattening everything in their path, but Noah is the picture of calm. He looks up at me, all professionalism. "Well, you know what the problem is here. I imagine this flares up somewhat regularly."

I sigh. Answer him earnestly. "Actually, I've managed it pretty successfully for years with Pilates and stretching, warm baths, arnica. It's only gotten bad like this a couple times before and not for a while."

"Have you done anything different lately?"

"I mean, I moved recently. To a new apartment. So I probably put strain on it then."

He nods like, *that would do it*. "With your . . . fiancé?"

Is it me or did he choke on that word? I do my own noncommittal cough-nod-headshake hybrid.

Because, sure. My fiancé relocated at the same time as I did. Just not to the same address. But I'm not about to tell Noah that we broke up any more than I'd lay that news on my best friend's doorstep during her un-wedding do-over.

"Obviously, lifting heavy boxes might have triggered it," Noah is saying. "Or trying to yank a gigantic suitcase one-handed off a baggage carousel like a maniac. Also, excess stress can tighten the muscles, which makes your body more susceptible to strain."

Excess stress? Who's been under excess stress?

Noah's hands are still on me. And just the word *body* on his lips sends shudders through me. Shudders of revulsion, I tell myself. But even I'm not convinced.

A breeze whispers past. My T-shirt suddenly seems so thin.

He takes one last look at my shoulder, then slides his palm down the inside of my arm to my wrist, turning it over in his hand so that it's face up. I am praying I don't have obvious goose bumps. "Also, carpal tunnel doesn't help because the muscles radiate through. So, if you're doing a lot of design and layout work at the computer or even answering a bunch of emails, that can exacerbate the issue."

Design work. Layout. Like he knows what I do.

And soon, when the news breaks about the magazine, I guess he'll know that I don't have a job too.

He drops my hand. And, right away, to my chagrin, I miss the contact.

"I'm hopeful that there's not a tear. But if the pain doesn't improve in a few days, you may need an MRI to confirm. In the meantime, I can prescribe you an anti-inflammatory and send it to the pharmacy in town to pick up today," he is saying. "And a painkiller if that would help."

As much as I hate accepting help, especially from him, I have to admit that it's convenient to have a doctor in the house—or suite, as the case may be.

"Do you have ibuprofen to take for now?" he asks.

I nod. "Thank you," I manage. It pains me to say it almost as much as it pains me to move.

Noah stands up, so I am overcome by his shadow. It feels nice and cool outside of the sun.

He glances at my mug on the side table. Raises his eyebrows at me like, *you must have really wanted to avoid me if you settled for tea.*

My caffeine addiction dates way back.

"If you want actual coffee, I made some—iced actually like we both like. If you still take it that way. There's plenty in the kitchenette. I'm going to go get dressed."

I shrug, like I could take it or leave it. But the truth is, I will definitely take it. I am now in his debt, both for the coffee and the medical consultation, and it's the worst.

Who is this man, so much like and also unlike the boy I knew?

Noah was always good like this, I remind myself, though sometimes it's hard to remember through the fog of so many years—a narrative rewritten countless times and finally cemented. But is memory truth?

One thing is for sure: We were always good. Until we weren't.

Him being caring, thoughtful, that was never the problem. Until it was.

As he walks away, I try not to watch him. His muscular back, the slope of his shoulders, his tight . . .

At the French doors to his room, he stops and looks back, and I glance quickly away like I've been studying my nails and not his ass.

There's a glimmer in his eye. Like he *knows*.

"Nice T-shirt," he says, then disappears inside. A minute later, "Pack the Pipe" starts to play from his room.

Was that sarcasm? An acknowledgment of our shared history? A nod to the fact that my shirt is totally transparent?

I'd ask what he meant. But there are too many whys.

8

NOAH
TODAY

It's too early in the day to feel this mind-fucked.

I almost need to go on a second run, just to exorcise the frenetic energy agitating through me like a coffee grinder. Shaking my shit up.

That *fucking* woman.

Nell was always challenging. Even when she trusted me. She always acted like accepting help was like admitting weakness. Maybe because she had an older brother who demanded endless attention—mostly the negative kind.

She liked her independence. Maybe she didn't want to stress her parents out. I don't know.

But God forbid you try to order her around or give instructions; she was not a fan of authority. I used to joke that the best way to get her to do something was to tell her to do the opposite.

Only it's not really a joke. And it's all coming back to me now, along with a flood of other memories I'm not ready for. And *shit*.

I don't know how I'm going to make it through the next five days without drowning in it.

Because when I touched her shoulder—which I intended in a completely innocent way—I barely managed to pretend I was fine. That it wasn't like being blown sky-high by an electric shock, waves of history rocketing through me like in a sci-fi B-movie. Details I'd thought I'd lost years ago. Details that both wrecked me and gave me life like some Frankenstein monster. Flashes of skin. Visceral heat. Like what it felt like to *be* with her.

I thought I'd come on this trip. We'd be polite. We'd exchange banal pleasantries about our lives now; I'd impress her with my shiny-ass career. Maybe—after a few glasses of wine—we'd even laugh and reminisce about the way things were when we were kids. Because we were *kids* then. Children. And how could any of that matter now? It wasn't real, right?

But I completely underestimated the situation—myself, her, maybe even what we had. Of course, throughout the years as I periodically broke up with girlfriends out of boredom or just incompatibility, struggled to find footing, I thought about Nell from time to time. About how well we'd worked—until we imploded catastrophically. But I figured I'd romanticized or at least exaggerated our relationship.

First love. First sex. The heightened fervor of teenage experience, raw and uncut.

But now, seeing Nell in the flesh, I'm not so sure.

Literally in the flesh. All beautiful and rosy from sleep. In that see-through T-shirt and no bra.

So, maybe anyone would respond to that, right? Maybe this is just me reacting like any red-blooded dude. And I'm overanalyzing, which is something I don't usually do. And now she has me using phrases like *red-blooded*.

Who am I?

Even telling Nell about my job, the fact that I'm a surgeon, that I went to school for three billion millennia so that people could trust me with their lives and limbs, with their *careers*, wasn't as satisfying as I'd imagined. I don't know how I pictured she'd react—but maybe I at least expected an eyebrow raise. Instead, she called me a *chiropractor*.

The truth is, I might as well let this go anyway. Whatever this is roiling through me. Because, as an added impediment, the woman fucking *hates* me.

And, though it barely matters, she drives me insane, too.

Now, as I tear off my running clothes and throw them in the seagrass hamper, I can't help but ask myself, insane in what way?

That's when the doubt creeps in. *Was she the one?* Is there even such a thing? Can you meet the right person when you're only seventeen? Can you fuck it up forever when you're just old enough to vote? Can you really get that one chance at supreme happiness when your brain isn't yet fully formed and you're too dumb to know that there's life beyond baseball and hanging out with your wasteoid friends?

Disgusted with myself or maybe with life in general, I jump into the shower, lather up roughly, let the stream wash away this stupidity. Turn the water to cold plunge and refuse to give in when my mind drifts back to her pouty lips, her citrusy perfume, her smooth upper thighs peeking out the bottom of her oversized shirt.

When I climb out and the steam settles, I am resolute. I'll go back to giving her space, which is what she wants anyway.

Once I'm dressed, I pop open the door to our common room, grabbing my key card and wallet and stuffing them in the back pocket of my jeans, so I can meet the others to head into town. I don't check to see if Nell took the iced coffee I offered because I'm not a stalker—but she did.

And when I hear her faint voice from behind her closed door, I don't move closer to that side of the room and strain to hear, in case she's on the phone with *him*—her fiancé. I just happen to be checking out the record collection nearby, which actually does include some pretty dope albums.

She said they just moved apartments. Did they move in together?

There's something itching at the edge of my consciousness, something bugging me about this absentee fiancé with his journalism pedigree and stupid British name. I mean, it tracks. Don't get me wrong. Of course she'd be with some super-cerebral political writer. That's not surprising at all. Too busy to fly across the country to hang with her silly high school friends. That's who—in my heart of hearts—I always figured she'd choose. Not some jock like me. Not when she was coming from an intellectual family like hers. I was always going to be an anomaly.

But still, something feels off.

I hear her murmuring, but I can't make out most of the words.

"You can do this," I think I hear her say.

I picture this guy nervous about some big interview. Calling her for support. Kind, fortifying words. Inside jokes. And suddenly I hate him with every fiber of my being.

"You can do this!" I hear her say again, this time with more feeling.

And then I happen to catch my reflection in a wall-mounted mirror, ear practically pressed to her door, and it is a wake-up call. What the hell am I doing? I'm suddenly aware of what a fucking clown I'm being, eavesdropping on my ex-girlfriend from high school in some hotel suite. I shake my head and step toward the main door.

But then she yelps. And it's loud.

"Fuck . . . me!" she shouts. But not with enthusiasm.

And I realize maybe she's not on the phone at all. Maybe she's talking . . . to herself?

I pad back over to her door. Exhale. Knock lightly with my knuckle. "Um, Eleanor?"

There's a rustle inside and then, "Yup?"

"Everything okay?"

"Fine. Great! All good," she says, but her voice is muffled.

"Really? 'Cause it kind of sounds like you're talking to yourself."

"If I am, then your participation is not required."

"Right. But it's a little concerning."

"Feel free to ignore."

"If you say so," I say, shrugging at my reflection. "Then, I'm headed out to meet the group."

"Great. Leave! Good riddance! Bye!"

This is not my problem. Nell made that clear. And I'm already running late, which means she is too, so I walk toward the exit of our suite and place my hand on the knob . . . but I can't help but double back again.

"Nell. *Eleanor.* Is it possible that you maybe, just maybe, need help?"

"Not from you."

"Fine," I sigh. "You want me to go get Cara or Sabrina?"

There is a prolonged silence. Then a loud exhale. "Yes. But I think that'll take too long. I don't want to screw up Cara's schedule. Everyone is probably already waiting on us."

That is not untrue. "So, what then? I just leave you here to die alone?"

"That's fine," she mutters. "It's better for everyone."

I hear a bump and a groan, like she's given up and slid to the floor against the wall.

"Right. But it kind of goes against the oath I took."

"Thou shalt not be a dickhead? Too late."

I lean my forearm against the door and my forehead against my arm. "Yeah. That. And also, 'Do no harm.'"

She goes silent for a beat, and I do too.

Finally, I say, "So, what's it gonna be? You going to let me help you or not? Because this holding pattern is getting us nowhere."

"Fine," she grunts. "You may enter. But don't look."

"I think that's kind of going to make it hard to help."

"Ugh. Fine! But don't you dare laugh."

The doorknob turns and the door wheezes open a crack. I push it wide to reveal a room that's the mirror image of my own. Under dimmed lights, Nell is standing tangled up in the straps of a flowered dress.

For a second I do almost laugh. In my defense, the scene is pretty funny. The way she's standing there, all flustered and mad, with her dress in a twist and metaphorical panties in a bunch. I at least deserve clearance for a smirk.

But then I take a step toward her and see that her hair is tangled up too. And I realize we'll have to start from scratch, take the dress off completely, if I want to get her out of this. And I don't know if I'm more upset for her or for me.

I am being tested. But I make a fist, close my eyes for a second to steel myself, and ignore what riots through me.

"Turn around," I grunt because it's the best I can do.

She pouts but does as she's told.

I step close behind her and start to unwind a strand of her hair from the zipper at the back, easing the metal slowly down and revealing more skin as I go.

"What are you doing?" she snaps, all suspicious.

"Chill," I say. "Your hair is caught. It's a mess back here."

Gently, I brush the bulk of her thick wavy hair off her neck and work the strands out of the teeth, edging the zipper lower and lower until it hits bottom. And so do I.

My breath is shallow. I have the strong sense that I'm tangled up too.

"Okay," I say with genuine relief. "That part is done."

"What now?" she asks miserably, hoarsely. Like she is out of juice.

"I think," I say, careful to keep my voice even, "I need to pull the dress over your head and then put it back on the right way. The straps are crossed."

"Pull it *off*?" she says, despondent, glancing back at me. "But . . ."

"It's up to you," I say. "But I don't see another way. Not with your shoulder in this state."

"But I'm only wearing a bra and underwear under here."

I force my voice to stay level, though I am anything but calm. "It's nothing I haven't seen before," I offer.

"It's actually very much something you haven't seen in like twenty-plus years."

"Good thing I'm a doctor," I say. I have dissected cadavers. Examined bones poking through skin. Reset the elbows of NFL cheerleaders. I can totally keep this professional, *right*?

With a sharp exhale, Nell stands up straight. Keeps her eyes focused forward. Like she is prepared for battle. "Just do it," she says.

So I do. Slowly, carefully, I slide the soft cotton dress up against her body, edging her out of it bit by bit, until I'm able to slip it off over her head. And when I do, maybe it's an illusion, but I swear I see her shiver.

There is total silence in the room as she stands there practically naked. And I try not to look. I really do. But she's wearing a thong and there's so much bare skin and I'm only human and, though I try my best not to gape, my peripheral vision is horribly A-plus. I know immediately that the curve of her back, of her waist, of her upper thighs will haunt me for the rest of my days.

As quickly as I can, I untwist the straps of her dress in my hands.

"Ready?" I ask, holding it up.

She nods. Stepping just inches behind her, so I can feel the heat of her body warming mine, I begin to slide the dress back down over her head. She slips the arm she can lift beneath one strap, then I help ease the hurt arm through the other side, my hand sliding down her smooth limb to bend her elbow. Once her arms are clear, I take hold of the dress on either side of her rib cage and drag the fabric slowly down over her chest as it rises and falls—past her taut stomach, her hips. I bend to straighten it at her thighs, trying to ignore my hand's proximity to her ass.

And she's right. It's like I know her body and I don't.

And it's a fucking miracle that I don't just lose it right there. In the middle of this charming suite. At this quaint hotel.

It's a fucking miracle I can stand up straight, zip up the back zipper, and say, "Okay. I think you're good."

Neither of us move for a beat.

Then, very slowly, she turns around to face me. We are less than a foot apart. The air between us whirrs and twists like an engine revving. She meets my gaze, with her stormy-weather eyes, and in them I think I read the same pull I feel.

My heart is pounding like I've been sprinting, but I'm standing completely still. I'm afraid to breathe.

Then she leans in, so we are separated by inches. Parts her lips.

"This never fucking happened," she says in my face.

And she turns on her heel and leaves.

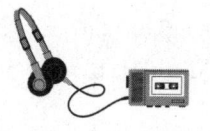

9

BOTH

BACK IN THE DAY

There are evening calls. Late-night calls.

You hang up. No you hang up.

My mom says I have to hang up.

There are group hangs at monuments in Riverside Park, at people's somehow empty apartments, at a local Burger King, where the teens all order nothing and sit for hours at orange tables that glisten with grease.

When Nellie and Noah are around the group, there's awkwardness between them despite how much they have shared over the phone about his absent father and her challenging brother and baseball pressure and art portfolios. About TV shows they like (*Friends* and *Twin Peak*s reruns), TV shows they love to hate (*Beverly Hills 90210*—except she still watches all the time).

In person, sometimes they acknowledge each other. Sometimes they don't. Most often, they circle each other, feeling their shared presence—stealing glances, talking loudly, trying to pull each other's focus—but rarely actually interacting.

In person, they *act* like they don't care.

They have not told their friends about what's happening between them.

What *is* happening between them?

For no good reason, this thing they're doing feels like a secret, something that isn't ready to survive out in the daylight under the gaze of their meddling social circle.

Until one day, they're hanging in separate groups side by side at Sheep's Meadow in Central Park, awash in late spring's rediscovered warmth. Their arms and legs bared, the crew is blissfully unaware that they're smoking joints, sunbathing, and cracking jokes where actual sheep once roamed or that, in an amusing twist, they are also sheep in a way, following each other's lead.

As if at a seventh-grade dance, they are split by gender. Girls in one group. Boys in the other. The only exception is the occasional girlfriend or hookup, an outsider the Upper West Side girls don't really know, lodged carelessly in the grass between her boyfriend's bent legs.

Seemingly out of nowhere, Cara and Ben have somehow discovered each other and solidified into a real couple—something about a shared love of *Star Trek*—even as Nellie and Noah have remained vague.

Today, Cara has a disposable camera and they're posing for shots. As usual, it's Nellie behind the lens. She is a believer in documentation. Also, the girls just like the thrill of picking the photos up from the twenty-four-hour photo shop and seeing how they were captured.

So, Nellie has taken her eye off Noah, forgotten to notice him for a minute, when she feels a tap on her shoulder. And she squints up from her crouched position to find him hovering over her, the sun beaming behind his head. He squats down to her level.

Two frogs.

"Wanna go hang out?" he asks.

"Just us?" Adrenaline rockets through her.

"Yeah."

"Now?"

"Yeah."

"Um. Sure."

Nerves. Excitement. Rinse. Repeat.

She pushes herself to standing, brushing imaginary dust from the back of her sundress. Grabs her prized black Agnès B. Lolita mini backpack. Kisses her friends on the cheeks, studiously ignoring their raised brows. He gives his friends pounds—ignoring their hoots and hollers, ignoring Damien's *Nellie and Noah sitting in a tree.*

K-I-S-S-I-N-G

Which is not something they have done.

Noah gives the group the finger—in a good-natured way—as the duo starts toward the gate at the exit.

Perhaps this is why Noah and Nellie have kept this a secret.

And then they are alone. With eight million people. In New York City. Set free to explore manicured streets and dingy corners, upscale shops and downscale delis. And that's what they do. They wander and soon start to talk like they do on the phone, laughing and disclosing in an uncensored way they don't do with anyone else. Like the calls were a warm-up for this big game.

They knock into each other playfully, giddily, pretending not to notice the tension building between them. Feigning indifference to the reverberations from even that fleeting touch.

Something. Is. Happening.

The park spits them out on the Upper East Side. The Met appears before them like a welcome surprise, its grand steps an offer they can't refuse.

"Should we go in?" she asks.

"Yeah," he nods. "For sure."

Inside it is cool. In all ways. *Dope* in these days. Maybe *bomb*. Their shoes click and squeal against the marble floors as they continue to meander without a plan. It's an adult kind of thing and a childlike thing, being in this museum without supervision with its mummies and paintings and suits of armor.

No teachers. No parents. No project partners.

Eventually, they explode into the brightness of the Temple of Dendur, blinding sun falling through its contemporary windows onto ancient ruins. They sit on a bench, make wishes while tossing pennies in the reflecting pool. Usually, when he's hoping for something, he wishes for a pro career. She wishes for art school acceptance.

Not today.

The hours slip by like instants. And in no time Noah and Nellie are back outside in the softer afternoon warmth, perched on an enormous park boulder they have managed to scale with iced coffee for her and lemonade for him. They're contentedly surveying their surroundings when he turns to her, a bit hesitantly, and says, "Can I tell you something?"

The way he says it, she thinks he's about to break bad news to her. Like the truth is, *I don't like you.* Or the truth is, *I already have a girlfriend.*

I am too good to be true.

Instead he says: "I like to draw, too."

Like it's an admission.

"You do?" She's surprised. Mostly that he hasn't mentioned this before. But, to his relief, she doesn't seem to find it funny or strange.

People keep telling them they're opposites. But maybe they're not as different as they think.

"Yeah," he says, eyes downcast. "I love comics. And I sometimes draw my own."

"That's cool!" She is touched by how shy he suddenly seems. "How come you never talk about it?"

"I feel like people are more interested in the baseball," he says with a shrug. "Even my mom is more interested in the baseball."

Nellie looks at him, hard, in the eyes. "Well, I'm not more interested in the baseball. In fact, I'm kind of relieved! I assumed you were just humoring me in European paintings. And when I freaked out over that Degas photography show."

"Well, I was," he says. "But only because I prefer dumb girls."

"Prefer dumb girls . . . for *what*?" she challenges.

It is the unspoken thing he has acknowledged. The *why* in why they're here.

She gives his arm a light shove. He grabs her hand before she can fully retreat. Something flutters in her chest as he weaves his fingers through hers, examines her palm.

"Damn," she teases. "I guess maybe I need to give Sebastian another chance after all. Maybe *he* likes artsy girls."

Noah frowns. Doesn't like the joke.

"I'm pretty sure your friend Lydia beat you to it."

Nellie's eyes narrow. "*Friend* is a loose term. Did she really?"

"Yup. By the time I got back to Ben's house that day, they were in a corner . . ." He shrugs like, *doing you know what*. They both know what. And it hangs in the air between them. "I don't like that idea anyway. You with Sebastian. Bad call."

"Oh, yeah?" Nellie says, tilting her head to peer playfully up into Noah's face. "Why not?"

"Because. I've got a better plan."

And then he leans in and, as she braces herself against the jagged surface of the rock with her free hand, he slides his palm to the small of her back and presses his full lips to hers. Softly first. Tentatively. Until she's kissing him back harder, her hands slipping around his neck as she edges closer to him. He tastes like lemonade, smells like the mowed grass of a thousand baseball diamonds. Heat rises between them. And she has never been so outside her body and in it at the same time as she sinks into him. Thinks, *Oh this is what this is supposed to feel like*, as he pulls her closer and, without realizing what she's even doing, she climbs on top of him, straddling him.

Their wishes from the fountain—the same silent prayers—have come true.

They have both been waiting for this for months. Been thinking about this moment for what feels like eons, especially in teen years—when a week is a month and a month is a year. Have wasted countless hours imagining a scenario just like this one, when, all the time, it was theirs for the taking. And now they can't hide their impatience. They are zero to sixty.

Under Noah's shirt, his skin is warm as Nellie slides her hand up his back, then down the hard planes of his stomach, until he inhales sharply. And finally, he loses his balance a bit as his arm slips just slightly against the boulder. And she yelps as they teeter and threaten to fall. And then they're both laughing against each other's mouths, self-consciously, suddenly remembering where they are.

Their hair, their clothing, their expressions—it's all askew.

Noah glances around. No one is watching except a single chunky gray squirrel, casing their drinks. This is New York City after all. And two teens making out barely registers.

Noah turns back to face Nellie. Her hair that smells like Creamsicles. Those wild gray eyes. He wipes a small smudge of eyeliner from below her lower lid with the edge of his thumb.

Her cheeks are pink. Her lips are the tiniest bit swollen.

"Can we do this again?" she whispers.

And he doesn't know if she means now or later or the walk or the museum or the hangout or the make-out. But the answer to all of it is *yes*.

10

NELLIE
TODAY

The transport Cara has booked is not your mama's van. It is black. It is sleek. And it is idling with a purr in the dusty estate parking lot, bordered by herb gardens, as it awaits our arrival.

I am almost bolstered by the sight of John, my beloved driver from the aiport, who is apparently squiring us around today. He welcomes me at the door with a wink, a chilled bottle of water, and a capped smile.

But, as expected, the rest of the group has the patience of a preschool class. That is to say, none. And when I mount the steps and board with Noah following close behind me and pause at the front to get my bearings, it's to hoots and hollers.

"What took you so long?" Damien calls from the back. "Play doctor on your own time!"

"Who's playing?" Noah jokes along.

"Yeah," quips Ben, popping up from the front seat. "Noah's the real deal!"

Cara—dressed in a white eyelet frock presumably to reference the bridal theme—grabs her husband's arm and shoots him a meaningful look. He sits back down, chastened. She smiles up at me.

"Sorry, CB," I say. "My shoulder is acting up. I had a wardrobe malfunction."

"Oh, no!" she says, her brow furrowed. "Are you okay to come? Please don't feel obligated to join."

"I'm totally okay to come."

"Good. Because I was going to make you come anyway." She grins, leaning in toward where I'm standing in the aisle. "But seriously, are you okay?"

She makes a not-so-subtle gesture with her head toward Noah.

"I'm fine," I say, glancing begrudgingly back at him. "Noah actually called in some prescriptions to the pharmacy in town for me, so that should be helpful."

"See?!" Ben says. "The real deal!"

Cara shoots him another look. He shrugs like, *what did I do?*

"Hurry it up!" Damien complains. "Some of us have places to go and alcohol to drink!"

That guy.

I make my way down the aisle, praying for a decent seat, like this is a middle school field trip and I'm the odd one out. The last thing I want is to sit at the back of the bus with Lydia and Damien and the other troublemakers.

Thankfully, Sabrina offers me a lifeline, waving me over. "For you," she says, removing the tote she'd been using to save the seat across from her.

"You're a saint," I say, and she nods in agreement, humming angelically.

Beyond relieved, I drop onto the cool leather and sigh.

Until Noah comes up short beside me.

"No," I say, as he eyes my adjoining seat. Like I'm supposed to make room.

I cannot sit next to this man. No more close proximity. Not after the humiliation I just endured in the suite. Not with all the discombobulated feelings currently swirling in my head and seeping into my body like something venomous. My brain is packed so full of crap, it needs its own decluttering show.

"Um," Noah says, tilting his head to look down the aisle, "I think this might be the last free spot."

"It's not free," I say.

"It looks free," he counters.

"Maybe stand?" I suggest. "You're health conscious. You're a doctor. Haven't you heard? Sitting is the new smoking! Think of this as a standing desk. But in motion."

"Eleanor," he says. "C'mon."

"Forget that! Come back here and sit with the cool kids!" Damien shouts, cupping his hands like a megaphone. "Lydia says you can sit on her lap!"

"Or on her face," I mutter.

If Lydia was anyone else, I wouldn't judge her for being on the prowl. In fact, I kind of admire that kind of brashness and wish I had more of the free spirit in me. So, I don't blame her for wanting to bone. I just blame her for wanting to bone Noah—and anyone else I show a modicum of interest in.

"He's right—I'll scootch!" Lydia says. "There's *always* room for you!"

I look up into Noah's pleading face and across the aisle to where Sabrina is gazing pointedly ahead, but Rita is giving me a point-blank stare like, *be reasonable*.

"Nellie, give the guy a break," she says.

"Fine," I grunt. I give in, scooting toward the window to make room.

I search the seat desperately for an armrest to pull down and separate us, but there is no such luck. We are simply next to each other and his oversized body takes up too much room to avoid. I squeeze myself all the way toward the wall to avoid his cooties. And, when my thigh accidentally grazes his, I jump away like I've been scalded.

Because I have.

Because what just happened in my room was embarrassing, sure. Never mind earlier in the morning when I basically flashed him on the deck. But, worse, it lit an ember in me that I cannot seem to extinguish.

I need some time away from this man to remember why I hate him. Why it's safer to play keep-away. Because there is an ache between my thighs that says otherwise. I need some distance from the feel of his large palms running gently up my arms, then raking down my sides. The feel of his breath on my neck, giving me goose bumps all over, as he operated on my zipper—ever a surgeon. The feel of his eyes on me, searing up and down my body, when I swear I caught him stealing a peek.

I need distance from how easy it would have been for him to pull off my dress and keep on going, slipping off the little I still wore and tossing it to the side. To let the van wait. And how easy it would have been for me to let him do it.

Just the thought sends shudders through me.

Fuck. I'm in trouble.

It seems like the more I try to hang on to all the reasons I hate Noah, the more I remember how attracted I have always been to him—the chemical combustion between us. It was something I once attributed to our age when we were together, teenage hormones running rampant, but now I wonder if it's just *us*. Or maybe things feel super charged because what we had together came first—before adulthood and dating and disappointments. Before Alfie and breakups and split rents and dinners. Logistics that sap all the fun. Something that existed, raw and unfettered, before life got so complicated and exhausting.

I chance a glance up at Noah now, at his five-o'clock shadow and chiseled face. The open smile he shoots Rita as they banter about some sports teams I know and care nothing about. The way that smile reaches his eyes. The scar on his cheek from when he was twelve and fell into a barbed wire fence trying to catch a fly ball in a deserted Brooklyn yard. He still caught the ball. I know because he'd told me at least twice.

Feeling my eyes on him, he glances toward me, shoots me a questioning half-smile with narrowed eyes. A private one. An old-school one. But I don't want it. I scowl and turn away. Throw it back.

Because we cut ties because he cut me deep. It wasn't arbitrary.

Because he can't be trusted to stick around when the going gets tough.

Because the boomeranging inside me is making me feel nauseous and confused—and the bumpy van ride isn't helping. (No offense, John! No one is a better driver than you!)

Noah turns back to Rita, having been rebuffed by me. They laugh some more, rib each other like old friends. High-five. They sure seem chummy. I shoot Rita a look: *Remember we hate him?*

She shoots me a sheepish shrug.

"So," says Noah, maybe catching our drift or thinking I'm sick of all the sports talk. "How's work going for you, Sab? How did the last show end up doing?"

"Fine," she says tightly, examining her nails. She doesn't expand.

I know that takes major restraint for Sabrina, who is an artisan potter—literally wearing her own ceramic earrings recently featured in *Vogue*—and loves nothing more than to talk about her creative process. Especially her last show in Silver Lake, which sold out lightning fast. It was a big deal.

Noah shakes his head like he's confused. Maybe even a little hurt. But Sabrina is Team NSA for life. She avoids his eyes. And I love her for it.

I decide to follow her lead. I focus out the window and ignore what's inside.

There are winding roads with kicked-up dust, kinetic shade under the canopies of massive oaks. We flicker in and out of speckled sunlight like we are captured in Super 8. There are sweet-looking fruit stands and creameries, with working barns and lofted terraces, and horses and cows that may or may not know how lucky they are to live in this Eden.

There are handmade signs for biodynamic farms and lavender fields, where they sell honey and soap; and large wineries with signs full of flourishes that mark lavish driveways like grand manors. There are ornate B&Bs in renovated Victorian homes and modernist hotels with sharp lines and sustainable style, designed to blend into the landscape. Indoor-outdoor spaces, everything delightfully blurred. And there are vineyards, of course, in every direction. Meadows and rolling hills bearing horizontal stripes, like so many French tees, a grid of grapes grown with love and care.

And then, finally, there is a town. One so sweet it looks like a soundstage. Only it's real. People *live* here.

I think about the mean cat at my crummy corner bodega and my faltering career and have some real questions about my life choices.

When we exit the van, I am feeling somewhat calmer, the view from the window a balm.

"How's it going?" John asks quietly, out of the side of his mouth, as I exit onto the charming street.

"Eh," I say, letting my face fall. I can't lie. Not to John.

"I'm here if you need anything," he says, patting me on the shoulder. "You're okay, kid."

It's work not to well up.

Before I can pull it together or fall apart, Cara runs up beside me, squeals, and grabs both my hands. At some point during the ride, someone put a tiara on her head to remind us that she is the un-bride.

"Isn't this the best?!" she cries.

And it is. It really is. There is nothing I love more than wandering a quaint town with my favorite people. But I need her to stop jumping up and down while holding my hands. Against my will, I wince.

"Oops!" she says, a hand to her mouth. "Shit. Your arm. I keep forgetting."

"Totally fine," I assure her. "All good."

I swivel around, taking in the delightful single-story tea shops and sundry stores selling olive tapenade and handwoven table runners; clothing and home decor boutiques; tasting rooms and eateries with al fresco dining areas strung with twinklers and cordoned off with blooming trellises. Vintage streetlights stand guard outside a town hall with proper archways and colonnades.

"Isn't it so cute?" Cara gushes.

"The cutest."

I love seeing her so happy and free.

"And," she adds, leaning in, "I may have the antidote to your problems."

I doubt it. But then she has no idea how myriad they are.

Still, I know this look on my best friend's face. It's the best kind of trouble. Cara is up to no good.

This is the look she gave me in sixth grade when she stole a cigarette from her stepfather for us to try in Riverside Park. This is the look she wore in tenth grade when she presented me and Sabrina with homemade—pretty believable—fake IDs. This is the look she gave us over fall break in college before she whipped out quaaludes and tickets to Liz Phair at the Troubadour in LA—and convinced us all to get tiny ankle tattoos.

It's good to see that look. I realize it's been a minute, and I've missed it.

"Okay, CB," says Sabrina, a hand in the back pocket of her high-waisted jeans. "Dish. Whatcha got brewing?"

"These!" Cara says, holding open a tote bag filled to the brim with every kind of edible imaginable. "Tada!"

Suddenly the Pharcyde song makes sense.

"Alright, alright, alright," says Rita, nodding like she's Matthew McConaughey in *Dazed and Confused*. "This works for me."

"Take whatever you want! There's plenty," Cara grins.

"Ooh!" Sabrina props her oversized sunglasses on her head and plucks a tin of pomegranate-flavored gummies from the assortment. "Good call. I was already psyched to wander galleries—and now it's going to be next level."

"Are there good galleries here?" Noah asks.

"Nope," says Sabrina. "Which will make it even better." She pops a gummy in her mouth.

Lydia grabs a weed lollipop, of course. Because she sucks. And she sucks.

Cara's college friends choose sour lemonheads. Damien sorts through each option until he finds the highest dosage product—a 20mg tincture with a skull and crossbones on the label.

Then Cara turns in my direction, sifting through what's left and presenting me with a package of grapefruit CBD gummies. "I know you're not really a weed person, so I got you these. No THC. Just straight chill. And they're good for pain, probably!"

Damien scoffs. "Good for pain but not for fun."

"What are you, an afterschool special?" Sabrina snipes, scrunching up her nose at him. "You're going to peer pressure Nellie into taking *drugs*?"

"Yeah. We're full adults," Cara agrees, unironically dropping a gummy bear on her tongue and tossing one in Ben's waiting open mouth. "Nellie is always fun, regardless."

Lydia scoffs.

I choose to ignore her.

"I'm not saying that Nellie isn't fun," Damien says, sliding an arm around my good shoulder, so that his hand rests on my bare back. "Nellie is the *best*. She knows I think that." He looks to me for confirmation. I nod like *sure*, because what is the other option? But I take a small step forward to escape his sweaty palm. "I just think you're underestimating her—she can handle *one* gummy."

"It's true that it might help with the shoulder," Rita says, fishing a pack of gum out of her Clare V. tote (clearly stolen from Sabrina).

"Yeah, but . . . have you heard the story about the bong hit at Ben's house?" Cara stage-whispers, her eyes widening meaningfully. "Nellie never recovered!"

"Hello!" I say, "I am literally standing right here. I don't need you guys to litigate my weed consumption.

"Thank you, Damien," I add, turning toward him and, only in that moment, fully taking in the cheesy pink polo he's rocking. "I do think I could handle one gummy . . ."

And I am about to finish with a big *but* and a hard pass on the THC when I hear someone cough behind me. But not cough cough. Like he's got allergies or tuberculosis. Cough with *meaning*.

I turn around to find Noah standing to my right, looking innocently up at the sky.

"Excuse me," I say.

He drops his gaze to meet my eyes, his hands behind his back, like, *can I help you?*

"What the hell was that noise?"

He shrugs. "Nothing."

"It sure sounded like something."

"And yet it wasn't."

"So, you *do* think I can handle a gummy?"

He opens his mouth, closes it again. "I mean, maybe if that's . . ."

"Cut the shit, Noah."

"No. Nope. Not at all. Not even a little bit. Don't take the gummy. You absolutely *cannot* handle it."

My eyes narrow at him; I swear the whole group holds its collective breath. Even strangers coming in and out of surrounding shops seem to go silent, like they can feel the weather turn.

I take a step toward him; I see him consider taking a step back.

"What—you think you fucking know me?" I demand, a finger in his face. "Because you felt me up two decades ago when I was a literal *child*?"

An older woman passing by on the street looks at Noah aghast.

"No, that's . . . I was a child too," he says to her. She hustles away.

I turn to Cara. "Hand me the fucking gummy."

Cara looks unsure of what to do. I have clearly hit deranged on the rage-o-meter.

She nods toward Sabrina, who is still holding a tin, maybe hoping she'll talk some sense into me. Sabrina is the direct one; the unafraid one.

"Nellie," Sabrina cautions. "Are you sure? 'Cause it's not worth it to prove a point."

"Positive," I say, my hand out. "Give me one. *Please.*"

Sabrina opens the tin, struggling a moment with the child proofing, and then places a gummy in my palm. It looks innocuous enough.

I throw it in my mouth.

"Maybe start with half—" she begins. But it's too late. I have already started eating the whole thing.

It's sweet and tangy. See? No big deal.

"You can still spit—" Sab says. "And you swallowed."

"That's what she said," Noah and I both respond.

I turn to Noah and give him the finger.

"Oh boy," he says.

And though I'd never admit it, I am thinking the same thing.

Two hours later, I am questioning my choices. Not just about the gummy or about forgoing the gallery crawl with Sabrina and Rita to go wine tasting with Damien, Cara, and Ben. But also about my career trajectory, love life, and the dress I'm wearing, which keeps slipping down so my cleavage is on parade.

Perhaps most of all, I'm wondering how I could possibly have sanctioned sitting at this picnic table in the direct sun, baking like a hot dog in a floral bun.

Cara and Ben seem unaffected—in fact, they're joyous. For one thing, Cara is, of course, slathered in sunscreen because she's responsible like that. She has surely made sure that Ben is too.

No one hates this kind of heat like I do—being out in the elements like this. I am sweating balls. But also the two of them—on their side of the slatted wooden table—have been in constant hysterics for the last thirty minutes about the convoluted tasting notes in the wine. And it has devolved into the kid-friendly version.

"Hmm," Ben is saying. "I taste top notes of gluten-free chicken nuggets and burnt broccoli that assault the palate with an aroma of full-bodied ketchup, but of course not touching the chicken nuggets or the broccoli."

Cara is literally sobbing with laughter and, despite a hand to her mouth, very nearly about to spit-take a gulp of a crisp Riesling.

I wonder how long it's been since they've had extended time alone together, without the kids.

Damien is oblivious. His pupils are so blown out from that high-intensity weed tincture, his once-frosty blue eyes so obscured, that he may have left the planet. It hasn't seemed to matter at all that I've been drifting in and out of listening while he talks about how day trading is like a metaphor for life—or maybe life is a metaphor for day trading. I can't keep track.

If I'm honest, I only kind of know what day trading is.

Besides, all I can think about is how my body temperature is so high that soon I am probably going to throw up and pass out simultaneously.

How there's a child with his family at the next table who I will traumatize for life. I can picture him as an adult, sitting on his therapist's couch, talking about how he can't even smell wine without flashing to the woman with the giant hair and overflowing boobs, sweating profusely into her vomit.

I want a glass of ice water so badly instead of the wine sitting in front of me, which is growing warmer by the second, but I no longer recall how to make that happen. Surely, I am not expected to stand up on my own, walk to the bar inside, and order from a total stranger! My mouth is glued shut. I can't even remember how money works.

Money. Money?

Where is my bag? *Shit!* Where is my bag? I left my bag. I lost my bag! The child at the next table stole my bag!

Nope. My bag is slouched next to me on the bench. Where I left it.

I heave a sigh of relief like something actually happened and place a hand on my purse so it doesn't flee.

"Anyway," Damien is saying, "you get it."

I nod. Yes. I totally get it. Whatever the hell he's talking about.

"And you always get it," he continues. "Or, I guess, I feel like you've always gotten *me*. Which is why I'm so glad that I got you alone for a minute—well, sort of."

He gestures with his chin toward Cara and Ben, who are too busy concocting plans to build a tower out of beer-branded cardboard coasters to notice anything else.

Damien looks at me expectantly, from under his blond lashes, like it's my turn to speak. "Yes," I say. Because I don't have other words.

"I get you too, you know," he says. "You and I are so alike. That's why I knew you could handle a gummy. Noah always wants to believe you're tamer than you are. But you're an undercover wild child. I know that."

This statement confuses me because I am now positive that Noah was one hundred percent right about the gummy. But also, *yeah!* I could be a wild child! Whatever that means.

"The thing is," he continues, "girls always liked me a lot growing up—and they still do now, to be honest. You know that. I'm not trying to be cocky. But, like, it's true."

I nod. And not just because I have lost all other functions. What he's saying is weirdly accurate, though I have never understood it myself. While not being the best looking or remotely trustworthy, Damien is deeply charismatic—in a sociopathic kind of way. He's an expert flirt. In high school, there were even periods when we would talk on the phone and I soaked up that singular focus. The more attention he got from women, the more alive he became. I cannot count the number of girls who confided in me back in the day that they were hooking up with him in secret. At one point, two close friends of mine revealed their respective secret relationships with him to me in the span of a single week!

How he convinced them all to keep it on the DL is beyond me. But the guy is funny. And successful now, I guess. And I will admit he is truly gifted at making you feel like you're in a secret club together—with everyone else on the outside.

Which is what he is doing with me right now. I assume out of boredom.

And I think I'm supposed to be flattered by his attention. But he has deeply misjudged my mental state. I'm not sure how I would handle this shit on a good day—but right now?

I cannot.

"Anyway," he says, running his thumb up and down the edge of a white paper napkin. "I guess I've always wondered: Why didn't *we* ever get together?"

What?! This just took a turn.

I am functional enough to bark out, "Noah!"

"Right, I know. But you guys broke up for a second once or twice during high school and I actually met you first. I guess I should have stepped in when I had the chance."

It's true that Noah and I took a couple of breaks, but we always got back together within days. Neither of us dated anyone else.

I am struck dumb. And I am so hot. And dizzy as hell. And all I can think about is the trickle of sweat trailing its way slowly down my back. I am also going down.

"And, like, now we both wound up back in New York," Damien is saying, eyes on the table in front of him and then shifting focus to me. "And I should have texted you or whatever—DMed you instead of assuming one day we'd run into each other. 'Cause now you're engaged, and it just feels like we missed our chance. And what if we were meant to be?"

It occurs to me, even in my only semi-lucid state, that if we were meant to be, we *would* be. That's sort of the point. But I do not have the tools to express that concept or somehow explain to this man—who I assume is just having a moment in the movie of his life versus expressing actual *feelings*—that we never got together because *ew*.

"You're just so stunning," he says, gazing at me.

"I have to go to the bathroom," I say, gazing back.

He crinkles his nose, thrown off for a moment, but then thankfully he's too high to clock the true weirdness of that transition.

And, so, despite my fear of moving at all, I take the opportunity while he's distracted to stand up, unstick my dress from my ass and thighs ever so elegantly, grab my bag, and go wander in search of a make-believe bathroom.

Make-believe, because I clearly don't have to pee. There is no liquid left inside me. I have sweat it all out.

"Be right back!" I lie as I reach the sidewalk and start walking away.

"I think the bathroom is this way!" Damien calls from behind me. But I don't turn around.

As quickly as I can, I round the corner into a patch of shade underneath the awning of an olive oil store.

Thank the fucking Lord.

This isn't the first time olive oil saved me, I think. *What?*

I lean back against the cool stone exterior and close my eyes and the sensation is like a dream. *Thank you, thank you, thank you.* There's even a slight breeze worrying the leaves on the surrounding trees.

Oh, sweet relief.

The good news is I have escaped the sun—and Damien. The bad news is, I can't ever move from this spot again. And it would be inconvenient to be arrested for vagrancy.

That's when I hear someone clear their throat.

A police officer already? Oh no! I'm high! Oh, wait. It's legal. It is legal, right?

My heart pounding, I peek one eye open to find Noah standing in front of me in place of a cop, all tall and smug and not at all sweaty.

He only glistens.

Fucker.

"Oh. It's just you," I exhale, relieved despite myself.

"Not the most flattering take, but okay yeah fine," he says, toggling his head. "Just me. More importantly, what are you doing?"

"Nothing."

He raises an eyebrow. "Really? I could have sworn you were leaning against a building, talking to yourself again."

"I was meditating," I insist. "You're not evolved enough to understand."

"No, I get it. You're at one with the facade."

"With all of Planet Earth."

"Really? Even with me?"

At that, I open my other eye. "No. Not with you. Only humanity."

He rolls his eyes. Looks me over, head to toe, which I do *not* feel like a laser scanning me.

"You look hot," he says, finally.

And I get a flash of heat between my legs. "Th-thanks," I stumble.

"No. I mean, sure. You look hot that way too. You always do," he says, now a bit flustered, his eyes glancing off and skittering away from my falling top. "But I meant hot like temperature. From the sun. Which I know you hate. Are you okay?"

Dammit. Why does this man know me so well? Have I really barely changed in twenty-some-odd years?

I don't have the will to fight it. I must confess.

"I'm *so* hot," I admit, letting myself droop. "And not at all in the good way—even *I* know that. Look at me!" I lift my hair up off my neck and lean my head back. "And I can't get water. Because I'm too scared to try to use Apple Pay right now because what if I can't scan it correctly because I'm . . . you know."

"Too high?"

I scowl. "Whatever."

His eyes say I told you so, but his lips—full and soft in a way I *don't* notice—say, "Come with me."

"No."

"Nell."

"Eleanor to you."

"*Eleanor*. Fine. C'mon."

"Why?"

"Because I can help you."

I shake my head. "Never go to the second location. It's the kiss of death."

"Except when you know the person can help you stop freaking the fuck out."

"What if you know the person is *deranged*?"

He rubs a hand over his hair like he might make a wish—for me to stop being a pain in the ass. "Eleanor!"

"Aren't you going to lecture me on how I should have known better?"

He shrugs. "I would, but it's not that fun."

"Why?"

"Because you're kind of pathetic."

My mouth drops open. "What the hell!"

"Just come with me." He reaches out a hand like there's a universe in which I would take it. He rolls his eyes, then motions for me to follow.

"Fine!" I relent. "But wherever we're going better not be hot."

Noah moves to touch my elbow and guide me forward, but I snarl, so he jumps back and gestures with his chin instead. He makes his way down a short block, past a cheerful children's bookstore and a hippie candle shop with batiked muumuus in the window. The smell of fresh-baked cinnamon buns wafts from a small bakery with a chalkboard sign outside that reads "Spice up your day!"

We round the corner and suddenly the street opens into a large town square. And looking at it, I feel like I can breathe again. The plaza is green and placid, and there are black metal benches shaded by trees—redwoods, cedars, spruces, and palms. In the center, there is a simple fountain by a small marigold garden. And just seeing the water bubble up and splash eases the tension in my chest a bit.

"Oh, thank God," I murmur. Apparently out loud. Because Noah smiles at me, seemingly against his will.

We cross to the small park area and settle on a bench, blessedly out of the sun. The relief is palpable, despite the mixed company.

"What time is it?" I sigh.

He looks at his watch. "I think the van is picking us up in about thirty minutes to take us to the restaurant for pizza."

Panic surges through me. "Thirty minutes?! Shit!"

"What's wrong?"

"I can't let John see me like this!"

"Who the hell is John?" he snaps more sharply than is warranted. "Your fiancé? I thought he wasn't coming? I feel like that wasn't his name."

"Fiancé?" Right. In theory I have a fiancé. "No."

"There's another guy you're dating?"

"No!"

"Then who's John?"

"The driver."

"The driver . . . of the van?"

"Yes!"

Is it me or does Noah look relieved? And then amused.

"And John can't see you high because . . . ?"

"I don't want him to be disappointed!"

Noah tilts his head, looks at me. Hard. And I think I see a flash of pity cross his face as his expression softens.

"I'm sure he wouldn't be disappointed," he says, quietly. Then, he starts digging into a market tote bag that I just now notice he's been carrying by the handle.

"What's in there?"

"The medicine for your arm, for one thing."

"You picked it up?"

"I figured you might forget . . . in your state."

"Why didn't you forget? Didn't you also take a gummy?"

"I did, stoner. But some of us are not lightweights—and know it."

Stoner. What he called me on that first day we talked.

When I first met Noah, he never really drank or smoked pot. At least not during baseball season. I guess he has since dabbled and learned his limits.

I open my mouth to protest, but what's the point?

"Here." He hands me an unopened bottle of iced green tea.

"You got this for me?"

"No. I got it for me. But if you're dying of thirst, you can have it."

I shrug. Beggars can't be choosers. I take a sip. "I prefer raspberry."

Noah rolls his eyes for the umpteenth time. But I don't care—because the drink is cold and refreshing like an oasis in my mouth and, as an added bonus, I have successfully annoyed him.

"This is pretty," I say, taking in our surroundings, the other duos on benches having no doubt more normal conversations. "How did you know about this spot?"

"I've been here before," he says.

Right. He is a California boy now. He might live in LA, but wine country is just a hop, skip, and a jump for him. I wonder who he's come here with—girlfriends, friends, the team? I glitch on the idea of his girlfriends. I wonder what they're like, how many there have been.

But I don't ask. Because I have no right. Instead I say: "Today is weird."

"Well, sure," he says. "Wait. I have something to help with that too."

And, from the gourmet market tote, he pulls out an individual box of Cheerios.

At the sight of it, something catches in my throat and I almost start to cry.

What is with me today? This week? This year?

How can dry cereal be a time machine? And yet, it is. Shooting me back through the space-time continuum to the day we first really spoke in Ben's kitchen, before all the hurt and the messiness. Before everything after that. Before now.

Our eyes meet. And there is so much there, I cannot even begin to unravel it. What lies beneath the yellow flecks in his irises that I'd forgotten were there. Years and days and no time at all.

Why is he sitting here with me? Is he tolerating me? Doing his duty by me? Or is it more?

Without a word, Noah hands me the box. I open it and start to eat and, just like that day so many millennia ago, I quickly start to feel more like myself. I scoop up a little handful and hold it out toward him, a peace offering. He takes me up on it, popping an *o* in his mouth.

I think about telling him about Damien's question about our romantic past—but why? It's meaningless and can only cause trouble. I decide to keep my mouth shut.

The breeze has picked up, cooling the damp nape of my neck and my thighs beneath my skirt. It ruffles the hem. Tickles my calves.

Having finished his Cheerios, Noah is leaning back against the bench beside me, his strong hands resting on the thighs of his perfect worn-out jeans. I feel like tipping my head onto his broad shoulder, giving in to whatever this is I'm feeling. My guard is down, I reason. That's why.

It's only nostalgia.

Just feet away, a small spaniel chases a rogue leaf. From inside a hexagonal pavilion on the other end of the plaza, a quartet starts playing, something big band and age-old. And, for some reason, I feel filled up.

11

NOAH

TODAY

In that moment I know. I am officially fucked.

Maybe before I could have pretended that I was just being kind. That the doctor in me—the son of a single mom and brother to an older sister—felt I had to take care of this woman, who I *knew* would need help. Because she is stubborn. And impossible. And defiant in the face of sound advice.

Maybe before I could have at least pretended that it was just chemical attraction driving me. Animal magnetism. Just sex. The way her strap keeps slipping off her shoulder. The way her sheer dress teases and sticks to her thighs. The way she licks the iced tea off her pink lips. Her gray eyes, high cheekbones, freckled shoulders.

The fact that I basically saw her naked earlier today. Pressed my hands against her hips.

And it's that—sure it is.

Of course I want her.

But when I hand her the Cheerios and her face changes, I know it's more than that. And I know that I'm screwed.

And I know I was screwed before that moment too. Because I bought her those Cheerios in the first place.

Now somehow I need to convince her not to hate me anymore and to like me instead.

I know something else too in that instant though, as she hands me that little mound of cereal to share. I know what was bugging me, what seemed off, when I examined her shoulder on our deck.

She's not wearing a ring.

"Tell me about your fiancé," I say now.

And maybe that's unfair. Because maybe it's her own business. Or maybe I'm being an idiot because she's just not wearing her ring because it's being sized or whatever. Or maybe she doesn't believe in that ring stuff, thinks it's all patriarchal bullshit. Which is entirely possible.

But as I watch her pause, I think I'm onto something.

She scrunches up her nose. "I'd rather not."

"How come?"

"Because you're *you*."

"Fair enough." I pause. "Do you wish he was here?"

"Right now?"

"Yes."

I hold my breath. Bite the inside of my cheek to keep from reacting either way.

"No," she says without hesitation. "Not at all."

Relief courses through me. We just sit and listen to the music for a minute, let the breeze blow past us. It feels like it could be any era, any time.

"You know, I do think it helped," she says, eventually.

"The Cheerios?"

"Maybe," she laughs. "But no, I meant the gummy. I think it maybe helped with my shoulder pain."

"That's good. You should try those CBD gummies Cara got you."

"Maybe." She nods. "Or some actual narcotics."

"That would probably work better." We both chuckle.

"I can't believe you're a doctor," she says, unfiltered in a way she hasn't been, I guess thanks to the pot. "I mean, I *can* believe it. I actually totally can."

And it feels like the nicest thing anyone has ever said to me. "Thanks."

"What made you do it? Like, how did you get from when I last saw you . . . to surgeon?"

I consider how to answer that giant question, loaded as it feels with minefields. I decide to keep my response literal. "Well, after I hurt my knee, I had to have surgery, as you know. During my recovery, I was really depressed and things were . . . well, I wasn't in a good headspace."

I watch her bite her lip, no doubt considering her own role in that reality. She nods in recognition.

"Anyway, it wasn't great. But then I got really lucky with my physical therapist. He was a young guy, really got me. And it was the first time I started to let some hope creep in again. By the end of working with him, I'd decided to become a physical therapist. And Henny had started dating the guy."

"No way," Nell laughs—and I love the sound. "Did it work out?"

"Yup. He's my brother-in-law now."

"Amazing."

I nod. "Amazing."

"So . . . ?"

"So, I applied to do my undergraduate and physical therapy degrees at Pitt—they have a strong program. But, once I was there, I started wondering about becoming a surgeon instead. I did a premed track, went to medical school at Johns Hopkins . . ."

"So you mentioned."

"I like to mention it as often as possible."

"Naturally."

I feel the corner of my mouth quirk up.

"I did my residency in Cleveland . . ." I watch recognition come over her face, like that helped fit some puzzle pieces together for her. "And now . . . here I am."

"Incredible," she says, and she's beaming like she means it. "I would never have guessed, but, somehow, it really makes sense, honestly."

"I mean, I guess I was looking for a way to work in sports without playing," I say, examining my hands. "But also . . . I don't know. I think I wanted to prove that I could do it."

I don't say that I wanted to show the world, show *her*, that I was more than what they saw. But that's the truth.

The light is starting to dim, the hour growing later. The sun is no longer at full mast, scorching the earth from above.

Nell looks down at her hands too, her ringless fingers.

"You said 'layout,'" she says, which, out of context, I don't understand.

"I did?"

"When you were talking about possible carpal tunnel. You said if I was working on 'design and layout' too much—like you know what I do for a living. That I'm an art director."

"Of course I do, Eleanor," I say, turning toward her. "You think I haven't wondered and googled you? Asked Cara and Ben about what you're doing? You're really talented. Always have been."

She seems pleased. "Thank you."

"Do you like it?"

"Yeah, I really do," she nods. "Most of the time. Lately, I've been feeling kind of stagnant though. Like I'm over magazines and commercials. Like maybe I'd like to try transitioning to TV and movies, even though that's a slightly different skill set."

"That sounds really cool," I say. "I'm sure you'll make it happen if you want to. You can do anything."

And I mean it. She can.

She blinks and looks down, like she doesn't know what to say.

A squirrel hustles by on its way to a nut. Nell takes a sip of iced tea.

"How's your mom?" she asks, back on safe ground.

"She's good. Sweet. Same old."

"She was always the best cook."

"Also still true. I miss her food."

"And how's Henny?" she asks with a wistful smile. "Besides being married."

"Henny is . . . *Henny*," I say. And we both laugh. Because I know we're picturing the same thing. Impatient eye rolls and groans and *ugh*s but so much warmth. My sister, Henrietta, doth protest too much. She may seem scary, but she is ultimately a teddy bear. Just one that shouldn't be crossed.

Back in the day, Henny loved Nell as much as she hated my other friends—maybe more. I know she felt a loss when we broke up, too. "We talk every week," I add. "Or, more specifically, she lectures me about my dumb choices every week."

"That sounds right."

There's a comfortable silence between us as we both sit with that. After a beat, I glance over at Nell beside me and I can tell she's about to say something real from the crease that pops between her eyebrows.

I wait, patiently.

She swallows hard, stares at the ground. "The last time my shoulder flared up like this . . . it was when my dad . . ."

I nod. Close my eyes against the pain that rises. My heart broke for her then too. When Ben called and told me. I can remember that moment exactly—I was standing in my office, taking the first sips of my morning coffee.

"I tried to reach you . . ." I say.

"I know."

"I wanted to come pay my respects, but I didn't want to make things harder for you. It seemed selfish."

"Yeah," she agrees. "That makes sense."

"Your dad was the best," I say. And I mean that, too.

"I thought so." She shoots me a weak smile, eyes welling. "He really was the best."

Because he was—gregarious and funny and talented and someone who saw the people around him for who they were and accepted them despite their flaws. He was an architect, and as soon as I saw what Nell was doing with her life, it made so much sense.

She has carried on his legacy in a way.

I didn't have a lot of male role models growing up. There was my baseball coach, though looking back, I'm not sure I could say he always had my best interest at heart. Plus, he had an unhealthy obsession with Limp Bizkit, which I could never unsee.

So, Nell's father, Jeff, was the closest I came to having a dad in those days. In the time Nell and I were together, I came to rely on his perspective.

When she and I broke up, I felt like he dropped me too.

"It was so long ago," Nell says now. "You think you're okay. That the grief—at least the acute kind—has passed. Then you meet John the driver who gives you fatherly advice and you take a gummy and suddenly you're crying in a town square, eating Cheerios with your ex-boyfriend."

I shoot her a small smile. "I'm not sure how universal that scenario is."

"You know what I mean."

"Of course I do."

And then she turns to look at me. Like *really* look at me.

"Of course you do," she echoes, like she's just realizing it. Like I am too. That our history was *real*.

"We were just children," she says, like it's puzzling but also a small piece of forgiveness.

"We were just children," I say back.

And something stirs inside me as I stare into her thundercloud eyes. My own gaze drops to her lips, which fall open like an invitation. In that moment, it feels like we're alone in the world. And I've got tunnel vision.

I want to make her feel better. I want to make *me* feel better.

I'm not sure who leans in first. I just know that, somehow, our faces are suddenly inches from each other, her eyes heavy, lashes black. Her breath sweet with that iced tea.

And I am about to kiss her, like I want to so bad, like I now realize I've wanted to since I first saw her standing at baggage claim struggling with that stupid suitcase, when a voice rings out from just feet away.

"Hey, you two!" Lydia squawks. "Get a room!"

She's approaching with another woman who I don't really know, a work friend of Cara's maybe who she has made a vacation disciple. Damien is coming around the corner too, but I don't know if he's caught the scene.

I wish I could freeze the moment, from just seconds ago. But it must be time to head out. And Nell is already up and standing.

"What the fuck with today," she says to no one in particular.

What the fuck with today.

12

BOTH

BACK IN THE DAY

"Truth or dare?" that girl Chloe asks. Chloe is pretty. She has a pierced septum, a pierced tongue, and a ripped Nirvana T-shirt and supposedly dabbles in smoking heroin—a chic amount. She is on the periphery of their world—appearing, compliments of Sabrina, for weeks at a time and then disappearing into the ether.

Tonight, she's here at Sab's house because Sab's parents are away. And now that the group is all varying degrees of wasted and draped on living room furniture in an amorphous circle, Chloe has suggested a game of old-school Truth or Dare.

It's possible that she's just trying to get some action.

It's Nellie's turn.

"Truth," she says, nerves fluttering despite the alcoholic lubrication.

Chloe leans back on her hands. Tick-tocks her head. Worries her tongue pierce with the tip of her tongue.

"What's your number?" she shrugs finally.

"My phone number?"

Cara and Sabrina giggle.

"No, your *number*. Like how many people have you fucked?"

"Dare," says Nellie, not skipping a beat.

Chloe laughs. She looks scary. Her pale skin, jet-black hair, skinny arms. But she's good-natured.

"Okay, dare then."

Noah furrows his brow, leans back into the plush L-shaped leather couch. Glances over at Nellie, lying across the way in a mid-century horsehair lounge chair, trying to read her face. He kind of wanted to know the answer to that question, too.

It's only been a few weeks since their first museum day, but, since then, they've been hot and heavy, meeting up whenever possible for long walks and even longer make-out sessions.

Why doesn't she want to answer? Is the number that high?

"Okay," Chloe says. "I dare you to take off your shirt, so you're only wearing your bra, straddle . . . hmm. Who should it be? Ah! Sabrina! And suck face for a full minute."

Nellie looks doubtful. "Wait, really? Sabrina? That seems . . ."

"Hey!" Sabrina complains. "What's wrong with me?"

"Nothing is wrong with you!" Nellie says. "But you're *you*."

"Do it, do it, do it!" the others start chanting.

Sabrina looks at Nellie, Nellie looks at Sabrina. They're drunk enough and close enough to shrug like, *okay*.

"Here goes," Nellie says, pushing herself to standing. She pulls her shirt over her head and places it neatly on the lounge. Like perhaps she is stalling. Then, in her baby-blue push-up bra, she crosses to the love seat where Sabrina is curled up.

"I need a lap," she says. "You're going to have to uncurl."

"Okay," Sabrina says, swiveling around so that her feet are on the ground. But her expression is unsure. Like maybe her earlier bravado was just that. "Come to Mama?"

Nellie and Sabrina both dissolve into laughter. It's doubtful that this will actually happen.

But Nellie moves to sit on Sabrina's lap, faces her friend, and settles there. "This is weird," she laughs.

"You're weird," Sabrina says.

"C'mon, guys," says Chloe. "Just do it. This isn't a big deal."

"Okay," says Nellie. "Speak now or forever hold your . . ."

"I'll speak now," Noah says, suddenly. He has been sitting across the room warring with himself. On one hand, this is the game. Also, part of him kind of wants to see this. On the other hand, he's feeling possessive. Why does Sabrina get to kiss Nell? That's his job.

Everyone has turned to face him. "What's the hang-up, slugger?" Chloe asks.

Noah shrugs like this is inconsequential. Like he is not self-conscious now, with everyone staring at him, waiting for an explanation for why he's the buzzkill stopping the game. "I just don't think Nell should have to make out with Sabrina."

"Have to?" Sabrina scrunches her nose. "Thanks a lot."

"No, what I mean is, I don't think Nell should make out with anyone . . . except *me*."

Chloe grins, deeply amused, while the others exchange surprised looks. "Well, that isn't the game, Baseball. Anyway, on what grounds?"

He rests an elbow on the top of the couch behind him, leaning back like this is no big deal. "Because," he says, "she's my girlfriend."

But this *is* a big deal. A very big deal. Because they haven't said the b-word or the g-word to each other. They haven't agreed to be monogamous—even though they both have been. And they still haven't told the others anything official.

Cara yelps and brings her hands together in front of her chest like a proud mama. Sabrina shrugs like, *who knew?* But Nellie, she looks over at him with a barely suppressed smile spreading across her face.

"You guys are together-together?" Ben asks.

"Apparently," Nellie answers, then she pushes herself up off her friend's lap.

She crosses to the lounge, picks up her shirt, and readies to put it back on.

"Hang on a second," says Chloe. "You're not off the hook! You at least have to do the dare with your boyfriend over there—you can't just do *nothing*."

Nellie shrugs. She is happy to oblige. She lays her shirt back down, crosses over to Noah, and, without a word, gestures for him to turn toward her.

He smooths the wrinkles out of the thighs of his jeans as she straddles him.

Once settled, she leans in and whispers in his ear, "Girlfriend, huh?"

"Is that okay?" he murmurs.

"That's okay," she nods.

"Hurry it up!" Chloe calls.

So, Nellie presses light kisses to Noah's neck beneath his ear, his jaw, his cheek, then nips his lower lip. The other eyes on them are strange, but, right now, she couldn't care less. He tips his chin up toward her, waits for her to return. And she does, her lips—progressively familiar—working against his own. Her tongue slips into his mouth, tasting of St. Ides forties and cold raspberry Snapple.

And maybe it's part of the dare, only maybe it's not, but she starts to grind against him, despite the audience. He pulls her closer to him, his hands on her ass, so that they're flush against each other. Her inner thighs squeeze the outside of his, his button fly pressing between her legs. The heat dials up quickly, and soon they are fully all over each other—his hands finding her pretty blue bra, him hard beneath her, both of them breathless.

"Okay, okay, time's up," Chloe is saying, but they're not stopping. "We should go to the party!"

"I think we lost them," Sabrina laughs.

And she's right. They are lost. To everyone but each other. Too drunk to care about the spectacle. Too into each other to care about some party, where they'll only want to escape together anyway. Too absorbed to even really notice as everyone else grabs their belongings.

"Hey!" Sabrina calls, before she leaves, forcing them to look up, heavy-lidded, for just a moment. "We're going. Be back in a few hours. Place is yours."

She winks.

And, with the slam of the door, they go back to their business.

Things get real. Quickly. This is the first time they've been truly alone for an extended period of time. Not just a few minutes. Not just outside. Not with friends around the other side of a monument or outside a closed door. Just alone.

Soon, that blue bra is discarded on the floor beside the couch—beside his jeans and T-shirt and her shorts, too. His boxer briefs are pushed down. And the two are horizontal on the couch, skin sticking to the leather, facing each other, entwined.

Their lips are swollen. Their cheeks are flushed. Their hearts are hammering, stomachs rising and falling fast.

He drags his hands down her sides to the elastic of her underwear, readying to slip them down and off. But then he pauses, narrows his eyes. Murmurs into her mouth: "Why did you pick dare?"

"What?" she breathes, distracted by the heat pouring through her body, by an anticipation she hasn't experienced before.

"Why did you pick dare?" he repeats, still breathing heavily. "Why didn't you answer the truth question?"

And she opens her eyes to gaze back at him. "I don't know," she says. "I guess I was embarrassed."

"Because . . . ?"

"Because," she shrugs.

He rests his head back against a patterned throw pillow, not separating from her, but creating the smallest amount of distance so he can see her whole face.

"Because the number is high?"

She pauses. Sighs. Slumps slightly back too. "Because it's not."

"It's low?"

"It's low."

"How low?"

She bites her lip. "Zero low."

His own lips part, then meet again, as he processes this.

"What about you?" she asks, her eyes searching his face. "High?"

He pauses. Considers his answer. "It's zero low too."

"What?!" she says in disbelief. "No! I don't buy that for a second. How is that possible?"

He tick-tocks his head. Brings a hand up to cover his eyes, embarrassed though their answers aren't different. "The same way it's possible for you?"

She shakes her head. "No way. There have been so many more girls for you—like, I know that. *Everyone* knows that."

"Yeah," he says. "For other things. But not . . . for this."

They're silent for a minute, searching each other's eyes.

"Well, good," she says finally. "No time like the present. Let's do this."

"Really?"

"Really."

"Here?"

"Here."

"Condom?"

"Sabrina has. In her bedside table. Her mom gave them to her 'just in case.'"

"But—are you sure?" he asks. "I could plan something more . . . special."

She gazes into his earthy eyes; he gazes into her overcast ones. "This *is* special."

Noah searches Nellie's face for any sign of doubt. Finds none. "Okay, then," he says, nuzzling her as he rolls her fully onto her back beneath him. She squeals, laughing.

He kisses his way down her long neck, past her collarbones, between her breasts, to her belly. Then, slowly, he slides her Victoria's Secret underwear all the way off, past her ankles, heels, and toes. He returns to hover above her, eyes full of a new kind of focus. "Let's do this."

13

NELLIE
TODAY

After the visit to town, I beg to be dropped off before the rest of the group heads to dinner. And when I get back to the room alone, I flop onto my bed—careful-ish of my shoulder—and pass the fuck out.

The combo of the gummy, heat, wine, and stress has officially done me in.

I sleep through the organic pizza feast. I sleep through the drinks. And, when I wake up, in a foggy disoriented state, it's pitch-dark out, the chirp of crickets the only sound. And I get the sense that even they're the last insects at the party.

I reach over and grab my phone. It's after 1 a.m. And, unfortunately, I am ravenous.

I haven't eaten since the Cheerios.

I stand up and pad over to a side table by the door where I've dumped my snack bag from the plane and retrieve a raspberry jam oat bar. It will have to suffice, along with those salted caramel truffles I've been eyeing. Beside the bag slouches the organic market tote from Noah.

Right!

Unwrapping and demolishing the bar, I carry the tote over to the bed to forage through it for my meds. But inside I find so much more than I expected.

There's a prescription anti-inflammatory. A pain medication, as promised, too. But there's also arnica cream, a cold pack, Epsom salts, and a heating pad—which I celebrate like it's a new car.

Yesssss.

There is also a second bottle of iced tea. Which makes me question Noah's claim that he bought the drink for himself—was it always intended for me?

And, if so, why was he being so kind? Was it guilt? Reparations for our past—though he has still never admitted fault? Or could he just not stand the idea of someone out there in the world not liking him?

Noah was always the most charming, well-loved guy. You couldn't *hate* him. If you got to know him well, you'd glimpse his darker dimensions, but he presented outwardly as accepting, sweet, and fun—like everybody's favorite puppy.

With a killer six-pack and panty-dropper eyes.

Well, it was no mystery why the ladies liked him.

Is he just trying to right a wrong, so his conscience is clear?

My mind wanders back to his abs, then roams around his body to unseemly places, as I wonder whether it's still the same.

Inadvertently, tangled in my dress, I'd shown him mine, but he hadn't shown me his.

But back in the day . . .

That relationship was so formative for me. So much so that he haunted me. Sometimes, over the years, I'd realize suddenly, with shame, that I was attracted to someone because of a certain physical quality that reminded me of Noah. And I'd chastise myself for that—for even remembering the particular slope of his lower back into his ass, the leanness of his build, the broadness of his shoulders, the smooth tan skin of his muscled forearms. The way his eyes crinkled when he smiled. Even Alfie, though fair and lithe and always in a vintage band tee, had a half-smile that evoked one Noah used for our inside jokes.

But it was a poor imitation. More caustic than clever. I know that now.

By the time I realized I'd been taken in by that familiarity in part, that I'd endowed this new man, Alfie, with a kind of warmth and affection he didn't possess, I was in deep.

I groan, running a hand as far as it will go through my tangled hair.

I am hot and bothered enough, but still I pop a pill and plug in the heating pad. I dim the light, lie back down, and place the warming fabric on my injured shoulder.

Every part of me feels pulled tight, the dial turned up.

Moonlight falls through the shades, turning everything blue. Even my mood. A tree branch taps the window like Morse code.

Am I reacting this way because I'm roiling from a breakup? It would be easier if that was the case. Only, I know that's not true. Because Alfie and I were over ages ago, though I'd let the relationship sit out, thawing, until it turned. Change is always challenging, and another failed relationship didn't feel *great*, but I'd felt mostly relief when he walked out the door carrying his last box of political tomes and politely wished me well like I was his least favorite colleague.

One thing I know for sure: I will not be lying in bed decades from now, electricity thrumming through me, sheets nervy against my skin, thinking about *him*.

Clearly I'm in crisis of another kind. It's true that I've been feeling stuck. New York is home, but somehow I've grown sick of the Brooklyn neighborhood I once loved. Even of the curmudgeonly bodega cat with whom I used to trade haughty glares. I am no longer excited by the prospect of the next fancy project or timely "collab"—the parties, the cocktails, the sometimes-famous people.

In about two months, the magazine will fold, cast aside along with its staff.

Which, I suppose, is the push I need. I'm ready for the next challenge. The next stage. But what does that mean?

Because here I am in the dark with my eyes closed against reality, fantasizing not about a new future but about the past. About what—or who—lies just on the other side of this suite's common room. About putting on some of those old records and inviting him in. And isn't that the exact opposite of what I should be doing?

Grasping at old versions of myself out of desperation? Backsliding into old habits? Giving credence to bad ideas, a person I know is bad news, from before I knew better?

Why am I even entertaining this? The truth is, I realize now with a sense of profound embarrassment, I don't even know if there is a *this* at all.

And I definitely know there *shouldn't* be.

And yet I keep returning to that almost kiss on the plaza bench earlier in the day, the way his lids dipped heavily as he leaned in.

I need to focus on the future! Heal my (psychosomatic?) arm! Be my best self for Cara. Then go home and figure out what's next. Not daydream about making out with my ex-boyfriend from a time when I was also crushing on John Starks, George Clooney, and Christian Slater.

I shift to my right and feel around on the bedside table for a bottle of orange blossom and chamomile pillow mist that is apparently distilled on the property. I spray it around in place of sage to clear the air. Clear my head.

And it does smell incredible.

See? I'm fine! Great, even. I can go back to avoiding Noah. Rejoin Team NSA. Use my shoulder as an excuse to skip the booze bus to wineries Cara has planned for tomorrow—Day 3: *You booze, you snooze!* Song: "My Own Worst Enemy" by Lit—and use the time to get my shit together instead.

Screw my head on right.

You've got this, I hear my dad say. Or maybe it's John the driver.

But the heat enveloping my shoulder, radiating all the way down my body, and coiling at my core, is saying something different. Gingerly, I grab the heating pad and move it to my stomach, then I turn on my side and let it curl with me, offering comfort.

The next morning, I do in fact beg off the booze bus. Which I object to anyway on the basis of terminology alone.

I believe in buses. And I believe in parties. But, in an ideal world, never the twain shall meet.

There's too much potential puking involved in both.

Cara is totally understanding and practically offers to stay behind too, but obviously that's out of the question.

Once she's given me a pass and I've promised to be *extra* fun later, I wait to hear the main door to our suite wheeze open and slam shut before I climb out of bed and venture into the common room. Noah has made coffee again and, though I am intent on avoiding actual contact with him today, I feel like it's still acceptable to drink his brew.

He has left his door open and I can't help but notice—when I walk over and fully snoop—that his bathroom mirror is still steamed up from a shower. Horribly, I instantly flash to an image of him lathering up—and scurry away, pulling my mind out of the gutter.

Besides, I have big plans for the day and I'm pretty excited.

Though I have wandered around the property a bit, visiting the chicken coops periodically en route to meals to say hello, I have yet to enter the spa barn. And based on the scents emanating from its recesses, it is not to be missed.

After all, this is where the amazing distilled flower mist was born! How else can I pay homage?

I figure the spa will be good for my shoulder and my brain. So, I'll commune with my higher mind. And drink some cucumber water.

I am so zen. *Om.*

But when I meander the quiet dirt path to that corner of the grounds and pop inside wearing my robe, I find an abandoned reception desk. It's in the style of a bleached-out paddock, behind which a birch shelf is lined with natural beauty serums and creams. There is no one to be found. I peek in and around the area, by the racks of impossibly soft yoga pants and a crystal display, down the treatment room corridor featuring gathered sprigs of hay mounted along the walls.

They've really doubled down on the farm theme.

Unsure of what to do, I peek back outside, returning to the property's main path, and fortunately bump into a member of the staff, a young woman with blue hair and a soft-spoken voice.

"Can I help you?" she asks.

Oh, if only.

"I was just interested in the spa . . ."

"Ah," she nods. I feel like she gets me. Just like Damien thinks he does. I gag. "When the property is rented out in this capacity, it's not staffed unless there are specific massages and treatments scheduled. But the hydrotherapy area is open for use—and it's wonderful. Help yourself!"

So I do.

I head back inside past the desk and push through raw wood barn doors to reveal another world: Under a lofted ceiling, adorned with modernist pendant lights, plush but sharp-edged daybeds form single-file lines on either side of hot and cold plunge pools. Each lounger is appointed with a succulent in a ceramic planter to create a sense of organic symmetry. Light spills in through rows of windows, illuminating a countertop bearing bone broth, hibiscus tea, lemongrass elixir, and trays of fresh fruit and date bars. Instead of cucumber water, there is green grape water. This is wine country, after all.

As I step onto the stone-tiled floors, I realize they're radiant, emanating heat from deep within—kind of like me. I shake my head, defiantly.

Will. Not. Go. There.

Once again, I can't help but note the photographic potential for this space, at once immaculately designed but not at all stuffy.

Down a short corridor on one side, I find a eucalyptus steam room—with its glass door properly fogged up—beside a cedar sauna with steaming coals.

And it's all mine! The booze bus has ferried my favorites and least favorites away for the day and left me alone in paradise.

I slip off my robe—noting that my shoulder is already feeling a bit improved—and hang it on a hook outside the sauna, which is where I plan to begin. I grab a rolled-up towel to lie on and one for behind my head, then quickly dig through that organic market bag Noah left me. It's cute. I'm now using it as a tote.

See? I am resourceful!

But when I find my hair tie at the bottom of the bag, I also find my muscle relaxers, which I had completely spaced on. It feels fated. I may not be a weed girl, but I am most definitely a fan of benzos.

I pop one, happily, hang my tote under my robe, then head into the sauna. I spread my towel out on the top level and lie on my back, letting the dry heat envelop me.

Yes. *This*, I think.

I feel like, even through the towel, the wood against my skin is sending healing vibes to my shoulder. I can just sense it getting better.

Only, the tie at the back of my bikini top is stabbing me in the spine. So, I sit up, slip off my top, and cast it to the side.

Free bird!

There is one more problem: no distractions. The longer I lie here, my skin exposed to the warm air, dry heat prickling up and down my body, the more I feel a stirring inside me as my thoughts wander back to Noah. To his arms straining against his workout shirt. To that almost kiss. To what it would have been like if his lips brushed mine, even for the briefest moment. To his tongue slipping into my mouth and . . .

Suddenly, there's a rush of cool air and an "Oh, fuck" that doesn't come from me.

My eyes pop open and I turn to the door to find Noah himself standing there in swim trunks—perfectly fitted, of course—his eyes averted.

"Oh, fuck!" I say too, grabbing the towel from beneath my head and using it to cover my chest.

There's an awkward pause, as we freeze in our respective spots.

Since I'm the one in the more compromising position and he's looking away, I seize the opportunity to surreptitiously check him out. And, yes, the six-pack has endured since our teen years. Only now, instead of being willowy and young, he is filled out and cut. It's a less sharp kind of tone; a more rugged, natural one. I bet he still plays a lot of sports.

I am basically fucking ended.

"Sorry," he mutters. "I had no idea anyone would be in here. I thought the whole group was gone."

"Yeah," I say, "so did I. Hence the . . ." I gesture to my once-bare chest, now *mostly* covered with what turns out to be more of a hand towel. "All clear," I add, so he can look up.

He allows his gaze to travel to my face, though it flits briefly back to my chest for an almost imperceptible beat.

I guess maybe there is a *this* after all.

I should be freaked out. At least more so than I am. Considering that I spent a good portion of the night and much of the morning trying to push similar imaginary scenarios from my brain. But, for whatever reason, the situation strikes me as kind of funny.

I giggle.

"What?" he asks, still lingering in the doorway.

"Nothing," I shrug, but start giggling harder.

He looks at me impatiently. "Nell. *Eleanor*. I was going to spend a few minutes in here first, but do you want me to give you privacy? Hit the steam instead?"

I shake my head, trying to suppress my laughter. "No. It's fine. The more the merrier. I mean, of course this is happening!"

He takes my go-ahead earnestly, and lets the door close behind him, settling his towel on the lowest level, as far from me as possible. He opts to remain sitting up, almost formally, and I can't help but admire his toned thighs and calves from above, though one leg is bouncing with agitation.

I lie back down, keeping the towel across my chest. But the more I lie there trying to be cool, the funnier it strikes me. I giggle again.

"For the love of God, Eleanor! What is so funny?"

"This!" I say, dissolving into full laughter.

He shrugs, sighing. Rolls his eyes. "I mean, I guess this is better than you freaking out."

He's right. I should be in full panic mode. And the thought of that gives me pause. Why am I not also sitting up ramrod straight and ordering him out of here? This is my nightmare—and illicit fantasy come true.

"Oh," I say, recognition settling in.

"What?"

"I took a muscle relaxer."

"You took a muscle relaxer and then went to lie alone in a sauna? Where you could have potentially passed out? With no one to find you?"

"Pretty much," I shrug happily. "Want one?"

He considers this for a moment. Shrugs back. "Sure."

When he returns from grabbing the pill, he takes his seat again, leans over his thighs like *The Thinker*, his head in his hands. He has started to sweat a bit in the steam, and there's a sheen rising on his neck and shoulders that's creating more of a challenge for me. I look away.

We're quiet for a bit. My eyes are closed; I'm doing a decent performance of calm. But inside I am buzzing.

"Is this weird?" Noah says, finally.

"Totally!" I chirp. "I am literally topless in a sauna with Noah-who-must-not-be-named."

"Sorry—what?"

"Don't worry about it." I wave him off, which accidentally knocks my towel to the side, exposing my chest momentarily again. "Oops. Sorry!"

"No problem," he sighs, staring at the ceiling.

"We can handle this," I say.

"Of course," he says. "We're adults."

"Adults," I agree. "And old friends. Sharing a sauna."

"Yup," he says. "*Friends.*"

I close my eyes again, trying to ignore the tingling migrating from my fingers to my toes with a pit stop between my thighs. Trying to ignore the terrycloth towel rough against my breasts.

"It's hot in here. Is it hot in here?" I blurt out, suddenly unable to handle the tension.

"Yes," he says, popping to standing. "Really hot. I'll let you . . ."

His voice trails off and he shakes his head as he gathers his towel and practically sprints out the door, giving me a second to snag my top and wrap my larger towel around my rib cage.

Walking out into the plunge area feels awesome, the way leaving a sauna always does. I am a clean, mean, spa-ing machine. And definitely slightly inebriated.

I find Noah in the cold plunge. I dip my toe in—it is truly frigid. It's the kind of iceberg chill that should only be associated with summer drinks.

"How long are you going to stay in there?" I ask.

"As long as it takes," he grumbles, gritting his teeth.

I pad over to the refreshments for some grape water. It's crisp and yummy and mostly tastes like . . . water.

Noah has finally emerged from the cold and is sitting on the edge of a daybed, his hands resting slightly behind him. He leans back and rotates his neck. He is a sight to behold. My dirty thoughts are not my fault, I reason. A man this handsome is impossible to ignore, even if he once stomped on your heart.

I make a show of *not* looking. Because I am respectful. And impervious to his charms.

"How come you didn't go on the bus?" I manage.

"Honestly, I'm not that big a drinker," he says. "Especially a day drinker."

"But day muscle relaxers. That's okay."

"Desperate times call for desperate measures."

"Are you," I ask, "desperate?"

It comes out hoarser than I intend.

He rakes his gaze up my body to my face, something ragged in his eyes. "Do you want me to answer that?"

Maybe it's the meds taking effect, but this is as direct as he's been.

"I don't know," I answer honestly.

He sighs. Pushes himself to standing. Crosses to the hot tub and begins to wade in, down some steps.

"How does it feel?" I ask.

He bites his lip. "Perfect."

"Is it weird if I get in too?"

He shakes his head. "Not any weirder than anything else."

I am about to shed my towel when I remember I'm holding my top in my hand. "I should probably put this on," I say.

"Probably." He rubs a hand roughly at the back of his neck.

"One second!" I scurry behind a dracaena in a large planter and fasten my bikini at the back. I make sure I have full coverage and then reemerge.

"Tada! All respectable!" I say.

"Great," he grunts, looking truly miserable.

I join him on the steps, ankle-deep in warm water.

We stand next to each other for a beat, hands on our respective hips, then swap sideways glances.

I see his Adam's apple bob beneath stubble. He clears his throat. "I'll just go first."

Noah wades all the way in, his body disappearing below the foamy surface. And he groans in a way that moves through me, leaving trails. But I'm fine. *Totally* fine. I cross one leg in front of the other. "This actually feels amazing."

"Well, you were literally just on ice, so."

"The cold water is good for circulation, stimulates the lymphatic system."

"It's still frigid as fuck."

"You afraid?" he asks, an eyebrow cocked.

"No. I just don't see the point of subjecting myself to pain."

"You know what they say about pain . . ."

"To avoid it?"

"That it's just the B-side of pleasure," he shrugs, holding my gaze for a beat—like he knows what's in my mind. "I'm just saying, the hot water feels better because of the cold. But if you can't handle it . . ."

"I can handle it."

"Like you handled the gummy?"

I gasp. *How dare he!*

"One thing has nothing to do with the other."

"Right," he says, his mouth ticking up at one corner like he's suppressing a smile. "Except for the part where you're a lightweight. In all the ways."

He's having a good ole time now that he's roasting me, and I'm not having it.

Outraged, I stomp out of the hot tub and over to the cold plunge. Then, glaring at him, I wade in, quickly at first, and then slower as the reality of the temperature takes over. "Oh my God!" I squeal. "This is freezing!"

"Get your shoulders under!" he calls. "It doesn't count without the shoulders!"

As quickly as humanly possible, I dip my shoulders under the water and then rush out of the cold, hurrying back around to the hot tub and splashing in, out of breath.

"That's psychotic!" I say. And it's only then that I realize I have sat directly next to Noah—inches from him—instead of all the way across the tub as I planned.

The jets hit me from all directions, pushing my buttons.

I try to act like it's all normal.

He looks down at me, his eyes twinkling. "Just look at that lymphatic system pumping at full force."

I bring my hands to my face, sure it's flushed. "Is that even really a thing?"

His lips quirk again—too amused. "It got you in the ice water."

I shoot him a dirty look and then he starts to laugh. It's a snicker and then a full-throated thing I haven't heard in decades, but it takes me instantly back.

To a time when I was less mature.

So, I splash him in the face.

His mouth drops open in mock shock. "Oh, you do not want to mess with me."

So, I splash him again. Which starts us roughhousing. And lands us, somehow, with his back to the edge of the tub and me pinning him in place, our faces inches apart.

Our laughter stops dead.

I lick my lips. Watch him watch me. I am all wet in all the ways. Maybe fantasy should become reality.

"Is this weird?" I ask.

But I kiss him before he can answer.

14

NOAH
TODAY

Nell kisses me and it's all the things at once.

Because it's like we've done this a million times, but also never before.

And it's zero to sixty. Like I'm starved.

She isn't careful with me, either. She presses her lips against mine, at once pillowy and rough. My hands migrate to her thick hair, threading in where it's damp at the nape of her neck. I trace her flushed cheek, her jaw, her smooth back, as we go deeper. My palms flex around her hips as she starts moving against me.

Holy fuck.

I groan. Or maybe she does. I can't even tell. I'm lost in the fog of her body drenched and flush against mine again, the hot water churning around us, chaotic and fevered.

I flash to Nell at cocktails that first night in that teasing lowcut top. To the sundress catching on her thighs in the town square yesterday. To how hot and rosy she looked lying in the steamy sauna, her towel threatening to drop from her chest.

I want her so badly, it's like my brain has left the building. There's just skin against skin, droplets of water, straight lines that curve into sharp turns.

I can't fucking believe this is happening. This isn't at all how I pictured today.

I pull back for a second, blink my eyes open to make sure it's real. She looks up at me like she knows, mischief in her eyes below dark lashes. And it's better than anything I could envision—*have* envisioned, if I'm honest—in my mind.

I kiss down her throat, as she arches to give me clearance, sighs. It's so easy to get lost in it all, as she straddles me, body slick, lips and teeth teasing again, then pulling away.

And maybe I should leave well enough alone—but, even in the midst of this fever dream, something gnaws at the edge of my consciousness, and I know I can't stay silent.

"Eleanor," I groan as she grinds against me, making me fully insane.

"Yes, Noah?" she says, nipping my ear.

"Can I ask you a question?"

"If you must."

I tighten my grip on her ass, but say, "I must"—I guess with enough conviction that she pauses to look up and into my face. We're both breathless, chests rising and falling fast.

"Okay?"

"Is there a fiancé?"

She bites her lip. Pauses for a brief beat while I have a small heart attack. Then shakes her head.

"Was there ever a fiancé?"

She nods. "We broke up six weeks ago. But my friends don't know."

This is the best news I've heard in a while.

"Okay. Are you rebounding? Like, is that what this is?"

She considers the question for a second. "I don't think so."

"Okay. Cool."

Satisfied, I lean in to kiss her again. This time she stops me, her arms still wrapped around my neck.

"Wait. Now, I have a question."

"Go for it."

I'm listening but also distracted by a drop of water dripping down her neck from her now-wet hair and into her cleavage. I'm dying to stop it in its tracks with my tongue.

"Do Cheerios really mitigate the effects of pot?"

Without meaning to, I laugh out loud.

"What?!" she says. "Don't be mean! I don't know anything about weed."

I rearrange my face into a more serious expression. "No. There is no correlation between oats and level of highness."

She pouts. "I swear it helped."

"And you've wondered all these years?"

"I mean, I thought it was unlikely."

I snicker.

"Shut up," she says.

"Make me," I say.

And she's about to when, against her lips, I say, "One last thing . . ."

"Ugh! What, dude? So damn chatty."

"Why are you making me call you Eleanor?"

"Oh." Her smile drops just a bit. She scratches her neck, looks down. "It's just . . . you're the only person who calls me Nell. And not Nellie."

"And you hate it?"

"No. That's the thing. Not at all."

15

NELLIE
TODAY

I grant him permission to call me Nell, and then things go from PG-13 to R-rated.

He kisses me rougher now, harder, slipping his tongue into my mouth. He tastes like he drank that grape water too. His hands scrape down my chest, yanking my bikini top free. I arch against his palm, pinched and tight.

"Good thing I put my top back on," I laugh into his mouth. "That was a waste of time."

"Nah," he says, all gravel. "I liked taking it off."

His voice reverberates through me and I grind into him, feeling him go rock hard against me. Not everything from the past is smaller than you remember it.

And I don't know if we're making out like teenagers because that's how it started or if it's the frustration of twenty-plus years coming to call.

But the water is making me feel weightless, like we might just float away, intertwined. On an X-rated lazy river. His thumb grazes my jaw, then slides down my neck, his palm cupping my breast, getting waylaid there. I run my hands over his shoulders and down his sculpted arms, scratching at his back. I squeeze his thighs between mine.

I can't be sure where I begin and he ends.

But it's when I raise my hand to run it over his hair at the back of his neck that I yelp loudest—from a shock of pain.

Right. My arm is still injured.

"Are you okay?" he asks, out of breath. His brow is crinkled.

"I'm fine," I say, catching a drop of water trailing down from his temple with my fingertip.

But something glitches in his expression.

"What now?" I ask.

He sighs. "I'm probably going to regret saying this, but . . . are you sure you're good with this?"

"Have I not shown enough enthusiasm?" I laugh. "I'm literally topless on your lap."

I lean into him, pushing my boobs against his bare chest as if to demonstrate.

He nods. Sweeps a palm across his forehead. Like he's suddenly stressed. Why is he *stressed*?

"That's true," he says. "But you're also under the influence of a muscle relaxer. That I prescribed to you."

Is he fucking kidding me? I wonder. "Are you fucking kidding me?" I say.

"It's just that, you were pretty anti this until about fifteen minutes ago—and I just want to make sure you're not doing something you're going to regret."

"Didn't you also take a muscle relaxer?"

"Yes, but . . ."

"Yes, but what?"

He shrugs. "Lightweight."

"You know, you're right," I say, irritation rising. "You must be impervious to meds. Why else would you still be so uptight?"

I start to back up off his lap. Sink down lower into the water and cross to the opposite side of the pool, so that the froth shields me. I am shaking my head—at him? At myself?

Because I know what this is. This is an excuse. This is Noah panicking. This is second thoughts.

"I'm sorry," he says, a pained look in his eye. I assume from the discomfort of the situation. "Maybe I shouldn't have said anything."

"Do not say sorry to me," I say to him, careful to keep my voice at the horizon line. "Like this was your *bad*. I'm a big girl. I make my own decisions."

I will not give him the power to make me sad. To reject me. Not again.

"I know. Of course you do. It's just there's been a lot of miscommunication between us before and I don't . . ."

"Just stop," I say, holding a hand up like, if I try hard enough, I might be able to hold him back against the side of the pool using only the power of my mind. "This was dumb."

"It wasn't dumb, I just . . ." He runs a hand along his closely shorn hair again, clearly unsure of what to say.

"It *was* dumb," I say. "But I'm not. If you're not interested, you can just say that. I don't need this bullshit."

"It's not bullshit," he says, his hands out of the water and facing the ceiling like I'm the one being unreasonable. "We aren't just some random people to each other. This could mean something and I . . ."

. . . *am freaking out*. I finish his sentence for him in my head.

"Stop!" I say firmly now, and I know I'm getting upset, but I will not allow this man to give me some kind of easy letdown or talk. I will not hear it. Not so many years later like nothing has changed.

Ugh! Why did I do the same thing and imagine a different outcome? Why did I expect this Noah to be mature and consistent and present when that's not his MO? Here he is, playing the same old shell games with my emotions.

This man literally spends his time with professional athletes, probably traveling from city to city and banging a nameless, faceless many. I realize in that moment that I actually know nothing about him, the Noah of today. He could have his own fiancée for all I know.

"I get it," I say, as I reach for my towel, which slouches on the slate-tiled floor beside the pool, and begin to climb out. "It was a thrill-of-the-chase thing. You thought maybe you'd time travel for a second, but it got old."

"What? No! I didn't plan this, Nell," he says, starting to rise out of the pool himself. "You were the one letting the towel drop in the sauna and I was trying to . . ."

The rage that rises in my chest at his words surprises even me—at teenage Noah, at today's Noah, at Alfie. At all the deeply disappointing humans along the way. It courses through my veins like venom, transforming me into something sinister.

"Oh, so *what*? Now I threw myself at you?"

"No! That's not what I meant."

I wrap the towel around my chest fully, grab my top and my tote, and stomp toward the barn doors. "Fuck you, Noah. Good for you. You convinced your gullible high school sweetheart to make out with you. Mission accomplished. Now, you can move on. Go tell Damien or find Lydia or something."

"Lydia?" he says. "Really, Nell?"

I swing the spa doors open and whip around to face him. "It's *Eleanor* to you."

In the afternoon, time stretches. It downward dogs. It planks. It rolls its neck.

I check work email and the clock eight hundred times, both anxious for the crew to return from their booze bus excursion and dreading having to act like everything is normal. Like nothing *happened*.

I sit on the deck, where the breeze is so slow and warm that you'd miss it if you blinked. The air smells of jasmine, of whatever the nearby yellow flowers are, of summer coming. Every so often, a chicken bawks. And I balk too.

I'm angry at Noah for sending mixed signals. I'm angry at myself for getting swept up. But most of all, if I'm honest, I am *deeply* embarrassed.

Because I thought I was in a safe place with a safe person. And when he flipped the switch, I felt like maybe I wasn't.

I know it's partially my fault—I should have followed my instincts and avoided this situation altogether. Not just because Noah is changeable and only operates on his own terms. But also because, as much as I want to pretend it's all in the past, I'm lugging enough baggage around for some socialite on a European tour.

As much as I hate to admit it, I realize now—as I inspect my coral toenail polish and relive the spa debacle again and again—that I have to be real with myself: Once upon a time, Noah hurt me. A lot. It was a million years ago and, yes, we were kids. But the sting remains.

In this situation, there is no such thing as a clean slate.

When it comes to interacting with him, I'm never starting at zero. My feelings are already at a fever pitch, my teeth already bared. I'm waiting for him to wrong me.

When my phone pings, I look down half expecting the text to be from him. Which is silly, because does he even have my number? That's how little we've interacted, how little we actually know each other at this point.

Sabrina

> We're baaaaack! Come upstairs and hang out with us! It's happy hour. Meaning we're on the deck and we just ordered the whole room service menu—and I'm happy about it.

Oh, thank God. I smile. That sounds like a plan.

Rita and Sab are staying on the top floor, so I climb the winding bleached-wood staircase to their room. Before I can knock, the door swings open to reveal my two friends—already very drunk and with full goblets in their hands.

Sabrina's usually immaculate bob is in disarray, her shades perched on her head as she has surely forgotten them there. Her black tank top is haphazardly tucked into her black pleated skirt and her purple eyeliner has smudged practically down her cheek. Rita's free arm is slung around her wife's shoulders, and her denim overalls are hooked on only one side, like she is the Fresh Prince of Bel-Air. And if I think *my* hair is untamed, Rita's curls look poised to swallow us all whole.

"Come, come!" says Rita, waving me inside. "There's cheese! And more cheese!"

Indeed there is. I look around expecting I might find Cara too, but she is nowhere to be found.

Meanwhile, Sabrina did not lie. In the time it took for me to throw on shoes and head upstairs, the room service has arrived. The duo has already started in on a cheese plate so enormous that it takes up half a dining table on their deck. Beside it sits some kind of tuna tartare, deviled eggs, chilled shrimp cocktail on a bed of crushed ice, and a massive order of French fries. Now, the two women plop back down on a love seat to continue gorging their wasted asses. It's hard not to laugh as I settle in across from them and watch them ooh and ah over the various creamy Bries and hard goudas.

"Holy shit," says Sabrina, her sunglasses falling crookedly onto her face. Startled, she removes the shades and casts them to the side, so she can return to scarfing, unencumbered. "Sorry, hon. But I think I might leave you for this apricot jam."

Rita shakes her head, her mouth full. "I can't blame you. I've never been big on the idea of ethical nonmonogamy, but maybe for this almond-stuffed olive."

"I guess the booze bus was a success," I say, thinking not for the first time about how lucky they are to have found each other—partners who share a mutual love of salumi and fried food.

"Mm. Kinda," Sabrina says. "The first few wineries were great—one in particular, Scribe? Super-cute design. Spanish style. Great wine. You would have loved."

"Ah. Sorry I missed it!"

I was busy getting busy with my high school boyfriend and archnemesis.

"Well, you don't have to be," Rita says, "because, by that point, we were super drunk and may have ordered their entire cellar. So, you can have a bottle—or *five*."

Sabrina nods in agreement. "That might have happened. Anyway, after that, things deteriorated a bit. At the next spot, Lydia started cozying up to the winemaker—or she thought he was the winemaker. I think he was maybe just an intern at the tasting room. By that time, Cara started to feel a little woozy and Damien was forcing the driver to blast Wu-Tang on the van's sound system. It was weird."

Rita nods, stuffing a shrimp in her face. "But not as weird as how many times Damien asked where you were."

"So true. After like the eighth time, I started to wonder if all those blunts in the nineties did permanent damage."

What the hell is up? How bored is he?

"So, what did you do?" Rita asks, all innocence.

"Yeah, what did you do?" Sabrina adds.

They exchange a look in a not-so-subtle way and then, as if choreographed, they look simultaneously back at me.

I must blush some kind of insane crimson, because Sabrina stands up and starts pointing at me with her reverse French-tip nail and, though she can't get the words out because of all the crackers in her mouth, I know where she's going.

"Shhh!" I say.

"Mmph!" she says.

"What's happening?" Rita asks.

"Noah!" Sabrina finally blurts out.

"Oh," says Rita. Then, "OH!" She leans in, eyes wide. "What happened?"

I motion for them to keep their voices down. The balcony Noah and I share is only one floor below.

"They hooked up!" Sabrina stage-whispers.

"How did you know?" I whisper back, mortified, but also a little relieved to have it out in the open. "Are you a witch?"

"I mean, yes, obviously," Sabrina says, sitting back down. "But we didn't know anything except that you both stayed behind—on purpose?"

"No," I say, shaking my head. "Definitely not on purpose. It was a total accident—and a mistake."

They stare at me expectantly. I stare back at them.

"Well, dish!" Rita yelps. "C'mon. We're old married folks. We don't get dirt like this ever!"

"It's not dirt!" I protest.

"Sorry, smut," Sabrina says. "We don't get smut ever. C'mon—what happened?"

So, I swear them to secrecy and then tell them the basics. And though I start out planning to censor certain parts, I wind up revealing it all.

When I describe storming out, Rita whistles. "Sorry, Nellie. But that is definitely dirt."

"I'm proud of you," Sabrina says, leaning over to pat my shoulder. "You got some! Also, I'm not going near that hot tub for at least forty-eight hours. That does not sound sanitary."

"Yeah," I scowl, grabbing some kind of candied nut for myself and stuffing it in my mouth—it is indeed fantastic. "Too bad he's such an asshole."

That's when both women avert their eyes, look down, look away. A hummingbird flits by. Rita points to it like it might distract me from what's happening directly in front of my eyes. "Nellie. Did we ever tell you about the time we saw like twenty hummingbirds when we were visiting my family in Mexico City?"

"Rita."

"Yes?"

"You don't think he's an asshole?"

She presses her lips together. Shakes her head.

I deflate. "I thought we were Team NSA."

"We are, we are," Sabrina says, popping another olive in her mouth. "It's just that . . . you didn't really hear him out."

"Hear him out?"

"Yeah. I mean, it kind of sounds like he was looking out for your best interests. I get that stopping was a buzzkill. But I'm not sure that makes him an asshole, per se."

"I mean, we're just two drunk witches," Rita nods apologetically. "So, take what we say with a grain of salt."

"A grain of this smoked paprika sea salt," Sabrina says. "It's to die . . ."

I try to adsorb what they're saying. Did I overreact? It's true that I distrusted him from the get-go. Or did I not do the incident justice in the retelling?

"But . . . he panicked."

"Well, he pushed pause, which is pretty Herculean for a dude in his position if you think about it. And I know you're assuming he changed his mind about you, but did he ever actually say that? I feel like maybe he was trying to make sure you were all good. That you were really consenting. And, no offense, but I'll just say this because I'm drunk and can't be held responsible for what comes out of my mouth—but you're not always the best at accepting help."

Sabrina eyes me sideways like she's not sure if I'm going to attack. But honestly, it's not exactly a revelation—that's something I've been working on unsuccessfully for a while now. I don't like to need people. I don't like to be a burden.

Sometimes, I know I take an offer of help as an insult.

"Well, that's partially because when I asked Noah for help all those years ago, he didn't just say no," I say. "He disappeared."

"Help with *what*?" Sabrina asks, leaning in. "Why did he disappear?"

I shake my head. I can't go there. I've kept the truth about what broke me and Noah to myself for so many years. It's going to take more than great olives to open me up.

"Maybe—*maybe* he was trying to make sure I didn't get too attached," I concede. "Before things went too far."

"And acting like a grown-up?" Sabrina suggests.

"Don't push it."

She shrugs, sheepish. There's a beat while we all stuff more appetizers in our faces.

"But anyway," I say, "don't you think this is just another nothing conquest for him? Like he's just got a girl in every port, up and down the coast?"

"Is he in the navy in this scenario?"

Rita is shaking her head, her curls bobbing. "No. No. Because he's literally had one serious girlfriend since I've known him and, when that didn't work out, he wouldn't even go on a date or let anyone set him up for eons. In fact, he even shot down that one woman from accounting—the intelligence-challenged one with the big boobs." She turns to Sabrina, gesturing at her chest. "Remember her?"

Sabrina is nodding. "Totally, totally. I think. The one with the shiny hair or the one with the vintage Corvette?"

And I am staring at them both, absorbed in this run-of-the-mill memory jog when what they're saying starts to crystalize for me. Rita and Noah being so buddy-buddy. Their warm greeting, despite never having had any reason to overlap before. The way Sabrina's unwillingness to talk to Noah seemed to hurt his feelings.

"Oh my God!" I yelp. And now it's my turn to point a finger. "You guys have been hanging out with Noah. In LA! And you do it *a lot*!"

Sabrina's eyes go wide. She freezes like a bunny in a floodlight. Only she is no innocent cottontail.

Rita eyes us both anxiously, bites her lip, starts binge-eating a dish of Marcona almonds.

"It just happened!" Sabrina bursts out, finally, covering her eyes with her palm.

"I can't believe you! With all your bullshit Team NSA crap! Lies!"

"I know, I know," she groans. "I'm the worst. But I didn't know how to tell you."

"Um, how about just calling me? And telling me? Like maybe, 'Hey, Nellie. You know that boy who shattered your heart into a billion pieces? He's my new bestie.'"

"And Rita's colleague," Rita adds. She raises her shoulders to her ears, her hands meeting in front of her chest as if in prayer. "Sorry. I figure we might as well say all the things now."

"You work together? Is that how you reconnected?"

How could I have been so dumb? I knew Rita worked in events for a sports team. I just didn't know which one. They're all the same to me.

Sabrina toggles her head, grits her teeth. "Rita may have recommended Noah for the job."

"Oh my God! You're that close?!"

"I posted about one of my gallery shows a few years ago, around the time he moved to town," she says. "I guess he saw it and he came. Now, I know that's just what he's like—he *always* shows up. For events, for occasions, for birthdays . . ."

"*Birthdays?* You spend your birthdays with him?"

"He's not just some jock, by the way," she says, ignoring me. "He really loves art. He's very knowledgeable. Did you know that about him?"

I did. Of course I did.

My mind is blown though, as I contemplate how many ridiculous conversations I've had with Sabrina since they became friends again—about how much *we* hated Noah and how he was the worst.

She never even liked him much back in the day, even when I did. Never took him seriously.

I cover my face with my hands. Too much humiliation for one day. "I can't believe you let me go on and on about Team NSA," I whine. "It's so cringey. Ugh!"

Sabrina pops out of her seat and comes to kneel in front of me like I'm a knight and she's a squire. Like she's Noah examining my arm. She grabs my hand—and it would be funny because it's so absurd if I wasn't feeling so betrayed. "I am *so* sorry. Truly. But I love you. And I didn't think it mattered much because you're so rarely in LA and you never see him or anything. Well, today you've seen a lot of him. Like *a lot*. But you know what I mean. It seemed like it would just cause you unnecessary pain."

I sigh. "I guess I can see that."

"Also, just as a reminder, I still don't even know the details about what happened back in the day. And Noah won't dish either, out of respect for you. One day, you were happily ever after—at least mostly—and the next you were putting a hex on his house."

"I thought *you* were the witch."

"Can't there be two?"

"Three!" Rita volunteers, her hand up.

"Anyway, I am so sorry."

"*We* are so sorry," says Rita, leaning in.

I grumble and cross my arms.

"Do you still love us?" Sabrina asks, tipping her head sideways and shooting me her best doe eyes.

I groan. Roll my eyes. Give in too easily, my shoulders dropping. I don't have it in me to hold a grudge. "Well, obviously. But please. In the future, do not lie to me again!"

Rita and Sabrina mutter all manner of *definitely not* and *of course not* and *never again*.

"And now, as punishment, I am going to eat all your truffle fries," I pout.

"Fair enough," Sabrina says.

She returns to her seat beside Rita, rests her feet on a nearby ottoman.

"Does Cara know? That you're friends?" I ask, the thought of them discussing it paining me. "Actually, don't tell me. I don't want to know."

Rita and Sabrina exchange another of those coupley glances. The sky is turning to a bruised peach, readying for sunset. This is the world's longest day.

I eat a few of their French fries but can't quite make good on my threat. Anyway, we have places to be. It's time to get dressed for dinner. I skipped last night and today, so I shouldn't be late. "I better go get ready," I sigh. "It takes me an extra fifty years with my shoulder."

"Can I just say," Rita says, as the three of us creak to standing and head back into the suite. "At least this means you know you can trust our opinions about him. Noah is a good guy. We know him—*now*. Not as a teenage boy. And I don't think he would feel you up in a hot tub and then just toss you to the curb."

"You'd be surprised," I mutter.

"But what I mean is," Rita continues, as I reach the door, "I've seen how he looks at you."

I flash to Lydia, so many years ago on the street outside my drawing class. *"How come that boy was staring at you?"*

Against my will, a small part of me has the same response today as I did then. A streak of joy alights through me like a comet. I tamp it down.

"I've never seen him like this before," Rita continues, as she opens the door for me. "I think he maybe still has legit feelings for you. So, look at it this way: there's nothing standing in your way!"

Except for a massive dumpster fire.

But I nod, humoring her, as if it's all simple now. As if Noah and I are capable of getting along, even if he is decent. Even if this was a misunderstanding.

And I am about to exit into the hallway when Sabrina suddenly slams the door shut with me still inside. She turns on me, backing me toward the wall, with pursed lips. I almost trip over a standing lamp.

"What the hell—?"

"One second, young lady!"

"Um. Okay," I say. "Old lady."

She points a finger in my face. "What about Alfie?"

"Oh. *Oh!*" says Rita, her eyes widening again. "What about Alfie? The plot thickens!"

And now it's my turn to look sheepish. I shrug my shoulders, tilt my head. Scratch at an imaginary itch at the back of my neck.

"We broke up," I murmur. "There is no Alfie. At least, not in my world."

"I knew it!" Sabrina celebrates. She turns to Rita: "I told you! I told you something was fishy."

"Well, he definitely stinks," I say, collecting my hair in my hands and holding it off my neck for a beat. I need a vacation from this vacation.

"Who's the liar now, huh?" Sabrina says, dancing in a circle. But then she stops and lays a hand on my good shoulder. "Wait. Are you okay? What happened? Why didn't you tell me?"

"I'm fine. It happened a little over a month ago. And I didn't want to make Cara's celebration all about me."

"But you could have told me *weeks* ago. I would have helped you. I would have listened. I would have sent you sad-song playlists and trashed his ass. I would have resurrected my campaign to get you to leave New York and move back to LA."

I smile, a small sad smile. She's right. I know it. Of course, I should have told Sabrina and Cara. But this private part of me, that's afraid to share when life goes off track, is strong. It's hard for me to overcome.

In my house growing up, I was rewarded for being the easy one, the low-maintenance one, the one who never had to be bailed out. That's my whole identity.

I take a moment to mourn the conversations and support I could have had if I had simply trusted my friends. Let them help.

"I know," I say, my eyes welling for the umpteenth time on this trip. Though tears are rare in my normal life, I keep landing on Water Works here. "I think sometimes I'm afraid that if I start to talk about one thing, it will all come pouring out."

"Then let it rain, baby!" Sabrina says, pulling me into a hug.

I sigh, sinking into her arms, into the smell of her figgy perfume, so appreciative of the comfort.

"Sometimes it's embarrassing," I say into her hair, so that it's safe and I don't have to look her in the eye while I make this admission.

"What is?"

"To be the single one. The one who never seems to make it work. While you guys and Cara and Ben have it so figured out."

Rita and Sabrina exchange a glance over my shoulder, then start to giggle.

"Look," says Rita. "We do not have it together. Trust me. We just spent two hundred dollars on cheese."

"Right," I say, pulling back. "But you wasted that money together."

"Well, let's not go too far. Cheese is never a *waste*."

A breeze blows in through the open door to the deck, bringing with it the slightest chill. I think I'll wear my jean jacket to dinner, sit near the heat lamps.

Rita gives me a hug too, then disappears into their bedroom to get dressed.

This time, I walk to the door committed to actually leaving. But just before I step into the airy halls of this charming cottagecore house, I turn around to face my friend again.

"Are you disappointed in me?" I ask Sabrina, eyes downcast. "Because I broke up with Alfie?"

"Are you ever getting back together with him?"

I shake my head.

"Then hell no, woman. I hated that dude. And that's a fact."

In some ways, it's the acknowledgment of another lie—at least of omission. The fact that she hated my fiancé and never had the guts to tell me. One of many unspoken truths in a lifelong friendship.

But as the door clicks shut behind me and I start to descend the stairs, step by creaky step, past bud vases of wildflowers perched on windowsills, I feel a bit clearer than when I arrived.

16

BOTH

BACK IN THE DAY

There are awkward family introductions and school breaks and movies and sushi dinners and parties with friends. There are teenage arguments and petty jealousies—that result in a couple of very short-lived breakups—and failed attempts to teach Nellie baseball. There are Hamptons weekends and her rotator cuff injury—damn that baguette!—and professions of love that flush them both from head to toe.

So, when the time comes for the next stage of their lives, they have a plan. A different path. So they won't wind up broken like all the rest.

It's inevitable, everyone tells them. *Long distance won't work.*

He has nearly committed to playing Division One baseball at a college in Southern California; she has applied to three colleges there too—a safety, a target, and a reach.

They will go together to the West Coast. To the land of palm trees and neon billboards and an abundance of avocado and lemon trees. They won't fall victim to crossed calls, tonally confusing voicemails, Jell-O-shot-fueled dorm room temptations, the slow stretching in opposite directions toward separate lives.

They will stay together.

Until one day, a glitch in their plan. A hiccup of gargantuan proportions. One of life's before and afters.

A stolen base that steals a future. A massively torn ACL, a pop in his knee that sends shockwaves of pain. A trajectory forever altered.

Nellie isn't at the field watching the game when it happens. She's at home, studying for her midterms. Midterms that Noah keeps insisting don't even matter because it's spring semester of senior year.

He doesn't understand why she cares. Because academics have never mattered to him. Nothing has mattered—except baseball.

So, he's mad at her already for not showing up. Even though she tried to explain that she can't leave a project unfinished. It's just not how she's built.

And, maybe, Nellie reasons later, that is part of the reason why Noah's anger seems directed largely at her after the accident happens—after he is taken to a hospital and the doctors tell him, with kind but unyielding faces, that he's facing surgery, a long recovery, may never return to the same level of play.

He will miss key years in the development of his game.

If he was further along in his career, this might have been surmountable. But now, in this nascent stage, it's catastrophic.

And when Nellie tries to tell Noah it will be okay—he is more than baseball. So much more. That he will still have a remarkable life. They can still go to California together and have their adventure, he looks at her like, *how dare you*. He looks at her like he never has before. Like she doesn't know him—or maybe anything at all.

Noah sulks and droops, and she exchanges meaningful looks behind his back with his mother and sister, Henny. Her own parents raise their eyebrows, observing from a distance. He stops returning her calls promptly. Stops making plans to hang out.

And then, one day, he finally agrees to meet up with her—at the foot of their Central Park boulder, since he can't currently climb—after an unprecedented two-week hiatus in which she tries to be understanding and reason that his world has been rocked. And he breaks down, actual tears streaming from bloodshot eyes she barely recognizes as he asks her not to go. To give up their dream. To make a new one. California will only remind him of what he's lost.

And she considers what he's saying, though she has just *that* day received the big envelope saying she's been admitted to her reach school in LA. Her dream school. With the design program she has always imagined.

Nellie feels pulled in all directions. Her heart will break either way.

But she reasons that maybe she could be just as happy here. On the East Coast. At home. Near her father and mother—and everything she knows. Near the grocery salad bars and Tasti D-Lite ice cream shops and Dr. Zizmor subway ads; in muggy summers that smell like rot and crisp autumns that smell like the passage of time.

So, she agrees. "Thank you," Noah says, burying his face in her neck as Nellie runs a soothing hand over his warm head and neck. Down the back of his hoodie, over his shuddering back.

And she almost says, "You're welcome"—but is he? To this great sacrifice on the altar of desperation?

She can already hear her parents questioning why she's changed her mind. Why no California? Why not this program—it's all that she has talked about for years?

And weeks later, as Nellie slumps on a couch watching Noah stumble drunkenly through a friend's house party—in a way that is so unlike the Noah she first knew but she fears is exactly like this new post-baseball incarnation—she is not at all sure she has made the right call.

And maybe, just maybe, that's why she still hasn't informed the LA school that she will not be accepting admission. Maybe that's why she has not informed the East Coast university that she *will* be joining their first-year class.

She's not ready to remove the safety net. She is unsure of their staying power.

She feels someone plop heavily down beside her, unsettling the cushions, and she turns toward the disruption.

"Whattup, Nellie?" Damien says.

"Not much," she sighs, crossing her arms over her chest in a self-hug.

He follows her gaze to Noah, who is placing some sort of pill on his tongue. Some girl Nellie doesn't know is giggling and holding his chin shut like he's a dog taking roundworm medication. The girl's hands are on Noah's body and he's laughing.

"My man's a wreck." Damien gazes unblinking from below blond lashes.

And, though it's disconcerting that he has so aptly read what is in Nellie's mind, though she doesn't want to betray Noah, it's hard for her to deny the obvious.

"It's not great," she admits.

"He says you're staying in New York for him," Damien says, rotating his baseball cap sideways on his head and looking down at her. "That true?"

She nods. Bites her lip.

He leans on his thighs, facing forward, then turns to examine her again. "If anyone asks, I never said this, but let's just say he's not considering you on the same level. You deserve to hear that."

She knows she shouldn't take the bait, but how can she not? She can see the shift in Noah like night and day. He has started returning her calls again since they agreed to forgo their California plans, but still sometimes it feels like he's avoiding her—and she has heard rustlings about him and other girls.

What she is watching now from across the room doesn't help. And that's happening in her presence. What goes on when she's not around?

"What does that mean, Damien?" she asks, working to keep her voice even, empty of desperation.

He laughs lightly. "You're the only one who calls me Damien," he says. "You know that?"

She really doesn't care. Not right now.

"What are you trying to tell me?" This time, her voice catches in her throat.

She is appealing to Damien's best self, which she knows even then barely exists. But she has already been sensing what he is implying and some part of her needs confirmation.

"Look," he says, leaning in. "That's my boy. I'd do anything for that kid. And he's hurting right now. But you're too good for him. You could do better."

Is Damien dropping wisdom or fucking with her?

Unbeknownst to her, her boyfriend has wondered the same thing when Damien has suggested that Noah should let Nellie go, too—*what's the fun of college with the same old girlfriend?* And if Nellie stays for him, isn't that just pressure? Damien keeps asking. Won't he feel trapped?

"D! I *need* you!" Some drunken girl calls from across the room, bangled arm outstretched. Damien jumps to standing. "Catch you later," he says to Nellie.

Alone on the couch again, Nellie tries to catch her breath, but she can't. She wishes her girls were here. But they're not. Cara and Ben are off planning their future at Stanford together. Sabrina is hanging with Chloe and her new art world friends, dating girls openly for the first time.

Nellie wouldn't want to bother them anyway.

But she has been dragged to this party to be ignored. Which only compounds what Damien is suggesting.

She watches Noah, who is leaning on his crutches, laughing too loud at that same girl's joke. He never used to drink, really. He never used to be like the other neighborhood boys.

He doesn't feel her eyes on him this time or, if he does, he doesn't turn to look. She has become an appendage.

She can feel it like a fact.

And in that moment, Nellie knows, she is done with *all* of this. Has already mentally moved on to the next thing. Ready for her new life to start, now.

Will she be able to move forward here with Noah? To find that new life in New York? Will he even want her to?

"I'll Be Missing You" plays on the stereo like a sick joke.

And, as she watches her boyfriend, she wonders if they are both already gone.

17

NOAH
TODAY

Dinner is a subdued event, mostly because the crew is already halfway to hungover.

Anticipating the group's exhaustion after a long day of wine tasting, Cara has arranged tonight's festivities at the farm-to-table restaurant on property. Everything has been sourced within mere miles. There are gem lettuces, squash blossoms, red wine reductions, and slices of steak so tender they melt on the tongue.

Nell huddles at one end of the long wooden table with Sabrina and Rita, who both look a bit worse for the wear. At least Sab seems to have returned to her usual warm self instead of ignoring me. She waved when she walked in and now she keeps sneaking peeks at me and winking.

Maybe she's still drunk.

Nell, looking relaxed in an oversized jean jacket and another floral dress, is avoiding me altogether.

Eye contact. Physical contact. Contact sports.

You name it. She's avoiding it.

Despite all her thoughtful planning, Cara herself didn't even make it to dinner, apparently having majorly overdone it on the winery tour. I can only imagine how much so if she's skipping her own event. Ben is tight-lipped about her state, but it is clearly no bueno.

She has tomorrow to recuperate and then it's un-wedding day.

So, mostly I get to hang out with Ben, which is actually what the doctor ordered for me. It's the most chill. We ate some pretty outstanding radishes with butter and sea salt and braised short ribs as he ribs *me* about working for the Dodgers (he's a diehard Yankees fan). He asks me how I can show my face as a New Yorker, but then—as always—has a million questions about the players I've met and worked with.

As the others start to disappear back to their rooms, Nell included, giving us more cover, I ask Ben how things are at home.

"Good!" he says. But then he frowns. "Okay."

Ben is always the most positive, so I take his frown seriously. "What's up?"

He runs a hand through his hair and rests his forehead in one palm. I realize he looks pretty stressed out.

"I'm really tired," he says.

"I'm sure."

"No, but *really* tired."

He and Cara have two kids under five, so I guess that's to be expected. But he looks beat, even for that.

"Don't get me wrong, the kids are great—except when they're not. But it's a lot. And lately . . ."

He hesitates, so that I start to imagine he's going to confess something truly bad. Lately he's been thinking he can't take it anymore? Lately he's been thinking about other women? Lately he's joined a pickleball league?

None of that would be in character, but I am loyal to my best friend for life. We are ride or die. So, whatever it is, I'm here for it.

"Lately, what? You can say it."

He sighs, tracing the grooves in the table with his finger. "I feel like an asshole saying this out loud. It feels so disloyal."

"Okay . . . no judgment. Promise."

He exhales. "Lately, Cara is kind of struggling, I think. And it's *challenging*."

This surprises me. Cara has always had her shit together. Maybe more so than anyone else in our friend group. Even since we were kids, she was the one who organized every gathering, every night out. As far as I know, she works her ass off rising through the tech ranks by day, then manages to make it home to cook some elaborate nutritious dinner at night.

"Struggling how?"

"Well, at first, she was sad a lot of the time and kept talking about how she didn't know who she was anymore."

"Right. I get that," I say, leaning back in my chair. "I mean, it's easy to lose sight of yourself when you've got so much shit to do for other people."

"Right. So, like, I tried to be more helpful, pitch in. But she wants things done the way she wants and I can't always do it the 'right' way, so . . . she does it herself. But then she's overwhelmed."

He fiddles with the blue cloth napkin and unused butter knife lying askew in front of him, like he's going to use the components to build a fort. And it's hard for me not to see Ben as his eight-year-old self, creating scenarios for his action figures. I always wanted to play sports and he always made me play He-Man.

"Have you talked about it? How you want to help, but don't know how?"

"Yeah—and maybe it sort of helped for a minute. But then things took a turn."

"A turn?" My heart rate elevates ever so slightly. 'Cause if there's a real problem, if Ben and Cara can't make it work, then there's no hope for *any* of us.

"Yeah, she said she realized she needed to, like, blow off steam. And now suddenly she wants to go out all the time, try every new restaurant and bar, get wasted, do drugs again—and she planned this whole thing," he says, gesturing around like he doesn't know how it all materialized. "And like, she wants to have sex *all the time*, which—at first—I admit seemed like a good thing. But now, man. It's like she's out for revenge. And I can't keep up! I am just fucking *exhausted*. And honestly, I think she is too, if I could get her to admit it. She doesn't seem happy! I mean, right now, she's literally lying on the bathroom floor of our suite, groaning. I don't know what she's trying to recapture, but I am an old man—and I like it that way. I want maybe a little scotch with dinner and bed by ten p.m., so I can be up at six with the kids and do it all over again. I want our old boring life back."

He rubs his eyes with his fists. Yawns. Like he's the toddler.

"Oh, man," I say, 'cause I'm not sure what else I have to offer. "That's tough."

"We have these few days off of parenting," he says, his hair now standing on end from all the messing with it. "I just want to *chill*, you know? Just for a sec."

It's hard to age gracefully. Hard to accept new versions of yourself, when that also means saying goodbye to the old versions, the formative ones, the ones that made you *you*.

I know that firsthand even from way back after my injury. When you feel like you've lost your identity, where do you look? Where do you go?

I understand Cara's dilemma. But also Ben's.

"What's up with tomorrow?" I ask, because I know it's the one day without any real itinerary.

He groans. "Cara has this idea that we're going to drive to the coast and pick up all this shit for the big party on Saturday. Some flower farm and oyster farm and I don't fucking know. Things we could have paid someone else to do—we're already spending a billion dollars on this whole thing. It wouldn't have mattered."

I took for granted that Ben and Cara both wanted this days-long debauched celebration. It never occurred to me that he might have wanted off the roller coaster.

"I know people have much bigger, way more legit problems," he continues, "but I just want to do nothing—lie by the pool, play Connections, and read the latest Erik Larson for one damn day."

"No problem," I shrug. "Done."

"No problem?" He scrunches his nose.

"I'll do it for you," I say. "Cara will probably feel like shit tomorrow, anyway. I bet you can convince her. Let me pick up all the stuff on the coast. I have a car. I've got nothing scheduled. I'm not going home to two toddlers in a few days. Let me go and give you your free Friday."

Ben gazes at me like I'm an archangel descended from heaven. "Really?"

"Really. I've never even been to the Sonoma coast. Seeing it sounds nice."

The relief on Ben's face is palpable—like he's just been awarded a stay of execution instead of been released from a day of errands. "Thanks, man," he says, resting a hand on my upper arm. "You're the fucking best. I mean, for a Dodgers fan."

I feel a small pang of guilt. Because of course I would have done this for him anyway. But it's also self-serving. I need to escape this place for a day, solo. Get my head on straight. Try to shake off this shit with Nell. Because it's all I can think about. And judging by the massive implosion at the spa, something between us is probably not workable. She can't get over her distrust—and maybe vice versa too.

She can't see that I've changed. And, the truth is, I get it.

Somehow, some way, I need to stop feeling whatever I'm feeling for her. I need to move on, for real.

But how do you move on from something that's been haunting you since some night under strobe lights when you were seventeen?

"How are things with *you*?" Ben asks, now, like he's read my mind. And maybe he has. We've been friends for that long. "How's seeing Nellie?"

I rub at my shoulder absently. Adjust in my chair. Open my mouth to speak and then close it.

Ben's eyes go wide. "That bad, huh?"

"It's just—" I start.

"Yo! Whattup, losers?" Damien booms, collapsing into a chair beside us, condensation dripping from his pint of beer.

And that's enough for me to clam up.

I realize looking at him now that I haven't had as much fun hanging out with him on this trip as I expected. He's always had a shitty side, but he also had this endearing, thoughtful core.

A crunchy outer shell, but a chewy center.

But it's been all crunch and no give on this trip. It's a lot. I wonder now if growing up for him has meant releasing that chiller side of himself instead of expanding it. Hardening against any vulnerability.

"Man, this is a crew of lightweights," he says. "Am I right?"

Ben nods, agreeably. "We're old, dude."

"You're old," Damien says, leaning back in his chair like he owns the place. "I'm just getting started. I'm gonna be like Al Pacino, having babies with babies even when my balls are as wrinkled as your face."

"That's a visual I didn't need," I say.

Damien turns on me, his ice-blue eyes narrowing. He gestures toward me with his chin. "Where were you today? Speaking of lightweights. How come you bailed?"

"I just had shit to do," I shrug. "Emails to catch up on, patient notes. That kind of thing."

"Gotta pay the bills," he nods, taking off his baseball cap, then settling it back on his head. "For a minute, I thought maybe you stayed back with Nellie."

Whatever disparaging things you might say about Damien, and there are a lot, his EQ is scary high. He is not to be underestimated. Not much gets past him. Now, his assessing gaze is homed in on me.

I'm careful not to shift in my seat or avoid his eyes as I say, as casually as I can, "Nah. I didn't even know she was staying back too."

"Yeah?" he says, his head tilted. "So, you didn't hang out?"

I shake my head. "I ran into her at one point for a sec, but that's it."

He nods, studying me. *Why do I feel like I'm being interrogated?*

The air has thickened with caveman tension, and I honestly don't know why. It's like I'm being sized up by one of my oldest friends.

I don't care what he thinks, but no way I'm betraying Nell by revealing what happened. Damien has never been the most trustworthy and my antenna is definitely up now.

"I had a good talk with her *alone* in town yesterday," he says, taking a swig of his beer as if it's no big thing. Like they hang out all the time. "She was saying she felt like we always connected."

Now it's my turn to narrow my eyes. "Connected?"

"Yeah, that we always got each other. She was asking if we could hang out more in New York." He shrugs like it's whatever—like he could take it or leave it. "I guess I could give that a shot. Give her what she wants."

The idea of Damien and Nell hanging out in New York and what that implies—the idea of her saying she'd want to spend time with him—makes me want to break something massive over his head. But I just let the corner of my mouth tug upward in a half-smile.

"That's cool," I say, gritting my teeth. "I never remember you guys hanging out back in the day."

"Well, that was then," he says. "Now is now."

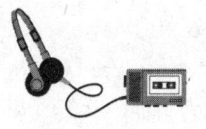

18

BOTH

BACK IN THE DAY

That was then. But then was not so simple either.

Then is when Nellie realizes she has missed her period.

Just as she's having doubts about her future with Noah in New York and weighing her options, she realizes there may be yet another unexpected glitch in the plan. In all of the plans, actually.

Because she is alone in her family apartment, her brother finally away at school, her parents on a trip upstate with friends, when realization sets in.

She dials Cara's number. Hangs up before anyone answers. With Cara, she is in for a lecture.

Why wasn't she careful? Is she crazy?

She dials Sabrina's number. But Sabrina has been busy lately. Busy with her new friends.

When Sab answers, she is breathless and a tangle of strange voices crisscrosses in the background. "Hey! Just heading out the door to this opening in SoHo. What's up?"

"Nothing," Nellie says. "It's not important."

"Okay, cool. We're late, so I'll call you tomorrow, okay? Miss you!"

"Yeah, totally," Nellie says, trying to disguise the wobble in her voice. "Have fun tonight!"

She goes to dial Noah. But she realizes she's not ready.

So, instead, she throws on a navy-blue, oversized Champion pullover, grabs her keys from the cluttered tray by the front door, and walks to Duane Reade alone. Swallowed whole by her sweatshirt with her hands pulled inside her sleeves, she makes her way to the correct aisle at the pharmacy. Eyes the pregnancy tests with trepidation. Pluses and minuses circle in her head like unsolved equations. Like so many SAT questions.

Only she has no clue what to do. And this is not multiple choice.

"That one's pretty good," says an employee who is restocking nearby, a young woman with her dark hair pulled back. Her name tag reads DEBBIE and there is kindness in her eyes. "At least, it worked for me. It's easy to read. But get two, just to be sure."

But what does it mean for them to work, thinks Nellie. And she wonders, as she says thank you, what answer this woman got when she took her tests—and if now she's working this shift for diaper money.

Nellie buys green Tic Tacs at the counter, not because she wants them but because she wants to buy something besides this radioactive purchase. To somehow defuse the shame of the pregnancy tests sitting threateningly on the counter.

Then she walks home, clutching the white plastic bag to her belly, a wintergreen mint on her tongue.

She hovers over the toilet, pees on the stick.

The test is positive. The girl was right. It *is* easy to read.

Nellie bursts into tears, the kind of heavy sobs that are reserved for being alone. They subside just as fast.

A thunderstorm in summer.

She takes a deep breath, knowing what she must do. Pages Noah. He calls her back.

"I need to talk to you," she says between shudders.

He is distracted. She can hear music in the background. Is everyone out living their lives except for her?

"Hang on," he half shouts. "Let me find somewhere quiet."

There are muffled voices and footsteps as he finds a nook. The sigh of a door. Maybe he's in a closet or a bathroom.

"Where are you?"

"This sick apartment on the Upper East Side. It has three floors! Remember that kid Chino? I guess his dad is some kind of diplomat."

She does not. Nor does she care. She says nothing.

"What's up, Nell?" he asks, exhaling.

She steels herself. And then, in a burst, she tells him. And there is silence on the other end of the line.

"Fuck," he says finally.

"Fuck," she agrees.

"Are you sure?"

"Yeah," she says, like it's an apology. "I'm sure."

"Fuck." Again. "What now?"

And she is annoyed by the way he expects her to have the answers. It's her body, yes. But why should she know more than he does about what to do?

"I don't know," she breathes. "I guess maybe I need to go to the doctor . . . and then make an appointment and . . ." She breaks off, losing her voice in the enormity of the thing, and starts crying as recognition of her situation descends again.

Will she tell her parents?

She has so much on her plate right now. How will she even make time for this—an enormous error? Her breath turns shallow again. She's panicking.

"Okay," he says. "It's okay. Do you want me to come to you?"

He is asking. He is not insisting. And she realizes in that moment what a tremendous chasm there is between those two things.

He's not jumping in the nearest cab to race to be with her, to face this problem that they have, in fairness, created together. He is asking her—*do I have to leave the party? Do I have to deal with this right now?*

Is it her or does his tone sound *inconvenienced*? Put out by the fact that he might have to leave this *sick* apartment to be by her side?

"Yeah," she says, even though asking for his help in this moment—when she already feels like a burden to him—is the last thing she wants to do. But she's out of options. She's in this with him. For better or worse. "That would be good, Noah."

There is tension in her voice.

He sighs. With frustration? Irritation? Resignation? "Okay. Fine. I can probably leave here in twenty."

She hangs up the phone. And sitting on her bed, hugging her knees to her chest, she waits. And waits. And waits. And waits.

And he never comes.

He calls her not the next day, but two days later. And what he has done is so egregious, so shameful, that she can't bring herself to admit any of it to anyone.

If she tells the people who love her, they will no doubt hate him.

Is she ready for that?

In that time, thankfully, she has awoken to her period. She has never been so happy for the ache of cramps.

If it was a real pregnancy, it has not stuck.

But what has happened is enough to change her path.

She is willing to allow that Noah's injury, the loss of his baseball scholarship and accompanying dreams, has transformed him into someone else entirely—at least temporarily.

That this pregnancy scare—yet another vision of a possible hitch in his future—may have been enough to render him unable to function.

Maybe he'll even return from the farthest reaches of asshole-dom in time for them to work it out.

But Nellie will not be making plans around Noah. Not now. There's too much to lose.

"Oh, thank God," he says, when she tells him she's not pregnant. "Look, I'm so sorry. I just, there's been so much going on. I freaked out. I froze."

She will not let him off the hook so easily.

"Right," she says, her voice tight. "Well, I was kind of freaking out too. But now I'm not."

"Okay . . . I mean, that's good?"

"I'm glad you think so," she says, like she couldn't care less what he thinks.

And the numb formality in her voice is more severe than any shouting.

"Nell," Noah says, as he realizes he may have finally pushed too far. And wasn't that his deep, dark intention maybe? But he realizes in this moment that separation from Nellie isn't what he wants. Not at all. He has made a huge mistake—one from which he may never be able to recover. "I am so sorry. I can't tell you how sorry."

"I hear that," she says. "But I have to go."

"You have to go? But we just got on."

"Yes," she says. "But I have things to do. I'm taking driving classes starting today."

"You're taking driver's ed? Why?"

"Because. If I'm going to live in LA, I need a car."

The weight of her words lands just as she hoped. On his chest like the last brick. His mouth drops open. He adjusts his grip on the phone, begins to sweat.

She feels real satisfaction as she waits for him to piece this puzzle together.

"Live in LA? What do you mean? I thought we decided..."

"Well, *I* decided that I need to do what's good for me. I need to look out for myself. Because no one else is."

And he gets it. He does. He knows he has done something unforgivable. But *this*? This is all it took for her to let him go? To decide not to choose him?

It confirms his worst suspicions. That she was just looking for a reason. That she has never thought he was enough.

Maybe it was all a lie. Maybe he wasn't more than baseball to her, any more than he was to anyone else. If all it took was this one transgression, albeit a big one, maybe she was looking for a way out all along?

"Okay," he says. Because what else is there to say. "Are you still going to Chloe's party tonight?"

"I might stop by. Probably not."

"But we had plans?"

"Plans? Like when you told me you were coming over two nights ago? And left me alone, terrified, and fucked up?"

"Nell."

"Noah."

There is a heavy pause.

"What would you have done if I was still pregnant today?" she demands. "Would you have disappeared for good?"

Like your dad. The subtext hangs in the air.

"Nell." His voice has gone hoarse, desperate. "You can't possibly think that."

"Actually, I can. Lately you haven't given me a reason to believe anything else."

There is the twist of a knife. There is a blank space where there used to be words.

"Fine. Maybe I'll see you," he grunts, and hangs up before she can beat him to it.

And she sits on her bed, in the aftermath of the call, holding the receiver in quaking hands and feeling broken.

The loneliness that descends is total.

The conversation went just as she planned. And yet she only feels empty.

She will go to California. But does she want to leave like *this*?

That night, though Cara and Sabrina are busy again, Nellie goes solo to Chloe's party.

Because Noah has massively disappointed her. She is deeply angry. But she knows he's good at heart. Somewhere in there, the good, funny, caring Noah still exists. And he is hers. While she is definitely going to California with or without him now, this doesn't have to be the end.

Maybe she can still convince him to come.

They're pissed. They're hurt. They're both going through a lot. But they can do it together.

But when she shows up at the party, there is only crash and burn.

Because as she kisses Chloe hello at the door and then weaves her way through the throngs in the dark club—one with the same strobes and press of bodies and half-spoiled smell as the night when they first saw each other—she searches for Noah everywhere. It's Lydia who runs into Nell first and points him out. And when she follows Lydia's gesture, she sees he's not seated on a platform like that first night. He is leaning against a partition at the edge of the dance floor.

And his tongue is down the throat of a girl she has met a couple of times before—some friend of Lydia's.

Chastity or Crystal or Christa?

Her mind stops. Her world goes dark. It teeters on its axis again.

Nellie brings a hand to her chest as recognition—oily and viscous—sears through her, decomposing all she understands. Light turns to midnight. Her heart pounds like it's trying to escape. There is a strong possibility she will throw up.

He feels her eyes on him. Looks up. Sees her see him.

Sees the slack look on her face.

His mouth drops open—in shock? In awe? In recognition of the decision he has made?

Because this is a decision. Make no mistake. Punishment for not choosing him.

Lydia stands beside Nellie, following her gaze to Noah, still twisted up with her friend. "Sorry," she says, barely containing her grin. "But I told you he was out of your league."

Colossal destruction. Thunderous collapse. It's not what either of them planned. And yet, they have masterminded this.

Nellie takes one last look at Noah, who has untangled himself as if to make his way toward her.

But the abyss between them is too deep. There is nothing left to say.

She turns to go. Bass thunders in her ears. And he can't get to her fast enough. He watches her recede and disappear into the crowd.

And this is when the rest of their lives begin.

19

NOAH
TODAY

Nell and I are in my rental car, cruising down the 101 South. I'm in the driver's seat and she's the passenger, huddled in a hoodie and shorts. A progressively cooler breeze is blowing in through the partially open windows, but neither of us makes a move to close them.

And this is literally the last place I expected to be today—at least with her.

Last night, after Damien threw a grenade into my sense of world order and then Ben excused himself to go bring a Coke to his barfing wife, I lay in bed trying to figure out who to be most annoyed with—D, Nell, or myself.

She wants to "hang out" with Damien in New York? *What the fuck?*

Even the idea of her agreeing to that platonically makes me want to blast the roof off this place. Why is she willing to spend time with Damien and not me? Why are they even talking alone? Do I really need to tell one of my oldest friends how uncool that would be?

(Apparently, since he seems to think he's clear to make a move and was maybe even warning me to step off—warning *me*?)

Nellie clearly didn't want to share the suite with him. I assumed that was because he isn't her favorite. But maybe it was actually for the opposite reason—because she felt self-conscious, living alongside a guy she's attracted to.

I shuddered, the thought of them together like pure torture.

I was losing it.

On the other hand, Damien definitely wouldn't have been dumb enough to pause a hot tub hookup—a fucking mind-blowing one, if I'm honest—to check in on her sobriety.

So maybe I deserve whatever I get. When I think about our history, now, in the light of day, I think I definitely do.

I'm such a fucking tool.

It was just that, in the hot tub, I had suddenly imagined her face afterward, eyes potentially filled with regret, and I wanted to make sure that wasn't where we were headed.

Because I didn't think I could handle that.

Only that's exactly where I put us.

I didn't realize how far that would take us off the rails.

I took a pillow and covered my face with it, so I could scream into the void.

Maybe this infatuation was just about me? My feelings of attachment just an expression of some early midlife crisis about unfinished business from my youth, things I didn't accomplish, proof that I still had it. That's what Nell had suggested when she got angry. Could she have been right?

But, lying in my bed, I knew that wasn't true. This was all about her. A woman I met way too early, before I was ready for her, and who I now know in my gut is the one for me.

Unfortunately, there is just going to have to be more than one *one*. Because this one is not interested.

I had come on this trip still harboring some resentment, I realized now. But seeing Nell had changed all that, had made me realize it was worth pushing through that pettiness for the promise of what could be.

Was there anything I could do to win her over, at this point? Was there any way to surmount our history?

No. That was the resounding answer. She was never going to be able to see me differently.

I threw my pillow across the room. And I decided resolutely, then and there, to let this—and her—go. I am a focused man. A surgeon. Not easy to ruffle. I wasn't going to let this thing derail me.

I would be polite and avoid her as much as possible for the remaining couple days and then head home and get back to my functional, full life—which was totally fine before I saw her again.

So, in the morning, I woke up with a renewed commitment to forgetting Nell. Which lasted about three seconds until I headed into the common room to make a cup of coffee and found her already awake, on the phone. There she was, leaning over the desk, taking notes on the estate-branded pad, her wavy hair falling around her face and her ass—in throwback velour gym shorts—in the air.

I thought: *I am so screwed.*

She looked up at me, actually *looked* at me, which felt in my pathetic head like progress, and then glanced away.

"Uh-huh," she was saying. "Yes. Totally. Got it."

I crossed the room and grabbed a pod to start making coffee for us. She held up a to-go cup from the property's café.

I have never been so offended to have my coffee rejected.

"I got it, CB," she said. "I wrote it down. And yes"—she took the phone away from her ear and scrolled on it, then returned it to her ear—"I just got your list over email, too. Yes. I will cross-check them. I will not forget," she said, standing up and shaking her head. "I've got this. You've picked the right woman for the job."

I poured coffee into a mug and then, as quickly as possible, turned to go back to my room to hide until Nell was gone.

"Hang on," she whispered at me, a finger in the air.

So I did. Stood there waiting like an idiot. Because I'm a fucking sucker.

"Cara," she said. "I am literally a professional. People entrust me with million-dollar budgets. Please just have a little faith. Yes. Fine. Bye. No, don't call me to check in. No, don't!"

But Cara had clearly hung up.

"God help us all," Nell groaned, looking up to the ceiling and then at me. "Okay. So, here's the deal: Cara feels like shit. She and Ben need a day to chill, but they have a bunch of errands they need to do on the coast, like forty-five minutes away."

"Yeah. I know. I told Ben I'd handle it for them last night."

"Right," she said, a hand on her hip. "That's cute. I love that both of you thought Cara would entrust that task to you alone."

"Excuse me, but I'm a functional adult. Why can't I handle it?"

"Well, for one thing, you're not Cara."

"Cara doesn't want to go."

"Right. So, that's why she asked me."

I shake my head at the absurdity of it all. "Okay—so you're going instead?"

"Yes. But I need a car."

I shrug. "Okay. You need to borrow my rental?"

Nell bit her lip. Sighed, clearly steeling herself. "Unfortunately, I need your driving skills too."

I cocked my head to the side. "Wait. Are you one of those New Yorkers who never learned to drive?"

"No!" she protested. "I went to school in California."

"I know," I said quietly, because I know that one stings for us both. And suddenly I was reminded of her driver's ed classes.

The ones she mentioned that day when I finally called. After . . . everything.

I felt like scum.

"I learned to drive," she said. "But . . . I haven't driven in a really long time and I'm rusty. Too rusty to drive those windy roads. It's John's day off, and no one else here seems to have a car and no plans today, so . . . I'm out of options."

I leveled her with an amused look. "You're out of options?" Like I was the bottom of the barrel and she wasn't bothering to pretend otherwise—fair enough. "Hey, thanks."

"Actually, *we're* out of options," she said, clearing her throat. "Unless you want to call Cara back and tell her we can't help."

And so here we are—driving toward the Sonoma coast. In complete silence. And the view, both in and outside the car, is breathtaking.

I have lived in California for a while now. I resisted it at first. Turned down the multiple opportunities that kept landing in my lap, drawing me out here like it was inevitable. I guess because of what the place represented about my past. But, since I finally gave in and made the move, I have fallen head over heels for this state.

And one of the things I love most is how much it changes from place to place. There is so much variation in such close quarters.

People are fond of saying that in California you can go to the beach in the morning and ski in the afternoon. That's technically true, I guess, though, if those locations are anywhere near each other, the water will be freezing, and the snow will be pretty damn spotty.

But there's so much more than that here. I have visited deserts to drink date shakes in the shadow of towering dinosaur statues. I have seen Central Coast rocks crowded with gluttonous elephant seals, and old mission towns with Spanish-style porticos above New Age hipster wellness shops. An entire Danish-style fairy-tale town that would make

Hans Christian Andersen proud; and the "Garlic Capital of the World" that reaches your nose miles before you reach your destination.

I have seen impossibly bountiful farmers' markets, perused by world-famous chefs, and mini-mall parking lots crowded with Hollywood types waiting hours for the best soup dumplings, the most luscious al pastor tacos, the most decadent Italian subs. I have eaten pie and burgers in Pasadena and West LA, and burgers from drive-thrus that can't be beat. I have tubed down rivers and surfed waves in the ocean and taken dusty hikes around reservoirs blocks from art galleries and cool kids boutiques. I have sat below fairy lights in the countryside; and behind home plate all over the state. I have even checked out the LA River, which is nothing like a river at all.

But I have never seen anything in California like this.

Because, for a second, my mind plays tricks, and I wonder if this is the Scottish moors instead.

"Wow," Nell gasps, pressing her palm against the glass. "It's like hobbit green out there."

It's been so long since she last spoke that I'm almost startled. "Is that an official Pantone color?"

"It should be. Hobbit Green. Jane Austen Green. Cotswolds Green."

The art director would know. Even if she wouldn't be caught dead within a mile of anything *Lord of the Rings*.

It's a gray day today. Even inland at the estate, the weather felt changeable before we left, the clouds low and heavy above us. It's not like a late-spring storm brewing on the East Coast, where you can almost smell the rain before it comes, humidity building like it has no choice but to give. This feels cold in a way that's more heedless of humans and their convoluted seasons—cold to the bone.

The closer we get to the coast, the more the temperature drops. And the scenery grows more rural. Nurseries and garden stores replace wine and sandwich shops. There are cows and sheep behind brown metal fencing, roaming meadows of grass so thick and verdant that it looks thatched.

Craggy rock formations and eucalyptus trees line the narrow dirt road beside wildflowers with free rein. It is shamelessly ample. And it's impossible not to be moved.

Nell sighs. Almost contentedly.

I love the sound.

I wonder if she likes road trips. I never got to learn that about her. We were too young when it all came crumbling down.

"Have you ever been to Ireland?" she asks now, tapping the window absently with her knuckle.

"Yes," I say. "But only Dublin. I really liked it though."

"I went abroad to London in college," she says. "I never got to Ireland, but I visited Scotland. And it's so weird, but it kind of looked like this."

Great minds.

It feels so odd. To know someone so well and also not at all.

"I was just thinking that," I say. "It's crazy that this is forty-five minutes from the town plaza where we were baking in all that sun."

The mention of the town plaza is probably a misstep. I can't be sure where Nell's mind wanders, but mine veers directly toward that almost kiss in the shade, her lips parting with a nearly inaudible sound that echoed through me. And maybe that's why she goes silent again.

It's better than thinking about the hot tub, which it's now my goal in life to move beyond. Forget becoming the world's most renowned surgeon. Instead, I just want to forget the feel of her body on mine. I'm pretty sure it will haunt me for the rest of my life, no matter what happens. Her hair wet at the ends, curling into ringlets, dripping rivulets of water down her neck and chest, as she leaned in and nipped my lip, shot me a secret smile.

Focus on the road.

I take this as encouraging though, I tell myself. The fact that she's willing to engage at all. The fact that we can talk without biting each other's heads off, if only for a short reprieve.

"My fiancé was from London," she says, finally, still gazing out the window. "Not that I met him when I was abroad. It was years later in New York. But we went to England together a bunch of times, to see his family."

"That sounds nice."

"You'd think."

Not for the first time, I wonder why that moron let her go. I wonder about the morons before him, too. The ones who came after me.

"Didn't Cara say he was a political journalist? Does he cover American politics?"

She nods.

"But he's a Brit."

"Oh, yeah. And very high and mighty about it. Don't get him started on 'your American system' and so on."

"He sounds fun."

She actually lets a small laugh fly. "He wasn't the *most* fun."

"Was he smart?"

"Yes."

"Was he funny?"

"I thought so at first. And then I realized it was ninety percent accent and ten percent bitterness."

I nod in recognition. "Was he at least a nice guy? Or I guess, *is* he a nice guy, since he's still alive?"

"Eh. He's dead to me."

I snort. "It kinda sounds like you dodged a bullet."

"Yeah," she says, turning toward me, so I can feel her eyes on the side of my face. "Apparently that's my move."

"Ouch," I say, because we both know what she means. I'm not gonna lie. Being equated with some pompous asshole with no sense of humor. Being someone with whom she narrowly avoided being saddled. It stings.

We go silent again, but maybe more companionably so. Outside, it has started to mist. She puts up her window and suddenly it feels like we're cocooned in our own little cozy warm bubble.

And I realize that, even in this state, with all the tension and the bad blood, I'm happy to be marooned with her.

Which is probably a terrible sign.

It starts to drizzle.

We pass a small cemetery, a ravine that bottoms out in a creek. And then we're coming up on the coast at our first destination—an oyster farm.

When I pull to a stop, she pulls her hood up over her head, gets out, and jogs toward an outdoor area with an overhang for cover. I am close behind.

20

NELLIE
TODAY

I can't help it. I can't help making the barbs and I can't help feeling bad for Noah as I watch them land.

I can't help studying his jawline, his scruff, the crinkle of his eyes. His biceps in his T-shirt, his tan forearms, the cords of muscle in his neck.

Noah is officially under my skin.

And I can only partially delude myself that he hasn't always been.

I jog from the car to avoid getting wet, an automatic response after years of experiencing the frizz effects on my hair. But he just saunters and, dammit, even the way he walks—all casual and confident—is sexy.

I am so fucked.

But I'm going to have to suck it up (a terrible choice of words). Because, now that my ego has had about twenty-four hours to recover, I realize that even if Noah stopped what was happening between us because he changed his mind, he was at least trying to spare my feelings. And, as undignified as that feels, I have to admit that puts his heart in the right place.

His other organs less so.

This man is maybe not the same boy who left me stranded so many years ago.

When he reaches me now, there's rain beginning to patter harder on the tin roof above us. I look up at him, his T-shirt damp and clinging to his defined chest, his short hair tufting up just slightly as he ruffles it with his hand. And I shiver, but not from cold.

He notices, frowns. "I'd offer you my jacket, but, like an idiot, I didn't bring one."

But I'm glad he didn't. And not just because outerwear would only have blocked the view. But also because this is romantic, in an almost absurd way. It's hard enough to bear without him gallantly offering me a coat. We are literally by the sea, alone together, caught in a storm.

And it's because I can't handle *The Notebook* of it all—and feel guilty about being a jerk in the car—that I turn to him and blurt out, "Truce!" And then stick out my pinky finger. Like I'm in fourth grade.

"What?"

"Truce. It's when two sides agree to stop fighting for the greater good."

"Yes, I've heard of that," he smirks. "But, for the record, *I* wasn't fighting."

I roll my eyes big, my frustration ramping up like a race car at the starting line. "Do you want to try to get along or not? 'Cause I can take my pinky elsewhere."

"No, no, no!" he says, rearranging his expression into something more solemn. "Okay. I'm in."

He hooks his finger around mine and, against my will, something unholy vibrates through me, buzzy and electric. I flash to the hot tub, his fingers knotted in my hair.

Now, his hazel eyes zero in on mine and seem to hold them there like some Jedi mind trick. Like he's thinking about the same thing. His hands are big and warm. And *big*. Did I mention big?

"But," he says, before I can pull my pinky back to safety or, better yet, to a nunnery, "what are the deal points of this truce? If it's official, there must be terms, right?"

Every second I spend physically touching him spells more disaster. I know I should inch away, but instead I find myself pulled into his orbit, answering his flirty side-eye with my own.

"Oh, there are terms," I say, taking a step forward. "Major terms."

He raises an eyebrow. "Major terms, huh? Not minor terms. Okay, then."

"Are you ready? Can you handle it?"

"Yup. I've *been* ready." For a second, I'm disoriented—I'm not sure what he means.

"For this?" I manage, with all the false bravado I can muster. "Never."

He steps in close too, so that now our hands, intertwined, are the only things separating us. The air between us is kinetic and charged. I can see his chest rise and fall. And it's hypnotic.

My breath feels shallower too. I need to get it together, break this spell or risk jumping his bones. Would he reject me again? Am I this glutton for punishment? A few more seconds and I can't be held responsible for where my lips land. And I don't know for sure what's going through his head, but his eyes are wolfish like he's about to eat me for lunch.

"So," he says, leaning in closer, "what are the rules? Tell me. No promises. But I'll do my best to follow them."

Behind us, someone clears their throat. My face flashes red hot.

What am I doing? Falling down the same black hole, that's what.

"Just don't be an asshole," I mutter and tear my hand away.

Noah's hand is left stranded, dangling in midair. He exhales sharply. And I feel that pang of pathos again. *Dammit.*

He shrugs, lowering his hand and sliding it into his pocket for safekeeping. "I'll try," he murmurs.

To our right is a man who must be Mike, the oyster farm's "head of sustainable agriculture" according to his name tag. He's the dude Cara says we are meant to meet. He is goofy looking in a floppy fisherman's cap and rubber waders. But beneath it, I see he is about our age—and not un-handsome.

"Welcome," he says. "You must be Ben Goldstein and Cara Faustin."

"There's been a slight change of plans," I say.

"They couldn't come, so we're here in their place," Noah explains.

"We're not married," I over-explain.

"Or even a couple," Noah grumbles.

"Oh," Mike says, eyes widening slightly. "Okay! Well, nice to meet you then."

He directs this only to me.

"Are you ready to begin the tour?"

Tour? I thought we were picking up oysters on ice and hauling ass out of here. There's a tour involved? But of course there is, because . . . my bestie loves a tour.

Noah shoots me a questioning look.

"Cara," I say.

"Ah," he nods.

"Right this way," says Mike with a flourish, like he is ushering us through Versailles and not past massive basin flats of water with oysters being cleaned inside. The air is ripe with brininess, but this somehow offers even more sense of place. It's hard not to feel transported—and I realize it's been too long since I've been somewhere truly new.

On Cara's itinerary, today read, "Day 4: *Free Parking!*" The song? "Freedom! '90" by George Michael.

I think there's something you should know, I think it's time I told you so
There's something deep inside of me, there's someone else I've got to be

A Cara classic.

And right now, it's feeling like it kind of makes sense.

Because when Mike leads us out to the back, I realize we are not just near, but right on the coast. It's nothing fancy. The shoreline's dirt and sand—littered with the fragments of cratered oyster shells—gives way to the placid water of Tomales Bay, serene and glossy. Patches of overgrown grass crest like small islands and, farther out, fishing and sail boats glide. On our side of the bay, the shore is lined with small houses on stilts that jut into the water. There's something in them of faded gentry, weathered by the seasons but designed to withstand the changing tides.

They have been here, and they will be here.

Across the water are low green hills under a layer of fog and peppered with trees like so many broccoli florets.

I exhale, big.

Here, Mike begins his spiel, explaining the forty-year history of the oyster farm, where they currently lease over one hundred and fifty acres of the bay. He references sticks protruding from the water that mark the beds and describes another site, a nursery, where they grow oysters from inception. And he delivers all this information directly to me—and me alone.

"It's beautiful here," I say.

"Well, beauty knows beauty," he winks.

Noah clears his throat.

The rain has let up for a moment, the sun feebly fighting the good fight. So, next, Mike suggests we jump ahead and leads us to a picnic table where all the necessary components wait for oyster shucking. There are two kinds of hot sauce, lemons, a special basil mignonette made by a local chef—and, of course, oysters on ice.

And there are flutes of Prosecco, too.

Handing us knives, an unwittingly questionable choice considering the way we've been bickering, Mike demonstrates the how-to—first on his own and then placing his hands over mine and guiding me, as he leans down over me.

It is a lot of contact with Mike. I wonder if next he's going to rest his hands on my hips and show me how to hit a fastball.

On the bench across from me, my ex-boyfriend seethes. Which makes enduring Mike easier.

"Amazing job!" Mike says to me. "You're a natural."

"Thank you," I bask.

He ignores Noah, who is struggling.

"You're terrible at this," I say to Noah, who is still unable to open a single oyster after several minutes. "And you are literally a surgeon."

Noah shoots me a death glare. "My patients don't have shells."

"We can't be good at everything," Mike says. Then he nudges me and winks again. "These are some of our classics," he continues, describing the varieties before we try them. "Pacific, Deep Water, Cold Water."

"Isn't that the name of a cologne people wore in the nineties?" Noah grunts.

"That's Cool Water!" I say, giggling.

Neither man seems amused.

But when we finally sample the oysters, everything else melts away. They taste like sea, salt air, something ephemeral and hard to grasp—days of leisure, of easy breezes, of escape.

I must groan out loud because Mike says, "You know, some people say oysters are aphrodisiacs."

Then he makes eyes at me.

"You don't say," I reply.

"Maybe you want to try one with hot sauce? Something a little *spicy*?"

"She doesn't like hot sauce," Noah practically barks.

"How do you know?" I am tempted to ask as annoyance rises in me. Maybe I've changed! Maybe I'm a new and exciting hot-sauce-loving woman now!

But he's right. And I will not relive the gummy episode or the cold plunge by dosing myself to prove a point. I down the rest of my wine instead.

It's begun raining again and there's a definite chill.

Time to move on.

Before we leave, Mike takes us—well, me, with Noah trailing behind—around to see the various machinery. The farm is small and rustic, but mighty, supplying oysters to some of the highest-end restaurants in Northern California.

"Wow," I say, as Mike lists the recipients of their harvests, eateries helmed by James Beard award winners and the like. "That's impressive."

"Oh, yeah," he agrees. "The chefs around these parts are next level. Everything is local too. They source their milk from Straus Family Creamery down the road and the oysters from here and cheese from another farm up the way . . ."

"Yum!" I say, with maybe a little too much enthusiasm. Mike is clearly very proud of this operation and I want to seem suitably impressed, especially because Noah—usually so charming and chatty—has gone uncharacteristically silent.

It is possible he wants to kill Mike.

"You know," Mike says, stepping toward me and pushing his hat off his head, so that it dangles by the neck strap like he's a Boy Scout. "I know all the best spots. If you're in the area for a few days, I'd love to take you to try some of my favorites."

I chance a glance up at Noah, who rolls his eyes so wide I'm surprised they don't fall out of their sockets.

"Unfortunately, I'm only here for the day," I say, letting Mike down easy.

"We're actually leaving," Noah says at the same time, placing a hand on my shoulder and nudging me toward the car.

"Too bad," Mike says. "It could have been great."

And I will never know if he means us or the food.

We leave with a cooler full of oysters and Noah's bad attitude.

"That was so unprofessional!" he says, once we're in the car.

I raise my eyebrows. "Would it have been unprofessional if Mike was a hot lady?"

"Are you calling Mike hot?"

Touché.

The oyster farm had its own shop. And, before we left, I tried to convince Noah to buy himself a hoodie, since he was clearly cold, goose bumps rising on his arms, but he refused. Would not give Mike the satisfaction. Though, as I pointed out, Mike was not likely pocketing the cash.

Noah would not give in.

I myself am regretting my choice of jean shorts instead of proper jeans, fingering the fringe and mourning the loss of their lower half as I crank the temperature on the dashboard.

"What's better than a heated car seat?" I sigh.

"A hot tub," Noah says.

Then he steals a glance at me with wide eyes like, *did I say that out loud?* And I can't do anything but laugh.

I am high on oysters—or, more likely, a sense of abandon. It feels so good to be out of my usual routine, away from schedules and computers, even social demands.

Next, according to Cara's notes, we are headed to a small goat dairy farm and creamery, where they make their own cheese. I turn on the radio as Noah pulls back onto the winding road. The Dixie Chicks' "Cowboy Take Me Away" comes blaring through the speakers. Noah pulls a face, but, when I start belting it out and swaying in my seat, he can't stop the smile from spreading across his face.

"There it is!" I say, and poke him in the dimple.

My mood has improved and maybe his will too.

By the time we get to the farm, the rain has begun again in earnest, so we are immediately shepherded to a nearby barn, standing tall between two pastures.

This is a woman-led operation. So, of course they have thought to have umbrellas on hand. Always prepared.

The wind-stripped barn has a proper red roof and, inside, mile-high ceilings and wooden pens for the animals.

It smells like a barn and it's lousy with hay. But it takes me about three seconds to forget that and make a beeline for one particular stall, where a warming red light glows. Inside, four baby goats are snuggled together in a corner; others romp and frolic, tails wagging like puppies.

The cuteness is almost unbearable.

"Oh my God!" I yelp, like the cliché I am. "How old are they?"

The answer comes quickly: "They were just born this week." I glance beside me to find a tall older woman with salt-and-pepper waves, a fleece vest, and a warm grin leaning against the barrier. "Adorable, aren't they? This stage doesn't last long. They grow fast."

Maggie introduces herself to me and Noah as the "steward of this land and head goat," but I think she is actually the head farmer. She gives us some background on the property, which I don't hear because one of her farmhands has entered the pen and picked up a black baby goat and is now transferring it into my arms.

It. Is. So. Cute.

"Bah," I say to it, speaking in its native tongue. I figure it's still learning to talk and don't want to confuse it.

I look up to find Noah also cradling a goat, though his is all white. He has a goofy grin on his face.

"Excuse me for one second," Maggie says, walking a few yards away to chat with another staff member.

"Bah," I say again to my goat. It seems to understand. "That's it," I add. "I'm taking you home."

"He'll need a tough name if he's heading to New York," Noah says. "To make it on the mean city streets."

"I already picked it," I say. "Humbug."

"Humbug?"

"Yeah, like bah . . ."

Noah tilts his head, wearing a doubtful look. "That's not tough."

"Yes it is! Like, don't fuck with Humbug!"

"You could say 'don't fuck with' before basically any name and it would sound at least a little tough."

"I don't know. 'Don't fuck with Noah' sounds pretty soft."

He shoots me a dirty look. "That's fine. I'm in touch with my softer side."

I almost let a comment fly about how I was recently in touch with his *harder* side, but that is definitely the giddiness talking. Would only usher in awkwardness. I can't remember when I was last this relaxed—but I press my lips closed.

"Anyway," I say instead, petting my goat's head. "What's *your* goat's name?"

"That's easy," he says. "The GOAT. As in, the greatest of all time."

"Oh God!" I groan. "You and the sports. So on the nose."

"Don't hate just because you know it's good." Noah shifts and looks down at his new friend. "Do you think Maggie is ever coming back?"

I glance over at her; she's clearly still in heated conversation. "Why?"

"Because I'm afraid the GOAT is going to pee on me."

I can't help but laugh and then I can't really stop, which unnerves the farm workers and two come forward to take our goats back to their mothers in the pen.

Noah shoots me a crooked smile, as he leans his forearm on the ledge of the pen.

"They were cute," I say to him.

"Well, cute knows cute," he deadpans. And I start laughing again.

For the second time, we have underestimated Cara. Meeting the baby goats is incredible and we assume that was the special experience connected to picking up the cheese, but there is so much more. Describing the operations on the farm, Maggie leads us over to the main office past at least one grazing cow. But "the office" turns out to be a gorgeous modernist farmhouse that blends geometry with authenticity—it's all original wood but also granite countertops. Windows, windows everywhere.

One entire side of the farmhouse is lined with a sweeping porch. This is our destination. She gestures for us to sit at a reclaimed wooden table—polished but still with its beautiful knots and imperfections—waiting with two deceptively simple place settings. Matte ceramic dishware, French blue Madre linen napkins, pristine stemless wineglasses. Above us hangs a vintage chandelier and honeycomb lanterns. Globe lights are strung through the surrounding trees and, though it is still daytime, they shed some light beneath the ever-darkening clouds.

It's pouring now and Maggie ducks her head beyond the porch, looking up at the sky like she doesn't like it. But I think this is a pretty amazing view—and the air smells like damp earth. Like fresh. Like alive. I have always loved watching a storm from the protection of a porch.

"How long have you had the farm?" I ask her.

"It's been in my family since before I was born."

"Wow," Noah says. "A native Californian. You're a rare breed."

She nods, proudly, standing taller in her wellies. "Fourth generation. Of course, things weren't so polished in the olden days. We didn't always make goat gouda." She smiles conspiratorially at us like we're in on the joke and not part of the bourgie gouda crowd—which we totally are. "Enjoy."

Members of the kitchen staff, casually dressed in jeans and tees, arrive next with heavy pours of dry rosé and charcuterie trays so bright and colorful that they put the estate's—which was not so shabby—to shame. And, as the staff explains, everything is local, from this farm or from West Marin. There are soft fetas and chevres and harder Manchego-style cheeses. There is wildflower honey, lavender preserves (and sprigs!), sliced baguette still warm from the oven. There are salamis and salumi and bresaola too. There are dried strawberries, fresh apricots, and crisp crackers with sea salt.

And it is all for us.

"Thank you so much," I say politely to the server.

"Holy fuck," I say to Noah when she's gone.

"Holy fuck," he agrees.

I lose the next few minutes to tastes and sighs. Tart wine, creamy cheeses, sweet fruit. It is a true feast.

When I finally look up, Noah is staring at me.

"What?" I say, wiping at my face.

He shoots me a half-smile. "Nothing. I just like when you like something. And you *definitely* like this."

"Of course I do! The presentation, the flavors, the care that's gone into all of it. It's a masterpiece!"

He nods, eyeing me and not the food. "It is."

I've had more wine than he has. My edges are blurred. He's the driver. But he's looking at me unguarded now, his bright eyes swallowing me whole.

I pick up my glass of wine, lean back in my chair. Take a sip. He watches me lick my lips.

So I lick them extra.

"Didn't your mother teach you not to stare?" I say.

"Yup," he answers. And he keeps on staring.

"What are you thinking about?" I ask finally, shifting in my seat.

"Goats," he says. "Mostly goats."

"Oh, yeah? What about them?"

"Mostly about how lucky that baby black goat is that you don't have official naming rights."

"Hey! Humbug loves me, okay?"

He shrugs. "Who can blame him?"

I look across the table at Noah, at the angles of his face in the dim light. It would be helpful if he wasn't so damn good to look at.

"What were you really thinking about?" I ask, if only to keep talking and distract myself.

"Honestly?"

"Preferably."

"The first time I saw you."

"Oh." I'm surprised, by both that fact and his frankness. "Outside my drawing class?"

He shakes his head.

"Um, excuse me," I laugh, leaning in, loosey goosey. "Are you saying you don't remember meeting me that day?"

He shoots me a look, rubs a hand over his stubble. "Of course I remember. I remember your V-neck sweater and your attitude. I remember coming back to introduce myself, properly. I remember it all."

"Okay, but?"

"Okay, but that wasn't the first time I saw you."

I am stunned. In the narrative that is my relationship with Noah, that run-in on the sidewalk was, for sure, the first time he knew I existed. I realize it's so cemented in my head—our story—that it feels earth-shattering for it to change.

What else have I taken for granted as the truth? What else from our history needs a fact-check?

"When then?" I ask.

"A couple weeks or maybe a month before," he says. "I was at a club..."

My mouth drops open. Mind blown. I even lift out of my seat, which is no small feat, as I have melded to it. And before he can even continue, I say, "No. Wait—seriously?"

"Yes?" He looks at me like I've lost it. "Why?"

"Because!" I say. "I saw you for the first time that night too."

"Wait, really? But how do you even know it was the same night? We went to a lot of parties."

But I know. And so does he. Because something magnetic happened in that moment between two strangers that left an indelible mark.

We never discussed it, all those years ago, each letting the other believe that our first meeting was on the sidewalk (at least after Noah confessed to recognizing me in Ben's kitchen). I never wanted to admit that I'd seen him first from afar and pined. It sounded crazy.

We gape at each other now, not unlike we did on that first night. I examine his changeable eyes, the faint scar on his cheek, the pout of his lower lip. Only now, instead of our view being obscured by bodies, what's in our way is something harder to name.

"I saw you," he says.

"I saw you first," I say.

And it's maybe true if only by a few minutes.

"It's weird though," he says. "There were so many of those parties. I met so many people, so many girls."

"Yes, yes," I say, rolling my hand. "I know. You were very popular."

"No. What I'm saying is, I remember you so well. Even though we didn't speak. I saw you. I didn't know you. But I couldn't look away."

The impact of his words thunders through me. We really did feel inevitable in that moment and even in the period afterward, when I lay in bed at night, imagining him.

With this irrational sense of knowing him.

Neither of us knows what to say.

"The magazine I work for is folding," I confess. It's the first time I've said it out loud to anyone and it feels like heaving a gigantic weight off my chest.

Noah's brow furrows like he actually cares. "Shit. I'm so sorry."

"Thanks." I drop my head back, my hair falling away from my face. "I'm starting to think it might be a good thing."

"I get that."

That's all I really want to say for now, and he seems to sense this. He lets it go.

The rain is coming down now. In sheets. In pillowcases. In winter-weight duvets. The once muddy farm beyond is now streaming with water, rushing past in newly formed creeks.

I guess it's cold, but I don't feel it.

"What else is on that list?" Noah asks me, nodding his chin toward where my phone lies between us on the table.

Right. Reality. Cara and her errand list.

I grab my phone and scroll through to her email. "The flower farm. A chocolatier. And then a dinner reservation at some place called Nick's Cove where, apparently, we have to try the deep-fried saltines." I look out toward where our car is parked a distance away.

"I don't want to leave here like . . . ever," I say. "But maybe we should get going."

"That's what I'm thinking," Noah nods, that crease popping between his brows. "This looks kind of intense. Maybe we should try to escape before dark."

As we start to rise, stretch, a blueness comes over me. I guess I'm sad that this is ending. Likely seeing movement, Maggie pops back out through the door. "How was everything, folks?"

"Incredible," I say. And I mean it.

"We figure we should probably grab the cheese and get on the road," Noah adds. "We've got to get back to the Healdsburg area tonight."

Maggie's eyes go wide. "Well, I'm afraid that's not in the cards," she says, sighing like she's often the bearer of bad news and is sick of it. "There was flooding on the pass. It looks like it should subside by tomorrow morning. But there's no getting off the coast tonight."

"What?" Noah and I exclaim in unison. And it would be comical if it wasn't real.

Suddenly, I flash to a yellow sign we passed on the road in: FLOODED DURING STORM.

Welp. They tried to tell us.

Noah scratches at the back of his neck, visions of sleeping in his rental car no doubt dancing in his head. "Is there anywhere nearby to stay?"

"There's Dillon Beach Resort just a few minutes from here. I can't guarantee they'll have a room, but it's not quite high season, so maybe? I'd offer you a bed here, but I've got family in town and we're all filled up. Unless you want to sleep with the goats."

A bed. As in *one*. Singular.

I guess Maggie has assumed we're a couple. And why not? But still, even the suggestion has me avoiding Noah's eyes.

Regardless, this is not an option. And I do not want to sleep with the goats. I picture myself curled up in hay under the red incubation lights. Suddenly, Humbug and his friends seem slightly less cute.

"Okay," Noah says. "We'll try Dillon Beach."

"But what about the cheese?" I ask, trying not to think about the reality of what is essentially a night away with him—to keep the panic out of my voice. "What about the oysters? There's really no way to get back?"

"It's not too hot," Maggie says, an understatement. Suddenly, it is bone-chilling. "I think the oysters and cheese will be fine. I'll pack the coolers with extra ice. As for whether you're really stuck . . . I'm afraid so."

I push the thought of a night with Noah out of my mind. I can keep it together, keep my hands to myself for one night. Not subject myself to more potential disappointment. I got this. *Do I got this?*

The truth is, I have to keep it together. Because, while Noah has been teasing a bit, I know he would flirt with a cement pole if it stopped in front of him. He's always been that way, just charming and radiating warmth. (Well, when he's not being a pain in the ass.) He put a stop to what was happening in the hot tub. Out of wisdom, I now believe. So, if he has self-control—if he's maybe not even super tempted anyway—then I can surely handle this, too.

I mean, how sex-deprived am I? Mental note: If I ever make it home, I need to get out more.

We thank Maggie and ready to get on our way. While she adds extra ice to the coolers, Noah tries calling the hotel up the coast, but there's no answer. We will have to roll the dice.

Consummate hosts, Maggie and one of her farmhands walk us to our car. The umbrellas have gone from helpful to a nice gesture, purely symbolic. The rain is blowing sideways. My feet are sloshing in my sandals. I am a drowned rat.

Thanking them, we climb inside the Jeep's warm embrace and then, at the last minute, I roll down my window a fraction. "Maggie!" I shout over the drumming of the rain against the windshield. "What's the black baby goat's name?"

"Mike," she shouts back and keeps on walking.

Despite our current predicament, I cannot stop laughing.

Maybe it's the wine. Maybe it's nerves. Maybe it's the way Noah's right eyebrow dips when he's surly.

But I cannot stop pushing that button.

"Maybe it's a sign," I say, grinning. "That Mike and I are meant to be."

"Meant to be what?"

"Meant to live out a quiet life of oyster farming and oyster shucking and oyster eating in West Marin, of course."

"There might actually be worse things," he concedes. "Minus the Mike part."

"But Mike is the whole game!"

Noah frowns. "Mike isn't the whole anything."

"Hmm. If I didn't know better, I'd say you're jealous."

"I am," he says. "Of Mike's attention. Why didn't he teach me to shuck too?" He smirks at me and then glues his eyes back on the road.

It is truly torrential. And I should stop needling Noah since we're driving down perilous roads during a perilous storm. The trees are drooping with the weight of the water, swaying with fatigue. The tall grass is getting a beatdown, the wooden fence posts teetering. But I figure I'm keeping it light.

I am airy. Breezy. Not freaking the fuck out.

I don't love the feeling of being trapped in general, and it doesn't help that I'm alone with Noah, carrying this slightly punchy energy—somewhere on the spectrum between goofy and breakdown. I have had more than one vision of us slipping down a mountainside to our sure death in some disaster-movie-style mudslide. But it's been such a relaxing and delightful day, such a pressure-free break from all the things (despite the fact that I brought a major source of my stress along), that I'm almost game for whatever comes next.

What comes next—after we drive through what is more a single intersection with a cute café, antique store, and post office than a town—is the hotel, though we pass it twice before we spot and pull into the small parking lot.

Whatever I pictured, this is a thousand times better!

Though the fog is so low that the details are hard to make out, a cluster of tiny prefab houses line a grassy cliff above a wide sandy beach and churning gray ocean. A sign—so distant I can hardly decipher the words—announces this is the Point Reyes Seashore.

Sign. Me. Up.

The cottages themselves sit on paving stones the color of overcast days, protected by raw wooden fencing at the cliff's edge. But beyond that, the view gets wild. Windblown cypress trees are frozen as if petrified like supersized bonsais with splintered trunks.

Looking at them is like seeing the Earth change in real time.

"I wonder if geology is my missed calling," I say out loud, as Noah cuts the engine.

"I'm pretty sure that requires math," he says, sliding a dubious look my way.

"What are you trying to say?"

"That you're terrible at math."

"Why?" I say, propping a hand on my hip. "Because I'm a woman?"

"No. Because you—*specifically*—are terrible at math."

I want to tell him once again that he doesn't know me. I want to not feel comfort at the fact that he does. I want to announce that since he last saw me, eking by in pre-calculus thanks only to Cara's help, I have taken up coding and stock brokering and volunteering for NASA in my spare time. Those are math things, right?

But alas. It's only a matter of time until he sees me use the calculator on my phone just to figure out a tip.

"Ready?" he asks me, as we prepare to run toward a shop marked GENERAL STORE—the only building that looks open. There's a restaurant that is clearly shuttered currently, an office that—probably thanks to the evening hour—is dark and closed for the day. I am praying that not only is there a room, but that there's someone there to give us a key—if only because the art director in me needs to see the decor in these adorable houses.

"Ready!" I say with more bravado than is real.

"Go!" he says, and we both shove open our doors and bust out into the storm. It's raining so hard that I almost lose my footing trying to slam my door shut. Seeing me struggle, Noah jogs around the car and helps me.

Then, he grabs my hand.

Together, we run like the wind through the rain. But it's all for naught. Because when we jog up the stairs to the covered porch and arrive on the threshold of the shop, breathless and huffing, we are soaked like we just went swimming fully clothed.

"It's like we jumped in a pool," I say, gazing down at my sopping-wet clothing.

"Or a hot tub," he says.

And my face gets hot. I am suddenly conscious that we're still holding hands—and the dampness is doing nothing to tamp down the wattage searing up my arm. But I'm afraid to let go, because, honestly, I don't want to. And also won't that make it more of a thing?

"Haha," I say. "Maybe don't humiliate a lady in a hot tub and then tease her for it."

"Sorry, sorry," he says. Then he squeezes my hand, sending another wave of something torrid through me.

I play my shudder off as chills. Then, under the pretext of opening the door, I let his hand go—and immediately miss it.

Inside, once I get over the fact that we are literally dripping water all over the wood floor, I look around and realize we have landed in my happy place.

This store is part gourmet market, part home decor boutique, and part surf shop.

And those are all the things I love.

One side of the space is stocked to the gills with local snacks like garden veggies with citrus hummus, sandwiches, pasta salads and, of course, more wines, beers, ciders, and cheeses. There are artisan chips aplenty, with West Coast flavors like jalapeño and chili lime, and a bakery counter with what smells like outstanding coffee. There are fresh donuts and signs for some kind of straight-from-the-cow soft serve. Moo.

On the other side of the store—beyond a dishware array and Turkish kitchen towels that I vow to peruse at length later when I'm not straight from a dunk tank—is everything you might need for a beach vacation. And I mean *everything*.

Big-ticket items like wetsuits and bathing suits; small-ticket items like playing cards and old-school bulk candy. There are neon woven beach blankets that need to be mine.

I am ready to pounce. But before I can step toward it all, a young woman—in a hoodie and board shorts—steps out from the back, sees us, and gasps.

"Oh, no!" she says. "You're all wet."

"Are we?" deadpans Noah. He winks at her and that's all it takes.

She giggles. And it's annoying to me that he is so adorable that even twenty-five-year-olds are still in his demo.

"One second," she says, flustered. "Don't move."

"I don't think I could if I wanted to."

She reappears minutes later with plush towels, and it's a bit like trying to staunch a gunshot wound with a miniature Band-Aid. But at least we can wander around now without creating puddles.

I let Noah handle the room situation with her at the counter while I examine all the adorable things, and I am smelling a candle scented like "moonbeams" when he appears beside me again. It's like I can sense him there before I see him—like I have Noah radar.

"There's space," he says.

"Oh, good," I breathe, though my pulse jumps. I regard him warily. "How much space?"

"It's one suite, but it has two bedrooms."

One suite. Two bedrooms. I can handle that! After all, that's our thing.

I try not to think about how truly tiny the tiny houses appeared.

The restaurant is indeed closed, so Emmy, the woman who is working the shop, takes us over to a tucked-away fridge and freezer area stocked with all sorts of ingredients for all sorts of dinners.

"The houses have full kitchens," she explains.

"Do they have full chefs?" I ask.

She looks confused. This zone is irony-free.

I turn to Noah: "I do not cook," I say without apology.

"I don't cook either," he says. "Pasta?"

We buy penne and marinara sauce, some fresh veggies sourced from a nearby farmstand, and several Charleston Chews—which feature prominently in my summer camp memories. I grab two toothbrushes and toothpaste, and we're good to go. Except we are drenched. Which feels like the perfect excuse to buy some replacement clothes and, within moments of stepping into our house for the night, I run into the bathroom and change into dry sweatpants, a cozy T-shirt, and socks that are fluffy like a Pomeranian. They are buttery soft, and I have never been happier.

The look inside the homes is mid-century with modern touches. The cottages themselves are gray and slatted, with giant picture windows and cream-colored Adirondack chairs parked out front, facing the sea. Inside, atop bleached wood floors that I am deeply hoping I didn't ruin with my soggy sandals, there is a cushy couch in front of a gas fireplace, a granite kitchen island, and a vintage 1950s-style mustard-yellow fridge and matching turquoise microwave. In the back I find a single bathroom (*gulp*) and two bedrooms, as promised—a primary and, just above up a short staircase, a lofted option with a low ceiling, probably designed with kids in mind.

It all feels thoughtful but unfussy. Like these are rooms that families are supposed to use but also love.

I immediately fall for this place, hard. I can't believe how much they've fit into this tight space without it feeling cluttered. Which is why, instead of ruminating about which bedroom I should take, I flop on the couch, flip on the fireplace, and am already snuggled beneath a fleece throw when Noah emerges from the bathroom in his matching outfit.

He should look silly, right? Or at least basic in a random tee and sweats. After all, we are twinning. Instead, he looks top notch. Like he has just toweled off after a refreshing swim.

His hair is still damp and is just long enough to be ruffled. He is lean, not bulky. Not overly worked out. But the T-shirt is maybe the slightest bit snug across his chest, which only accentuates his cut arms. And when he reaches up to run the towel over his hair and the stubble on his jaw one last time, his shirt rises to reveal a sliver of firm abs and twin indentations leading down to . . . places I shouldn't be thinking about.

I'm thrown back in time to our first real conversation in Ben's parents' kitchen again. When he reached for a cereal bowl, and I was distracted by a similar sight.

Only this time it's way worse. Because they didn't sell underwear at the store—or at least we didn't think to look. So, I am painfully aware that there is nothing under his sweats.

I am also commando. And braless.

I pull the blanket up higher.

"So," I say to stop my brain from spinning and my body from overheating. "Hungry?"

"Starving," he says. "Which is weird since I feel like I just ate all the goat cheese in Sonoma County a couple of minutes ago."

I scrunch my nose. "True. But, if you think about it, we haven't had an actual meal all day."

"True."

Noah volunteers to play chef and, as he puts a pot of water on the stove to boil, I busy myself with my phone, entering the Wi-Fi password. I haven't had legit service all day, so I am suddenly flooded—mostly with texts from Cara.

Cara

How's it going?

Did you get the oysters?

Did you find the place okay?

I just looked at the radar and I think there's a storm coming.

There's definitely a storm coming!

Shit. Are you guys okay? Have you drowned? Killed each other? Did I send you both to your deaths?

Ben says it wouldn't be my fault. But I think he's just trying to make me feel better. It's not working.

Please let me know as soon as you get this.

> (It's not because I'm worried about the oysters—although I am a little bit worried about the oysters.)
>
> Sorry—I know I'm freaking out. I haven't seen my kids in a few days and I think maybe you're getting the full force of my mama bear energy.
>
> But still. Please text back. Like SOON.

"I think Cara is worried about us."

"What makes you say that?" Noah turns his phone to face me, revealing a similar barrage of messages from Ben.

"Wait—Ben is having a neurotic meltdown too?"

"She took over his phone."

"She doesn't have your number?"

"No, she definitely does."

Noah returns to cooking, which is sort of funny to watch—he is very determined, his tongue peeking out the side of his mouth as he concentrates on the instructions. I suspect this is what he looks like in surgery. Meanwhile, I text Cara and let her know that we'll survive but not be back until tomorrow.

Cara
> Thank God!

I see the telltale dots appear. Disappear. Then appear again.
I roll my eyes.

Nellie
> Yes, Cara. The oysters are fine.

Cara

Oh. Okay, cool. I wasn't even going to ask.

Sure.

I know that she ran directly to Sabrina and told her that Noah and I are stuck because, a few minutes later, I get a text from Sab with multiple eggplant, taco, and winky face emojis. And that's when I decide I was happier without service and turn off my phone.

Good timing because dinner is ready!

Noah and I sit across from each other on stools at the small breakfast bar. We each have a cider open in front of us. It's . . . intimate. It feels domestic and homey in a way that I both love and hate.

I throw my hair in a sloppy bun. And look up to find him watching me.

"I like your hair like that."

"Apocalyptic from the rain?"

"No. Wild and like . . . natural."

"Thanks," I smile.

If he thinks I have natural highlights, I am not going to tell him different.

I bite into the pasta on my plate and whoa, this man does *not* have talent in the kitchen—it is all reserved for medicine, sports, and sex stuff—because, somehow, he has messed this up. The pasta is so undercooked that al dente doesn't begin to describe it.

"Delicious," I say, as a piece of pasta crunches audibly in my mouth. "Thanks for making dinner."

He takes a bite too, then pauses mid-chew.

"You're welcome." He scratches his head. "I think I may have undercooked the pasta."

"Did you?"

"Did I what?"

"Cook the pasta at all?"

His mouth drops open and then he cracks a wide grin, shrugging with his palms up. "I told you I couldn't cook."

"No. No. *I* can't cook. You can't boil water."

He laughs, loud and big. And it fills up the entire tiny cottage. Completely infectious.

"Fair enough." He takes a big bite anyway. And I follow suit.

Honestly, the food is bad, but, after our day and in this little house with the rain pouring down outside, it tastes oddly good.

I look at him sideways, wonder about him in the world. Noah, in his twenties, in his thirties, navigating medical school and summer jobs, internships and relationships.

I snag on that last thought. And get suddenly curious. In a dangerous way.

"So," I say, oh so subtly. "Did your ex cook?"

He looks up at that, wariness in his eyes. "My ex?"

"Well, I mean, maybe I should say 'exes'? I honestly have no idea. But Rita mentioned someone . . ."

"Avery," he nods.

Avery? I hate her instantly.

"What was the deal with . . . Avery?"

"The deal?" He pauses to look up at the ceiling and consider what comes next. I try not to stare at the way the dim lighting casts shadows across his face, accenting his cheekbones and strong chin. *Damn.* Why does he have to look like that? "She's a d-girl—like a development exec at a studio," he starts. "One of the guys on the team—his wife—introduced us at a pool party."

"Be honest: Did you meet in the pool? Or the hot tub?" I gasp. "Wait! Do you seduce all your women in water?"

"Um. First of all, no. She didn't even swim that day."

Of course. I roll my eyes.

"Second, I did not seduce you."

"What would you call it?"

"Mutual. At least, I hope?"

He is asking and so, against my will, I nod. Yes. Fine. If I must. *Mutual.*

Probably he is being generous. I'm the one who would have let it play out, let the chips—and his hands—fall where they may.

The memory of it ricochets through me. I cross my legs and will it away.

"Anyway, she was smart and from the East Coast and, *yes*, she could really cook," he says.

I was with him for the first two.

"So, what happened?"

"What do you mean?"

"Well, it obviously didn't work out," I say, sweeping my arm around the general space to indicate that she's not here. No Avery in the cabinet or under the chair. "So why did it end?"

"Honestly," he says, scratching his temple. "It's kind of hard to explain."

"Did she hate that you travel a lot?"

"Oh," he says, surprised. "I don't."

"You don't travel with the team? I just assumed." Now, I'm surprised.

"I mean, occasionally, but mostly I'm on the ground for home games. And a couple of times a week, I'll head to the training room the day before or after a game. Or my partner in my practice will. But most of the time, I just see patients at our office."

Interesting. Then maybe not so much a girl in every port—or airport lounge.

"Anyway, it's not that anything was wrong per se, which is part of what made it hard to end it. It was time to commit for real or move on and . . . it just didn't feel right."

Suddenly, I feel defensive on Avery's behalf, outrage rising in my chest. "So, what? You just dumped her after she wasted all this time on you? Ghosted her? Cheated?"

Like you did me.

I don't say the words, but they hang between us all the same.

"No," he says firmly. "It wasn't like that. I wanted to feel the way I was supposed to—but I couldn't. I told her upfront, a few months before the end. We went to therapy, but I just couldn't get there."

I nod, quieted. Remind myself he's not eighteen-year-old Noah. He is not the same.

"Honestly," he continues, "this has happened over and over with me. There's nothing wrong on paper. There's just something . . . missing. I don't know. Maybe my expectations are too high."

I don't want to relate to this but I do. So close, yet so far. My relationship mantra. And I never wanted to settle.

Because, somehow, I always sensed that there was something better. And now, with a sharp intake of breath, I fear I know why.

"I wonder the same thing," I say carefully. "But—and I mean this more than anything—I would always rather be alone than with the wrong person."

He nods solemnly. "Exactly."

His gaze falls to my face, which he examines so intently that I no longer know what to do with it—part my lips, blink, arch my brows.

It's like he can read my thoughts.

I stretch my neck, side to side, pretending not to feel the effects of his focus on me, hot and heavy.

"I owe you an apology," he says finally, eyes downcast for a moment but then flitting back up to find mine.

"The pasta *was* pretty undercooked." I smile, taking a sip of cider.

"Not for that."

"Oh. For . . . it's okay." No part of me wants to discuss this, but I charge ahead. I am trying to be a grown-up, which is not my strength. "Look—when you stopped things in the hot tub, I got angry. But I think I was mostly embarrassed. Because I thought . . . but now I realize that, even if you panicked, you did the right thing. By stopping things before they got out of hand. Well, *more* out of hand."

"I don't mean that either."

And then I let myself know what he means.

There's a silence as the weight of his sentiment descends, landing inside me so differently than when I'd imagined him saying these words to me. So many times. Over so many years. Until it cycled almost entirely out of my daydream rotation.

It doesn't make me feel vindicated; it makes me feel sad.

"When I think back to the day you reached out and told me . . . that you might be pregnant, and the way I acted—" Noah pauses, his brow furrowed, his palm flat on the island like it might keep us steady. "I would have killed any guy who treated my sister that way. I was . . ."

"A child."

"Yes. And no."

"Noah. We were kids. It was a million years ago. And you were already grappling with watching your future, as you thought you knew it, crumble under your feet."

And I realize I mean it. Maybe I really can begin to forgive that eighteen-year-old boy.

"We were, but it still mattered—and it matters *now*," he says, his eyes dark and haunted. "It's still the moment I regret most in my life. Because what I did, that choice in that instant, kickstarted a domino effect that destroyed everything in its path."

"Not everything."

"No?"

"No. Because look at you," I say, with what I realize is genuine fondness and maybe even a little awe. I rest my palm on top of his strong hand. I don't notice how nice it is or how the contact reverberates through me because I am impervious. "You're a *doctor*. And a good guy. A full person. With friends and a life, away from the toxic shit we grew up around. And maybe that would never have happened for you if those dominos hadn't fallen."

He looks at me, a little slyly, glancing from my face to my hand and back again. Feeling exposed, I'm tempted to pull my palm away, but don't. Instead, I play chicken with myself. "Thanks for saying that, Nell . . . can I call you Nell, again?"

"Let's just assume yes. For now."

"The truth is," he says, avoiding my eyes for a beat again. "A big part of what motivated me all these years was . . . you."

"Me?"

"Yeah," he shrugs, now resolute and gazing at me fiercely. "I wanted to show you what I could do. I wanted to prove . . . anyway. You're being generous, but the truth is it's *not* okay. What I did was unforgivable. And I know even if you're trying, it may never be possible for you to fully let that hurt—that betrayal—go. Which I hate. But I don't blame you for being pissed. Even so many years later. I treated you like shit. You didn't deserve that."

And I can't tell him it's untrue. That would be disingenuous. Because let's be honest—I *am* still angry after all these years. At least I was, as recently as this morning. Even before Noah left me waiting all by myself, scared and destroyed that night, I had already begun to mourn him—at least the version of him I had loved and who had loved me. It was like the boy who was everything to me had disappeared. I had never felt so alone.

"Thank you for saying that," I say now. Because that's what I can offer. That's what is true. I'm grateful for what he's saying, how it's releasing me from the shackles of this decades-long hurt. "I think I owe you an apology too," I add, forcing the words out. "I hated that feeling of needing you, of not having you show up for me so much that a switch just flipped inside me. And I decided I wasn't going to consider you in any of my plans."

"I'm not going to lie," he says, exhaling. Even now, some light goes out of his face at the memory. "It stung so bad. But that was the smart thing to do, after what I did. Considering how I'd been acting."

"Maybe," I nod. "Like I said, I'd rather be alone than wrong. So, I wiped you out of my future."

"Well, to be fair, I wiped myself out of your future—at the party. As long as we're airing all the dirty laundry."

I open my mouth to respond, but all that comes out is an almost inaudible "Why?"

He closes his eyes for a brief beat, shakes his head. "I think I was just in search of an escape . . . from myself, from reality. It's hard to explain, but it was torture for me to see *you* see *me* in those days. I felt like garbage every time you looked at me—pity or confusion or hope in your eyes. And, with you, I couldn't hide. You have always been able to see me. Like *actually* see me."

I nod. Because this all makes sense but also doesn't change anything.

"But that's not an excuse," he adds, as if he knows exactly what's in my head. "The first mistake was egregious enough. I didn't need to compound it by hooking up with someone else."

I sigh. "Yeah, maybe let's not dwell on that." Because, even so many years later, I can't think of that night without hurt taking over. I shake my head, memories flooding through me like something visceral. "God. If you could have seen the look on Lydia's face when she told me—"

"Told you?"

I cringe. Am barely able to form the words: "She made sure I saw. Pointed you out, kissing her friend."

He swallows, hard. "Lydia pointed us out?"

"Yeah. And she was over the fucking moon."

He nods carefully. "Explains why you hate her."

"I always hated her."

"Fair enough."

But now I'm worked up. "She beelined for every good-looking guy who showed a modicum of interest in me," I say, still irate after all these years. "Even you! And when that didn't work, in a vulnerable moment for us, she basically pimped out her friend to you."

He rubs a hand across his eyes, sighs. *That's fact*.

"I'm so sorry I took the bait, gave her extra ammunition."

He looks like he really is.

But now I'm on a tear. "She still does it, by the way—chases every hot dude who looks at me anytime we're forced together for Cara. I mean, she hasn't been able to keep her hands off you this whole trip!"

"Wait." He cocks his head to one side, a bit of fire sparking in his eyes. "Are you calling me hot?"

"That's what you took from what I just said?"

"Pretty much." He shoots me a small smile that takes me down. "At least that seemed like the good part."

"Yeah, well. You're *okay*."

He gives me a look that calls me on my bullshit. "You're okay too," he says, his gaze dropping from my eyes, down to my lips, down my body, and then back up again.

With effort, I stop myself from doing the same to him.

My hand is still covering his, but now it feels conductive. It's hard to focus on anything else. But again I feel like moving it is even more conspicuous.

"Anyway," I say, trying to play it cool. "Now it's all water under the bridge."

"Right," he says, eyeing me. And it feels like I'm being lit up from within.

"Now we can be friends!" I say.

"Right. *Friends*."

He flips his hand over and grasps mine before it can flee. His forearm flexes and I die a little.

The "friendship" between us is palpable.

So, gently, I take my hand back, reach across the table, and punch him in the arm. Maybe harder than intended.

"Buddies," I say with a forced grin.

He shakes his head at me. "Nell."

There's just too much history and too much distance now, between my life and his. This can't be a thing. Because I can still feel how seminal this all is and was, for both of us. It's not light, even if I want it to be.

I realize that's what Noah meant in the hot tub. This can't be casual.

Needing something to do, I stand up and start clearing, coming around to his side of the bar to grab the pasta bowl. He watches me move, and I feel a little like stalked prey.

And, the thing is, I like it.

A lot.

Part of me wants him to grab me by my sweatpants pockets and yank me toward him. Send plates flying. Pasta sauce on the pretty wood floor. And me, bent over the kitchen counter.

But I shake my head to let that go. What am I thinking?

I don't know whether to stop drinking or down the rest of my cider. I go with the latter. Because my nervous energy has ramped up a notch.

We manage to clean up dinner, avoiding contact in the narrow kitchen. But I can feel him like a pulsing inches from everywhere I move.

I had figured we'd hang out for the rest of the evening, but now I don't think I can handle it. Full darkness has descended outside, even the light emanating at a distance from the general store seems to have gone out, and the wind is whistling past the windows like a tease.

"Do you want to watch a movie?" he asks.

I do. But I shake my head.

"I think it's bedtime," I say.

Noah raises his eyebrows. "Tired?"

I shake my head, temporarily forgetting to lie. I have never been less tired. If I sleep for a single minute tonight, it will be a miracle. A croissant with Jesus's face. An oil lamp that burns for eight days.

"If you're not tired, why don't we hang out?" Noah flops onto the couch, pats the seat beside him.

But there is no way. I am not strong enough. And I'm not wearing underwear.

I shake my head.

He cocks his. "If you're not tired, why go to bed?"

"I'm cold," I say. Which makes zero sense.

He holds up the throw blanket. I shake my head. "That's too fleecey."

He meets my gaze for a beat, then nods slowly—with some version of understanding. "Okay," he says. "Let's go to bed."

For a second I'm not sure if he means *together*.

"You don't have to just because I am!" I say more quickly than is normal.

"Nah," he says. "I should get sleep too."

Noah offers to take the loft bed, though at some point he will definitely smash his head on the ceiling. But that's just how he is. He is a take-the-loft-bed kind of guy.

As he starts up the stairs, I head toward the bathroom to brush my teeth. "Good night, Noah," I say as lightly as I can manage.

He pauses and looks down at me, almost mournfully. Smiles what kind of looks like a pained smile. I'm sure I'm mistaken. "Sleep well, Nell," he says.

I finish brushing my teeth, then head into my room and climb into bed.

Soon, I hear him pad back down the stairs, make the rounds, turning off lights throughout the bungalow. Through the crack in my door, I watch them go out, one by one, the communal space blackening until only a sliver of light remains, probably from the bathroom.

My whole body is vibrating. It's like someone flipped a switch and now I am on. Night is day. Rest is an impossibility. Instead of relaxing me, the cider has turned up my volume to maximum horniness. And I can't think of a single thing besides Noah lying in the bed directly above me in few, if any, clothes, rumpled sheets grazing his warm skin—his strong forearms, thighs, firm stomach, calves. His dark lashes closed against his cheeks.

I don't know what the hell to do with myself. I even briefly consider stepping outside to cool off, but it's pouring rain and I'm in the middle of breathtaking nowhere.

But I cannot stay still.

So I stand up and tiptoe to the bathroom, careful not to wake him. Aware of every creak as I cross the floor. But as I reach to slide the door open, Noah steps out—in the middle of pulling off his shirt, exposing the top of those low-slung sweatpants. And I gasp, like he's a ghost. The hottest apparition. And, to be fair, he *is* haunting me.

My palm lands on his chest as he drops his T-shirt back down and we nearly slam into each other like we're characters on a laugh-tracked sitcom. I snatch my hand away like I just got burned.

I try to pull myself together, bring a palm to my heart to stop it from pounding. Because I am not on edge. I am a *completely normal person*.

"Sorry!" he says, also flustered. "I didn't mean to startle you. I was just brushing my teeth. I thought you were asleep."

I shake my head. "I can't sleep."

"Well," he says. "It's only like nine thirty."

"Is it really? It feels like two a.m."

"It's been a long day."

"Long," I agree. "But weirdly good, right?"

He shoots me a crooked smile that almost ends me. "One of the best."

He holds my gaze. If he can't hear my heart thumping, it's a fucking miracle.

"Well, good night," I say before I do something dumb—dumb*er*. And turn back toward my bedroom.

"Weren't you going to the bathroom?"

"Yeah," I say, looking back at him and his crinkled brow. "But— I'm good."

Deranged. But good.

"Are you sure you're okay up there?" I add. Because that's all I can think about. Him. *Up there, up there, up there.*

"I'm fine. It's actually pretty cozy," he says.

"Ah, I want to see it!"

He arches an eyebrow. "You want to see it . . . *now?*"

There's so much going on with me that I can no longer differentiate between the emotions—longing, anxiety, hope, regret, fear, want, a compulsion for cute design. I'm sure it's all printed in black and white across my face.

I have to escape.

"Tomorrow is fine!" I say with a forced smile. Oh so casual. I shake my head. I take a step toward the bedroom. But Noah stops me, reaching out and gently resting a hand on my shoulder—which I realize in that moment hasn't bothered me all day.

"Hey," he says, and I turn back around to look up at his stupid handsome face. That face I've thought about for all these years, that I fell in love with when I was just a kid, that has been, at times, both my favorite and least favorite face. His expression is inscrutable. At least to me, in my current fugue state. "I just want to say because I didn't get to before," he says, "about the hot tub: For the record, I didn't panic."

This is unexpected. And also, I suspect, untrue. "You did panic, actually."

"Fine. But not about being with you."

"No?"

"No."

"Was there someone else there? Hiding in the cold plunge?"

"Nope," he says. "It was just me and you. Alone." There's a meaningful pause. "Just like now."

And those words send shivers of possibility through me that I can't shake off.

"What was the panic about then, if not me getting the wrong idea?"

He looks down at the ground, then seems to steel himself, exhaling a rush of breath. He looks back up, his eyes boring into mine. "About *losing* you again."

The silence takes on weight as our eyes lock.

I try to speak, but all that comes out is the quietest sigh. Like a whistle.

"Anyway," he says, an almost apologetic smile playing on his full lips. "I just wanted to say—I *liked* that things got out of hand. And I wouldn't mind if that happened again. As soon as possible."

I am heated up like a brick oven. No, I am on fire. And I know Noah can tell.

Because when I don't move, he does. He reaches out and takes hold of my elbow, runs his palm down my forearm, stopping to encircle my wrist. Like when he examined me that first morning. Only this time it's different. He leaves trails in his wake.

He yanks me lightly toward him. And I am gone.

I look up into those hazel eyes, the ones I know and don't, flecked with doubt and reason and need. And I realize I want more. And I don't care about the fallout.

He can examine me all night long.

"Maybe oysters *are* aphrodisiacs," I say, like I don't know I'm speaking out loud.

"Maybe," he says. "Or maybe I just want you."

Noah pulls me closer to him, firmly, like he's taking the reins. He's towering over me, so that I'm suddenly extra aware of how much bigger a human he is than I am. By how much I want him to subsume me.

He brings a warm hand to my cheek. I lean into it.

I can't take it anymore. I am in.

And, as soon as I am, I don't feel hesitant anymore.

I am on a mission.

Now, I take a step closer, so that my body is brushing up against his, my breasts—through my thin tee—brushing against his chest. I look up into his face, let my eyes drop to his lips.

My breath is shallow. His is ragged.

"I swear to God, if you stop this time . . ." I start.

He shuts that down. "I'm not going to stop."

As proof, he reaches down and pulls my T-shirt over my head in one quick movement. Tosses it—like the baseball player he is—behind us and out of sight.

So, I do the same to him. Tit for tat.

I watch—and feel—his eyes rake down me, as I cock my head sideways and smirk up at him.

He bites his bottom lip.

In the plunge pool, I felt his body against mine, but the froth hid most of him from view. Now, he's all laid out in front of me.

And it's all fucking mine.

The scars from years of playing, roughhousing, skateboarding—the boy I knew. And the definition, smooth planes, and rough edges of now. I place my palm on the side of his sculpted neck with purpose now, watch him swallow hard as he tries to remain still, like he's afraid he might frighten me away. Then I drag my hand slowly down the terrain of his chest, past his collarbone, pecs, the hard ridges of his abs—tracing the V that leads down.

He inhales a shuddered breath.

I slip my fingers into the very top of his sweatpants, and let them hang, teasing, from the elastic band. The tension between us—years in the making and intensified with every barb, glance, and not-so-accidental touch today—is now nuclear.

And we are about to blow.

What choice do we have but to save the world from our combustion?

Which is why Noah takes action. His darkened eyes still glued to mine, he grabs me roughly by the hips and backs me toward the wall, until I'm pinned against it. Then he leans down and, pausing just centimeters from my lips so I can feel his breath on my face, says, "Thank fucking God."

And then he kisses me. And it's not slow and patient; it's urgent like the time is *now*. Like we both needed this yesterday.

Like it might not happen again.

We crash together. His lips snag mine, his stubble delightfully rough against my face. His grip tightens around my hips, his large hands flexing, as I tip my chin up for him to go deeper. He tastes like that cider and toothpaste, smells like our rainy day by the sea.

And I am all in.

My hands are everywhere I can reach. In his hair, behind his neck, at his broad back. His skin is warm and hard as I pull him toward me, so that we're flush against each other. So that I am a Noah-and-wall sandwich.

And that's when he scrapes his hands down to my ass and lifts me up, propping me against the wall as he steps between my legs. And we're grinding against each other—*dry humping* as the kids used to call it—like it's still those days. Like we're still teenagers, impulsive, hungry, hormones coursing through us and blurring our choices.

And it's like a release. Of expectations. Of demands. Of hangups.

I bite his lip. It's my turn now. He pulls back slightly to look me in the face, his expression amused, like it's a dare. Like this is a warning.

And then he dives back toward me, his tongue slipping into my mouth, as I feel him get so hard between my legs. I press myself into him.

I can't get enough.

And it's a time warp, back and forth. Now and then. Yesterday and today.

I think of all the times we were desperate for each other as teens, but there was nowhere private to go. Frustration, need. The closets we hid in amid rain jackets and dust. The cold porcelain of restroom walls. The dark house-party bedrooms with mountains of coats.

My breath is coming faster now, shallow and heated, as he presses into me, our twin sweatpants the only barrier. And I am no longer a solid. I am liquid mercury—shapeshifting and shiny.

I need more.

And he must have the same thought because suddenly he is carrying me, never breaking contact, then setting me down on the stairs. He kneels on the step in front of me and wraps his fingers around the elastic band of my bottoms just like I did to him, hesitates for a beat, messing with me.

Like this is the moment where there is no turning back.

But that train has already left the station.

Even in the dim light, his hazel eyes sparkle with a badness that ramps up my heart rate.

"You feeling okay?" he whispers, leaning over me, his lips parted.

"Pretty good actually," I say, my voice a rasp. "Right now."

"Right," he says. "But I should make sure—don't you think? That you're okay?"

I'm about to protest because, is he going to pause hooking up to check out my arm? But then he slips his hand inside my pants and between my legs.

His fingers roam so gently I might scream.

Instead, I gasp. At least I think it's me. And he groans. My hand squeezes the banister as he presses his fingers inside me. Because, if I haven't already, surely I'm about to fall—hard.

I am dead. Or I don't care if I am. If this is it, I'm okay with that. Time is no longer a thing. Space is what I don't want between us.

My body is trembling, pulsing—like we're back in that club where we first saw each other and I am the bass. I reach for him too. Try ineffectually to pull at his pants, but he's tied the drawstring tight.

Who ties the drawstring?

And that's when Noah pauses for a second, despite my protests, leaning hot and heavy against me, and says, "Condom?"

I shake my head. "I'm on the pill. You?"

"I should be good—all clear and no one since Avery."

"Clean bill of health for me too," I say.

He narrows his eyes and cocks his head. "We'll see about that."

The doctor is in.

21

NOAH
TODAY

There is life after death. And it's in West Marin.

Because we have been resuscitated. Brought back from the brink.

That's what I decide as I lead Nell through the dark into the bedroom. Pull her down onto the platform bed. Finally drag those sweatpants down her smooth legs and throw them in a corner—so that now I've got all of her.

It's faint with all the clouds, but there is a feeble moonbeam falling through the small windows. It bounces off her skin like a circle light, making her glow.

Despite the shadows, I can see her lips are a little swollen from all the kissing. Her cheeks are flushed. Her eyes have a dreamy quality, though they're also laser-focused on me.

I hover over her, holding myself up on my forearms.

"Poor Mike," I say.

"Why?"

"He doesn't know what he's missing."

"Hmm," she says, shooting me a wicked smile. "I think he does though."

And as I dive for her, she giggles, wrapping herself around me. I let myself drop to one side, so we're entangled, lying facing each other. I run a hand slowly up her bare side because I can—her thigh, her curved hip, the ridges of her rib cage. I cup her breast, my thumb brushing back and forth, as she closes her eyes and arches against me.

I am fucking toast. And not just for tonight. I know it then as I watch her not watch me.

This girl is it for me.

But I can't worry about that now—not when she's here in the flesh, all the flesh, directly in front of me. Like a fucking impossibility. The least likely gift.

Nell tugs at my sweatpants impatiently, at the knot in my drawstring. And even as she sighs against my skin, she says, "Were you worried someone was gonna break into your pants? Were you worried there was going to be a robbery?"

"You can never be too safe," I smirk.

"You can definitely be too safe. For example, right now."

She pulls uselessly at the knot, gives up, and rolls on top of me, kissing down the side of my neck, then moving lower on my chest, dragging her insane body against mine, making me fucking crazy.

My dick has never been so hard.

I sit up to untie my pants. She yanks them down and off. Then, pushing me down on my back again, climbs up toward me on all fours.

Then, as she narrows her eyes, with aching slowness, she lowers herself onto me, so we are fully fused. She gasps as I groan. And then there's no holding back.

We rock against each other, harder. I want this to last forever. But nothing does.

And right now, I have a job to do.

I wrap my arm around her and flip her onto her back. She presses her face into my neck. Sighs my name.

I'm not that fumbling teenage boy anymore. And I need to show her.

22

NELLIE
TODAY

I wake up in the morning, tangled up in Noah. I am dazed and toasty. And it's a stellar way to start the day.

Today at five p.m. is Cara and Ben's big un-wedding party—the culmination of the whole trip. If the song on the Saturday itinerary isn't "White Wedding" by Billy Idol, I'll eat every single oyster in the cooler myself—shells and all.

Outside, the sun is clearly shining, blasting through the windows like it's finally back from vacation and it's got some stories to tell. The storm is over.

It was a long night in all the best ways. And, on top of being . . . on top, I feel like it was really cathartic too.

We got resolution. We got satisfaction.

Sleep is overrated.

This felt like the kind of night that's an end and a beginning. And considering how formative my relationship with Noah was—or first love always is—and how long I carried anger toward him, and maybe myself, this feels like a major step forward.

So, I am bright-eyed and bushy-tailed.

The day is rife with possibilities. Possibilities that extend beyond this hotel room, all the way to my life in NYC. My friendships, my work, the bodega cat—what's next.

In the dark last night, while I traced my finger back and forth across the scar by Noah's knee, we talked and talked and talked; we ate Charleston Chews and drank cider at midnight; we did other things that will haunt—and sustain—me for the rest of my days. Things that make me blush in the light of day.

But now it's the morning after. *The day after.* That sounds so ominous.

Clearly, neither of us is making breakfast—because we got no skills. And that leftover pasta should be put out to pasture.

Plus, we have oysters and cheese to ferry back. So we can't linger in bed forever.

I sigh, burrowing for a blissful moment further into both the plush bedding and Noah. Press my front into his side. His body is warm with sleep.

For one more brief instant, I am an ostrich with my head in the sand.

Though I have done a good job—by my standards—of pushing questioning thoughts of the future out of my head until now, they're starting to pop in, uninvited. They carry casseroles of chaos, twelve-packs of panic, cases of doubt.

As much as I don't want to face reality, it's coming to call. I surely have at least three hundred texts from Cara already.

I twist my head and peer regretfully up at Noah, who is still sound asleep. Groan quietly against his chest. Resist the urge to press kisses across his rib cage. He is a sight to behold in the dawn's early light, sun particles percolating around him like fairy dust.

How did I ever tolerate Alfie?

Noah's lashes are black against his cheek, his lips parted, the scruff on his jaw just a little heavier than the previous day's. His chest, which I've been using as a pillow, looks even more sculpted in daylight and he's got one perfect tanned leg sticking out from beneath the comforter. Basically, he's like a not overly worked-out Greek god. And the last thing I want to do is get up.

But I must. Because—as much as I now acknowledge that there's something real between us, that there always has been, that he is not the same boy he was when I knew him and yet still *is* in the good ways—I also know that there's no future for us. I live in New York. He lives in LA.

We have full lives that we're not just going to uproot for each other. We wouldn't do it then, and we won't do it now. The truth is, just because we've both caught feelings and a license to bone, doesn't mean that we would work in the real world.

There's so much more to a relationship than that.

And I am looking at him likely with as much doubt as affection when he opens one eye, peers at me, and murmurs, "Stop freaking out."

"What makes you think I'm freaking out?"

"Because," he says, "you're freaking out."

I sit up and he pulls me back down. "Noah, I have to get up."

He shakes his head. "I have better ideas."

I giggle because of course I do. But I am also all business. "Look, mister," I say, poking him in the chest. "Take your ideas elsewhere. We need coffee and we need food. And we need to get the fuck back to Sonoma, assuming the flooding has subsided—because Cara is probably mid-coronary."

"She'll survive," Noah yawns, turning on his side to face me and nudging me with his knee. "Besides, I'm also mid-coronary."

"Really? Your heart seems just fine to me."

"No, really," he insists. "Feel it."

I roll my eyes but lean forward and press my hand flat to his chest—but it's a trick! He grabs me and pulls me on top of him again.

"Okay. All better," he says, his arms wrapped around me as I straddle him.

"Oh, thank God. I'm a miracle worker. Take me on the road."

"Okay." He shrugs. "I'll take you anywhere."

It's a pretty convincing argument—the hard planes of his body under mine. A perfect fit. His lids still heavy with sleep.

I bury my face in his neck. Breathe him in. But then I escape, scooting to the bathroom before he can stop me.

I will get my head on straight.

Cara has indeed texted. *A lot*.

She is worried about the oysters. But also us. But mostly the oysters.

And she's a little bit worried about the explosive combination of me and Noah.

Cara

> I'm so sorry! I would never have sent you without me if I thought you'd get stuck with HIM!
> Are you okay?

Nellie

> I'm okay.

Cara

> Was it torture?

I consider that question: Has being with Noah been torture? A little at first. And then it's been a dream. But there's more punishment coming down the pike when we part ways, I let myself admit.

Part of me wants to confess it all to her, share in ways I have historically been hesitant—the good and the bad. But that would involve revealing so much at once—the truth about Alfie, the truth about the hot tub, the truth about last night. And this is her big day. Or un-big day.

I will not make this about me.

Also, the last twenty-four hours with Noah have been so special, as if protected by some kind of magical force field. I kind of want to keep them to myself, at least for a little while longer. I'm afraid, once they see the light of day, weather the storm of other people's eyes, questions, thoughts, they'll start to morph and fade. And I can't have that. Because I need them to carry me for a bit.

Nellie

No worries! We did just fine. Almost behaved like adults.

It's true-ish.

Noah eventually gets up, though he tries to fool me back into bed at least twice more.

Outside, the sun is indeed making an appearance, but it's a bit overcast intermittently here—marine layer fogging up the sky. There's a chill in the air that I know will lift once we make our way back toward the estate.

We get dressed to both of our chagrin. We go for a walk, down tiny wildflower-lined streets to a flat sandy expanse of beach that is almost entirely our own—a best-kept-secret spot. We laugh and tease and hold hands and chase each other like idiots. The sea air styles my hair.

We return our key. We leave. We pick up the flowers at the flower farm, regretfully declining the tour of the meadows and the floral design class Cara had booked for the day before. We're short on time. Next, we pick up sea salt honey, chestnut meringue, and wineberry pies from a bakery that smells like joy, but decline the sourdough-bread-baking experience.

And though we don't get to have the incredible dinner with Rhode Island clam chowder and fried saltines on the water at Nick's Cove, we do pick up the world's best breakfast sandwiches with eggs and apple-smoked bacon from a counter restaurant along the road that Cara texts us to try.

She has missed her calling as a travel agent, as much as that's still a job.

And so we are driving up the coast inhaling our sandwiches, the rental car's trunk packed with local delicacies, when I finally get up the courage to have "the talk" with Noah. And by "courage" I mean that for the past few miles, I have been staring at the side of his ruggedly handsome face willing myself to broach this topic without ruining the trip at the very end.

"What?" he says, finally.

"What, what?"

He tears his eyes away from the road long enough to shoot me a cut-the-crap look.

"You've been staring at me mournfully since the vineyards reappeared."

"Grapes make me sad."

"Said no one in history." He sighs. "Out with it. Whatever it is, you're going to say it eventually, so you might as well cut to the chase."

When I don't speak, he lays a hand on my thigh and squeezes lightly. I never want him to take it away—which sends my mind down another perilous neural pathway.

I can't *need* him.

I will do this! I clear my throat. "Noah, the last day with you has been . . . so special. *You* are so special."

"Uh-oh. Is one of us dying?"

"No!"

"Okay. That's a relief. Continue then."

I exhale. "When two people are attracted to each other . . ."

"Oh!" He grins. "I get it. This is a sex talk. You don't need to bother. I already know how it works . . . although if that wasn't obvious last night *and* early this morning, maybe I have bigger problems."

I shoot him an impatient look. "Noah. Be serious. Listen. Long ago . . ."

"In a land far, far away called New Amsterdam . . ."

"Noah!"

He is cracking up and, though his laugh is adorable, I want to kill him. On the upside, my frustration is a motivator for me to blurt out: "Shut up for a second, please!"

And he does.

"What I'm trying to say is that last night was so great, all of yesterday was amazing. *Beyond* amazing. But it can't happen again because we have no future together and I live in New York and you live here and we've broken each other's hearts enough and it feels really good to finally not be mad at you anymore after so many years and so, yeah. Okay?"

There's a moment of silence while he absorbs this and I catch my breath.

"No," he shrugs.

"No?"

"Yup, that's what I said. No."

"No to what?"

"No to all of it."

"Noah . . . you can't just say no!"

"Yes, I can. And I just did. Anyway, is it my turn to speak now? You had your chance. And, honestly, it was not your best work."

I cross my arms over my chest and purse my lips. "Fine!"

Without warning, he pulls the car over onto a little patch of grass by a dirt road and turns to face me.

"What are you doing?"

"Having the talk you wanted."

"But the oysters . . ."

"The oysters are headed nowhere good. They won't mind stopping."

I grumble but give in.

We're back in full sun country and the light is blasting bright behind Noah's head like a sign. Like he is destiny. Which I'm worried I'm starting to feel he is. And that's dangerous. I need to have this talk, create ground rules, because it's the grown-up thing to do. But it's also about self-preservation. I am not at all sure I trust myself.

"You're not wrong," he says. "About our history, about our separate lives, about how much I rocked your world last night."

"I didn't say that."

He toggles his head. "Mm. I'm pretty sure you did."

"Maybe that's what you heard."

"That is *definitely* what I heard—multiple times." He raises his eyebrows at me. I try not to blush. "But you're wrong about a few things, too. First of all, I don't live here. I live in LA. A city you love. Where you have lived before. Where there are many opportunities for art directors should they decide that winter is kind of bullshit and the sushi is better. Second of all . . . well, I can't remember second of all. But the gist is this: You're getting way ahead of yourself."

"Am I now?" I roll my eyes. "Tell me more."

"The long term may be complicated, but this moment is not," he says. "We have one more night together before we all leave tomorrow. I get that the idea of the future scares you. Okay. That's fine. Maybe you're right. Maybe it's impossible. But there's no reason why we can't see what happens before then, let tonight unfold however it will. There's no reason to shut it down."

He has a point. Maybe I am getting ahead of myself. Maybe the new me can just be in this moment and get what I can out of my time with him, then carry it with me as I reapproach my real life. At the very least, this experience has reminded me not to settle—not for the Alfies of the world. Not for anyone.

Noah sees me wavering and goes in for the kill.

"Please don't tell me I never get to kiss you again." There is so much earnestness in his face that I fold on the spot. "Deal?" he says, offering his hand for a shake.

Can I do this? Can I trust myself not to get too invested? Not to overthink? To just enjoy the time I have?

Maybe. But only if I can maintain real clarity.

"Not so fast," I say, leaving his hand hovering over the center console. "I will agree not to rule anything out completely if, and only if, this all stays between us. I can't deal with having to answer questions or hear opinions or process judgments or anything like that. I need to know that all decisions, questions, and concerns are my own."

He considers this. "Fair," he says. "So we good? Not to pressure you, but there's a giant flock of wild turkeys running toward the car and I'm a little scared."

I swivel around and indeed the giant birds are squawking toward us at full speed.

I link my own finger around his pinky and wiggle.

"I was really going for more of an actual handshake."

"Shut up, Noah," I say and kiss him hard on the lips.

"That works," he says, once I pull away. Then he pulls back onto the road before the wild turkeys go wild on us.

23

NOAH
TODAY

The party is in an actual tree house. Or at least, it feels that way.

We are seated in white wooden folding chairs, on a large, open-air platform, almost like an apartment without walls, hovering high above the ground. Globe lights are suspended from branches above us like our very own galaxy.

They'll glow brighter when night fully descends, setting the mood for what will be the dance floor.

Cara and Ben stand at the front and John, the driver, is acting as officiant. Apparently he is ordained—not that he needs to be.

After all, they're already married.

"I don't understand," I whisper to Rita, Sabrina, and Nell, who are seated in the row beside me. "What were they planning to do if the driver didn't wind up being so distinguished?"

"It was supposed to be Cara's cousin," Sab says.

"What happened?"

"He got in an accident. Tiny little temporary coma."

Nell's eyes go wide. "Really?"

"No," Sabrina says. "Stage fright. He chickened out."

For reasons I don't understand, Nell heaves a sigh of relief.

I am trying not to pay special attention to her, to respect her desire for no one to know what's up with us, but it's hard.

Maybe it was the twenty-four hours of relaxation, the fact that she didn't have time to change her hair after the beach, or maybe—I congratulate myself—it was all that life-altering sex, but she is luminous. Her gray eyes are full, her skin is smooth, her lips are slathered in some kind of shimmery pink.

I wonder how it tastes.

I want to sweep the waves off her neck with my palm and bite her shoulder. I want to rest my hand on the exposed skin of her thigh, inch it higher and higher.

But I can't. Because, according to everyone else here, we are not a thing. Though we agreed we can at least tell everyone we buried the hatchet and are good to hang out, so we don't have to avoid each other all night.

I focus my attention back on the ceremony, which has been sweet and corny in all the ways it should be. This may be an un-wedding, but the details have felt pretty classic. Cara walked down the aisle in all white, clutching a bouquet we picked up on the coast, to "Wild Horses" by the Rolling Stones—and all of us in the cheap seats cheered. (I know where Ben falls in the Beatles versus Stones debate, so I assume the song was his suggestion.) Like a real-deal officiant, John the driver mused about complementary qualities he'd observed in the couple, including the way Ben took care of Cara when she overdid it on the booze bus. That one got some laughs.

I hope Ben and Cara had the day they needed yesterday to recenter. I hope they're both feeling more themselves.

It looks like it. Whatever stress my best friend was feeling is gone from his face now as he gazes at his wife like she is the beginning and the end.

"I love you even though you're terrible at making beds," Cara is saying now, her eyes welling. "Seriously. No one is worse. I love you even though you still put Ansel's diapers on backward sometimes—and it's been years! You really should figure that out. Stickies at the front. At least you also clean up the leaks."

Laughter titters through the crowd. Ben offers up a sheepish shrug.

And it occurs to me that maybe there is value in knowing the best *and* the worst of someone before you agree—or in this case *re-agree*—to spend your life together. Maybe Ben wasn't sure he wanted this whole crazy celebration, but he looks full up right now as they choose each other again.

"But, most of all," Cara says, "I love you because you are my partner in crime. Not today. Not tomorrow. But always. Of course, you're the father to our incredible children—and I can give you *some* credit for them. But having this time to be with you here without the kids has also been so incredible because it's allowed us to just be *us* again—the us we have been since we met so many years ago. The us we still are. And the *us* I hope we will be for the rest of our days."

I know in that moment that Cara has gotten the confirmation she needed that, though time has passed and life is bedlam, she is still herself, that they are still *them*.

There is not a dry eye in the house. Even Damien, sitting on my other side, has misty eyes.

When Nell and I got back after our adventure, it was hard not to experience a little comedown. It was such a gift to retreat from the rest of the world together. It didn't help that the first person I saw—after she and I parted ways and I began unloading the trunk full of party stuff—was Damien.

"What's up, man?" he said, giving me a pound.

"Not much," I said, immediately tense. I wasn't even sure why.

But then he leaned up against the car without offering to help, chewing his gum with his mouth open. And I remembered. Right away, he started in: "So, you got stuck, huh? Alone with Nellie?"

"Yup," I said, tight-lipped, as I pulled out the cooler of oysters. Turns out maybe Mike was extra strong 'cause that thing was heavy as hell. Got to give credit where credit is due.

"How'd you swing that?"

Setting the cooler down, I paused and looked up at Damien, this old friend of mine who hasn't been feeling like a friend at all. "I didn't *swing* anything. There was a flood. Turns out I don't control the weather."

"Right," he said, staring me down. "So, did you tap that?"

Everything in me wanted to stand up to full height and punch him in the face in that moment. Because of the way he cheapens things. Because he's circling this girl he knows I love. Because I can't tell him the truth—that something *did* happen between me and Nell, and I've never been so fucking happy for even a modicum of a chance to win her back.

I wanted him to back the fuck off before he tainted this.

Instead, I exhaled. "D, grow the fuck up."

"Is that a yes?"

"No. That's a grow the fuck up."

"I'm pretty fully grown," he said, pulling out a dab pen and dragging on it. He slipped it back in his pocket and rose to standing, stepped in closer to me than he should. "You don't have to tell me, anyway, bro. Doesn't matter. This is just a trip."

I didn't have to be a genius to figure out what he meant. This is a short vacation, but he lives in the same city as Nell. He can play the long game.

"Good luck, D," I grunted, because I couldn't say anything else without revealing the truth—something I promised Nell I wouldn't do.

"I don't need luck, baseball boy," he said, close enough to my face that I could smell the stale weed on his breath. "We're not in high school anymore."

He shot me a peace sign, then strutted away.

I watched him retreat, my face pulsing with anger, wondering how I never saw him clearly all these years.

I always thought Damien kind of had a thing for Nell. I guess I can be honest with myself about that now, sitting next to him watching our friends tie the already-tied knot. I remember he once told me I was lucky because I'd snagged "the perfect girl." But I never cared. Because I knew there wasn't a chance in hell. The sentiment seemed almost sweet. And it was convenient, having my best friend and my girlfriend mostly get along, at least on the surface.

Plus, as far as I was concerned, Damien wasn't interested in being with one girl, ever. Nell worried that was true about me too, occasionally, which is why we broke up for super-short stints those couple of times. Because she lost patience. With how much I liked the attention. With how much I sometimes flirted.

So, when she and I were on one of our pauses, and he started talking to her regularly on the phone, it seemed a little weird. But I figured it was helpful to have someone in my court.

Now, I'm wondering if he was ever in my court at all.

Now, I'm wondering if he has a lingering thing for Nell—or if that thing is really about competing with me. About how I sucked up too much of the limelight for him. About how he felt cheated somehow.

And I'm wondering it while I sit next to him, pretending we're all good, and clapping as Cara and Ben consummate their un-wedding with a kiss.

In that moment, I am hit like a ton of bricks with the reason why I've kept so many of my childhood friends around for so many years, even if I'd outgrown them—the ones like Damien, who my sister, Henny, never trusted: I have unconsciously been trying to hold on to the past, to some small connection to Nell.

As backward as it seems, I know it's true. And now I don't need them anymore. Not the ones who take advantage. I don't need *him*.

I'm so happy for Cara and Ben, who seem truly blissed out, but I am suddenly so glad this ceremony is over. I've got radioactivity seated on either side of me, and it's too much to hold.

After the happy couple makes their exit, we all rise and file out toward another area of the tree house for cocktails.

"Drink?" I ask Nell.

She nods. "Drink."

Before we make it over to the bar, a server comes by with a tray bearing some sort of signature cocktail. It's orange. There are bubbles. I have no idea what it is, but I don't care.

I snag two—hand Nell one. And we wander over to where Sabrina and Rita are taking turns on a rope swing.

"I don't know," Rita is saying, tugging the rope to test it and eyeing the steel chains at the top suspiciously before sitting down. "I don't trust this thing."

"It held me," says Sabrina.

"Yeah, but you're not a real-sized person," Rita says. "You're a peanut."

Sabrina sets her hands on her (admittedly narrow) hips. "Short people are people too."

Rita nods. "Agreed. Just shorter people."

"Anyway, let's talk about something more interesting—let's talk about the FLOOD!" Sabrina says, turning her attention on us. "Was it crazy? I can't believe you guys got stuck."

"We didn't really see the flood," says Nell, looking up at me for confirmation. "So it wasn't *that* crazy."

"No. I mean, I actually don't believe you guys got stuck. Did you *really*? Or was it just an excuse to escape the un-bridezilla and all of us for twenty-four hours?"

"Why would we want to escape you?" I say.

Sabrina shakes her head. Points a finger at me. "You're good, Williams. Too good."

A server comes by with another tray, this one holding hors d'oeuvres.

"Oyster with toasted sherry mignonette?" the waiter offers.

"The oysters!" Nell exclaims.

"The oysters," I nod.

"They made it," she says.

"Sort of," I say.

I realize we're grinning at each other like idiots when Sabrina says, "Some people say oysters are aphrodisiacs."

Nell snickers, shoots me a private smile.

"Some people do say that," I say.

Sabrina studies us with narrowed eyes. She looks at me, then at Nell, then at me again. She raises her eyebrows knowingly. Sucks her teeth. But she doesn't say a thing.

Which wins her points in my book.

It's warm tonight, especially compared to how it felt on the coast. And instead of loose and floral like the others, tonight Nell's dress is short and black. It's tight and low across the top, flares into a miniskirt.

She is wearing it like nobody's business.

It would be so easy just to reach right up under it and . . . *fuck*. I swipe a hand across my eyes. I have got to get my shit together.

After everything that happened, it's just hard to be near her and not touch her. I restrain one hand with the other.

That's when Damien and Lydia saunter up together, the bad news bears. I shift away from Nell, so as not to attract attention, and find myself right up against Lydia.

"Hey, stranger," she says.

"Hey . . . Lydia," I say back.

I glance at Nell, who is now wearing a consternated look. But not for long.

"Damn, girl," says Damien. "You look smokin'."

"Oh." Nell looks down at her dress, up at Damien, and smiles. "Thanks."

I can't tell if she's actually flattered. I want to end him.

Damien is wearing one of his specials. A white polo and white pants with a white baseball cap. What I once thought was idiosyncratic, even charming, is suddenly dumb as hell.

Also, who wears white to a wedding?

There's an awkward silence. The crickets get their moment.

"So, what did we miss yesterday?" Nell asks, maybe to draw attention away from herself.

"Nothing!" says Cara, popping into the circle with Ben close behind. "But we missed you!"

"Aw shucks," Nell says, giving her bestie a squeeze. "Hey! We should have a toast! Sab?"

"Yes!" Sabrina seconds. We all raise our glasses. "To our luminous friends who we love so dearly! Congratulations on being the cutest! May the best of your past be the worst of your future together! Cheers."

"To us all being together!" Cara says.

I might be projecting, but Nell looks less sure.

We all clink glasses.

"Hey, Nellie," says Damien. "You need to make eye contact when you toast, girl. Otherwise, you get cursed—seven years bad sex, starting now."

I nudge her lightly so no one can see.

"Oh," she says, suppressing a smile, and maintaining eye contact with Damien. "I'm all good."

Cocktails lead to dinner, dinner to a cheese course (the goat cheese!) and then dessert—the pies! By the end of it all, everyone is toasty, dancing to "Real Love" (old-school!) and Taylor Swift (new-school).

The cheese factor is high.

Like it's a real wedding.

I've managed to keep my distance from Nell to an extent, hanging with Ben and a couple of his work dudes, when he's not dancing with Cara. I'm dodging Lydia's advances without outright insulting her, though they get more overt with every sip she takes.

But no matter where I am, I find myself stealing peeks at Nell from across the space. And it's only when I approach the bar solo to grab myself and Ben another scotch that I lose sight of her. From the other direction, she sidles up next to me and taps me on the shoulder, catching me off guard.

"Hey, you," she says, smiling. She seems relaxed, loose, happy.

"Hey," I say, feeling a grin spread across my face. "How's it going?"

"It's going good," she says. Then she looks me up and down. "I feel like I haven't seen you at all."

I shrug. "I've been around."

"Not *around* me." She is clearly a bit tipsy—and, frankly, so am I.

"Gotta keep my distance," I say quietly. "Stay well behaved. Keep my hands to myself."

"As it turns out, well behaved is not as fun." She scrunches up her nose.

A breeze blows past, billowing Nell's skirt. She catches it like she's Marilyn Monroe—but not before I catch a glimpse of the curve of her upper thigh and ass.

She sees me see. Giggles. Sighs.

"You look pretty incredible tonight," I say.

"You look pretty incredible yourself." She tilts her head, looks up at me. Bites her lip. I wish it was me.

The bartender crosses over to us. "What can I get you?" he asks.

We straighten up like respectable citizens, and I gesture to Nell like, *after you.*

"May I have another glass of that orange wine? It's kind of amazing!"

The bartender peeks under the bar, picks up a bottle, shakes it, holds it up to the light. "I'm so sorry, but it looks like we're all out," he says. "I can grab some more bottles in a bit, but the other bartender is on break right now, so I can't leave my post until she gets back."

"You know what?" Nell says. "It's just in the pool house shed, right—beside the barn? The overflow fridge? Cara pointed it out to me. I'll grab them myself."

"Really? Thanks so much," the bartender says.

"No prob."

She looks up at me again, shoots me a wistful smile. Like another place, another time, and heads toward the shed, humming some song as she goes.

I watch her leave. I survey the scene. Everything is . . . less without her.

"Whatcha getting?" Lydia asks, suddenly beside me out of nowhere.

"Nothing," I say. "Just running to the bathroom."

And that's truly my intention. At least I think it is. Until I find myself stopping by the pool house, afterward, to see if Nell needs help. I'm not sure how much wine she has to carry, and I don't want her to re-aggravate her shoulder. It's been feeling better.

I find her just outside on a path between the shed and the back of the barn, struggling with a box.

"Hey, need some assistance?" I ask.

"Oh, thank God," she says, and sets the carton carefully down in the grass. I try not to watch her bend over, but I definitely watch her bend over.

And she sees me do it. Stares at me long and hard. Leans back against the barn wall behind her.

She looks up at me, standing in front of her, hands in my pockets.

"Hi, Noah," she says.

"Hi, Nell."

"I hate that we can't just hang out."

"I hate that too." I cock my head. "We could though."

"We could?"

"Just for a minute."

"Here?"

"Here."

"But shouldn't we get back?" She stays rooted to the spot.

"I don't think anyone is looking for us."

The moon is big and bright. It casts spells in the dark. Softens the edges, turns everything otherworldly.

Nell sighs. "I like it here."

"Me too."

"Isn't it beautiful?"

"It is," I say. But I'm looking at her.

I've got visions of last night flashing in my head in succession like a stereoscope slideshow from when I was a kid. *Click, click, click.*

I wonder if she can see it in my eyes.

She reaches out her hand to touch me, weaves her fingers through mine. Swings our hands lightly back and forth.

And it's like a conduit, electricity crackling on a loop between us.

I take a step closer, forgetting the case of wine in the grass.

And it's not a choice. It's gravitational pull.

She tilts her chin up toward me, shoots me a sly smile as she brushes her thumb up the side of my hand. "Hey," she says, a little breathless. "What are the rules again?"

"The rules," I say, "are that there are no rules."

And then I'm stepping within an inch of her and leaning in and pressing my mouth lightly against hers, teasing her bottom lip until I make her say my name.

She is sweet and tart—and I think I like that orange wine too.

I've wanted her so badly all night, I can barely contain myself. And, judging by the way she's grinding against me, she feels the same.

My hands are tangled in her hair, my mouth is on her neck, my fingers are unbuttoning the front of her dress until she gets frustrated and just tugs it down.

"Christ," I mumble. "It's so fucking hard to keep my hands off you."

"You should definitely keep them *on* me," she says, breathing ragged.

"You mean, like this?" I ask, slipping a hand inside her bra.

She hums against my mouth. "Yup. For starters." I slide the straps off her shoulders and unhook her bra, so it drops and she's exposed in the light. Rake my hand back across her ribs and up and brush a thumb over her nipple.

"Holy fuck," I say, dazed, looking at her.

"Holy fuck," she says, looking at me.

We hear a creak to our right and both freeze. Turn in slo-mo. But it's just a chicken.

"What if someone comes?" she whispers.

"Then they're going to get a show."

She laughs. But then she doesn't.

Because there is no way either of us are stopping. No matter what happens. Because then my mouth is on her chest and she's arching against me, her hands clawing at my shoulders, at the bulge in my pants.

And then I'm slipping my palms up under that skirt I've been trying not to fixate on all night long and pinning her hips against the slatted wall. My hands are rough against her insanely smooth skin. Our breath is heavy, in sync. My hands slide to cup her ass, as my fingertips graze the lace edge of her underwear and I pull her closer to me. I slip my thumbs into either side of her underwear at her hip bones and drag them down, so they fall to her ankles.

"Here?" she asks, surprise in her voice.

"Here," I nod.

And she doesn't protest.

Because then she's stepping out of them in her heels and I'm bending to kneel in the grass, dropping between her legs and resting her thigh on my shoulder as I kiss up her inner leg and get to work.

24

NELLIE
TODAY

We are out in the open. Outside. Anyone could stumble past. I can feel the breeze blowing by my exposed skin. It gives me goose bumps. But I don't care.

Not anymore.

In this instant, I'm glad we kept things a secret. Because that secret let me keep what's brewing between us for myself just a little longer. Hoard it away. That secret led us here, to this barn wall, rough against my back, my hands in his hair, so insane for him that I have to bite my cheek to stay quiet.

As everything pulls tight in me, I lose track of where the outer world ends and my insides begin, the stars populating the sky melding with the fireworks popping off behind my lids.

I'm kinetic, inside and out, as I tug on his shirt at the shoulder and pull him to standing.

"Had enough?" he asks, his lids heavy.

I shake my head, huffing. "I need more."

He props a strong hand on the wall behind my head and leans in to kiss me again and, as much as I want it, I stop him, put a finger to his lips.

"Oh, see, but, wait. Because, well, look at you. And look at me."

His eyes drop down to his own fully clothed body and then scan up my almost fully naked one.

"Looks right to me."

He's not wrong. I like the rub of his clothes against my bare skin. But I shake my head at him. Slowly, one by one, I undo each button on his shirt, torturing us both. I slip my hands inside, let them road trip across his warm chest, taking their time, then venture down to his taut stomach, slowly unzipping his pants and sliding my palm inside.

"Shit," he groans, low and gravelly, burying his face in my neck. The sound travels through me like a drive on a bumpy road.

"Was it always like this?" I say, almost a whisper. "With us?"

Because I remember. But I don't.

"I thought so," he says. "But that was before I knew *this* existed."

This thing, this revelation.

In my mind, I remember fevered make-out sessions, stolen kisses, urgent pawing when we could find the space. I remember pining for him, missing him even before he lumbered out of sight, a lingering want that sat equally in my heart and between my thighs and could never be satiated. Never enough.

But this is something different—something I didn't think was in the cards. This is all of that plus time. Plus lost years. Plus experience and knowledge and even *skill*. Confidence. Swagger. This is a deep résumé, a strong, banging CV.

Noah is my ideal candidate. And I think maybe, finally, I am looking to fill the position. All the positions.

Including the one we're in right now, his pants around his ankles, my skirt pushed up high, him pressed against me, rock solid.

"Okay," I say, breathless. "Now, we're even."

He lets his gaze travel down me, raises an eyebrow, his chest rising and falling quickly against my own. "Okay," he says. "Now what?"

"Now," I say, "you fuck me."

He is happy to oblige.

My hands come to his muscular back, and he kisses me hard and then harder as I wheeze his name.

I lose all sense of time and place. I'm outside on a vineyard estate in wine country, yes, but I am everywhere else too. Against a stone wall in Riverside Park. Against a bathroom door, precariously pushed shut. On my childhood twin bed when no one is home.

And, afterward, we are breathless, collapsing into each other and laughing lightly.

And we are still chest to chest, when he murmurs, "I want to change the rules."

"I thought there were no rules."

"The new is rule is that there are rules."

I tip my head back against the wall, so I can better see his adorable face shadowed in the darkness. "Who is making these rules?"

"Me," he says. "And only me."

"That seems fair," I laugh.

"Fair is overrated."

He is kidding, but he is not kidding. I can see it in the intensity of his eyes, glowing like their own moons, inches from my own.

Even a day ago, I would have been afraid of what he was about to say. Afraid that he was about to set boundaries that would hurt my pride, that he was backing slowly away, having scratched some kind of childhood itch.

But I know better now. I know Noah *now*. Adult Noah. Who is kind and funny and thoughtful and a little bit irritable when other men hit on me.

I know Noah—who knows *me*.

"Alright," I say. "I'll bite."

He raises an eyebrow. "That I know."

I roll my eyes but also smile. Rotate my hand, to suggest he should say the thing.

"The first new rule is that this isn't over."

"I see."

"The second rule is that you don't get to freak out about it and run for the hills."

"Hmm. Which hills exactly?"

"The third rule is that you are open to the idea of coming back to LA. Of trying to transition to art directing for movies or TV because you have a skill set that could transfer even though it's not totally the same. To see if maybe it's for you. Because your job in New York is ending. And you love LA and you wanted to try something different anyway. And Sabrina lives there. And Rita does. And also, as it happens, so do I."

I purse my lips, amused. "'Cause it's that easy. And?"

"The fourth and final rule is that instead of going back to the party, you come back to our suite with me and let me do stuff to you and you don't leave again until I have to go to the airport in the morning."

Sounds like heaven—except for the part where he leaves. I push that out of my head.

"Well, I'm going to have to draw the line there," I say, toying with the collar of his open shirt. "I have a best friend who just got not-married who is going to be not happy if I don't go back and dance and belt out power ballads with her."

Noah stares at me hard, like maybe he was joking just then, but he is *not* joking. And he says, "What about the rest of it?"

I look back at him—his bright eyes, his stubbly jaw, the scar on his cheek. And I realize, I won't say no to him. Whatever happened in our past, whatever complications exist now, I need to at least be open to finding a path for us to be together. Because all of my resolve has melted. As unlikely as it seemed just days ago, I found the man for me when I was just a teen. And I'm not going to let him go again.

I'm scared. I'm unsure. There are definitely flutters in my chest.

But I have to trust him.

He is not the boy from before—Sabrina told me, Rita told me, Noah himself told me.

And I can see it for myself.

"I will take that all under advisement," I say with a half-smile.

"I'm going to need some clarification on that."

"I like you," I say, even though inside it makes me squirm, even though the words aren't big enough for what I actually feel. "I like you and I'm willing to try. Is that enough clarity for your stubborn ass?"

He smiles, big now. Smooths a hand over my hair, then tucks it behind my ear. "I'll take it."

"Okay. Now let me get dressed before I have a humiliating run-in with a cater waiter."

"Right," he says, as if just remembering where we are.

And as we put ourselves back together, as I watch him button his shirt as I pull up my dress, I feel warm inside. There is a light blooming in my chest.

"I'm glad you aren't in a coma," I say.

And he shakes his head like I've lost it and smiles.

"Should we tell people we're together?" I ask Noah, as we start back toward the party. "Like, screw it, maybe?"

I sort of want to shout from the rooftops.

He thinks, then shakes his head. "I kind of like having this just be our own thing for now."

I'm mildly disappointed by his answer even though I'm the one who originally suggested the secrecy, but I accept it and let it go. The truth is, I know he's right. Telling people will change things. We scatter our re-entry to the party—with a promise from him to carry the carton of orange wine. Not because we're hiding anything anymore, but because there's no reason to complicate the night.

We're feeling good. Why welcome other opinions?

With a single glance back at Noah in the dark, so damn handsome, leaning on his shoulder against the overflow shed, I walk back to the party—hopefully not in too much disarray.

I'm about to start up the stairs back to the treehouse space, when a voice startles me in the dark.

"If it isn't Eleanor Hurwitz," says Damien, standing there like maybe he's been waiting.

"You scared me," I say, a hand to my chest.

He tips his blond head, laughs. "Nellie, are you afraid of the dark?"

I roll my eyes. But he is not done talking. He is *never* done talking.

"I remember you still slept with a stuffed animal in high school," he says. "And I remember its name: Hairball."

I have to admit, I'm surprised he remembers that very specific detail about my matted stuffy. "Wow," I say. "Good memory."

He's right. I slept with Hairball coiled against my chest until I was way too old.

"Yeah, I have a good memory," he says. "But I also always paid special attention to you. Like we talked about. The other day in town."

I'm afraid of where this conversation is going and so, despite the discomfort I feel, I decide to get ahead of it. "Damien, I've always liked you," I lie. "But you know I didn't mean it *that* way, right? Like, we were always friends."

"Yeah," he shrugs, though I see a twinge of something else pass over his face too. "I know. It never happened for us. But who knows what the future holds?"

"Well, I do," I say. "Because the thing is, even if there was something like that between us, I couldn't do that because . . ."

He sighs. Shakes his head. "Because of Noah."

"Because of Noah," I say. "There's just too much history."

He stares at me, hard. Even in the dark, his blue eyes are piercing. Unsettled, I set a hand on the railing, like it's my escape route. Like I can't get away fast enough.

He sees it. Sees me wanting to leave. "Or maybe it's not just history," he says.

"Oh, well, I mean . . . no. It's just . . ."

"I'm not an idiot, Nellie," he spits.

"No," I say. "You're not."

We stand there considering each other for a beat. A breeze blows past carrying a new chill. And suddenly I wonder how long he's been standing here. What, if anything, he saw.

"Cara is probably looking for me," I say, as lightly as I can manage, and turn toward the stairs, taking them two at a time.

25

BOTH

BACK IN THE DAY

Noah calls. He does.

He leaves messages on her answering machine. They are brief. Because someone else might hear. But also they're brief because he is angry too.

Nell. Call me.

Nell. Just trying you again.

Nell. We should talk. Before you leave.

He doesn't say he's sorry. Nell notes this as she sits on her pinstriped beanbag chair and listens to them over and over, analyzing the cadence of his voice.

When she's not listening to "Fuck and Run" on repeat.

He knows he was wrong. He knows he acted like a scumbag. He knows he should have shown up when she reached out about the pregnancy scare, that she was frightened and alone. He knows he shouldn't have gotten drunk and kissed some other girl, especially one Lydia served up. *Of course not.*

He knows he has pushed Nell away.

And she is probably the best thing that ever happened to him—or ever will happen to him.

But also, she is leaving. And she is leaving him *behind*.

And actually, with each day she doesn't call back, he feels more like she already left.

And she's not the first person in his life to do that. Which she knows. She knows about his dad.

And she is freezing Noah out when he is in all kinds of pain—physical, emotional. When he is a mess because of his injury. When he has lost what feels like everything.

Nellie thinks he can't take it when things get tough—but what about her? Now that he is no one's golden boy, she isn't sticking around either.

She can't muster up empathy for him. Though he has no plan now. Though he will have to take a gap year. Though he is untethered, floating through space toward a giant black hole.

And so he tries to reach her. A few times. But it's no grand gesture. He walks by her building, once. Sees her father coming home from work, his jacket slung over his arm. Hides behind a scaffolding pole.

Wonders how much the family knows.

Wonders how this man who welcomed him with open arms—at family dinners, at birthdays, to architectural unveilings, when he needed fatherly advice—would react to seeing him now. Noah can't face the awkwardness, the probable rejection.

And so he goes home. And he doesn't try again.

26

NELLIE
TODAY

There is dancing. There is singing—way off-key. There are kamikaze shots I haven't done since college. There are joints for other people—the ones who can handle it. There is Britney and Kelly and Taylor and Olivia and Patti Smith and Pat Benatar and Queen Bey. There is A Tribe Called Quest, De La Soul, Biggie Smalls, Eminem, a little Nicki Minaj. There are bathroom breaks and late-night pizza orders. There is yelling above the din of the music. There is laughing, hugs, sentimental tears, laughing again. There is Cara's smile and Sabrina's snark and Rita's slightly deranged line-dance moves—enacted even more terribly by Ben.

There is a picked-up breeze, a whistle through the trees. Twinkle lights that sway with the ghosts of parties past. Flower arrangements that topple and are saved. Spilled glasses of wine splashed along once-white tablecloths. The smell of night-blooming jasmine. Cozy table blankets for staying warm during dancing breaks; hair swept into buns when it gets hot on the dance floor.

There is a night. One we'll remember. And, all the time, I see Noah mostly across the room.

I know we agreed not to mention what's happening between us to anyone, but it feels like maybe he's keeping too much distance. As much as I hate to admit it, those old vulnerable feelings are creeping in, just the tiniest bit.

I try to push them back out the door.

I avoid Damien, too. Maybe that's part of why I don't see Noah that much. It feels like Damien is an appendage, always lurking at Noah's and Ben's side, dark and stormy, yet another drink in his hand.

But I don't do a good enough job. Because, finally, as we are nearing dawn, light just beginning to encroach on the night's edges, I collapse into a chair next to Cara with a tall glass of water (not Noah, an actual one).

"I have to pee," she says to me. "Again. I don't want to. It sounds boring. Like a waste of time. But I have to all the same."

"Sad story," I say.

"Do you have to pee again too?"

I shake my head. "You're on your own, lady."

I love drunk Cara. I love every Cara.

"Damn shame," she mumbles, as she pushes herself to standing, slips her heels back on, and wanders toward the restrooms. "Save my seat!" she calls, before she disappears down the stairs.

I place a hand proprietarily on her chair. Which is unnecessary because I am surrounded by empty seats. And that proves unfortunate because that's when I feel a shadow overtake me, as someone settles on the other side of me.

"Having fun?" Damien asks.

I *was*, I think.

"Yeah," I sigh instead. "It's nice to all be together again."

He laughs, but it's sharp and ugly. "Right. Together again. One big happy family."

I know I shouldn't take the bait. But he is raining on my parade and, if I can't escape him, at least I can tell him to shut the fuck up. In the kindest way, of course.

"Is something wrong, Damien?"

"Lots of things are wrong. It's all wrong."

I am not a patient woman. And right now I just can't. I turn to face him. "What's your problem?"

"My problem?" he scoffs, pointing at me. "I don't have one. You, though. You have a problem."

He is drunk and slurring and I should ignore his stupid ass. But I can't help myself, so instead I say, "What's my problem? That you know so much about?"

"I thought you were engaged," he says, in place of answering me.

"Oh," I say, looking down. "Well, I'm not."

He stares at me with bloodshot eyes. "I never took you for a liar."

"Well, I always took you for one." It flies out of my mouth before I can stop it. I am the old me. The sparring me. The me who says the thing. It is unwise; it is not helpful. But, if I'm honest, it feels good.

He squints at me, considers me. Like he's seeing me in a new light. And then he smiles, which I think I like less than his frown.

"You always called it like you saw it," he says, almost appreciatively. And, for a moment, we both watch Ben attempt the Kid 'n Play because we are old as fuck. "It's nice to see that side of you again. I thought you'd gone soft. Ironic, though. That you're so sure about who's a liar."

I roll my eyes. "And what's that supposed to mean? Who's the liar? That's what you want me to ask, right?"

He just shakes his head at me. "I can't believe you fell for that shit—*again*."

"Fell for what?"

"For Noah."

"Who says I fell for—?"

"And the thing is," he steamrolls over me, "I tried to warn you. Back in the day *and* this time. I tried to tell you, but—just like everyone else—you're so on his jock that you can't see."

"Excuse me. I'm not on anyone's jock," I say. "Partially because no one has said that since 1994."

But there's a fluttering starting to rise in my chest, an unease that sets everything at an odd angle. Feeling at sea, I scan the dance floor, the space, the bar, looking for Noah. I just want a visual on him, so I can remind myself that I know who he is, no matter how his supposed friend is trying to gaslight me.

I am not back on that couch, at that awful house party, watching Noah disappear before my eyes. I am not back where I started.

Damien laughs loudly. Only it's not really a laugh. It's more like a jolt, a stab, a punch to the gut. "You sure looked like you were on his jock back by the barn . . ."

My cheeks go hot. I'm sure I turn red. Maybe even purple. Because I am embarrassed. Of course I am. But I'm also *real* mad.

This feels like an invasion. A corruption of something good. Like he's stolen something from me.

I turn to face him, willing myself to discard the humiliation and go with the rage. "What? So now you go around spying on people?"

"Well, honey," he says, smug as fuck, "if you don't want an audience, then get a room."

I shoot to standing, so that my chair topples over behind me with a loud crash. I glower down at him.

"You know, I never liked you," I say, above the pounding in my chest. "I never trusted you. I put up with you, faked it, to keep the peace. I watched you plant toxic seeds in Noah's head, try to plant ideas in mine. You were always so fucking jealous of him. And you still are."

And now it's Damien's turn to flush, his pale skin going blotchy and heated. "Jealous of Noah? Please! Why? Because he had everyone fooled? Thinking he was so fucking charming when he was really just fucked up. I wasn't jealous. I was disgusted. It was pathetic. *You* were pathetic. And you still are."

Inside me, the pendulum has swung so far. It's impossible to imagine that only minutes before, I was awash in a love fest with my best friends, relaxed and free and literally crying with gratitude for the wonderful people in my life. And now, this asshat has corroded everything, coating it with a layer of tar and grime.

And I think I'm more angry about that than anything else. How dare he ruin this incandescent memory for me?

"Just stay the fuck away from me," I say, and turn to escape—to anywhere else. Adrenaline tsunamis through me.

But now he is on his feet, following close behind me. "Wait, Nellie. Please. I'm sorry. I'm drunk. Don't fucking listen to me. I don't think you're pathetic. I never thought you were pathetic."

I turn to face him, my heart thundering in my chest. "You don't get it: I don't give a shit what you think."

"I was trying to protect you!"

"This is your version of protecting someone? Violating them? Humiliating them? Degrading them?"

He looks to the sky, presses the heels of his hands into his eyes. "This isn't what I wanted to happen."

"What did you want?" I ask him.

"I just wanted to protect you from *that*!" he says, gesturing behind a tall wall of speakers. "Where's your boy now?"

And then I see it. Catch a glimpse from the side where there's a gap in the sound equipment. I see *him*. Noah. Standing half-hidden, facing Lydia, the strap of her dress pushed off her shoulder, his hand on her side. He's leaning toward her, so they're only inches apart.

And I flash to the moment not long before when we were that close. When he pushed the strap of my dress down too.

With fucking Damien watching.

There is an intake of breath. Mine. Before the full weight of what I am witnessing descends, crashing down on me like another tidal wave.

That's when Noah feels my gaze on him, like he always does. He looks up, meets my eyes, cocks his head, and then sees what I'm seeing. He bolts away from Lydia and toward me.

"No, no, no," he says, as he comes closer. "It's not what it looks like. I know that sounds like bullshit, but for real."

I shake my head, too stunned to move. Too disappointed. Too sad.

As I force myself to turn to leave, Noah gently grabs my upper arm to stop me. I shake him free. "Don't touch me!"

At that, the music stops. And suddenly all eyes are on me. The last thing I want in this moment.

"Nell, Lydia had an injury she just wanted me to check out."

I roll my eyes. "How dumb do you think I am?"

"If you believe it was more than that, pretty dumb."

"Is that supposed to be *funny*?"

"Nell," he says, taking a deep breath to steady himself. "I'm telling you the truth. D, back me up! He was there. Lydia came up and asked me to check out her shoulder. Right?"

Damien shakes his head. "I'm not covering for you anymore, dude. I'm done. She deserves better."

Noah's mouth drops open like an escape hatch. Stunned that his boy has turned on him. "Wow," he says, staring at Damien with a mash-up of confusion and anger. "Just fucking wow."

I look from Noah, to Damien, to Lydia, who flashes me a wink and a smile.

I've never cared enough to even wonder why she despises me so much. But in that moment, I realize she hates me a thousand times more than I hate her.

Noah takes a step toward Damien like he might punch him in the face. And the tension in the space ratchets up, as others consider stepping in. I don't care if they pulverize each other into tiny particles—but I don't want to be here to see it.

"I'm leaving," I say, and turn toward the stairs. And I mean it. I am leaving this party, this property, this state, maybe this hemisphere.

I will set up a new Planet Nellie. Somewhere very far away from these assholes.

"Nell!" Noah calls, turning back to me. "It's *me*. You know me. I wouldn't do this."

"I don't know what the hell is going on," I say, my eyes starting to well, "but I know I don't want any part of it. I don't like this *at all*."

I don't want to feel this way. I will not cry in front of these people. I will not give any of them the satisfaction.

"What's happening?" Cara says, returning from the bathroom and coming to stand beside me. Her makeup is smudged from our night of festivities, but she looks otherwise happy, glowing—or she did moments before. "What's going on?"

I have already robbed her of something.

This brings me back down to earth, helps me grab at the pieces and try to press them back together in my mind. "Nothing, CB. Go back to the party! I'm so sorry."

She looks at Noah, looks at me. "Did something happen? Why are you fighting?"

Neither of us answer. We have sworn each other to secrecy. Noah's lips part, like he wants to speak, but he's likely not sure what to say. Let alone how to defend what he's done.

Cara turns to Sabrina and Rita, who have joined the crowd of onlookers. "Why are they fighting?"

They share an unsure look. Also don't answer.

"Someone fucking tell me what's happening?!" Cara demands. And it is so out of character that we all go still. "Sabrina!"

"I think," Sabrina says, shooting a tentative look at me, "they're together."

"Who? Noah and Nellie? They're together?" Cara's brow, so relaxed moments before, is now crinkled in confusion. "You're *together*?"

"Yes," says Noah, just as I say "No!"

"Since when?" When Sabrina doesn't answer, Cara shoots her another commanding look. She is not suffering fools.

"Since the day they skipped the booze bus, I think," Sab mumbles, avoiding my eyes.

But I'm not mad at her. I'd rather she betray me than the un-bride.

"But that was days ago," Cara says, puzzling it all together. She turns her gaze on me. "You didn't tell me. I kept apologizing for sending you on those errands together. I kept checking in when you were stuck in the storm. And you never said a thing."

I open my mouth to apologize, the crushing weight of my mistakes rooting me to the spot. Paralyzing me. But before I can speak, Cara cocks her head and says, "What about Alfie?"

I clear my throat. I glance at Sabrina and Rita. I glance at Noah. Even Damien. They're all watching me expectantly. "Um. We broke up," I say, quietly. "Over a month ago."

"Broke up?" The hurt on Cara's face is undeniable. It's like something vibrant has gone out of her as she frowns. "Why wouldn't you tell me?"

And when I look into my best friend's face, her earnest bewilderment reflected in every angle, no viable excuse presents itself. So I tell her the truth: "I don't know."

"We're supposed to be best friends," Cara says. She looks from me to Sabrina, her eyes welling.

"I'm sorry," I say, as Sabrina mumbles the same.

"I don't know why I planned this stupid trip," Cara says, shaking her head. "It was obviously a mistake. Do whatever the fuck you want. I'm done." And then she rushes away, Ben close behind her.

He glances back from the top of the stairs, shooting us a disappointed look. Me most of all.

Sabrina sighs, her eyes downcast.

"I guess I should have told her," I murmur.

"Which part?" Sabrina asks, a sharp tone to her voice.

"I don't know. All of it."

She huffs impatiently. "Yeah, I think a lot could have been avoided if you were just honest."

"I didn't want to make this trip about me."

Sabrina looks at me, her own anger playing on her face. "Yeah? How's that going?"

She shakes her head and stalks off, too.

27

NOAH
TODAY

She looks so small. That's what I think as I watch Nell standing in the wake of Cara and Sabrina storming off. In the wake of this epic combustion.

Her arms are wrapped around her body like she is protecting herself. Only she can't protect herself from the reality of what she—and I—have caused.

Her eyeliner is smudged.

I take a step toward her, thinking maybe I could offer comfort, but she backs away.

And that's when I know—there's no coming back from this.

The music has started up again. The crowd is beginning to disperse. Damien has skulked off to some corner of hell. I'll deal with his ass later.

That relationship is obviously over. I wonder for a moment when it actually ended. Was it always this twisted or has the decay collected over time, eating away at layers of friendship until there was nothing left but trumped-up memories and hidden resentment?

But I can deal with that loss. It will take time, but I can sort out how I missed the truth about him, how I tolerated what I knew was unacceptable for so many years. I can even confront the role I played in the ugly thing this friendship became, letting him play beta to me for so long that he finally lashed out.

I can deal with almost anything, if Nell will just talk to me. But her face is a slammed door. And I'm stuck on the other side.

She grabs her clutch, makes her way toward the stairs. And I follow behind that little black dress that seems to droop now. I know she needs space, but we have so little time.

The sun is starting to come up. The night sky is overexposed, lifting slowly to muted violet. Even the birds have begun to awake, stretching their wings and making plans for the day.

Today, we go home. My flight is in a matter of hours. And the chance of me fixing this from a distance is slim to none. I've got to make her talk to me now.

So, I follow her down the stairs until we're out of earshot of all the others. Until we are with the chickens again, but this time without the magic. I call her name. But she doesn't turn around.

Finally, I catch up to Nell, put a hand on her upper arm to stop her.

She stills. But she doesn't turn to face me. I can see her shoulders starting to quake, and then she's racked with sobs. And I feel horrible, like a fucking monster. I want to wrap my arms around her, hug her close, kiss her head, her cheeks, make it better. But I know this woman well enough to know that isn't an option.

Not right now. She won't accept my help.

"Nell," I say again, softly. "Please turn around."

"Leave me alone," she hiccups.

"I can't," I say.

Slowly, she turns to face me. Her eyes are pink-rimmed and flooded. And the sadness in her expression, in her wobbling chin, is almost too much to bear, especially in contrast to the way she looked at me just hours before—with trust, need, amusement.

"What you saw with Lydia," I say, "was literally nothing."

"It wasn't nothing."

"Nell, it was. I'm not interested in her. I've never been interested in her."

She sniffles. "I don't know what's true," she says carefully. "And I think that alone is an insurmountable problem."

"I don't totally understand what happened myself," I say. "But Damien volunteered me to take a look at her injury and then... well, you know the rest."

There is a weariness in Nell's face that scares me more than the previous anger or the impatience. Like she doesn't have the energy to fight for us, to push past the bullshit.

Like we've time-traveled to somewhere neither of us wanted to go and can't get back to present day.

"Maybe that's true," she says. "But why would you even agree to that? She's not your friend. She's definitely not mine. You know our history. You know how she treats me. You have never truly been able to put me first; you've always been too worried about being liked to take that stand. And you're not hearing me—I don't *trust* you."

"Nell!" I say, running a hand over my head in frustration—though some of what she says rings true. Does my need for approval—my need to people-please—overshadow my judgment? "I'm not a cheater."

"It's not just that," she says, smearing the tears beneath her eyes with the back of her hand. They are only replaced by more. "It's not just about other women. It's bigger than that. I don't trust you to choose me or to make the right decisions. I don't trust you with my heart. You're not careful with me—and I can't just forget that. I warned you a *million* times about Damien. Henny did too! And you never listened—you always swore he had your back!"

"I was wrong, but—"

"You didn't listen to me! He *saw* us tonight, you know. He saw us. *Me*. Here. And he made sure to let me know. It's already ruined!"

A raw rage tears through me, stronger than I think I have ever felt before. I want to find Damien and destroy him. Like he's destroying this for me. Like he has destroyed something for this remarkable woman in front of me.

Like he has disrespected her.

"A million years ago, I thought we were forever," she says. "And you didn't show up for me when things got hard and then you broke my heart. And you *still* didn't choose me! Even after all that—the pregnancy scare, that kiss—you didn't fight for me. You just let me leave your life forever!"

"Nell," I say, squinting against the rising sun. I can feel myself losing my grip on this. "I asked you to stay. I asked you not to go to California. I *begged* you not to leave me behind. But you didn't choose *me*! You closed yourself off and left. And now you're doing it again. What was I supposed to do?"

There is quiet between us for a beat as my question settles, sees the looming light of day.

"I don't know," she says, crossing her arms over her chest. "But you don't either. And that's the problem. You still think I didn't choose you, but the options were only on your terms. You always expect me to be the one to adjust for you. We tried this out and look—it's a disaster again! My two best friends are barely speaking to me, we just ruined the celebration that Ben and Cara worked so hard to plan. You're asking me to forget the past, uproot myself, come to LA, risk the life I've built, risk getting hurt—I can't do all that."

"I'm asking you to be with me!" I plead, hating the desperation in my voice.

"But you have no idea what comes next," she says. "So, *I'm* deciding now."

"Nell, please . . ." I say because I know I'm losing her. I can see her disappearing like some flickering hologram. She is already gone. Her mind is made up.

Her incredible, impossible mind.

"I'm not mad at you," she says, running a hand through her hair and exhaling a shuddering breath. "Not like before. I want you to know that."

And I wish she was. Because mad I can work with. Resigned not so much. Defeated not so much. Goodbye not at all.

But now *I'm* starting to get mad. Because she's doing it again. She's not choosing me again—*us* again. She's not *trying* again.

She looks at me for an extended moment, like either she's trying to memorize or erase my face from her mind. "Take care," she says.

She turns her back on me. So I do the same.

And I am left feeling noxious, toxic, ready to burst. And I'm thinking I know exactly who to take it out on. My hand curls into a fist.

But it's like she can read my mind.

"Noah," she says, and I turn back around. "He's not worth hurting your hands."

And then she leaves.

I watch her recede again.

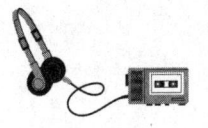

28

BOTH

BACK IN THE DAY

On Nell's plane to LA for college, there are tiny bags of peanuts. A window seat, thank God. Room in the overhead compartment, though she struggles to push her suitcase up and in.

"Can I help you?" asks a guy just a few years older.

"No thank you," she says.

She doesn't need help. She will not make that mistake again.

The flight is smooth. The middle seat next to her is empty. The movie is *Four Weddings and a Funeral*. For Nellie, the weddings also feel like funerals.

There is a woman with a baby, which sends Nellie's brain to dangerous corners, considering what she has just been through. She calls it back from the edge. Out the window, there is the platonic ideal of clouds. White, fluffy. But she knows they're just vapor.

She takes a deep breath. Inhales recycled air. Smiles at the nice grandmother-aged lady in the aisle seat, who keeps offering to share her peanut butter crackers. She asks where Nellie is headed.

"College," she says, forcing the expected smile.

"Wow! That's so exciting," the woman sighs. "But it's hard to leave home behind."

Home, *yes*. And her parents. Even her brother. But that isn't all she's leaving behind. She has also abandoned innocence. Hope. Stranded faith, trust. Deserted impulsivity, familiarity.

Childhood.

She has already left it all behind. Like so many stuffed animals. Like Hairball.

"Are you going to miss anyone in particular?" the woman asks.

Nellie nods. "Yes," she says. "My cat."

At home, Noah feels her leave, physically. Even though he hasn't seen her in months. Feels her board the plane. Teeter down the runway, ears popping as she ascends—up, up, and definitely *away*.

At home, everything looks the same. Noah lies in bed, stares up at his ceiling. There are the same posters—Mariano Rivera, Derek Jeter, Dave Winfield. *The Low End Theory*. *Ready to Die*. Nirvana's *Nevermind*. The same cracks in the moldings. Same smell of garlic sautéing in the pan as his mom cooks dinner—Thursday is sausage and peppers night.

But nothing is the same. And nothing is okay.

His crutches lean against his desk, one threatening to fall. His knee is bandaged. His pre-op appointment is tomorrow.

His future has turned from gold to dust. But that is not what's worst. What's worst is that he's mad. But he can't tell at whom.

He is mad at his knee. At the grade-three tear in his ACL. That's for sure. At the kid who hit the fly ball that sent him running and sliding into second. He is mad at his dad—because he is always mad at his dad. He is mad at his mom for trying to make him feel better, and at his sister for saying, "Your life isn't over." For wondering aloud what happened with Nell.

It's none of her business.

He is crazy mad at Nell, too. More so now than when they first stopped speaking.

Of course he is. For abandoning him, for leaving him. For not understanding that his life imploded. For expecting him to be the same even though everything had changed. For forcing him into corners where he made bad decisions—which he otherwise clearly would not have made.

And he's mad at her family because he suspects, on some level, that they never thought he measured up. Never thought he was smart or driven enough. And no doubt they *definitely* urged her to get as far away from his ass as possible.

Mad at her dad because they were close and—now what? Now Noah is just erased from the picture?

But, if he is truly honest, which he would rather not be, he is most angry at himself. Because *what has he done?*

What. Has. He. Done.

Another wave of nausea overtakes him.

He places his palms on either side of his head, squeezes, like he might fix his brain. Stop thinking all the thoughts.

His beeper buzzes. He picks it up. Calls the number back.

"D," he says. "What's up?"

"Come over, bro," Damien says. "We're playing *Street Fighter*."

"I don't know," Noah says.

"Yo! Forget that girl already! She's old news."

"It's not that easy."

"Noah," Damien snaps. "Don't be a pussy."

And so he goes.

29

NELLIE
TODAY

By the time I wake up, Noah is gone. I can tell by the way the space feels before I see the clues. The actual negative space. The holes he left.

The suite feels empty.

And so do I.

I pick up the itinerary. The final day says: "Day 6: *Goodbye to All That* . . ." I scan the code and Semisonic starts belting out "Closing Time." Because . . . of course.

And it's silly, but I am an easy target and even that makes my eyes well.

There's a lump in my throat the size of Texas—or maybe it's California. Either way, it's obstructing my airways. I feel like I can't breathe.

And I know this feeling. Because I have been here before. Decades ago. When I left for LA alone.

Only today, I am making the opposite journey. I am leaving California for New York. For home. And instead of being unsure of what to expect, of what adventures might be in store, I know exactly what awaits me—right down to the Jenni Kayne and Clare V. catalogues waiting in my mailbox. The Con Edison bills. The flyers for Thai and Mexican takeout and cheap movers wedged into my doorjamb.

The bodega cat has surely missed snarling at me.

I am packing up my suitcase, burying my face in my Dillon Beach T-shirt, which still smells vaguely of him, and trying not to cry, when I hear someone come up behind me. I whip around, hoping it's Noah. But it's someone much shorter and less complicated. Someone to whom I owe a massive apology.

"CB," I say. "You came."

And then I burst into tears.

She crosses the room and hugs me, hard. Lets me blow my nose on her super-soft top.

"It's okay," she keeps saying. "It's going to be okay."

And not for the first time, I think, her kids are so lucky to have her as a mom.

I finally take a wheezing breath and pull back, looking into her concerned face.

"I'm sorry!" I say. "I should be begging for your forgiveness and instead I'm weeping all over you."

"No, don't apologize," Cara says. "I like it."

"You like it?"

"Well, *like* might be the wrong word. But at least you're letting me in. That's all I really wanted."

We settle quietly beside each other on the bed, my rattled breaths coming slower and slower until I am almost calm.

I bite my lip, toy with the seam of the T-shirt in my hands, then I dare to sneak a peek at my best friend. She is no longer trying on the new boho vibe. Instead, she's wearing one of her signature French striped tees, tailored army-green shorts, her hair back. And when

I look at her, I can see the her from today, of course. But I can also see so many versions of her—the kid I first met, the math genius, the teenager, the college student, the twentysomething, the career woman killing it, the mom.

The person who took so many shots last night and is somehow still standing.

There's a clear path from the beginning to now. Yet, she scratches her head like she's confused about how we landed here.

I know I am so lucky to have her. I can't believe I ruined her party—there's a knot in my stomach that feels like it will never loosen.

And that's what I deserve—because what kind of lifelong friend destroys your un-wedding? That's been in the works for months and months, maybe even longer? Because Cara has been talking about getting us all together—our *Big Chill* moment sans the funeral—for *years* now.

The self-loathing is real.

"I'm so sorry," I say again, when I can finally will myself to speak, though it isn't enough. "I know I can say that a thousand times and it won't change how last night ended. But I'm still just going to keep saying it: I'm sorry, CB. That's not how I wanted *anything* to go. That's not what you deserve."

She toggles her head and, because she's a better woman than I, she says, "I know, Nells. It's okay."

"It's not okay," I say, shaking my head. "But that's how it went. And I'm still trying to unravel where I went wrong."

"I think maybe it was when you stopped telling me ... *everything*."

"Yeah," I say, bringing a hand to my shoulder and kneading where it has started to feel sore again. "That definitely didn't help."

She turns to face me then, propping her knee on the bed between us. And the look on her face kind of breaks me further. Because instead of angry, she looks hurt. Now her big brown eyes are welling too.

"Nellie. Why didn't you tell me? Do you not feel close enough to me anymore? Were you worried I would judge you?"

I have to think about that for a second, consider the truth versus the narrative I have told myself for so long, as I stare at the vaulted ceiling. "No," I say, finally. "It was never that. I don't feel less close to you—at least I don't want to. And I don't ever feel judged by you. I mean, I'm the judgmental one."

We both shake our heads and mumble something similar simultaneously like, "Not counting Sab."

We smile at each other.

"The thing is, Cara, you have so much on your plate. More than I can even understand. Two small kids and a husband and this giant job. Your time is so precious. I never want to bother you with my petty shit. You have *so* much going on in your life."

"But that's what you don't understand," she says, frustrated. "I have *nothing* going on in my life. I mean, yes. All those things—but also nothing. Every day is the same. I wake up, I get the kids to school or day care, I get myself to work, I sit on Zoom, I sit in conference rooms, I drink the same iced latte, occasionally with oat milk. I leave work, I get home, I make dinner. *Again.* Some members of my family maybe eat it. Mostly they whine for dessert. And then I basically pass out from fatigue and, before it feels like I've even really slept, I wake up and start again. I feel like the most boring person alive!"

How have I missed this? This struggle she is having. How have I been so self-involved that I didn't notice my best friend was wrestling with her own growing pains?

I have been so obsessed with feeling left behind in some way, with thinking that I didn't have a right to her time, that I forgot that moving forward is hard too.

"You're not the most boring person alive," I say. "I know that for a fact. Because that's definitely Ben's friend Percy from college. I know because I had to talk to him at cocktails the first night about his mortgage, and I fell asleep with my eyes open."

She giggles, despite herself. "Poor Percy."

"Poor Percy." I put a hand to my heart.

"The point is, I need to hear your petty shit," Cara says. "I live for your petty shit. And your less petty shit, too. Because it helps me feel like *me*." She sighs, places her hands slightly behind her, and leans back. "Nellie, it's been a really hard stretch." She drags a hand across her forehead. "I feel like I don't even know who I am anymore. It's like I've totally lost myself—and now I'm just a snack dispenser and a lady in waiting for two tiny lunatics—and one larger, lovable dumbass."

Suddenly, I can see the exhaustion in her face like it was always there. Only I hadn't been looking. Like one of those optical illusions. An autostereogram. Where the image emerges when you stop trying to focus. "Oh, CB."

"I used to be fun! Right? Didn't I used to be fun?"

"You're still fun! The most fun!"

"Meh," she says, frowning. "I feel like a fun killer. And I've been dragging Ben all over the city, to Japanese whisky bars and like Peruvian hand roll restaurants and God knows what else Instagram served me, trying to recapture something. I just wanted to feel . . . free or something again." She smiles sadly. "I'm not even sure he wanted to do this party. But I pushed him into it. And, actually, I do think having a little time together without the kids helped."

I study her face for a beat, the crease between her brows. "Why didn't you tell me you were feeling this way?"

"Maybe one thing we have in common is that we don't like other people to know when it feels like we're failing."

"I hear you," I say, placing a hand on her forearm. "But you are literally never failing. If you're failing, the rest of us are dead in the water. The human race might as well just lie down in defeat."

She sighs. We both do. Then she says, "I'm sorry about Alfie."

I tilt my head, narrow one eye. "Are you, though?"

"No." She shakes her head, definitively. "I hated him. He actually really sucks."

Then it's my turn to shake my head. "I mean, you guys should have told me he was the worst so long ago!"

"What were we going to say? 'Sorry to inform you, but the guy you're planning on marrying is the wettest blanket since we potty-trained Olivia'?"

"Yes. Something like that would have done the trick."

"Next time."

"Oh, God. Please don't let there be a next time."

She squeezes my hand, letting me off the hook too easily. "No next time."

I gaze at the floor, a patch of sunlight falling across the rug like a tiny sliver of hope. "CB, I really do feel awful about last night."

"Eh," she waves me off. "Don't. That was some real-life soap opera drama. No one is going to forget *that* meltdown! It just made the night all the more memorable."

This is a very generous spin. But of course it is. Because that's how my best friend rolls.

"Let's both try to be better about sharing when things blow."

"Let's both be better at asking for help."

We pinky swear. Because on some level, we are still eight years old.

I am absentmindedly folding and refolding the T-shirt in my hands, when she asks me, "So, are you sad? About Noah-who-must-not-be-named?"

I exhale sharply. Will my chin not to quiver. Nod because speaking is out of the question. I am definitely sad. But also, there is no good solution. Not with the lack of trust and the distance and the fact that he expects me to uproot my life. The fact that, on some level, he still thinks *I* have abandoned *him*.

She leans in and hugs me again. We rock a little back and forth. We're quiet in the wake of it all. Everything has already been said.

She pulls back and we just sit there for a minute, soaking it all in. I feel wrung out. But at least the air is clear.

"So, putting you and Noah in this suite together," she says finally, peering around my room and out the door into the common area. "That went well."

We look at each other and chuckle. It's the kind of laugh that starts as a titter, becomes a snicker, morphs into a hiccup and, eventually, graduates to full-on hysteria. Minutes later, Sabrina wanders in to find us both crying and rolling around on the king-sized bed, clutching our bellies.

"Is it safe?" she asks.

That just makes us crack up harder.

"What is happening?" Her eyes are wide, like we've both finally lost it. "And why wasn't I invited?"

"Total disaster!" Cara squeaks, when she can manage to breathe.

"Complete mess!" I sigh-wheeze-laugh.

"Oh, good," Sabrina says. "As long as no one is mad anymore."

As the laughter dissipates, I lie back on the bed on the row of too many pillows, with Cara next to me. Sabrina jumps on too and scoots over to one side, so I'm in the middle.

"I'm exhausted," Cara says. "I think we need a vacation."

I nod. "A just-us vacation."

"A do-nothing vacation," Sabrina says. "Rita likes too many activities. Activities are for the birds. I challenge you to name one good activity!"

"Sleeping in," Cara says.

"Lying by a pool and going back to sleep," I say.

"Eating French fries and talking shit," Cara says.

"Eating cake and talking shit," I say.

"Right?" Sab says. "You guys get it."

I hold up the T-shirt in my hands, examine it. "Should I throw this out?"

"No way!" Cara says, petting it with her palm. "It's too soft."

"Let's not throw out the baby with the bathwater," Sabrina adds.

"Is Noah the baby or the bathwater?"

"Unfortunately for you," Cara says, "I think he's both." Then she turns on her side to face me: "So, what really even happened?"

And so I tell her. I tell them both. Everything. *Finally*. And it comes out in a rush, a full purge. I tell them about my job ending, since the news will break any day. And I tell them everything about Noah. Not just the details about what went down on this trip, but about the history too—the parts I redacted years ago in hopes of protecting . . . I guess myself.

Maybe him on some level?

I think maybe there was a part of me that always thought we'd get back together. And I didn't want them to judge me if I made that choice. When I left LA to live in New York again after college, it was in part to be closer to my family—which proved so fortunate when my dad got sick shortly afterward. But also, I think some part of me believed maybe Noah and I would find each other again. In our city. With our spots. And our rough edges.

And somehow all the history would evaporate. And I didn't want my friends to think I was weak for taking him back.

But then he was gone.

He evaporated instead.

And my anger grew.

I caught myself looking for him sometimes, in boys I saw rushing down the subway steps or carrying their baseball equipment in a duffel on the train. In young men on green fields with dusty paths to white bases, the changing of the guard from childhood to adulthood.

I tell my friends what happened between us all those years ago.

About the pregnancy scare and him standing me up and my decision to leave for school and his decision to stay behind—and then the kiss. That *kiss*. With that random girl. That took something fluid, that still had at least the possibility of movement, and made it solid—immovable.

Over.

I tell them that the first time I saw him was at that club, that night. And that I obsessed over him, though I never said a word. One of many debauched nights to them maybe, but so significant for me. That I thought about him from that night on—and how I kind of never stopped.

"I had no idea," Cara sighs, like it's romantic and not a stupid tragedy with a side of oysters. "I can't believe you came here after losing your job and breaking up with your fiancé and didn't say a word!"

"I know," I nod.

"No wonder you're a mess!"

"Hey!" I elbow her lightly, smile.

She's too busy reeling to notice. "I can't believe Lydia never told me about him kissing that girl!"

"I mean, it was her friend. She orchestrated it. It didn't exactly make her look good."

"That's true." Cara considers this for a second. "I know she's kind of horrible. But I feel bad for her. I mean, Nellie, she resents you because she doesn't feel good enough."

"True," Sabrina says. "But she's also a dick."

There is a long silence as we digest this. "What Noah did was bad," Cara says, sliding a hand between her head and the pillow. "Really bad. I mean, I understand now why you hated him *so* much. I think if I knew then, I might have trouble forgiving him now, even on your behalf. But now, so many years later, I don't think he's the same mixed-up guy he was then."

"That's probably true."

"We all make mistakes," Sabrina says. "Like some of us throw up in tiny water bottles."

"That seems like a less egregious mistake."

She nods in agreement. "Fair enough."

"But are you sure you can't make it work?" Cara asks, propping herself up. "With the Noah of today?"

"Move to Cali and be near us?" Sabrina says, her eyes brightening. "You need a new job anyway! You guys seemed so psyched together yesterday. Before it all happened. I haven't seen you that lit up in years."

And I know they both just want me to be happy.

"I just can't," I say gently. "It requires more faith than I have left."

30

NOAH
TODAY

She wasn't wrong. Nell.

Well, she was. But not about this.

I'm a surgeon. Better not to hurt my hands. Not over some asshole I outgrew decades ago.

Maybe at some point I would have seen something worth saving in my friendship with Damien. Some relic of a boyhood brother who deserved a chance, simply because of our shared history.

But I've learned a lot about history this week. A lot about the past. There are things worth saving. And there are things it's wiser to let go.

Now I realize he was never who I wanted him to be, who I told myself he was despite all evidence to the contrary, because it was convenient. Because he presented a certain version of himself to me—one that flattered my weakest parts. Made me feel secure.

He was always two people. At least two. And I don't like any of them.

So, when I see him seated near the Japanese stall at SFO's food court, eating ramen out of a red plastic to-go bowl, I just keep walking. And later, when he rolls into the Hudson News as I'm leaving and puts a hand out for a pound, I keep walking too. No fuss, no foul. Just like I don't know him.

Because I don't.

"C'mon, Noah!" he calls after me.

But I've got nothing to say.

"Stupid fuck," he mumbles, loud enough for me to hear.

I shake my head and keep on moving.

And, honestly, it doesn't haunt me. It's like it's something I've known for a long time that I have finally looked at in the light.

Anyway, I have more important parts of the past to ruminate over. Parts that are harder to leave behind. Parts that I revisited and proved even more valuable than I could ever have imagined, not *less*.

I board the plane. I wait patiently while people try to force their enormous bags—the ones we *all* know are too big—into small overhead compartments. I stand up twice to let others into the middle and window seats. I try to work. I fail to work. I watch a third of a *Spider-Man* movie I've seen twice before. I put my seat back in the upright position.

And all the time all I can think about is her.

And it doesn't stop after we taxi and I deplane. Or after I grab my car from the airport parking lot, settling back into something that at least feels familiar, and pay the obscene long-term parking bill via the person in the booth. Or when I drive up La Cienega toward the green hills in stop-and-go traffic, past billboards for movies that will come and go.

It doesn't stop back at my house, up in the hills. Where I gaze out my picture windows at the canyon below—and it feels empty instead of full like it did before. Or even the next day, when I go to the office and leave a box of Sonoma County lemon cookies in the shared kitchen as a peace offering for having temporarily abandoned my staff. Or when my administrators, Peggy and Marco, tell me the gossip that I missed—how Carl at the radiology practice down the hall mixed up the charts *again*.

Nell is everywhere and she is nowhere. And I can't escape this feeling, like somehow I failed. Like, for a second, I had something precious in my grasp but I let it drop. Wasn't quick enough to save it.

I think about the baggage claim area and that stupid green suitcase and her crazy hair. I think about making iced coffee and walking in on her in the sauna and shucking oysters—or not shucking oysters. I think about arguing and getting soaked and making terrible pasta. I think about her citrus perfume lingering on my clothes. I think about her body in the dim light, how she groaned when she bit into that Charleston Chew. The way eventually she fell asleep on her side, her forehead almost touching mine.

I think about her. And it's eating me alive.

I am a fucking wreck.

Because she could have tried! And this is the same problem as before. Years and years ago when she opted to leave without me. Not to find a new plan for our new life, together. I fucked up, sure. But she could have tried; *we* could have tried. To find a solution, an answer, at least some attempt at seeing if this thing could withstand our respective stubbornness this time.

And, sometimes, if I'm honest, I'm even confused about who I'm angry at—is it the Nell from now or the Nell from before?

Who is the most frustrating Nell?

What is the statute of limitations on mistakes? On being flawed?

We were just children.

That's what she said. But either that's true and she should forgive me, or it's a lie and she should acknowledge that we were—and are—so much more.

Cara posts two photos on Instagram, one after the other.

How it started, how it's going.

The first picture is of the group of us as teenagers in the Meadow. And I know right away, it's the day when Nell and I first went to the Met. Nell was almost always the photographer in our crew, but, this time, someone else clearly took the photo. Because there she is. It's grainy and it's from far away, but, when I zoom in, I see how she is just barely sneaking a glance up at me with a small smile, though we're not touching. How I am mugging for the camera, my boys at my sides, so fucking clueless about what I had and what I'd lose.

The second picture is from the un-wedding party, after we went to fetch the wine but before the terrible shit went down. This one is new. I have less baggy pants. And the image offers much more clarity. In this one, she is stealing a glance at me too, but at least then I had the sense to glance back.

I look at the photo eight hundred times a day. It twists the knife every single time.

But I don't text her. I don't call her. I don't send an email, a DM, or a carrier pigeon.

I can't yell at her. Or make my strong arguments. Or even plead with her to consult a doctor about her stupid shoulder—make sure she doesn't need surgery.

Because I am respecting her space. And I'm trying to move on.

Which is why I call Ben, daily, and yell at him instead.

"I know," he says, as I rant.

"I know," he says again.

But we are getting nowhere. And, at this point today, I'm not even sure he's listening. Because, though I am on my way to Dodgers Stadium to work with the team, this is the third time I've called him this week on my commute to rail about the same thing.

He has replaced all my podcasts. All my music. All my other calls. Although really it's not him, it's me.

I groan. For the umpteenth time.

"Dude, I've never heard you like this," he says, as he has earlier this week. "You sound . . . *bad*."

I stop at a red light. Glance over at the overly injected blonde in the Audi beside me, who shoots me a wink. I run a hand over my eyes. "I feel bad."

"That's . . . bad."

Well, we agree on one thing.

Everything is bad.

"I need to let it go," I say, resolute. "I need to drop it."

"Yeah, I mean, maybe you do just need to let it go." He is sick of trying to convince me otherwise. And I don't blame him. I'm sick of myself.

I hear murmuring in the background. A distinctly female voice at a stage whisper.

"What?" Ben whispers, then he returns to his full voice. "No, sorry, actually—I don't think you should let it go."

I shake my head. "Tell Cara I say hi."

"No, Cara's not . . . it's just me. Okay, yeah, Cara is next to me, and she doesn't think you should let it go."

"But Nell asked me not to call," I say, as traffic starts to move ever so slowly. Like everything in my life, it is stop-and-start. It's like moving through molasses. Yet I have no control. No way to pick up speed.

I don't see an alternate route.

"And so you're just going to listen? Not even try to convince her?"

"I don't have a choice!"

"Don't you, though?"

I go silent. What's the point of trying to convince Nell to give us a chance? She's already made up her mind. And she's not wrong—shit is complicated. Emotionally. Logistically.

Who cares what my heart wants?

"Dude, listen," Ben says. "I was with you when you broke up the first time and I'm with you now. I've been listening to you struggle with this shit for *weeks*. You're better together. Both of you."

"Both of us?"

"You think she's not a fucking wreck too?"

I honestly don't know.

"You say you don't have a choice," Ben says. "That you have to let her be. I think you don't have a choice . . . you *have* to go get her."

My knee is starting to bump up and down. Even if my mind isn't there yet, my body is starting to wrap itself around the idea.

"What's the worst thing that happens?" he asks.

She slams the door in my face. She says no again. We spend an amazing few days together, so I'm in even deeper, and then she sends me packing.

She doesn't choose me . . . *again*.

My heart combusts into a billion pieces. Again.

"There's nothing I can do if she still doesn't think I'm good enough, that I'm even worth a try."

"Maybe you're the one who doesn't think you're good enough," Ben says. "Maybe that's on *you*."

And that's when it hits me like a giant wave that I don't have time to dive under: Since we were kids, I've been asking her to choose me.

I've told myself over and over again that she didn't choose me.

But maybe it's time I chose *her*.

31

NELLIE
TODAY

"I think you should give him a chance," Cara is saying to me for the hundredth time.

I have been getting the same kinds of messages from Sabrina too.

But I am way past that. It's been weeks since I said goodbye to Noah. Weeks since he asked me to stay, to come to LA, to try some version of us being together, to ignore this feeling in my gut like I was still just one of his many followers—a sycophant in the cult of Noah.

Like he still just expected me to fold into *his* life.

Nothing has changed.

It's been weeks since the taxi pulled up at my brownstone apartment building, dumping me out onto a street that felt familiar and looked strangely smaller at the same time. A place I once really adored and is objectively lovely, but have maybe outgrown like so many once on-trend denim silhouettes.

Weeks since the bodega cat sauntered up, his plush belly almost brushing the ground, and shot me a dirty look like he'd hoped I was gone for good.

You can never go back, I tell my friends. The past is the past.

And Noah hasn't reached out. No call. No text. No snail mail letter or singing telegram.

And I get it. Because I didn't leave it open-ended. But it is still astounding to me how much this feels like the first time around. How I kept waiting for him to call *again*. To try harder. And how he didn't for literal decades and doesn't now.

In that time, it became a new millennium. Towers fell. Smartphones were born. Smartphones got cameras. Smartphones ruined the world.

My father died.

And then Noah did reach out. But by then . . . I had nothing left to say.

No words.

"CB," I say now. "There's no there there anymore."

"But there is though! Isn't it at least worth a try?"

What is this scenario? Where we try long distance and it's horrible like it always is—death by a thousand paper cuts in the form of missed calls, time differences, questionable photos posted on social media—and we break up all over again? Marinate in the pain all over again?

I wouldn't do either of us the injustice.

But I do miss him. God, I miss him. Even though I barely had him.

"I think we kind of did try," I say. "And it didn't end well."

"He didn't hook up with Lydia, for what it's worth," Cara insists. "I know that for sure! She said Damien told her to go ask him to examine her—and then made sure you saw it. She may have been trying to get in Noah's pants . . . Okay, she was. But she didn't succeed and Damien, well, we all know he's garbage. Even Ben is done with him."

I know that too. About Lydia and Noah. Really, I knew that almost instantly. She was never his type and there was Damien at his old shenanigans again. But that shot of adrenaline—of seeing Noah with her and that moment of not knowing—was enough to convince me that what we have is not enough for me to uproot myself *or* trust him from thousands of miles and organic smoothies away.

Noah wants me. I can admit that. But he wants to merge me into his life. He wants me to be convenient. And what happens when I'm not?

"I know, CB," I say. "But it's just too hard."

So, I am sad, but I am working on other things. On finding new ways to replicate some of the feelings I felt when I was with him—like everything was in Technicolor. Like I was on to the next chapter. Like I was awake again.

I've been taking meetings about freelance art director gigs, ones for TV and film, as I finish up at the magazine. It's a big change and will involve a steep learning curve, but I think I'm up for it. I've been looking for new apartments—though I'm not sure exactly where I want to go. I've been digging up old contacts and going out for drinks.

For Manhattans, old-fashioneds, martinis—and advice.

And then I've been coming home and, yes, I have been allowing myself a few minutes to stare up at the ceiling and remember what it felt like to have his hands in my hair, his lips on my lips, his smile projecting a thousand-watt glow in my direction.

I've been staring at the photos Cara posted—I know partially for my benefit. I've been examining our faces for clues. To what, I'm not sure.

I've been coming home and, *yes*, letting myself cry until my pillow is damp, remembering how free I felt on that day in West Marin and wondering if I'll ever feel that right again.

If I will die alone and the bodega cat will celebrate.

"Will you at least promise to tell me if you need me?" Cara says. "No more secrets?"

"I promise," I say. And I do. Because I'm also working on learning to ask for support. On telling my friends when I'm feeling vulnerable or down. On accepting help.

I am working on letting in what might make me happy.

And so, today, as I root around in my purse for my keys after a fruitful meeting in SoHo, I'm planning to treat myself. I will order sushi—no oyster shooters. Too triggering. I will watch Hallmark movies. I will give myself an extra few minutes to think about Noah and wallow in aching for him. And then I will try out my new rose oil and jade gua sha facial tool and go to sleep early.

But, when I turn the key in the apartment lock, I open the door to something unexpected.

Wall-to-wall yellow. In the form of Cheerios boxes. Each featuring an image of a heart-shaped bowl.

Cereal bowls of love.

There must be hundreds of them. And when I tiptoe in, close the door behind me and look more closely, I see there are a few other types too.

Honey Nut. Apple Cinnamon. Multigrain.

Multigrain?

I turn in a circle, my apartment transformed. And it is only as I do this that the shock begins to dissipate and reality dawns. Who else could have done this? But did he orchestrate it from a distance? Or is he . . . ?

When the doorbell rings, I cross back toward it in a daze.

"Who is it?" I ask, not daring to look through the peephole.

"You really don't know?"

His gravelly voice hits me hard. I brace my forehead against the door.

"It's best to be safe," I say.

"It's Mike," he says. "From the oyster farm."

"Oh, thank God. I thought it was someone creepy."

I turn the lock and open the door. And there is Noah standing there—in all his tallness, maybe less relaxed than usual, handsome as always. A bit worse for the wear.

His denim shirt—the one I love—looks a little rumpled. His perfectly worn pants look like they've been through a thing or two.

Most likely a flight.

But it's in his face that I see the true toll. There are new dark circles under his eyes. His cheeks look drawn. His five-o'clock shadow is nearing midnight.

Right away, I want to step toward him, draw my fingertips along his jawline, kiss his cheek scar, his forehead, his lips—curved as they are in a small smile.

But then I remember. This is not Sonoma. We are not together. And there are four hundred boxes of cereal behind me in my apartment.

How will I eat them all?

"Can I come in?" he asks.

I glance behind me. "I'm guessing you already have."

"Your landlady is very kind," he nods. "A bit of a romantic. Not good with security."

Fair enough.

Is there anything this man can't talk his way into?

When we were growing up, Noah was so accustomed to being a god among boys. That high school athlete. That star. Can you ever outgrow that? That entitlement? That expectation?

I step back and let him pass through. Not because I miss him and seeing his face sends a fusion of joy and heat rocketing through me. Not because I am so fucking relieved that he's here that birds are singing in my head. Not because I still remember what it felt like when he pressed kisses down my side all the way from my rib cage to my ankle. But because when someone sends you enough Cheerios for a lifetime, you should at least hear them out.

That's just etiquette. Emily Post says.

I close the door. And then it's the two of us. Alone in my apartment. The one where I live as grown-up me. And it feels like two worlds—two versions of me—colliding. Like the quietest explosion. He feels alien and like he belongs at the same time.

"Nice place you've got," he says, glancing around.

"Thanks," I say. "It usually has less of a supermarket warehouse vibe."

He swivels his head to look at all the boxes. "I just wanted to make sure that, if you're ever freaking out, you have plenty of reinforcements."

"But I thought oats don't actually mitigate the effects of weed?"

"Well, it always seems to make you feel better," he says, raising an eyebrow. "So what do the scientists know? Plus, it smells better than hundreds of oysters or wedges of cheese."

The man has a point.

I cannot believe he is standing here. Actually standing here. Surrounded by so much breakfast.

I am suddenly overcome by nerves. And confusion. And a general sense that, for reasons I can't quite explain, I might burst into tears. Happy. Sad. Overwhelmed.

I motion toward the couch—kelly-green velvet and my favorite piece—so he can take a seat. So I can at least perform some semblance of normalcy.

"Can I get you a drink?" I ask. Because that's what polite people offer.

"Sure," he says.

"Milk?" I ask. "And a spoon?"

"Obviously," he says.

As soon as I'm alone in the kitchen, I close my eyes and press my back against the cool steel of the fridge, trying to keep myself calm. My heart is thumping out of my chest.

I need to get my head on straight. I need to calm down. Whatever this is, I need my mind to be clear for it. But the problem is, my mind is never clear with Noah around.

I know I'm not supposed to want him here. I know I said we should avoid each other, cut ties. I know this situation is complicated as hell. But the thing is, I didn't realize how much I would miss him. Or how much that would hurt.

I exhale, resolved to stay chill. I grab a beer and a cider from my fridge because that's what I have. And I come back to the living room all casual, holding the drinks up in front of me.

"Which one do you want?" I ask.

"Which one do *you* want?"

"I asked you first. You choose."

"Fine," he says. "I choose the Brooklyn Lager. And you."

I freeze, unsure of what to say next. I part my lips, close them. In a fugue state, I hand Noah the beer. Our hands graze each other. And it's like an electric shock when we make contact, lightning scorching its way through me.

Decades, years, eons—and this boy still does that to me.

"Thanks," he says, all cool. Like this is all just the most normal thing. Like he hasn't just said what he said. And he sits down on the couch. "Hey," he says. "Mind if I turn on the game?"

What is happening?

"The . . . okay? But you're going to need to be more specific because I don't know what 'the game' means?"

"The Yankees game," he says. "If you hand me the remote, I'll turn it on."

I feel like I'm in an alternate universe. As I hand him the remote and he starts scrolling through to some sports channel I've never turned on like it's completely regular, I am out of my body.

Did he fly from LA to sit on my couch and watch sports?

Suddenly, I can't play along anymore. I can't pretend this is normal and wait patiently to see what comes next. The shock and thrill of seeing his face is morphing into disorientation to the point where I remember that this isn't good for us. This isn't good for *me*.

What is he doing here?

"Noah," I say. "What's going on?"

"Well," he says, "we're having a drink and watching a baseball game 'cause I have something I want to show you."

I am still hovering over him.

"Right. I know literally what we're doing. But why? What are you doing here? I haven't seen or heard from you in weeks. We said goodbye in California and that was supposed to be it."

"Right," he says like we're discussing the weather. "I know. But I don't want that to be it. I don't think that *should* be it."

I narrow my eyes at him, prop a hand on my hip. "Well, maybe you don't get to decide."

He toggles his head. "Yeah, okay, fine. But I've solved the problem. So, the decision kind of makes itself."

"You've solved the problem?"

"Yup."

"Because you're going to bribe me with cereal to uproot my entire life for you?"

"No," he says, like I'm being ridiculous. "Because I'm going to uproot *my* life for *you*."

I take this in. At least I try.

What. Is. He. Saying?

Like a zombie, I sit down on the couch too because I'm not sure I can trust my legs to hold me up. I open my cider with a hiss. Chug half of it. Let it fizz, tart and sweet, on my tongue. Place it on a hexagonal coaster on my coffee table. The hexagonal coaster I bought at the MoMA store while I was living my regular adult life—and hating him.

"Sorry—what?" I say, finally.

"I'm moving back to New York. To be with you."

He says this like, *I'm going to order the burger.* Like it's that basic.

I choke. Belatedly. Like my body just realized it swallowed something. "What do you mean?"

"Well, I thought about it," he shrugs, "and the way I see it, it's my turn . . . to choose you. To show you I'm a different person than I used to be."

"Noah . . . what is going on?!"

He finally gives me his full attention. Slides over beside me so we are close, our thighs touching, so I can feel him next to me. And then he faces me full on, his expression taking on a new seriousness. It takes everything in my power not to trace the scar on his cheek with my thumb, his faint laugh lines. Not to lean in and kiss his parted lips, then and there. I can feel his presence like a hum beneath my surface. Like mini earthquakes that won't stop rolling.

Today, his eyes are a color I can barely describe—something earthy and green and brown and yellow all at the same time. Something grounded.

They hold it all. And they are zeroed in on me.

"I didn't realize until I saw you in California that you're what's missing from my life."

I open my mouth to interject, but he holds up his hand.

"Just let me get this out. I know you'll have thoughts—trust me. I know you."

Fine, I allow. I will listen.

"Before Sonoma, I had convinced myself—deluded myself—into believing that what we had was just a kid thing. Just a first-love thing. That there wasn't a chance in hell it would become something again. I mean . . . I figured we might still be attracted to each other. I figured there was a small chance we might bone or something, but—"

"Noah . . ." I motion for him to continue.

"Sorry." He slides a palm over his hair. "Anyway, then I saw you at baggage claim and you were, well, let's be honest, kind of mean. But also really hot. And most of all, you were *you*. Sharp and stubborn and funny and impossible—my *person*. And, from that moment on, as much as I tried to convince myself otherwise, rationalize what I was feeling in a million different ways, I've known that I can't live without you. That I don't *want* to live without you."

"But . . ."

"I know," he says, a hand coming to rest on my leg, to steady me. "We have history. We have baggage—exponentially bigger than the Jolly Green Hulk. I get that. I do. And no amount of cereal is going to erase that. But we're adults now. That's the beauty of it. We can figure out how to get past it. Because it's worth it. And because, honestly, it's going to take a lot more energy trying to get over you than it is trying to get . . . well, not under you. But you know what I mean. Under you is part of it."

I exhale a wobbly breath. Try to pull my mind out of the gutter as I flash to me under him—which is frankly where I'd like to live.

I want to buy what he's selling, but it feels too good to be true. And him uprooting his life . . . for me? It seems like so much.

"But what about your work?"

"I can work here. The good—and I guess bad—news is that everyone needs doctors."

"But you love your job."

He nods. Looks the tiniest bit glum for just an instant before he wipes any trace of negativity off his face. "And I'll be sad to leave. But I'll find work I love here, too. I have no doubt. Because the thing is, Nell—I love *you* more."

I am struck silent. Mind blown. Head reeling. Tornadoes spin through me, picking up my expectations and tossing them victoriously aside. Finally, I manage to make my lips form words: "You . . . love me?"

Noah grins at me, takes my hand in his strong own. I realize I'm obsessed with his hands. "Nell. Of course I love you. I've *always* loved you. I was just too young and stupid to know what to do about it."

How is this happening? Minutes before, I was walking into my apartment ready to spend the night wallowing in the loss of this man. And now he's sitting next to me, in the flesh, looking at me like the world begins and ends at my say-so.

"But . . . what changed?"

He looks down at my fingers, thinks about this for a beat. "For years I've been telling myself that you didn't choose me. I think I was so used to people catering to my every whim that I expected things to work that way forever. And, after the injury, I suddenly felt like all my power was gone—like I was nothing without baseball. And I retreated inside myself and pushed you away and then, when you actually left, I think it felt like proof that you also didn't think I was good enough. And so I spent all these years villainizing you in my head, telling myself that you gave up on me, that you didn't choose *us*. That all your talk about how I was more than sports was just bullshit. That even your family didn't like me. But it never occurred to me that I had never chosen *you*. I was so angry at you for going to college as we planned despite the fact that my world had imploded, maybe even angry at you for not dragging me with you, that it never even occurred to me that I was the one abandoning you and our plan—forcing you to go live our dream, our life, without me. Because I couldn't see why you'd want me anymore. I kept asking you to choose me. I kept testing you. But I never *chose* you."

What is rising in my chest is something I can barely describe. I am overcome. I am shocked. I am still processing.

And I am, it seems, in love.

For the first time in decades, I let myself admit it. And it steals my breath.

Fuck. I love him.

"So, you just came here."

"So, I just came here."

"Ready to stay."

He shrugs. "Basically."

I tilt my head. "That's pretty brazen. What if I don't want to try? What if I don't want to bone?"

He raises his eyebrows and gives me a look like, *please*. Then he jumps to standing. "Oh!" he says, gesturing toward the TV. "There it is!"

Noah pauses the game, then walks over, pointing to an LED screen behind home plate.

It's an ad on a digital monitor. For something called Humbug Medical.

It has a black goat logo.

I look at him. I look at it. I look at him again.

"What . . . ?"

"For my New York practice. I figured Humbug might be a pretty good name after all."

"You took out an ad at Yankee Stadium for your new East Coast medical practice?"

"Well, sort of," he says. "I called in a favor. It's just a mockup. To show you how serious I am. I'm a ways away from actually getting it off the ground."

And that's it. I am ended.

Maybe it's that adorable black goat. Or the crooked smile on Noah's face. Or the fact that he has finally seen us from a different perspective.

Maybe it's the weirdness of that name. Or how good he looks, with those broad shoulders, taking up space in my apartment.

But if I have more questions, I can't think of what they are. They've been subsumed into a swell of something much more powerful.

So, I launch myself at him. Or at least I think I do. All I know is that one minute I'm on the couch and the next I'm on him—my mouth on his mouth, my arms around his neck, my body pressed up against his. And there is heat pooling inside me.

He doesn't hesitate. He kisses me right back. There's no doubt here now. There are no questions.

He tastes like beer and something fruity, and I don't ever plan to let go.

32

NOAH

TODAY

She's on me in a flash and it takes everything in my power to contain myself.

Because this is all I want. Forever.

In just weeks—but also through years—I've missed her so much. The way her hair smells, tickling my skin as it pours over us. The way her mouth tastes, like cold cider. The way her body feels as I lift her up—like she's my perfect fit.

My other half.

My *missing* half.

I would happily live here. Among the cereal boxes. Subsisting solely on oats and beer—which is basically also oats.

I would build us a fort on the couch. Build us a pen for the goats. Build us a sex den in the bedroom—which I have yet to see.

Build us a life—and never leave.

But that won't be necessary because just as our kiss turns to something more, as we tumble toward the sofa knocking over cereal boxes, hands traveling in illicit directions, tearing off clothes, skin against skin, and breaking all the traffic laws, she mumbles something incoherent.

"What?" I say.

"I said I'm coming with you."

"Coming with me—to the couch?"

From a whisper away, she giggles into my mouth, which just makes me want to do all the things to her—*for* her.

"No, silly. To LA."

"To help me pack?"

She shakes her head. "To live."

"But what about Humbug?"

"Humbug will live forever in our hearts and in infamy."

I pause for real now. Pull back just a bit, as I peer into her face, threading my fingers in her hair at the back of her neck. "Are you serious?"

"Very. This was all very thoughtful of you. But I hope you didn't quit your practice yet. Because I'm coming to LA."

"But . . . are you sure? I thought you didn't want to uproot your life for me."

She shakes her head. "No. I didn't want you to *expect* me to do that. And anyway, I don't know if you know this, but my best friends live in California. And I lived there first, by the way, like way before you— so, it's really *my* place. Not yours. And they need art directors there whether at an ad agency or in entertainment. And also, as much as it will always be home, I need to leave New York before the bodega cat figures out how to make copies of my keys."

I look into her face, searching for a hint of doubt. "Are you sure?" I ask her.

"Positive," she says.

"You're incredible. Unhinged when it comes to that cat, but incredible."

"Thank you. You are also okay."

She pushes up and presses a lingering kiss to my lips, so that I chase her for more. "Oh," she says, like she's forgotten one detail, "and I love you too."

Warmth floods through me, so that I no longer know where she ends and I begin. I am amazed by how fucking lucky I am.

"That's good news," I say, unable to contain a massive grin spreading across my face. "There's just one last problem."

She raises an eyebrow. "Let me at it."

"How are we going to ship all this cereal?"

"That's easy," she says. "The Jolly Green Giant!"

More like ten Jolly Green Giants.

First love, last love.

That's what I think as I stare into the face of this beautiful woman, in whom I can still see that girl I fell in love with a trillion years before. The face I saw across the club, lit by strobes, and couldn't forget. The eyes that glanced at me one last time as she hurried toward art class. The expression of trust and longing she wore for all our shared firsts and that I can't wait to see again and again—as long as we both shall live.

Epilogue

BOTH
TODAY

There is a firepit. A spit. A smooth sand beach. A long communal table with a white tablecloth, set with brightly colored plates and cloth napkins with gold deco napkin rings. There are bud vases of wildflowers and goblets waiting to be filled to their brims.

There are beach blankets in neon at each seat. Hoodies that read DILLON BEACH—parting gifts for the guests for when it gets chilly.

There are twinkle lights strung above in the cypress trees. And a cocktail bar set up inside a mini retro airstream. There is beer on tap. There is rosé ready to flow.

There are bowls of cannabis gummies—but not for the bride.

There are oysters, prepared over the fire. Platters of shrimp cocktail. Multiple goat cheese plates—with apricot preserves. Dishes of dates and Marcona almonds.

It all awaits.

But before they dig in, there is a wedding. A ceremony on the beach, presided over by a driver named John, where the bride wears a white dress—a mod A-line mini—and the groom wears a collared shirt, the color of well-worn denim.

There is family in the seats—and friends who are family too. Moms and sisters and brothers and trusted confidantes. There is even a professional baseball player or two. And they all look on with joy and relief at something that has worked out in a world full of chaos.

There are vows and promises and titters of laughter, happy tears that flood the ducts of watching eyes. There are hands to chests, and tilts of heads onto neighboring shoulders, squeezed hands.

"They say you can never go back," the bride says, clutching her wildflower bouquet with ease thanks to months of PT. "And I think that's true. But it turns out, if you're lucky, you get to move forward."

There is a broken glass, shouts of *Mazel tov!* A *real* kiss. The bride dipped. Cheers and music as the newly married couple walks down the sandy aisle, hands woven together.

"So, what now?" Noah asks, as they retreat toward a secluded spot behind the dunes to quickly regroup, the sand cool beneath their feet. "Now that we've got everything we want."

"Good question," Nellie says, turning toward him, lifting her hand to toy with the buttons on his shirt.

"Do we try for goats?" he asks, his hands resting at her waist.

"Hmm," she says, tilting her head to gaze up at him. "I hear they eat shoes. And I like my shoes."

"A Cheerios farm then?" He raises a hand to untangle her necklace, lays it flat. His fingers are warm as they brush her skin.

"I think that's not how that works."

"I've got it then," he says, a glimmer in his eye. "An oyster bed!"

At that she smiles, sliding her hand down his chest and stepping in so close they're basically one. "Bed," she says. "Now *that* sounds like a plan."

THE END

Acknowledgments

I was born and raised in New York City, but I spent my college years and twenties living in LA. During that time, I fell in love with both Southern *and* Northern California, though they were pitted against each other as rivals. Even after I moved back east, I kept returning to the West Coast—especially to Sonoma County.

The day I had the idea of setting *Backslide* in wine country, I called my best friend, Rachel Leonard, who lives nearby in the Bay Area, and spoke the words out loud. And whatever you believe about the power (or magical thinking) of manifestation, somehow, miraculously, within hours, I received an unrelated email inviting me to visit the Sonoma Coast and cover the reimagining of a beloved hotel property for a travel feature. And, so, off I went to tool around the area doing the best kind of research—for a couple of days with Rachel as my local guide and then with the loveliest small group of West Marin locals and fellow journalists.

So, thank you to Tory Weiss and Leah Goldstein, who invited me on that trip and were the most delightful hosts. As a travel writer, I'm fortunate to visit many incredible places, but one of my favorite hotels in the world is the Farmhouse Inn in Forestville, California (which, up until recently, was run by members of a local family). "The estate" in this book is very loosely inspired by that property, with its cheerful energy and quiet luxury. Dillon Beach Resort stars as a version of its casual awesome self here, though the hotel I describe is truly an amalgamation. And while I've definitely taken some liberties, kept it a bit loose, I've hopefully mostly done it justice.

Of course, this would all be moot without my brilliant editor, Carrie Feron at Gallery Books, whose laser-sharp instincts, deep wisdom, and quiet power blows my mind on a regular basis. Your belief in me makes me believe in myself. So, a huge thank-you to Carrie, Jen Bergstrom, and their team of incredible Gallerinas—especially Ali Chesnick, Lucy Nalen, and Heather Waters, whose unchecked enthusiasm, hard work, and warmth makes everything smoother and more fun. I am truly so lucky to have you!

To Faye Bender, my agent, who is forever in my corner, I'm so grateful for your insight, encouragement, and groundedness (and for the "slippery sunshine" bouquet). You have been, and continue to be, the best partner in crime. Also, a *huge* thank-you for introducing me to the incredible Michelle Weiner and Olivia Blaustein at CAA, a true dream team whose collective knowledge is unsurpassed.

Thank you to Peter Hartogs, who introduced me to his friend Dr. Jeff Giuliani, when I decided I wanted Noah to be an orthopedic surgeon. Thank you, Jeff, for offering deep patience and clarity as you walked me through the ins and outs of that career—and also how to treat rotator cuff injuries. (You joked, but I did name a character after you!)

Because I wanted to make sure that Nellie's career also tracked, I had the pleasure of speaking with Nick Cogan, who schooled me on the various facets of art direction vs. creative direction and so much more. Thank you for taking the time!

Thank you to the Weiners and Tabers, who are always up for a game and a laugh and have taught me the value of escape to beautiful and interesting places.

Of course, I would be nowhere without my community of fellow writers: A huge thank-you to Sarah MacLean, whose unchecked generosity, humor, and commiseration—whether over salt and vinegar potatoes or during playdate pickups—keeps me sane. And a giant thank-you to Nicola Kraus, who kindly brought me into the fold many years and books ago and has allowed me to stay there, thank God. As always, I am so grateful to Emily Barth-Isler, Hanna Neier, and Katie Schorr for being touchstones as we all navigate this wild publishing world. Thank you to Zora Ginsburg for acting as my style consultant, wardrobe closet, and lifelong friend without complaint. And thank you to Lucinda Halpern, for being a model of female entrepreneurship and fearlessness.

To my sister, Claudia Zelevansky a.k.a. Claud Claudia and Aunt Clock, thank you for always being my first draft reader and for giving me honest—but not super mean—notes. You will have to make them less helpful if you ever want me to stop asking.

To my parents, Lynn and Paul Zelevansky, who have fully embraced my new romance author identity without missing a beat, thank you for funding all those Jude Deveraux novels during my teen years and for never questioning my circuitous path.

To my husband, Andrew, who has somehow survived many post-Covid years sharing a workspace with me while I grumble and groan: I believe it is truly rare—and so lucky—to have your greatest creative sounding board just feet away from you at all times. Thank you for solving every plot issue and for making me laugh as you do it.

Thank you to my children, who are incredible even when they're impossible. Your strength, imagination, and kindness gives me hope for the future every day.

And, finally, to the readers, thank you all. (Yes, even those of you who go in for the kill on Goodreads.) I think this one has some extra sweetness. I hope it brings you joy, escape, and so much more.

About the Author

Nora Dahlia is a lifestyle writer whose work has appeared in *The New York Times*, *Elle*, *The Wall Street Journal*, and *Vanity Fair*, among others. Nora is also a book doctor, ghostwriter, collaborator, and writing coach. She lives in Brooklyn with her husband, kids, and two fruitless lemon trees. She is the author of *Backslide* and *Pick-Up*.